ALEX RIDER

POINT BLANC

ANTHONY HOROWITZ

HARRAP'S

Published by arrangement with Walker Books Ltd, London.

21, rue du Montparnasse
75283 Paris Cedex 06
HARRAP's® est une marque de Larousse SAS
www.harrap.com

ISBN 978 2 81 870365 6

About the author

ANTHONY HOROWITZ is the author of the #1 *New York Times* bestselling[1] Alex Rider series of novels[2] and the award-winning[3] writer of PBS's *Foyle's War*, *Collision*, and *Injustice*, as well as many other film and television projects. He lives in London.

1. n°1 dans la liste des best-sellers du New York Times
2. série de romans
3. qui a reçu un prix

DIRECTION DE LA PUBLICATION : Carine Girac-Marinier

DIRECTION ÉDITORIALE : Claude Nimmo

NOTES EN MARGE : Patricia Seixas

RÉVISION DES NOTES : Giovanni Picci

RELECTURE : Joëlle Narjollet

INFORMATIQUE ÉDITORIALE : Philippe Cazabet, Marie-Noëlle Tilliette

CONCEPTION GRAPHIQUE : Uli Meindl

FABRICATION : Rebecca Dubois

Mot de l'Éditeur

Vous aimeriez lire en langue originale, mais le vocabulaire, les expressions figurées ou la syntaxe vous arrêtent parfois ?

Cette collection est faite pour vous !

Vous trouverez en effet, en note dans la marge, une traduction de certains mots et expressions qui vous permettra d'avancer facilement dans votre lecture.

Nous n'avons pas cherché à vous donner une traduction littéraire de l'ouvrage et nous nous sommes parfois écartés du sens littéral pour vous fournir le sens qui convient le mieux à l'histoire. Aussi les mots sont-ils traduits dans le contexte du texte original.

Les expressions figées anglaises sont, bien entendu, rendues par une expression équivalente en français.

Les allusions à des réalités culturelles du monde anglo-saxon sont expliquées également dans la marge, pour vous aider à mieux comprendre la trame de l'histoire.

Vous aurez ainsi, en regard du texte original, tout le savoir-faire d'un dictionnaire rien que pour vous et adapté à ce livre !

Notre objectif est de vous mener jusqu'au mot FIN en vous donnant les clés nécessaires à la compréhension du récit.

Laissez-vous gagner par l'angoisse, l'humour et le suspense qui règnent chez les maîtres de la littérature anglo-saxonne.

Lire en VO ? You can indeed!

Coup de pouce pour vous aider à bien comprendre le début de l'histoire...

New York, bureau de Michael J. Roscoe, richissime président de la Roscoe Electronics, au 60e étage de la Roscoe Tower, sur la Cinquième Avenue. Aujourd'hui, le « roi de l'électronique » doit déjeuner avec le sénateur Andrews.

La matinée n'est pas très productive. M. J. Roscoe a du mal à se concentrer : depuis le retour de son fils Paul de son école dans le sud de la France, il paraît très inquiet.

À midi pile sa secrétaire, Helen Bosworth, l'appelle au téléphone : sa voiture l'attend en bas pour le conduire à son déjeuner. Il est temps de partir. Roscoe met sa veste et se dirige vers l'ascenseur...

Contents

1 Going Down 9
2 Blue Shadow 21
3 Hooked 35
4 Search and Report 50
5 The Shooting Party 68
6 The Tunnel 86
7 Special Edition 103
8 Room 13 113
9 "My Name is Grief" 127
10 Things that Go Click in the Night 144
11 Seeing Double 166
12 Delaying Tactics 182
13 How to Rule the World 192
14 Black Run 208
15 After the Funeral 223
16 Night Raid 235
17 Dead Ringer 248
Afterword 263

GOING DOWN

Michael J. Roscoe was a careful man[1].

The car that drove him[2] to work at seven fifteen each morning was a custom-made[3] Mercedes with reinforced-steel doors and bullet-proof windows[4]. His driver, a retired[5] FBI agent, carried[6] a Beretta sub-compact semi-automatic pistol and knew how to use it. There were just five steps[7] from the point where the car stopped to the entrance[8] of Roscoe Tower on New York's Fifth Avenue, but closed circuit television cameras followed him every inch of the way[9]. Once[10] the automatic doors had slid shut behind[11] him, a uniformed[12] receptionist – also armed – watched as he crossed the foyer[13] and entered his own private lift[14].

The lift had white marble walls[15], a blue carpet[16], a silver handrail[17] and no buttons. Roscoe pressed[18] his hand against a small glass panel[19].

1. homme prudent
2. le conduisait
3. sur mesure
4. avec portières blindées et vitres pare-balles
5. à la retraite
6. était armé d'
7. Il n'y avait que cinq pas à faire
8. jusqu'à l'entrée
9. des caméras de télésurveillance le suivaient pas à pas
10. Une fois que
11. se refermèrent derrière
12. en uniforme
13. le suivit des yeux tandis qu'il traversait le hall
14. ascenseur
15. des parois en marbre
16. moquette
17. rampe argentée
18. plaqua
19. vitre

A sensor read his fingerprints[1], verified them and activated the lift. The doors slid shut and the lift rose to the sixtieth floor[2] without stopping. Nobody else ever used it[3]. Nor did it ever stop at any of the other floors[4] in the building. While it was travelling up[5], the receptionist was on the telephone, letting Mr Roscoe's staff know[6] that he was on his way.

Everyone who worked in Roscoe's private office had been hand-picked and thoroughly vetted[7]. It was impossible to see him without an appointment. Getting an appointment could take[8] three months.

When you're rich, you have to be careful. There are cranks[9], kidnappers, terrorists ... the desperate and the dispossessed[10]. Michael J. Roscoe was the chairman[11] of Roscoe Electronics and the ninth or tenth richest man in the world[12] – and he was very careful indeed. Ever since[13] his face had appeared on the front cover[14] of *Time* magazine ("The Electronics King") he had realized that he had become a visible target[15]. So when in public[16] he walked quickly[17], with his head bent[18]. The glasses that he wore[19] had been chosen to hide as much as possible of[20] his round, handsome[21] face. His suits[22] were expensive but anonymous. If he went to the theatre or to dinner, he always arrived at the last minute, preferring not to hang around[23]. There were dozens of different security

1. capteur scanna ses empreintes digitales
2. monta au 60e étage
3. ne s'en servait jamais
4. Il ne s'arrêtait jamais à aucun autre étage, non plus
5. Le temps qu'il monte
6. avertit par téléphone le personnel de M. Roscoe
7. avaient été triés sur le volet et soumis à une enquête minutieuse
8. Pour obtenir un rendez-vous, il fallait parfois attendre
9. des dingues
10. tous les misérables de la terre
11. président
12. classé neuvième ou dixième fortune mondiale
13. Depuis que
14. avait fait la couverture
15. cible
16. lorsqu'il était en public
17. rapidement
18. tête baissée
19. lunettes qu'il portait
20. pour cacher le plus possible
21. beau
22. costumes
23. ne pas s'attarder

systems in his life and although they had once annoyed him[1], he had allowed them to become routine[2].

But ask any spy[3] or security agent. Routine is the one thing that can get you killed[4]. It tells[5] the enemy where you're going and when you're going to be there. Routine was going to kill Michael J. Roscoe and this was the day death had chosen to come calling[6].

Of course, Roscoe had no idea of this as he stepped out[7] of the lift directly into[8] his private office – a huge room occupying the corner[9] of the building, with floor-to-ceiling[10] windows giving views[11] in two directions; Fifth Avenue to the north[12], Central Park to the west. The two remaining[13] walls contained a door, a low bookshelf[14] and, next to[15] the lift, a single oil painting[16]: a vase of flowers by Vincent Van Gogh.

The black glass surface of his desk was equally uncluttered[17]. A computer, a leather notebook[18], a telephone and a framed[19] photograph of a fourteen-year-old boy. As he took off[20] his jacket and sat down, Roscoe found himself looking at the picture of the boy. Blond hair, blue eyes and freckles[21]. Paul Roscoe looked remarkably like his father forty years ago[22]. Roscoe was now fifty-four, beginning to show his age despite his year-round tan[23]. His son was almost[24] as tall[25] as him. The picture had been taken the summer before,

1. même si cela l'agaçait autrefois
2. s'était plié à cette routine
3. N'importe quel espion vous le dirait
4. c'est la meilleure façon de se faire tuer
5. Elle révèle à
6. la mort avait décidé de s'inviter ce jour-là
7. en sortant
8. pour arriver directement dans
9. pièce immense, située à l'angle
10. du sol au plafond
11. offrant une vue
12. au nord
13. restants
14. bibliothèque basse
15. à côté de
16. un seul tableau
17. plateau en verre noir de son bureau était aussi dépouillé
18. carnet relié en cuir
19. encadrée
20. retira
21. taches de rousseur
22. il y a 40 ans
23. et commençait à faire son âge, malgré un bronzage perpétuel
24. presque
25. grand

1. passé la journée à faire de la voile
2. plage
3. l'une des rares journées heureuses passées ensemble
4. quitté son pays et son mari
5. en savourait chaque instant
6. travaillait
7. depuis
8. commis une erreur
9. déposa un dossier
10. derniers chiffres
11. Le prix de revient
12. réservé [une table] au
13. cligna des yeux
14. J'ai contacté le bureau d'Alan Blunt
15. correspondait au soir
16. joignable
17. organisé un rendez-vous téléphonique privé
18. le faire transférer
19. Dois-je vous faire apporter votre café ?

on Long Island. They had spent the day sailing[1]. Then they'd had a barbecue on the beach[2]. It had been one of the few happy days they'd ever had together[3].

The door opened and his secretary came in. Helen Bosworth was English. She had left her home and her husband[4] to come and work in New York and loved every minute of it[5]. She had been working[6] in this office for[7] eleven years, and in all that time she had never forgotten a detail or made a mistake[8].

"Good morning, Mr Roscoe," she said.

"Good morning, Helen."

She set down a folder[9] on his desk. "The latest figures[10] from Singapore. Costings[11] on the R-15 Organizer. You have lunch with Senator Andrews at twelve-thirty. I've booked the[12] Ivy—"

"Did you remember to call London?" Roscoe asked.

Helen Bosworth blinked[13]. She never forgot anything, so why had he asked? "I spoke to Alan Blunt's office[14] yesterday afternoon," she said. Afternoon in New York would have been evening[15] in London. "Mr Blunt was not available[16] but I've arranged a person-to-person call[17] for you this afternoon. We can have it patched through[18] to your car."

"Thank you, Helen."

"Shall I have your coffee sent through to you?[19]"

"No thank you, Helen. I won't have coffee today."

Helen Bosworth left the room, seriously alarmed[1]. No coffee? Whatever next?[2] Mr Roscoe had begun his day with a double espresso for as long as she had known him[3]. Could it be that he was ill? He certainly hadn't been himself recently … not since Paul had got back[4] from that school in the South of France. And this phone call to Alan Blunt in London! Nobody had ever told her who he was but she had seen his name in a file once[5]. He was something to do[6] with British military intelligence[7]. MI6. What was Mr Roscoe doing talking to[8] a spy?

Helen Bosworth returned to her office and soothed her nerves[9], not with a coffee – she couldn't stand the stuff[10] – but with a refreshing cup of English breakfast tea. Something very strange was going on[11] and she didn't like it. She didn't like it at all.

Meanwhile, sixty floors below[12], a man had walked into reception wearing grey overalls with an ID badge attached to his chest[13]. The badge identified him as Sam Green, maintenance engineer[14] with X-Press Elevators Inc. He was carrying a briefcase[15] in one hand and a large silver toolbox[16] in the other. He set them both down[17] in front of the reception desk.

1. très inquiète
2. Et puis quoi, encore ?
3. depuis qu'elle le connaissait
4. Depuis un certain temps, il n'était plus lui-même… plus depuis que Paul était rentré
5. dans un dossier, une fois
6. Il avait quelque chose à voir
7. les services secrets de l'armée
8. Qu'est-ce qui lui prenait, à M. Roscoe, de parler à
9. se calma
10. détestait ça
11. se passait
12. Pendant ce temps, 60 étages plus bas
13. vêtu d'une combinaison grise, un badge fixé sur la poitrine
14. technicien de maintenance
15. mallette
16. caisse à outils
17. Il les déposa par terre

1. légèrement gras
2. étaient faux, tout comme
3. ses dents irrégulières
4. était en fait plus près de la trentaine
5. dans son métier
6. pouvait se permettre
7. connu sous le nom du
8. des mieux payés
9. tueurs à gages
10. On lui avait donné ce surnom
11. lui jeta un rapide coup d'œil
12. ascenseur [en anglais américain]
13. même si
14. jamais passé
15. Qu'est-ce qu'il a ?
16. Des gens de chez vous sont déjà venus
17. Effectivement.
18. défectueux
19. pièces détachées
20. m'ont fait revenir
21. fouilla
22. en sortit une feuille de papier froissée
23. le siège social
24. instructions
25. employaient effectivement
26. même s'il n'était pas venu travailler depuis deux jours
27. au fond
28. couteau dans le dos

Sam Green was not his real name. His hair – black and a little greasy[1] – was fake, as were[2] his glasses, moustache and uneven teeth[3]. He looked fifty years old but was actually nearer thirty[4]. Nobody knew his real name but in the business he was in[5], a name was the last thing he could afford[6]. He was known as the[7] Gentleman and he was one of the highest paid[8] and most successful contract killers[9] in the world. He had been given his nickname[10] because he always sent flowers to the families of his victims.

The receptionist glanced at him[11].

"I'm here for the elevator[12]," he said. He spoke with a Bronx accent even though[13] he had never spent[14] more than a week there in his life.

"What about it?[15]" the receptionist asked. "You people were here[16] last week."

"Yeah. Sure.[17] We found a defective[18] cable on elevator twelve. It had to be replaced but we didn't have the parts[19]. So they sent me back[20]." The Gentleman fished[21] in his pocket and pulled out a crumpled sheet of paper[22]. "You want to call Head Office[23]? I've got my orders[24] here."

If the receptionist had called X-Press Elevators Inc., he would have discovered that they did indeed employ[25] a Sam Green – although he hadn't shown up for work for two days[26]. This was because the real Sam Green was at the bottom[27] of the Hudson River with a knife in his back[28] and a twenty-pound block of concrete[1] attached to his feet. But the receptionist didn't make the call[2]. The Gentleman had guessed he wouldn't bother[3]. After all, the lifts were always breaking down[4]. There were engineers in and out the whole time[5]. What difference would one more make?

The receptionist jerked a thumb[6]. "Go ahead![7]" he said.

The Gentleman put away the letter, picked up his case[8] and his toolbox, and went over to the lifts. There were a dozen public lifts servicing the skyscraper[9], plus a thirteenth for Michael J. Roscoe. Lift number twelve was at the end. As he went in, a delivery boy with a parcel tried to follow[10]. "Sorry," the Gentleman said. "Closed for maintenance.[11]" The doors slid shut. He was on his own[12]. He pressed the button for the sixty-first floor.

He had been given[13] this job only a week before. He'd had to work fast – killing the real maintenance engineer, taking his identity, learning the layout[14] of Roscoe Tower and getting his hands on the sophisticated piece of equipment[15] he had known he would need. His employers wanted the multi-millionaire eliminated[16] as quickly as possible. More importantly, it had to look like an accident. For this, the Gentleman had demanded[17] – and been paid – two hundred thousand American dollars. The money was to be paid into a bank

1. bloc de béton d'environ 10 kg
2. ne passa pas ce coup de fil
3. deviné qu'il n'en prendrait pas la peine
4. tombaient toujours en panne
5. qui allaient et venaient sans arrêt
6. agita le pouce
7. Allez-y !
8. rangea la lettre, récupéra sa mallette
9. desservant le gratte-ciel
10. livreur avec un paquet tenta de le suivre
11. Hors service, opération de maintenance.
12. seul
13. On lui avait confié
14. se familiariser avec le plan
15. dénicher l'équipement sophistiqué
16. qu'il élimine le multimillionnaire
17. exigé

account in Switzerland[1]; half now, half on completion[2].

The lift door opened. The sixty-first floor was used mainly for[3] maintenance. This was where the water tanks were housed[4], also the computers that controlled the heat, air-conditioning[5], security cameras and lifts throughout[6] the building. The Gentleman turned off[7] the lift, using the manual override key[8] that had once belonged to[9] Sam Green, then went over to[10] the computers. He knew exactly where they were. In fact, he could have found them wearing a blindfold[11]. He opened his briefcase. There were two sections to the case.[12] The lower part was a laptop computer.[13] The lid was fitted out with a number of drills[14] and other tools, each of them strapped into place[15].

It took him[16] fifteen minutes to cut his way into[17] the Roscoe Tower mainframe[18] and connect his laptop to the circuitry inside[19]. Hacking his way past[20] the Roscoe security systems took a little longer, but at last it was done. He tapped a command into his keyboard.[21] On the floor below, Michael J. Roscoe's private lift did something it had never done before. It rose up one extra floor[22] – to level sixty-one. The door, however, remained[23] closed. The Gentleman did not need to get in.

Instead[24], he picked up the briefcase and the silver toolbox and carried them back[25] into the

1. compte en Suisse
2. l'autre moitié une fois le travail terminé
3. servait essentiellement à
4. citernes d'eau étaient installées
5. géraient le chauffage, la climatisation
6. dans tout
7. coupa le courant de
8. clé de maintenance
9. avait appartenu à
10. se dirigea vers
11. les yeux bandés
12. La mallette était en deux parties.
13. Celle du bas contenait un ordinateur portable.
14. couvercle était muni d'une quantité de perceuses
15. tous maintenus par une sangle
16. Il lui fallut
17. pour percer un accès menant à
18. système central
19. au réseau interne
20. Pirater
21. Il tapa une commande sur le clavier.
22. grimpa d'un étage supplémentaire
23. resta
24. Par contre
25. les rapporta

same lift he had taken from reception. He turned the override key and pressed the button for the fifty-ninth floor. Once again[1], he deactivated the lift. Then he reached up and pushed[2]. In the top of the lift was a trapdoor that opened outwards[3]. He pushed the briefcase and the silver box ahead of him[4], then pulled himself up and climbed onto the roof[5] of the lift. He was now standing inside the main lift-shaft[6] of Roscoe Tower. He was surrounded on four sides by girders and pipes blackened with oil and dirt[7]. Thick steel cables hung down[8], some of them humming as they carried their loads up and down[9]. Looking down, he could see a seemingly endless square tunnel[10], illuminated only by the chinks of light[11] from the doors that slid open and shut again as[12] the other lifts arrived at various floors. Somehow the breeze had made its way in[13] from the street, spinning dust that stung his eyes[14]. Next to him was a set of lift doors which, had he opened them, would have led him straight into[15] Roscoe's office. Above these[16], over his head and a few metres to the right[17], was the underbelly[18] of Roscoe's private lift.

The toolbox was next to him, on the lift roof. Carefully, he opened it. The sides of the case were lined with thick sponge[19]. Inside, in the specially moulded space[20], was what looked like a complicated film projector, silver and concave with a thick glass lens[21]. He took it out, then glanced

1. À nouveau
2. il leva le bras et poussa
3. trappe ouvrant vers l'extérieur
4. devant lui
5. se hissa et grimpa sur le toit
6. cage d'ascenseur principale
7. cerné de tous côtés par des poutrelles et des tuyaux noircis par la graisse et par la saleté
8. De gros câbles en acier pendaient
9. crissaient en véhiculant leur charge de haut en bas
10. tunnel carré, qui semblait interminable
11. rais de lumière
12. se refermaient à mesure que
13. La brise avait réussi à s'infiltrer
14. faisant voler la poussière, qui lui piquait les yeux
15. l'auraient mené directement au
16. Plus haut
17. à quelques mètres sur la droite
18. se trouvait le dessous
19. parois de la caisse étaient doublées de mousse épaisse
20. compartiment moulé à cet effet
21. épaisse lentille de verre

at his watch[1]. Eight thirty-five. It would take him an hour to connect the device[2] to the bottom of Roscoe's lift, and a little more to ensure it was working[3]. He had plenty[4] of time.

Smiling to himself[5], the Gentleman took out a power screwdriver[6] and began to work.

At twelve o'clock, Helen Bosworth called through[7] on the telephone. "Your car is here, Mr Roscoe."

"Thank you, Helen."

Roscoe hadn't done much[8] that morning. He had been aware that only half his mind was[9] on his work. Once again, he glanced at the photograph on his desk. Paul. How could things have gone so wrong[10] between a father and a son? And what could have happened in the last few months to make them so much worse[11]?

He stood up[12], put his jacket on and walked across[13] his office – on his way to lunch with Senator Andrews. He often had lunch with politicians. They either wanted[14] his money, his ideas ... or him. Anyone as rich as Roscoe was a powerful friend and politicians need all the friends they can get[15].

He pressed the lift call button and the doors slid open. He took one step forward[16].

The last thing Michael J. Roscoe saw in his life was a lift with white marble walls, a blue carpet and a silver handrail. His right foot, wearing[17] one

1. montre
2. l'instrument
3. pour vérifier qu'il fonctionnait
4. beaucoup
5. Le sourire aux lèvres
6. tournevis électrique
7. l'appela
8. n'avait pas fait grand-chose
9. avait senti qu'il n'était qu'à moitié concentré
10. les choses avaient-elles pu si mal tourner
11. au cours des derniers mois, pour que tout s'aggrave à ce point
12. se leva
13. traversa
14. Soit ils voulaient
15. d'un maximum d'amis
16. fit un pas en avant
17. chaussé de

of the black leather shoes that were hand-made[1] for him by a small shop in Rome, travelled down to the carpet and kept going ... right through it[2]. The rest of his body followed, tilting into the lift and then through it[3]. And then he was falling sixty floors to his death[4]. He was so surprised by what had happened, so totally unable[5] to understand what had happened, that he didn't even cry out[6]. He simply fell into the blackness of the lift-shaft, bounced twice off the walls[7], then crashed into the solid concrete of the basement[8], two hundred metres below[9].

The lift remained where it was. It looked solid[10] but in fact it wasn't there at all. What Roscoe had stepped into was a hologram being projected into the empty space[11] of the lift-shaft where the real lift should have been. The Gentleman had programed the door to open when Roscoe pressed the call button, and had quietly watched him step into oblivion[12]. If the billionaire had just looked up for a moment[13], he would have seen the silver hologram projector beaming the image[14], a few metres above him. But a man getting into a lift on his way to lunch does not look up. The Gentleman had known this. And he was never wrong[15].

At twelve thirty-five, the chauffeur called up to say that Mr Roscoe hadn't arrived at the car. Ten minutes later, Helen Bosworth alerted security, who began to search[16] the foyer of the building.

1. faites à la main

2. se posa sur le tapis et passa à travers

3. basculant dans l'ascenseur, puis passant à travers, dans le vide

4. fit une chute mortelle de soixante étages

5. incapable

6. ne hurla même pas

7. dans l'obscurité de la cage d'ascenseur, rebondit deux fois contre les murs

8. s'écrasa sur le béton du sous-sol

9. plus bas

10. Il avait l'air réel

11. Roscoe était entré dans un hologramme projeté dans l'espace vacant

12. sombrer dans le néant

13. levé les yeux un instant

14. qui projetait l'image

15. ne se trompait jamais

16. commença à fouiller

At one o'clock, they called the restaurant. The senator was there, waiting for his lunch guest[1]. But Roscoe hadn't shown up[2].

In fact, his body wasn't discovered until the next day, by which time[3] the billionaire's disappearance had become the lead story[4] on American TV news[5]. A bizarre accident – that's what it looked like. Nobody could work out[6] what had happened. Because of course, by that time, the Gentleman had reprogramed the mainframe, removed[7] the projector and left everything as it should have been[8] before quietly leaving the building.

Two days later, a man who looked nothing like[9] a maintenance engineer walked into JFK International Airport[10]. He was about to board a flight for[11] Switzerland. But first of all he visited a flower shop[12] and ordered[13] a dozen black tulips to be sent[14] to a certain address. The man paid with cash[15]. He didn't leave a name.

1. invité
2. n'était jamais arrivé
3. entre-temps
4. faisait sensation
5. journaux télévisés
6. ne parvenait à comprendre
7. retiré
8. tel que c'était
9. qui ne ressemblait pas du tout à
10. [aéroport de New York : du nom du 35e président John Fitzgerald Kennedy]
11. sur le point d'embarquer sur un vol à destination de
12. alla chez un fleuriste
13. commanda
14. à expédier
15. paya en espèces

BLUE SHADOW[1]

The worst time to feel alone is when you're in a crowd.[2] Alex Rider was walking across the playground, surrounded by hundreds[3] of boys and girls of about his own age[4]. They were all heading[5] in the same direction, all wearing the same blue and grey uniform, all of them probably thinking much the same thoughts[6]. The last lesson of the day had just ended. Homework, tea[7] and television would fill the remaining hours until bed[8]. Another school day. So why did he feel so out of it[9], as if he were watching the last weeks of the term from the other side of a giant glass screen[10]?

Alex jerked his backpack over one shoulder[11] and continued towards the bike shed[12]. The bag was heavy[13]. As usual, it contained double homework ... French and history. He had missed[14] two weeks of school and he was having to work hard to catch up[15]. His teachers had not been sympa-

1. ombre
2. Se sentir seul au milieu de la foule, c'est ce qu'il y a de pire.
3. traversait la cour de récréation, entouré de centaines
4. d'à peu près son âge
5. se dirigeaient tous
6. pensaient probablement la même chose
7. Les devoirs à faire, le repas du soir
8. les occuperaient jusqu'au moment du coucher
9. se sentait-il aussi exclu
10. observait les dernières semaines du trimestre à travers une immense paroi de verre
11. balança son sac à dos par-dessus son épaule
12. en direction de l'abri à vélos
13. lourd
14. manqué
15. devait travailler dur pour rattraper

thetic[1]. Nobody had said as much[2], but when he had finally returned with a doctor's letter (...a *bad dose of flu*[3] *with complications...*) they had nodded[4] and smiled and secretly thought him a little bit pampered and spoiled[5]. On the other hand, they had to make allowances.[6] They all knew that Alex had no parents, that he had been living with an uncle who had died in some sort of car accident. But even so.[7] Two weeks in bed! Even his closest[8] friends had to admit that was a bit much[9].

And he couldn't tell them the truth[10]. He wasn't allowed to tell anyone[11] what had really happened. That was the hell of it.[12]

Alex looked around him, at the children streaming through[13] the school gates[14], some dribbling footballs, some on their mobile phones. He looked at the teachers, curling themselves into their second-hand cars[15]. At first, he had thought that the whole school[16] had somehow[17] changed while he was away[18]. But he knew now that what had happened was worse[19]. Everything was the same. It was he who[20] had changed.

Alex was fourteen years old, an ordinary schoolboy in an ordinary west London comprehensive[21]. Or he had been. Only a few weeks ago[22], he had discovered that his uncle had been a secret agent, working for MI6. The uncle – Ian Rider – had been murdered[23] and MI6 had forced Alex to take his place. They had given him a crash course[24] in

1. compréhensifs
2. ne l'avait vraiment dit
3. mauvaise grippe
4. hoché la tête
5. en se disant qu'il était un peu pourri gâté
6. D'un autre côté, il fallait être indulgent.
7. Mais tout de même.
8. les plus proches
9. c'était un peu exagéré
10. vérité
11. n'avait le droit de dire à personne
12. C'était bien ça, le problème.
13. les nuées d'enfants franchissant
14. grilles
15. se faufilant dans leurs voitures d'occasion
16. toute l'école
17. d'une certaine façon
18. en son absence
19. était bien pire
20. C'était lui qui
21. collège
22. Il y avait à peine quelques semaines
23. assassiné
24. formation express

SAS[1] survival techniques and sent him on a lunatic mission on the south coast[2]. He had been chased, shot at and almost killed[3]. And at the end of it he had been packed off and sent back[4] to school as if nothing had happened. But first they had made him sign the Official Secrets Act[5]. Alex smiled at the memory of it[6]. He didn't need to sign anything. Who would have believed him anyway?

But it was the secrecy that was getting to him[7] now. Whenever anyone[8] asked him what he had been doing in the weeks he'd been away[9], he'd been forced to tell them that he'd been in bed, reading, slouching around[10] the house, whatever[11]. Alex didn't want to boast about[12] what he'd done, but he hated having to deceive[13] his friends. It made him angry. MI6 hadn't just put him in danger. They'd locked his whole life in a filing cabinet and thrown away[14] the key.

He had reached[15] the bike shed. Somebody muttered[16] a "goodbye" in his direction and he nodded, then reached up to brush away the single strand of fair hair that had fallen over his eye[17]. Sometimes he wished that the whole business[18] with MI6 had never happened. But at the same time – he had to admit it – part of him wanted it all to[19] happen again. Sometimes he felt that he no longer belonged in the safe, comfortable world[20] of Brookland School. Too much had changed. And

1. [Special Air Service, commando d'intervention spéciale de l'armée britannique]
2. l'avaient expédié sur une mission de dingue, sur la côte sud
3. s'était fait traquer, tirer dessus et presque tuer
4. congédié et réexpédié
5. ils l'avaient soumis au secret d'État
6. en se le rappelant
7. ce côté secret qui le minait
8. Chaque fois que quelqu'un
9. pendant ses semaines d'absence
10. traînant sans rien faire dans
11. n'importe quoi
12. se vanter de
13. détestait être obligé de mentir à
14. enfermé sa vie entière dans un placard et jeté
15. était arrivé à
16. marmonna
17. puis repoussa d'un geste la seule mèche blonde qui lui tombait sur les yeux
18. souhaitait que toute cette histoire
19. quelque part, il avait envie que tout
20. avait l'impression de ne plus faire partie du cocon protecteur

at the end of the day, anything was better than double[1] homework.

He lifted his bike out[2] of the shed, unlocked it[3], pulled the backpack over both his[4] shoulders and prepared to ride away[5]. That was when he saw the beat-up[6] white car. Back again outside[7] the school gates. For the second time that week.

Everyone knew about[8] the man in the white car.

He was in his twenties, bald, and had two broken stumps[9] where his front teeth[10] should have been and five metal studs in his ear[11]. He didn't advertise his name[12]. When people talked about him, they called him Skoda – after the make[13] of his car. But there were some who said that his name was Jake and he had once been[14] at Brookland. If so[15], he had come back like an unwelcome ghost; here one minute, vanishing the next[16] – somehow always a few seconds ahead of any passing police car[17] or over-inquisitive[18] teacher.

Skoda sold drugs[19]. He sold soft[20] drugs to the younger kids[21] and harder stuff to any of the sixth-formers[22] stupid enough to buy it. It seemed incredible to Alex that Skoda could get away with it so easily[23], dealing his little packets in broad daylight[24]. But of course there was a code of honour in the school. No one turned anyone into[25] the police, not even a rat[26] like Skoda. And there was always the fear[27] that if Skoda went down[28], some

1. en fin de compte, tout était bon pour échapper à la double dose de
2. retira son vélo
3. déverrouilla l'antivol
4. ses deux
5. se prépara à partir
6. déglinguée
7. Elle était à nouveau devant
8. savait qui était
9. avait la vingtaine, était chauve et avait deux chicots
10. dents de devant
11. clous en métal à l'oreille
12. ne criait pas son nom sur les toits
13. comme la marque
14. que c'était un ancien [élève]
15. Si c'était le cas
16. fantôme indésirable, apparaissant et disparaissant en un éclair
17. d'avance sur les patrouilles de police
18. trop curieux
19. vendait de la drogue
20. douces
21. aux plus jeunes
22. des drogues plus dures aux première et terminale
23. s'en tirer si facilement
24. en plein jour
25. ne dénonçait qui que ce soit à
26. ordure
27. crainte
28. tombait

of the people he supplied[1] – friends, classmates – might go with him[2].

Drugs had never been a huge[3] problem at Brookland, but recently that had begun to change. A clutch of seventeen-year-olds[4] had started buying Skoda's goods[5] and, like a stone dropped into a pool, the ripples had rapidly spread[6]. There had been a spate of thefts[7], as well as one or two bullying incidents[8] – younger children being forced to bring in money for older kids. The stuff[9] Skoda was selling seemed to get more expensive the more you bought of it[10] – and it hadn't been cheap at the start[11].

Alex watched as a heavy-shouldered[12] boy with dark hair and serious acne lumbered over to[13] the car, paused by[14] the window and then continued on his way. He felt a sudden jolt of anger[15]. The boy's name was Colin and just twelve months ago[16] he had been one of Alex's best friends. In fact, Colin had been popular[17] with everyone. But then everything had changed. He had become moody and withdrawn[18]. His work had gone downhill[19]. Suddenly nobody had wanted to know him[20] – and this was the reason. Alex had never thought much about[21] drugs, apart from knowing that he would never take them himself[22]. But he could see that the man in the white car wasn't just poisoning a handful of dumb kids[23]. He was poisoning the whole[24] school.

1. fournissait
2. tomberaient avec lui
3. énorme
4. bande d'élèves de 17 ans
5. marchandises
6. les effets n'avaient pas tardé à se manifester [tel un caillou que l'on fait tomber dans l'eau, l'onde s'était rapidement propagée]
7. série de vols
8. cas de harcèlement
9. drogue
10. augmenter plus vous en achetiez
11. n'avait jamais été bon marché
12. large d'épaules
13. se dirigeait d'un pas lourd vers
14. s'arrêtait à
15. accès de colère
16. il y avait à peine un an
17. s'entendait bien
18. morose et renfermé
19. s'était dégradé
20. ne voulait plus entendre parler de lui
21. jamais beaucoup réfléchi à
22. il savait seulement qu'il n'en prendrait jamais
23. ne se contentait pas d'empoisonner une poignée de gosses idiots
24. tout entière

A policeman on foot patrol[1] appeared, walking towards the gate. A moment later, the white car was gone, black smut bubbling from a faulty exhaust[2]. Alex was on[3] his bike before he knew what he was doing[4], pedalling fast out of the playground, swerving round[5] the school secretary, who was also on her way home[6].

"Not too fast, Alex!" she called out[7], and sighed[8] when he ignored her. Miss Bedfordshire had always had a soft spot[9] for Alex without knowing quite[10] why. And she alone[11] in the school had wondered if there hadn't been more to his absence[12] that the doctor's note had suggested.

The white Skoda accelerated down the road, turning left, then right, and Alex thought he was going to lose it. But then it twisted through the maze of back streets[13] that led up to[14] the King's Road and hit[15] the inevitable four o'clock traffic jam[16], coming to a halt about[17] two hundred metres ahead[18].

The average speed of traffic[19] in London is, at the start of the twenty-first century, lower than it used to be in Victorian times[20]. During normal working hours, any bicycle will beat any car on just about any journey at all[21]. And Alex wasn't riding just any bike. He still had his Condor Junior Roadracer, hand-built[22] for him in the workshop that had been open for business[23] in the same street in Holborn for[24] more than fifty years. He'd

1. patrouillant à pied
2. le pot d'échappement défectueux crachant de la fumée noire
3. enfourcha
4. en deux secondes
5. évitant de justesse
6. rentrait aussi chez elle
7. lui cria-t-elle
8. soupira
9. un faible
10. vraiment
11. elle était la seule
12. à se demander si son absence ne cachait pas autre chose
13. zigzagua à travers le dédale de ruelles
14. menaient à
15. [la Skoda] tomba dans
16. embouteillages
17. s'arrêtant à environ
18. de là
19. vitesse moyenne de circulation
20. plus lente qu'à l'époque victorienne
21. va plus vite qu'une voiture, quel que soit le trajet
22. monté
23. atelier qui existait
24. depuis

recently had it upgraded with an integrated brake and gear-lever system fitted to the handlebar[1], and he only had to flick his thumb[2] to feel the bike click up a gear[3], the lightweight titanium sprockets spinning smoothly beneath[4] him.

He caught up with[5] the car just as it turned the corner[6] and joined the rest of the traffic on the King's Road. He would just have to hope[7] that Skoda was going to stay in the city, but somehow Alex didn't think it likely[8] that he would travel too far. The drug dealer hadn't chosen Brookland School as a target simply because he'd been there[9]. It had to be somewhere in his general neighbourhood[10] – not too close[11] to home but not too far either[12].

The lights[13] changed and the white car jerked forward, heading west[14]. Alex was pedalling slowly, keeping[15] a few cars behind, just in case Skoda happened to glance in his mirror[16]. They reached the corner known as World's End[17] and suddenly the road was clear[18] and Alex had to switch gears[19] again and pedal hard to keep up[20]. The car drove on, through Parson's Green and down towards Putney. Alex twisted from one lane[21] to another, cutting in front of a taxi and receiving the blast of a horn as his reward[22]. It was a warm day and he could feel his French and history homework dragging down[23] his back. How much further were they going?[24] And what would he do when they

1. il l'avait fait améliorer récemment, avec freinage intégré et système de braquets fixé au guidon
2. n'avait qu'un coup de pouce à donner
3. monter d'un cran
4. pignons en titane léger tournant en souplesse au-dessous de
5. rattrapa
6. angle
7. n'avait plus qu'à espérer
8. pensait qu'il était peu probable
9. c'était un ancien élève
10. proche voisinage
11. près
12. non plus
13. feux de circulation
14. bondit en avant, vers l'ouest
15. restant
16. regarderait dans le rétroviseur
17. [nom d'une cité, district de Chelsea]
18. dégagée
19. changer de vitesse
20. pouvoir suivre
21. voie
22. faisant une queue de poisson à un taxi qui le remercia d'un coup de klaxon
23. peser sur
24. Allaient-ils encore loin ?

1. tourna brusquement
2. s'était garé sur une aire mal goudronnée
3. la Tamise
4. laissant les voitures filer à ses côtés
5. en cours de réhabilitation
6. tour d'appartements de luxe heurtant l'horizon londonien
7. affreux squelette de poutres en acier
8. dalles de béton
9. nuée d'hommes casqués
10. les dominant tous, une grue géante, jaune canari
11. panneau indiquait

got there? Alex was beginning to wonder if this had been a good idea when the car turned off[1] and he realized they had arrived.

Skoda had pulled into a rough tarmac area[2], a temporary carpark next to the River Thames[3], not far from Putney Bridge. Alex stayed on the bridge, allowing the traffic to roll past[4], and watched as the drug dealer got out of his car and began to walk. The area was being redeveloped[5], another block of prestige flats rising up to bruise the London skyline[6]. Right now, the building was no more than an ugly skeleton of steel girders[7] and prefabricated concrete slabs[8]. It was surrounded by a swarm of men in hard hats[9]. There were bulldozers, cement mixers and, towering above them all, a huge canary-yellow crane[10]. A sign read[11]:

12. Adressez-vous au bureau du chantier

13. avait à faire sur le chantier
14. perplexe

Alex wondered if Skoda had some sort of business on the site[13]. He seemed to be heading for the entrance. But then he turned off. Alex watched him, puzzled[14].

The building site was wedged in between[1] the bridge and a cluster[2] of modern buildings. There was a pub, then what looked like a brand-new conference centre[3], and finally a police station with a carpark half-filled with[4] official cars. But right next to the building site, sticking out into[5] the river, was a wooden jetty with two cabin cruisers and an old iron barge quietly rusting in the murky water[6]. Alex hadn't noticed the jetty at first, but Skoda walked straight onto it, then climbed onto[7] the barge. He opened a door and disappeared inside. Was this where he lived? It was late in the day[8]. Somehow, Alex doubted he was about to set off on a pleasure cruise[9] down the River Thames.

He got back on his bike and cycled slowly to the end of the bridge, and then down towards[10] the carpark. He left the bike and his backpack out of sight[11] and continued on foot, moving more slowly as he approached[12] the jetty. He wasn't afraid[13] of being caught[14]. This was a public place and even if Skoda did reappear, there would be nothing he could do[15]. But he was curious. Just what was the drug dealer doing onboard[16] a barge? It seemed a bizarre place to have stopped. Alex still wasn't sure what he was going to do, but he wanted to have a look inside. Then he would decide.

The wooden jetty creaked[17] under his feet as he stepped onto it[18]. The barge was called *Blue Shadow* but there was little blue left[19] in the

1. encastré entre
2. ensemble
3. palais des congrès tout neuf
4. occupé à moitié par
5. s'avançant sur
6. jetée en bois avec deux bateaux de plaisance et une vieille péniche métallique rouillant paisiblement dans l'eau trouble
7. y monta directement, puis grimpa sur
8. tard
9. se doutait bien qu'il n'allait pas partir en croisière
10. vers
11. hors de vue
12. en ralentissant aux abords de
13. n'avait pas peur
14. se faire surprendre
15. il ne pourrait rien faire
16. à bord de
17. grinça
18. lorsqu'il monta dessus
19. il n'y avait plus beaucoup de bleu

flaking paint[1], the rusty ironwork[2] and the dirty, oil-covered decks[3]. The barge was about ten metres long and very square[4], with a single cabin in the centre. It was lying low in the water[5] and Alex guessed that most of the living quarters would be underneath[6]. He knelt down[7] on the jetty and pretended to tie his shoelaces[8], hoping to look through the narrow, slanting[9] windows. But all the curtains were drawn[10]. What now?[11]

The barge was moored[12] on one side of the jetty. The two cruisers were side by side on the other. Skoda wanted privacy[13] – but he must also need light, and there would be no need to draw the curtains on the far side with nothing there[14] apart from the river. The only trouble[15] was, to look in the other windows Alex would have to climb onto the barge itself. He considered briefly[16]. It had to be worth the risk.[17] He was near enough to the building site[18]. Nobody was going to try to hurt him[19] with so many people around.

He placed one foot on the deck, then slowly transferred his weight onto it[20]. He was afraid that moving the barge would give him away[21]. Sure enough[22], the barge dipped[23] under his weight; but Alex had chosen his moment well. A police launch was sailing past, heading up[24] the river and back[25] into town. The barge bobbed naturally in its wake[26] and by the time it settled[27] Alex was onboard, crouching next to[28] the cabin door.

1. peinture écaillée
2. parties métalliques rouillées
3. ponts couverts d'huile
4. très carrée
5. Sa ligne de flottaison était basse
6. songea que l'essentiel de la partie habitée était immergé
7. s'agenouilla
8. fit semblant de refaire ses lacets
9. étroites et obliques
10. rideaux étaient tirés
11. Que faire ?
12. amarrée
13. ne voulait pas être vu
14. de l'autre côté, car il n'y avait rien
15. seul problème
16. réfléchit rapidement
17. Cela devait valoir la peine.
18. assez près du chantier
19. lui faire du mal
20. son poids dessus
21. ne le trahisse
22. Et effectivement
23. s'enfonça
24. vedette de la police passait par là, remontant
25. pour rentrer
26. tangua naturellement dans son sillage
27. le temps qu'elle se stabilise
28. accroupi près de

Now he could hear music coming from inside. The heavy beat[1] of a rock band. He didn't want to do it, but he knew there was only one way to look in. He tried to find an area of the deck that wasn't too covered in oil, then lay flat on his stomach[2]. Clinging onto the handrail[3], he lowered[4] his head and shoulders over the side of the barge and shifted himself forward so that he was hanging almost upside-down[5] over the water.

He was right[6]. The curtains on this side of the barge were open. Looking through the dirty glass of the window, he could see two men. Skoda was sitting on a bunk[7], smoking a cigarette. There was a second man, blond-haired and ugly, with twisted lips and three days' stubble[8], wearing a torn[9] sweatshirt and jeans, making a cup of coffee at a small stove[10]. The music was coming from a ghetto-blaster perched on a shelf[11]. Alex looked around the cabin. Apart from two bunks and the miniature kitchen, the barge offered no living accommodation at all[12]. Instead[13] it had been converted for another purpose[14]. Skoda and his friend had turned it into a floating laboratory[15].

There were two metal work-surfaces[16], a sink and a pair of electric scales[17]. Everywhere there were test-tubes and Bunsen burners, flasks, glass pipes and measuring spoons[18]. The whole place was filthy[19] – obviously neither of the men cared about[20] hygiene – but Alex knew that he was looking

1. rythme endiablé
2. se mit à plat ventre
3. En s'accrochant au garde-corps
4. descendit
5. par-dessus bord et se pencha en avant, presque suspendu la tête en bas
6. avait raison
7. couchette
8. laid, la bouche tordue, et avec une barbe de trois jours
9. déchiré
10. réchaud
11. chaîne stéréo portable posée sur une étagère
12. n'avait pas d'autres aménagements
13. Plutôt
14. aménagée pour faire autre chose
15. transformée en laboratoire flottant
16. plans de travail
17. évier et deux balances électroniques
18. tubes à essai, becs Bunsen, flacons, pipettes et cuillères à mesurer
19. crasseux
20. ne se préoccupait de

1. centre névralgique de leurs activités
2. les recoupaient, les pesaient et les emballaient avant de les livrer
3. du coin
4. site de fabrication
5. à deux pas
6. c'était malin
7. se redressa et se glissa à nouveau
8. étourdi
9. Lorsqu'il s'était suspendu la tête en bas, le sang y avait afflué.
10. respira deux bons coups, essayant de se concentrer
11. pourrait prendre le relais
12. quelques mois plus tôt
13. Laisser quelqu'un d'autre s'en occuper.
14. pédalé jusqu'ici
15. repensa à la première fois où il avait vu
16. traînant des pieds vers elle
17. un bref accès de colère
18. munie d'un siphon
19. l'aurait débouché et tout fait sombrer

into the heart of their operation[1]. This was where they prepared the drugs they sold; cut them down, weighed them and packaged them for delivery[2] to local[3] schools. It was an incredible idea – to put a drugs factory[4] on a boat, almost in the middle of London and only a stone's throw away[5] from a police station. But at the same time, it was a clever one[6]. Who would have looked for it here?

The blond man suddenly turned round and Alex hooked his body up and slithered backwards[7] onto the deck. For a moment he was dizzy[8]. Hanging upside-down, the blood had drained into his head.[9] He took a couple of breaths, trying to collect his thoughts[10]. It would be easy enough to walk over to the police station and tell the officer in charge what he had seen. The police could take over from there[11].

But something inside Alex rejected the idea. Maybe that was what he would have done a few months before[12]. Let someone else take care of it.[13] But he hadn't cycled all this way[14] just to call in the police. He thought back to his first sighting of[15] the white car outside the school gates. He remembered Colin, his friend, shuffling over to it[16] and felt once again a brief blaze of anger[17]. This was something he wanted to do himself.

What could he do? If the barge had been equipped with a plug[18], Alex would have pulled it out and sunk the entire thing[19]. But of course it wasn't as easy as that. The barge was tied[1] to the jetty by two thick ropes[2]. He could untie them[3] – but that wouldn't help either[4]. The barge would drift away[5] – but this was Putney; there were no whirlpools or waterfalls[6]. Skoda would simply turn the engine on and cruise back again[7].

Alex looked around him. On the building site, the day's work was coming to an end. Some of the men were already leaving[8] and, as he watched, he saw a trapdoor open[9] about a hundred metres above him and a stocky[10] man begin the long climb down[11] from the top of the crane. Alex closed his eyes. A whole series[12] of images had suddenly flashed into his mind[13], like different sections of a jigsaw[14].

The barge. The building site. The police station. The crane with its great hook dangling underneath the jib[15].

And Blackpool[16] funfair[17]. He'd gone there once with his housekeeper[18], Jack Starbright, and had watched as she'd won a teddy bear[19], hooking it out of a glass case with a mechanical claw and carrying it over to a chute[20].

Could it be done? Alex looked again, working out the angles[21]. Yes. It probably could.

He stood up and crept back across the deck[22] to the door that Skoda had entered. There was a length of wire lying to one side[23] and he picked

1. attachée
2. gros cordages
3. les détacher
4. cela ne servirait à rien non plus
5. partirait à la dérive
6. ni tourbillons, ni chutes d'eau
7. mettrait simplement le moteur en marche et reviendrait
8. partaient déjà
9. trappe s'ouvrir
10. trapu
11. entamer la longue descente
12. Toute une série
13. lui vinrent soudain à l'esprit
14. pièces d'un puzzle
15. grand crochet pendant sous la flèche
16. [station balnéaire du nord-ouest de l'Angleterre, célèbre pour ses attractions et pour ses illuminations nocturnes]
17. fête foraine
18. une fois, avec sa gouvernante
19. nounours
20. en le crochetant hors de sa cage en verre avec une pince mécanique et en le transportant au-dessus d'un toboggan
21. étudiant toutes les possibilités
22. retraversa le pont à pas de loup
23. un bout de fil de fer, par terre, sur un côté

it up[1], then wound it several times round the handle[2] of the door. He looped the wire over a hook[3] in the wall and pulled it tight[4]. The door was effectively locked[5]. There was a second door at the back of the boat. Alex secured that one[6] with his own bicycle padlock[7]. As far as he could see, the windows were too narrow to crawl through[8]. There was no other way in or out[9].

He crept off[10] the barge and back[11] onto the jetty. Then he untied it, leaving[12] the thick rope loosely curled up beside the metal pegs[13] – the stanchions – that had secured it[14]. The river was still[15]. It would be a while[16] before the barge drifted away.

He straightened up[17]. Satisfied with[18] his work so far, he began to run[19].

1. le ramassa
2. l'entortilla plusieurs fois autour de la poignée
3. fit passer le câble sur un crochet
4. le serra très fort
5. bel et bien bloquée
6. verrouilla celle-ci
7. cadenas
8. pour s'y faufiler
9. entrée ou sortie
10. quitta discrètement
11. revint
12. la détacha, laissant
13. enroulée près des plots métalliques
14. bornes d'amarrage auxquels elle était fixée
15. immobile
16. Il s'écoulerait un certain temps
17. se redressa
18. Content de
19. courir

HOOKED

The entrance to the building site was crowded with construction workers[1] preparing to go home. Alex was reminded of[2] Brookland an hour earlier[3]. Nothing really changed when you got older[4]– except that maybe you weren't given[5] homework. The men and women drifting out of the site[6] were tired, in a hurry to be away[7]. That was probably why none of them tried[8] to stop Alex as he slipped in among them[9], walking purposefully[10] as if he[11] knew where he was going, as if he had every right[12] to be there.

But the shift wasn't completely finished yet[13]. Other workers were still carrying tools, stowing away machinery, packing up for the night[14]. They were all wearing protective headgear[15] and, seeing a pile of plastic helmets[16], Alex snatched one up[17] and put it on. The great sweep[18] of the block of flats that was being built loomed up ahead of him[19]. To pass through it he was forced into a

1. débordait d'ouvriers du bâtiment
2. se rappela
3. plus tôt
4. en grandissant
5. qu'on ne vous donne plus
6. qui quittaient le chantier
7. pressés de partir
8. aucun ne tenta
9. lorsqu'il se glissa parmi eux
10. d'un pas décidé
11. comme s'il
12. tout à fait le droit
13. le travail n'était pas tout à fait fini
14. transportaient encore des outils, rangeaient les engins, remballaient pour la nuit
15. casques de protection
16. des casques en plastique
17. en saisit un
18. L'immense étendue
19. en construction surgit devant lui

narrow corridor between two scaffolding towers[1]. Suddenly a thick-set man in white overalls stepped in front of him[2], blocking his way.

"Where are you going?" he demanded.

"My dad..." Alex gestured vaguely[3] in the direction of another worker and kept walking[4]. The trick worked.[5] The man didn't challenge him again[6].

He was heading for the crane. It was standing in the open[7], the high priest[8] of the construction. Alex hadn't realized how very tall it was until he reached it. The supporting tower was bolted into a massive block of concrete[9]. The tower was very narrow – once he had squeezed[10] through the iron girders he could reach out and[11] touch all four sides. A ladder ran straight up the centre[12]. Without stopping to think – if he thought about it he might change his mind[13] – Alex began to climb.

It's only a ladder, he told himself. You've climbed ladders before. You've got nothing to worry about.

But this was a ladder with three hundred rungs[14]. If Alex let go[15] or slipped, there would be nothing to stop him falling to his death[16]. There were rest platforms at intervals[17] but Alex didn't dare stop to catch his breath[18]. Somebody might look up and see him. And there was always a chance[19] that the barge, loose from its moorings[20], might begin to drift[21].

1. échafaudages
2. un costaud en combinaison blanche s'interposa
3. fit un geste vague
4. continua à marcher
5. L'astuce fonctionna.
6. ne l'embêta plus
7. se dressait en plein ciel
8. grand prêtre
9. tour était fixée à un énorme bloc de béton
10. après s'être faufilé
11. en tendant le bras, il pouvait
12. échelle, au centre, grimpait tout en haut
13. changerait peut-être d'avis
14. barreaux
15. lâchait prise
16. rien ne l'empêcherait de faire une chute mortelle
17. des paliers de repos à intervalles réguliers
18. n'osait pas s'arrêter pour reprendre son souffle
19. il était toujours possible
20. libérée de son amarrage
21. dériver

After two hundred and fifty rungs, the tower narrowed[1]. Alex could see the crane's control cabin[2] directly above him. He looked back down. The men on the building site were suddenly very small and far away. He climbed the last stretch[3] of ladder. There was a trapdoor over his head, leading into[4] the cabin. But the trapdoor was locked.

Fortunately, Alex was ready for this. When MI6 had sent him on his first mission, they had given him a number[5] of gadgets – he couldn't exactly call them weapons[6] – to help him out of tight corners[7]. One of these was a tube marked ZIT-CLEAN[8], FOR HEALTHIER SKIN[9]. But the cream inside the tube did much more than clean up spots[10].

Although Alex had used most of it[11], he had managed to hold onto the last remnants[12] and often carried the tube with him, as a sort of souvenir. He had it in his pocket now. Holding onto[13] the ladder with one hand, he took the tube out with the other. There was very little of the cream left[14] but Alex knew that a little was all he would need[15]. He opened the tube, squeezed some of the cream onto the lock[16] and waited. There was a moment's pause[17], then a hiss and a wisp of smoke[18]. The cream was eating into[19] the metal. The lock sprang open[20]. Alex pushed back[21] the trapdoor and climbed the last few rungs. He was in.

1. devint plus étroite
2. cabine de commande
3. segment
4. trappe au-dessus de sa tête, menant à
5. quantité
6. ce n'était pas vraiment des armes
7. pour se sortir de mauvaises passes
8. [crème anti-boutons]
9. pour une peau plus saine
10. faisait bien plus qu'éliminer les boutons
11. Bien qu'Alex l'ait presque tout utilisée
12. réussi à garder le peu qu'il restait
13. En se tenant à
14. Il restait très peu de crème
15. lui suffirait largement
16. fit couler un peu de crème sur le verrou
17. temps mort
18. sifflement et un peu de fumée
19. rongeait
20. s'ouvrit d'un coup
21. repoussa

He had to close the trapdoor again to create enough floor space to stand on[1]. He found himself in a square metal box[2], about the same size as a sit-in arcade game[3]. There was a pilot's chair[4] with two joysticks – one on each arm[5] – and, instead of a screen[6], a floor-to-ceiling window with a spectacular view of the building site, the river and the whole of west[7] London. A small computer monitor[8] had been built into one corner[9] and, at knee level[10], there was a radio transmitter.

The joysticks on the arms were surprisingly uncomplicated[11]. Each had just six buttons. There were even helpful diagrams to show what they did[12]. The right hand would lift the hook up and down[13]. The left hand would move it along the jib[14] – closer to or further from[15] the cabin. The left hand also controlled the whole top of the crane, rotating it 360 degrees. It couldn't have been much simpler.[16] Even the start[17] button was clearly labelled[18]. A big button for a big toy. Everything about the crane reminded Alex of an oversized[19] Meccano kit.

He pushed the button and felt power surge into[20] the control cabin. The computer lit up with a graphic of a barking dog as the warm-up program came into life[21]. Alex eased himself[22] into the operator's chair. There were still twenty or thirty men on the site. Looking down between his knees, he could see them moving silently far

1. pour avoir la place de se tenir debout
2. caisson métallique carré
3. qu'un habitacle de jeu d'arcade
4. fauteuil de pilotage
5. un sur chaque accoudoir
6. au lieu d'un écran
7. tout l'ouest de
8. écran d'ordinateur
9. installé dans un angle
10. au niveau des genoux
11. étonnamment simples
12. des schémas expliquant leurs fonctions
13. soulevait et abaissait le crochet
14. le déplaçait le long de la flèche
15. en le rapprochant ou l'éloignant de
16. Rien de plus simple.
17. de mise en marche
18. bien indiqué
19. géant
20. sentit l'électricité arriver dans
21. s'illumina, affichant un dessin de chien qui aboie tandis que le logiciel démarrait
22. s'installa

below[1]. Nobody had noticed that anything was wrong. But he knew he still had to move fast[2].

He pressed the green button on the right-hand control[3] – green for go[4] – then touched his fingers against[5] the joystick and pushed. Nothing happened! Alex frowned[6]. Maybe it was going to be more complicated than he'd thought. What had he missed[7]? He rested[8] his hands on the joysticks, looking left and right for another control[9]. His right hand moved slightly[10] and suddenly the hook soared up from the ground[11]. It was working!

Unknown to Alex[12], when he gripped the handles[13] of the joysticks, heat sensors concealed inside had read his body temperature[14] and activated the crane. All modern cranes have the same security system built into them[15], in case the operator has a heart attack[16] and falls against the controls[17]. There can be no accidents. Body heat is needed to make the crane work.

Luckily[18] for him, this crane was a Liebherr 154 EC-H, one of the most modern in the world. The Liebherr is incredibly easy to use – and remarkably accurate[19]. Now Alex pushed sideways[20] with his left hand and gasped as the crane swung round[21]. In front of him he could see the jib stretching out, swinging high over the rooftops[22] of London. The more he pushed, the faster the crane went.[23] The movement couldn't have been smoother[24]. The Liebherr 154 has a fluid coupling between[25] the

1. tout en bas
2. devait tout de même agir vite
3. commande de droite
4. vert pour « marche »
5. effleura des doigts
6. fronça les sourcils
7. raté
8. posa
9. cherchant d'autres commandes à droite et à gauche
10. un peu
11. décolla du sol
12. Sans qu'Alex le sache
13. en empoignant les manches
14. des capteurs de chaleur, dissimulés à l'intérieur, avaient détecté la température de son corps
15. intégré
16. crise cardiaque
17. s'affalerait sur les commandes
18. Heureusement
19. précise
20. de côté
21. étouffa un cri quand la grue tourna d'un coup
22. flèche se déployer et se balancer très haut au-dessus des toits
23. Plus il poussait, plus la grue allait vite.
24. plus souple
25. coupleur hydraulique entre

1. vitesses, alors il n'y a jamais d'à-coups ou de vibrations : elle glisse
2. immédiatement
3. la chance du débutant
4. sous réserve que
5. faisait un tour complet au-delà du
6. fut orientée juste au-dessus de
7. le chariot du crochet
8. glissa jusqu'à l'extrémité
9. au départ
10. au fur et à mesure qu'il s'approchait du sol
11. heurtait
12. serait démasqué
13. cm par cm
14. passa la langue sur ses lèvres
15. visa avec précaution
16. s'abattit sur
17. lâcha un gros mot
18. devait même se débattre
19. Avec un peu de chance
20. avait couvert le bruit
21. le ramenant vers lui au-dessus du pont
22. un gros plot métallique fixé sur

electric motor and the gears so that it never jolts or shudders – it glides[1]. Alex found a white button under his thumb and pressed it. The movement stopped at once[2].

He was ready. He would need some beginner's luck[3], but he was sure he could do it – provided[4] nobody looked up and saw the crane moving. He pushed with his left hand again and this time waited as the jib of the crane swung all the way round past[5] Putney Bridge and over the River Thames. When the jib was pointing directly over[6] the barge, he stopped. Now he manoeuvred the cradle with the hook[7]. First he slid it right to the end[8] of the jib. Then, using his other hand, he lowered it; quickly to begin with[9], more slowly as it drew closer to ground level[10]. The hook was solid metal. If he hit[11] the barge, Skoda might hear it and Alex would have given himself away[12]. Carefully now, one centimetre at a time[13]. Alex licked his lips[14] and, using all his concentration, took careful aim[15].

The hook crashed into[16] the deck. Alex cursed[17]. Surely Skoda would have heard it and would even now be grappling[18] with the door. Then he remembered the ghetto-blaster. Hopefully[19], the music would have drowned out the noise[20]. He lifted the hook, at the same time dragging it across the deck towards him[21]. He had seen his target. There was a thick metal stanchion welded into[22] the deck at the near end[1]. If he could just loop the hook around[2] the stanchion he would have caught his fish[3]. Then he could reel it in[4].

His first attempt missed[5] the stanchion by more than a metre[6]. Alex forced himself not to panic. He had to do this slowly or he would never do it at all. Working with his left and right hands, balancing one movement against the other[7], he dragged the hook over the deck and then back towards[8] the stanchion. He would just have to hope that the ghetto-blaster was still playing and that the sliding metal[9] wasn't making too much noise. He missed the stanchion a second time. This wasn't going to work[10]!

No. He could do it. It was the same as the funfair ... just bigger[11]. He gritted his teeth[12] and manoeuvred the hook a third time. This time he saw it happen. The hook caught hold of[13] the stanchion. He had it!

He looked down. Nobody had noticed anything wrong[14]. Now ... how did you lift? He pulled with his right hand[15]. The cable became taut[16]. He actually felt the crane take the weight[17] of the barge. The whole tower tilted forward alarmingly[18] and Alex almost slid out[19] of his seat. For the first time he wondered if his plan was actually possible. Could the crane lift the barge out of the water? What was the maximum load[20]? There was a white placard at the end of the crane arm,

1. à l'extrémité la plus proche
2. passer le crochet autour de
3. le poisson serait pris à l'hameçon
4. le remonter
5. tentative rata
6. de plus d'un mètre
7. en équilibrant chacun de ses mouvements
8. l'orienta à nouveau vers
9. coulissement métallique
10. marcher
11. en plus grand
12. serra les dents
13. attrapa
14. rien remarqué d'anormal
15. tira de sa main droite
16. se tendit
17. sentit vraiment la grue lever le poids
18. pencha en avant, de façon inquiétante
19. glissa presque hors
20. la charge maximale

printed with a measurement[1]: 3900KG. Surely the boat couldn't weigh that much[2]. He glanced at the computer screen. One set of digits[3] was changing so rapidly he was unable to read them[4]. They were showing the weight that the crane was taking[5]. What would happen if the boat was too heavy? Would the computer initiate an automatic cut-out[6]? Or would the whole thing just fall over[7]?

Alex settled himself[8] in the chair and pulled back, wondering what would happen next[9].

Inside the boat, Skoda was opening a bottle of gin. He'd had a good day, selling more than a hundred pounds' worth[10] of merchandise to the kids at his old[11] school. And the best thing was, they'd all be back for more[12]. Soon he'd only sell them the stuff if they promised to introduce it[13] to their friends. Then the friends would become customers too[14]. It was the easiest market in the world. He'd got them hooked.[15] They were his to do with as he liked.[16]

The blond-haired man he was working with was called Mike Beckett. The two of them had met[17] in prison and had decided to go into business together when they got out[18]. The boat had been Beckett's idea. There was no proper kitchen[19], no toilet and it was freezing[20] in winter ... but it worked. It even amused them to be so close to a

1. pancarte, au bout de la flèche de la grue, indiquait un poids
2. ne pesait pas autant
3. ensemble de chiffres
4. n'arrivait pas à les lire
5. indiquaient le poids levé par la grue
6. coupure
7. est-ce que tout allait se renverser
8. se cala
9. tira [sur la manette], se demandant ce qui allait se passer
10. en vendant pour plus de 100 livres sterling
11. ancienne
12. ils viendraient tous en redemander
13. la faire connaître
14. deviendraient aussi des clients
15. Il les avait rendus accros.
16. Il en ferait ce qu'il voudrait.
17. s'étaient rencontrés
18. à leur sortie
19. de vraie cuisine
20. on y gelait

police station. They enjoyed watching[1] the police cars or boats – going past[2]. Of course, the pigs would never think of looking right on their own doorstep[3].

Suddenly Beckett swore[4]. "What the...?"

"What is it?" Skoda looked up.

"The cup..."

Skoda watched as[5] a cup of coffee, which had been sitting on a shelf[6], began to move. It slid sideways, then fell off with a clatter, spilling[7] cold coffee on the grey rag[8] they called a carpet. Skoda was confused[9]. The cup seemed to have moved on its own[10]. Nothing had touched it. He giggled[11]. "How did you do that?" he asked.

"I didn't."

"Then..."

Beckett was the first to realize what was happening – but even he couldn't guess the truth[12]. "We're sinking![13]" he shouted.

He scrabbled for[14] the door. Now Skoda felt it for himself[15]. The floor was tilting[16]. Test-tubes and beakers slid into each other then crashed[17] to the floor, glass shattering[18]. He swore and followed Beckett – uphill now[19]. With every second that passed, the rake was becoming steeper[20]. But the strange thing was that the barge didn't seem to be sinking at all. On the contrary, the front of it seemed to be rising out[21] of the water.

"What's going on?" he yelled[22].

1. Ils s'amusaient à regarder
2. passer
3. les flics ne songeraient jamais à venir voir ce qui était sous leur nez
4. lâcha un gros mot
5. tandis que
6. qui était posée sur une étagère
7. glissa de côté puis tomba avec fracas, en répandant
8. loque grise
9. ne comprenait rien
10. bougé toute seule
11. gloussa
12. même lui ne pouvait deviner ce qui se passait
13. On coule !
14. rampa vers
15. lui aussi le sentit
16. penchait
17. glissèrent les uns contre les autres et s'écrasèrent
18. le verre se brisant
19. vers le haut
20. pente devenait plus abrupte
21. l'avant semblait se soulever hors
22. hurla-t-il

1. bloquée
2. d'un interstice
3. la retenait fermement
4. roulaient des tables et s'écrasaient
5. les assiettes et les tasses sales s'entrechoquaient et volaient en éclats
6. En pleurant et grognant à moitié
7. escalader cette paroi montagneuse
8. abrupt
9. perdit l'équilibre et tomba à la renverse
10. lui tomba dessus
11. enchevêtrés
12. grinçaient sous la pression
13. se brisa
14. se transforma en bélier et leur fonça dessus
15. os se casser dans son bras
16. hurla
17. à la verticale, suspendue
18. s'immobilisa
19. se soulever
20. avec stupéfaction
21. lentement, quelque chose s'était activé et avait pris la main, ralentissant l'opération

"The door's jammed[1]!" Beckett had managed to open it a crack[2], but the padlock on the other side was holding it firm[3].

"There's the other door!"

But the second door was now high above them. Bottles rolled off the table and smashed[4]. In the kitchen, soiled plates and mugs slid into each other, pieces flying[5]. With something between a sob and a snarl[6], Skoda tried to climb up the mountainside[7] that the inside of the boat had become. But it was already too steep[8]. The door was almost over his head. He lost his balance and fell backwards[9], shouting as – one second later – the other man was thrown on top of him[10]. The two of them rolled into the corner, tangled up in each other[11]. Plates, cups, knives, forks and dozens of pieces of scientific equipment crashed into them. The walls of the barge were grinding with the pressure[12]. A window shattered[13]. A table turned itself into a battering-ram and hurled itself at them[14]. Skoda felt a bone snap in his arm[15] and screamed out loud[16].

The barge was completely vertical, hanging[17] above the water at 90 degrees. For a moment it rested where it was[18]. Then it began to rise[19]...

Alex stared at the barge in amazement[20]. The crane was lifting it at half speed – some sort of override had come into action, slowing the operation down[21]

– but it wasn't even straining[1]. Alex could feel the power under his palms[2]. Sitting in the cabin with both hands[3] on the joysticks, his feet apart[4] and the jib of the crane jutting out ahead of him[5], he felt as if he and the crane had become one[6]. He only had to move a centimetre and the boat would be brought to him. He could see it, dangling on the hook, spinning[7] slowly. Water was streaming off the stern[8]. It was already clear of the water, rising up about a metre every[9] five seconds. He wondered what it must be like inside[10].

The radio beside his knee hissed into life[11].

"Crane operator! This is base. What the hell do you think you're doing? Over![12]" A pause, a burst of static[13]. Then the metallic voice was back. "Who is in the crane? Who's up there? Identify yourself!"

There was a microphone snaking towards Alex's chin[14] and he was tempted to say something. But he decided against it[15]. Hearing a teenager's voice[16] would only panic them more.

He looked down. There were about a dozen construction workers closing in on the base[17] of the crane. Others were pointing at[18] the boat, jabbering amongst themselves[19]. No sounds reached[20] the cabin. It was as if Alex was cut off[21] from the real world. He felt very secure[22]. He had no doubt that more workers would have already started climbing[23] the ladder and that it would all be over soon[24], but for the moment he was untouchable.

1. fatigant
2. puissance sous ses paumes
3. les deux mains
4. écartés
5. flèche de la grue déployée devant lui
6. ne faisaient plus qu'un
7. pendu au crochet, vrillant
8. ruisselait de la poupe
9. déjà hors de l'eau, s'élevant d'environ 1 m toutes les
10. comment c'était, dedans
11. se mit en marche en sifflant
12. Ici la station au sol. Qu'est-ce que vous foutez ? À vous !
13. un bruit de parasites
14. orienté vers le menton d'Alex
15. se ravisa
16. S'ils entendaient la voix d'un ado
17. regroupés au pied
18. montraient du doigt
19. en parlementant entre eux
20. Aucun son ne parvenait à
21. coupé
22. en sécurité
23. étaient déjà en train d'escalader
24. tout serait bientôt terminé

He concentrated on what he was doing. Getting the barge out of the water had been only half his plan. He still had to finish it.

"Crane operator! Lower[1] the hook! We believe there are people inside the boat and you are endangering their lives[2]. Repeat. Lower the hook!"

The barge was high above the water, dangling on the end[3] of the hook. Alex moved his left hand, turning the crane round so that the boat was swung in an arc along[4] the river and then over dry land[5]. There was a sudden buzz. The jib came to a halt[6]. Alex pushed the joystick. Nothing happened. He glanced at the computer. The screen had gone blank[7].

Someone at ground level had come to their senses and done the only sensible thing.[8] They had switched off the power[9]. The crane was dead.

Alex sat where he was, watching the barge swaying in the breeze[10]. He hadn't quite succeeded in what he had set out to do[11]. He had planned[12] to lower the boat – along with its contents[13] – safely into the carpark of the police station. It would have made a nice surprise for the authorities, he had thought. Instead[14], the boat was now hanging over[15] the conference centre that he had seen from Putney Bridge. But at the end of the day[16], he didn't suppose it made much difference[17]. The end result[18] would be the same.

1. Abaissez
2. mettez leur vie en danger
3. à l'extrémité
4. se balança en faisant un arc de cercle le long de
5. sur la terre ferme
6. s'arrêta net
7. était devenu noir
8. En bas, quelqu'un avait retrouvé ses esprits et fait la seule chose sensée.
9. coupé l'électricité
10. se balancer dans le vent
11. l'objectif qu'il s'était fixé
12. prévu
13. avec tout son contenu
14. Au lieu de ça
15. suspendu au-dessus de
16. au bout du compte
17. ne pensait pas que cela change grand-chose
18. résultat final

He stretched[1] his arms and relaxed, waiting for the trapdoor to burst open[2]. This wasn't going to be easy to explain.

And then he heard the tearing sound[3].

The metal stanchion that protruded from[4] the end of the deck had not been designed to carry the entire weight[5] of the barge. It was a miracle that it had lasted as long as it had[6]. As Alex watched, open-mouthed[7], from the cabin, the stanchion tore itself free[8]. For a few seconds it clung by one edge[9] to the deck. Then the last metal rivet came loose[10].

The barge had been sixty metres above the ground[11]. Now it began to fall.

In the Putney Riverside Conference Centre, the chief constable[12] of the Metropolitan Police[13] was addressing a large crowd[14] of journalists, TV cameras, civil servants and government officials[15]. He was a tall, thin[16] man who took himself very seriously[17]. His dark blue uniform was immaculate, every piece of silver[18] – from the studs[19] on his epaulettes to his five medals[20] – was polished until it gleamed[21]. This was his big day. He was sharing the platform with no less a personage than the home secretary himself[22]. The assistant[23] chief constable was there and also seven lower-ranking[24] officers. A slogan was being projected onto the wall behind him.

1. étira
2. s'ouvre brutalement
3. un bruit de craquement
4. dépassait
5. n'avait pas été conçu pour supporter tout le poids
6. qu'il ait résisté aussi longtemps
7. bouche bée
8. s'arracha complètement
9. il resta accroché d'un côté
10. céda
11. au-dessus du sol
12. chef
13. [police de Londres]
14. faisait un discours devant une foule
15. fonctionnaires et responsables du gouvernement
16. mince
17. se prenait très au sérieux
18. élément argenté
19. boutons
20. médailles
21. avait été poli jusqu'à étinceler
22. était sur scène avec le ministre de l'Intérieur en personne
23. adjoint
24. moins gradés

WINNING THE WAR AGAINST DRUGS[1]

1. Gagner la guerre contre la drogue
2. sur fond bleu
3. étaient assorties à
4. les plus grands journaux
5. Nous n'avons rien laissé de côté !
6. résonnant dans
7. noter la moindre de ses paroles
8. braquées
9. Grâce à mon implication personnelle et à mon travail
10. M. le ministre de l'Intérieur
11. éminent politicien
12. lui sourit à son tour de toutes ses dents
13. ne nous reposons pas sur nos lauriers
14. une nouvelle avancée
15. À ce moment, la péniche heurta la verrière
16. eut tout juste le temps de plonger pour se mettre à couvert
17. masse ruisselante
18. projeté en arrière
19. lunettes expulsées de son visage

Silver letters on a blue background[2]. The chief constable had chosen the colours himself, knowing that they matched[3] his uniform. He liked the slogan. He knew that it would be in all the major newspapers[4] the next day – and, just as important, a photograph of himself.

"We have overlooked nothing![5]" he was saying, his voice echoing around[6] the modern room. He could see the journalists scribbling down his every word[7]. The television cameras were all focused[8] on him. "Thanks to my personal involvement and efforts[9], we have never been more successful. Home Secretary…[10]" He smiled at the senior politician[11], who smiled toothily back[12]. "But we are not resting on our laurels[13]. Oh no! Any day now we hope to announce another breakthrough[14]."

That was when the barge hit the glass roof[15] of the conference centre. There was an explosion. The chief constable just had time to dive for cover[16] as a vast, dripping object[17] plunged down towards him. The home secretary was thrown backwards[18], his spectacles flying off his face[19]. His security men froze, helpless[1]. The boat crashed into the space in front of them, between the stage and the audience[2]. The side of the cabin had been torn off[3] and what was left[4] of the laboratory was exposed, with the two dealers sprawled together[5] in one corner, staring dazedly at[6] the hundreds of policemen and officials who now surrounded them. A cloud of white powder mushroomed up and then fell[7] onto the dark blue uniform of the chief constable, covering him from head to toe[8]. The fire alarms had gone off[9]. The lights fused and went out[10]. Then the screaming began.

Meanwhile, the first of the construction workers had made it to[11] the crane cabin and was gazing in astonishment at[12] the fourteen-year-old boy he had found there.

"Do you...?" he stammered[13]. "Do you have any idea what you've just done?"

Alex glanced at the empty hook[14] and at the gaping hole[15] in the roof of the conference centre, at the rising smoke and dust[16]. He shrugged apologetically[17].

"I was just working on the crime figures[18]," he said. "And I think there's been a drop[19]."

1. se pétrifièrent, impuissants
2. scène et l'auditoire
3. arraché
4. ce qu'il restait
5. affalés l'un sur l'autre
6. dévisageant d'un air hébété
7. nuage de poudre blanche se forma dans les airs et retomba
8. de la tête aux pieds
9. alarmes incendie s'étaient déclenchées
10. les plombs sautèrent et les lumières s'éteignirent
11. était arrivé à
12. regardait avec stupéfaction
13. bégaya-t-il
14. crochet vide
15. trou béant
16. la fumée et la poussière qui s'élevaient
17. haussa les épaules, l'air désolé
18. J'étudiais les chiffres de la criminalité
19. qu'ils viennent de chuter

SEARCH AND REPORT

At least they didn't have far to take him.[1]

Two men brought Alex down from[2] the crane, one above him on the ladder and one below. The police were waiting at the bottom[3]. Watched by the incredulous[4] construction workers, he was frog-marched off the building site and into[5] the police station just a few buildings away[6]. As he passed[7] the conference centre, he saw the crowds pouring out[8]. Ambulances had already arrived. The home secretary was being whisked away[9] in a black limousine. For the first time, Alex was seriously worried, wondering if anyone had been killed. He hadn't meant it to end like this.[10]

Once they got to[11] the police station, everything happened[12] in a whirl of slamming doors, blank official faces, whitewashed walls, forms[13] and phone calls. Alex was asked his name, his age, his address. He saw a police sergeant tapping the details[14] into

1. Au moins, ils ne l'emmenèrent pas bien loin.
2. firent descendre Alex de
3. en bas
4. Sous l'œil incrédule des
5. on l'entraîna du chantier jusqu'à
6. à quelques immeubles de là
7. En passant devant
8. foule qui en sortait
9. évacué
10. Il n'avait jamais eu l'intention que cela se termine comme ça.
11. Une fois arrivés à
12. se déroula
13. tourbillon de portes qui claquent, d'officiers au visage livide, de murs blancs, de formulaires
14. taper ces renseignements

a computer: but what happened next[1] took him by surprise. The sergeant pressed ENTER and visibly froze[2]. He turned and looked at Alex, then hastily left his seat[3]. When Alex had entered the police station he'd been the centre of attention, but suddenly everyone was avoiding his eye[4]. A more senior[5] officer appeared. Words were exchanged.[6] Alex was led down[7] a corridor and put into a cell[8].

Half an hour later, a female police officer appeared with a tray of food[9]. "Supper[10]," she said.

"What's happening?" Alex asked. The woman smiled nervously, but said nothing. "I left my bike by the[11] bridge," Alex said.

"It's all right, we've got it." She couldn't leave the room fast enough.[12]

Alex ate the food: sausages, toast, a slice of cake[13]. There was a bunk[14] in the room and, behind a screen, a sink and a toilet[15]. He wondered if anyone was going to come in and talk to him, but nobody did. Eventually he fell asleep.[16]

The next thing he knew[17], it was seven o'clock in the morning. The door was open and a man he knew only too well[18] was standing in the cell, looking down at him[19].

"Good morning, Alex," he said.

"Mr Crawley."

John Crawley looked like a junior bank manager[20] and when Alex had first met him he had

1. ce qui se passa ensuite

2. appuya sur ENTER puis eut l'air de se pétrifier

3. se leva précipitamment de son siège

4. évitait son regard

5. supérieur

6. Ils échangèrent quelques mots.

7. fut conduit au bout de

8. en cellule

9. plateau de nourriture

10. C'est le dîner

11. près du

12. Elle s'empressa de quitter la pièce.

13. des saucisses, du pain grillé et une part de gâteau

14. couchette

15. paravent, un lavabo et des toilettes

16. Il finit par s'endormir.

17. Et tout d'un coup

18. qu'il ne connaissait que trop bien

19. les yeux braqués sur lui

20. jeune employé de banque

indeed been pretending that he worked[1] for a bank. The cheap suit and striped tie could both have come[2] from a Marks & Spencer "Boring Businessman" range[3]. In fact, Crawley worked for MI6. Alex wondered if the clothes were a cover[4] or a personal choice.

"You can come with me now," Crawley said. "We're leaving."

"Are you taking me home?" Alex asked. He wondered if anyone had been told where he was.

"No. Not yet.[5]"

Alex followed Crawley out of the building. This time there were no police officers in sight[6]. A car with a driver stood waiting outside[7]. Crawley got into the back[8] with Alex.

"Where are we going?" Alex asked.

"You'll see." Crawley opened a copy[9] of the *Daily Telegraph*[10] and began to read. He didn't speak again.

They drove east through[11] the city and up towards[12] Liverpool Street. Alex knew at once[13] where he was being taken and, sure enough[14], the car turned into the entrance of a seventeen-storey building[15] near the station and disappeared down a ramp into an underground carpark[16]. Alex had been here before. The building pretended to be the headquarters[17] of the Royal & General bank. In fact[18], this was where the Special Operations division of MI6 was based[19].

1. en fait, il faisait croire qu'il travaillait
2. costume bon marché et la cravate rayée auraient très bien pu venir
3. collection « Businessman ringard »
4. était une couverture
5. Pas encore.
6. en vue
7. avec chauffeur attendait à l'extérieur
8. entra à l'arrière
9. exemplaire
10. [quotidien britannique de qualité]
11. roulèrent vers l'est, à travers
12. remontèrent en direction de
13. comprit aussitôt
14. effectivement
15. immeuble de 17 étages
16. en bas de la rampe d'accès d'un parking souterrain
17. siège social
18. En réalité
19. c'était là qu'était basée la section des Opérations spéciales du MI6

The car stopped. Crawley folded his paper away[1] and got out, ushering Alex ahead of him[2]. There was a lift in the basement[3] and the two of them took it to the sixteenth floor.

"This way.[4]" Crawley gestured to[5] a door marked[6] 1605. The Gunpowder Plot[7], Alex thought. It was an absurd thing to flash into his mind[8], a fragment of the history homework he should have been doing the night before. 1605 – the year Guy Fawkes had tried to blow up[9] the Houses of Parliament[10]. Oh well, it looked as if the homework was going to have to wait.

Alex opened the door and went in. Crawley didn't follow. When Alex looked round[11], he was already walking away[12].

"Shut[13] the door, Alex, and come in."

Once again[14], Alex found himself standing opposite the prim, unsmiling man[15] who headed[16] the Special Operations division of MI6. Grey suit, grey face, grey life ... Alan Blunt seemed to belong to an entirely colourless world[17]. He was sitting behind a wooden desk in a large, square office that could have belonged to any business[18] anywhere in the world. There was nothing personal in the room, not even[19] a picture on the wall or a photograph on the desk. Even the pigeons pecking on the window-sill[20] outside were grey.

Blunt was not alone. Mrs Jones, his senior officer, was with him, sitting on a leather chair[21],

1. plia son journal et le rangea
2. en faisant passer Alex devant lui
3. sous-sol
4. Par ici.
5. indiqua d'un geste
6. portant le numéro
7. [la Conspiration des poudres]
8. C'était absurde de penser à ça
9. où Guy Fawkes avait tenté de faire exploser
10. [le Parlement britannique, palais de Westminster]
11. tourna la tête
12. s'éloignait déjà
13. Ferme
14. Une fois de plus
15. face à face avec l'homme guindé et peu souriant
16. dirigeait
17. semblait faire partie d'un monde totalement fade
18. que l'on aurait pu trouver dans n'importe quelle entreprise
19. pas même
20. picorant sur le rebord de la fenêtre
21. fauteuil en cuir

wearing a mud-brown[1] jacket and dress, and – as usual – sucking a peppermint[2]. She looked up at[3] Alex with black, bead-like[4] eyes. She seemed to be more pleased[5] to see him than her boss was[6]. It was she who had spoken. Blunt had barely registered the fact[7] that Alex had come into the room.

Then Blunt looked up. "I hadn't expected to see you again so soon[8]," he said.

"That's just what I was going to say," Alex replied[9]. There was a single empty chair[10] in the office. He sat down.

Blunt slid a sheet of paper across[11] his desk and examined it briefly. "What on earth were you thinking of?[12]" he demanded. "This business[13] with the crane? You've done an enormous amount of damage[14]. You've practically destroyed a two million pound[15] conference centre. It's a miracle nobody was killed."

"The two men in the boat will be in hospital for months[16]," Mrs Jones added.

"You could have killed the home secretary!" Blunt continued. "That would have been the last straw.[17] What *were* you doing?"

"They were drug dealers," Alex said.

"So we've discovered.[18] But the normal procedure would have been to dial 999[19]."

"I couldn't find a phone." Alex sighed[20]. "They turned off[21] the crane," he explained. "I was going to put the boat in the carpark."

1. marron clair
2. en train de sucer une pastille de menthe
3. leva les yeux sur
4. ronds et brillants comme des perles
5. plus heureuse
6. que son patron
7. avait à peine remarqué
8. ne m'attendais pas à te revoir si tôt
9. répondit
10. qu'un siège disponible
11. glissa une feuille de papier sur
12. Bon Dieu, qu'est-ce qui t'a pris ?
13. histoire
14. fait des dégâts monstrueux
15. de 2 millions de livres
16. pendant des mois
17. La goutte qui aurait fait déborder le vase.
18. C'est ce qu'on a vu.
19. d'appeler la police
20. soupira
21. ont coupé le courant de

Blunt blinked[1] once and waved a hand as if dismissing[2] everything that had happened. "It's just as well[3] that your special status came up[4] on the police computer," he said. "They called us – and we've handled the rest[5]."

"I didn't know I had special status," Alex said.

"Oh yes, Alex. You're nothing if not special.[6]" Blunt gazed at him for a moment[7]. "That's why you're here."

"So you're not going to send me home?"

"No. The fact is[8], Alex, we were thinking of contacting you anyway[9]. We need you again."

"You're probably the only person who can do what we have in mind[10]," Mrs Jones added.

"Wait a minute!" Alex shook his head[11]. "I'm far enough behind[12] at school as it is[13]. Suppose I'm not interested?"

Mrs Jones sighed. "We could of course return you[14] to the police," she said. "As I understand it[15], they were very keen to interview you[16]."

"And how is[17] Miss Starbright?" Blunt asked.

Jack Starbright – the name was short for[18] Jackie or Jacqueline, Alex wasn't sure which[19] – was the housekeeper who had been looking after[20] Alex since his uncle had died. She was a bright, red-haired[21] American girl who had come to London to study law but had never left[22]. Blunt wasn't interested in her health[23], Alex knew that. The last time they'd met, he'd made his position clear[24].

1. cligna des yeux
2. agita la main comme s'il écartait
3. Ce n'est pas plus mal
4. statut spécial soit apparu
5. on s'est occupé du reste
6. Tu es tout ce qu'il y a de plus spécial.
7. l'observa un certain temps
8. En fait
9. envisagions de te contacter, de toute façon
10. ce que nous avons en tête
11. secoua la tête
12. J'ai plein de choses à rattraper
13. déjà
14. te renvoyer
15. Si j'ai bien compris
16. mouraient d'envie de t'interroger
17. comment va
18. le diminutif de
19. ne savait pas trop lequel des deux
20. gouvernante qui s'occupait d'
21. rousse, intelligente
22. pour étudier le droit mais n'était jamais repartie
23. ne se souciait pas de sa santé
24. il avait été très clair

So long as Alex did as he was told[1], he could stay living in his uncle's house with Jack. Step out of line and she'd be deported[2] to America and Alex would be taken into care[3]. It was blackmail[4] of course, pure and simple.

"She's fine[5]," Alex said. There was quiet anger[6] in his voice.

Mrs Jones took over[7]. "Come on[8], Alex," she said. "Why pretend you're an ordinary schoolboy any more?[9]"

She was trying to sound more friendly[10], more like a mother. But even snakes have mothers[11], Alex thought.

"You've already proved yourself once[12]," she went on. "We're just giving you a chance to do it again."

"It'll probably come to nothing[13]," Blunt continued. "It's just something that needs looking into[14]. What we call a search and report[15]."

"Why can't Crawley do it?"

"We need a boy."

Alex fell silent[16]. He looked from Blunt to Mrs Jones and back again. He knew that neither of them would hesitate for a second before pulling him out[17] of Brookland and sending him to the grimmest[18] institution they could find. And anyway, wasn't this what he had been asking for only the day before[19]? Another adventure. Another chance to save the world.

1. Tant qu'Alex faisait ce qu'on lui disait
2. Au premier faux pas, elle serait expulsée
3. placé dans un foyer
4. du chantage
5. va bien
6. une colère sourde
7. prit le relais
8. Allons
9. Pourquoi faire encore semblant d'être un élève ordinaire ?
10. avoir l'air plus sympathique
11. même les serpents ont une mère
12. déjà fait tes preuves une fois
13. Cela ne donnera probablement rien
14. qu'il faut vérifier
15. rechercher et rendre compte
16. se tut
17. qu'aucun des deux n'hésiterait une seconde à l'arracher
18. la plus sévère
19. ce n'était pas ça qu'il voulait, pas plus tard qu'hier ?

"All right," he said. "What is it this time?"

Blunt nodded at Mrs Jones, who unwrapped a sweet and began[1].

"I wonder if you know anything about a man called Michael J. Roscoe?" she asked.

Alex thought for a moment. "He was that businessman who had an accident in New York." He'd seen the news[2] on TV. "Didn't he fall down a lift-shaft or something[3]?"

"Roscoe Electronics is one of the largest companies[4] in America," Mrs Jones said. "In fact it's one of the largest in the world. Computers, videos, DVD players[5] ... everything from mobile phones to washing-machines[6]. Roscoe was very rich, very influential[7]—"

"And very short-sighted[8]," Alex cut in[9].

"It certainly seems to have been a very strange and even a careless accident[10]," Mrs Jones agreed[11]. "The lift somehow malfunctioned[12]. Roscoe didn't look where he was going. He fell into the lift-shaft and died. That's the general opinion.[13] However, we're not so sure."

"Why not?"

"First of all, there are a number of details that don't add up[14]. On the day Roscoe died, a maintenance engineer by the name of[15] Sam Green called at Roscoe Tower on Fifth Avenue. We know it was Green – or someone who looked very much like him[16] – because we've seen him. They have closed

1. prit la parole en retirant le papier d'un bonbon

2. les infos

3. ou un truc comme ça

4. l'une des plus grandes entreprises

5. lecteurs

6. machines à laver

7. influent

8. myope

9. l'interrompit

10. C'est vrai, on dirait que c'est un accident très étrange et stupide, même

11. concéda

12. aurait eu une défaillance

13. C'est ce que tout le monde pense.

14. certain nombre d'éléments qui ne collent pas

15. dénommé

16. qui lui ressemblait beaucoup

circuit security[1] cameras and he was filmed going in[2]. He said he'd come to look at a defective cable. But according to the company that employed him[3], there was no defective cable and he certainly wasn't acting under orders from them[4]."

"Why don't you talk to him?"

"We'd like to. But Green has vanished without trace[5]. We think he might have been killed[6]. We think someone might have taken his place and somehow set up[7] the accident that killed Roscoe."

Alex shrugged. "I'm sorry. I'm sorry about Mr Roscoe. But what's it got to do[8] with me?"

"I'm coming to that.[9]" Mrs Jones paused[10]. "The strangest thing of all[11] is that, the day before he died[12], Roscoe telephoned this office. A personal call[13]. He asked to speak to Mr Blunt."

"I met Roscoe at Cambridge University," Blunt said. "That was a long time ago. We became friends."

That surprised Alex. He didn't think of Blunt as the sort of man who had friends.[14] "What did he say?" he asked.

"Unfortunately[15], I wasn't here to take the call," Blunt replied. "I arranged to speak with him the following day.[16] By that time, it was too late."

"Do you have any idea what he wanted?"

"I spoke to his assistant," Mrs Jones said. "She wasn't able to tell me very much[17], but she under-

1. de télésurveillance
2. filmé lorsqu'il est entré
3. selon son employeur
4. n'agissait certainement pas sur leurs instructions
5. disparu sans laisser de traces
6. qu'il a peut-être été assassiné
7. d'une façon ou d'une autre, provoqué
8. qu'est-ce que cela a à voir
9. Je vais y venir.
10. marqua une pause
11. Le plus étrange
12. la veille de sa mort
13. appel
14. Pour lui, Blunt n'était pas du genre à avoir des amis.
15. Malheureusement
16. J'avais prévu de lui parler le lendemain.
17. n'a pas pu me dire grand-chose

stood that Roscoe was concerned about his son[1]. He has a fourteen-year-old son, Paul Roscoe."

A fourteen-year-old son. Alex was beginning to see the way things were going[2].

"Paul was his only son[3]," Blunt explained. "I'm afraid the two of them had a very difficult relationship[4]. Roscoe divorced a few years ago and although the boy chose[5] to live with his father, they didn't really get on[6]. There were the usual teenage problems[7], but of course, when you grow up surrounded by[8] millions of dollars these problems sometimes get amplified. Paul was doing badly[9] at school. He was playing truant[10], spending time with some very undesirable friends[11]. There was an incident with the New York police – nothing serious[12] and Roscoe managed to hush it up[13], but it still upset him[14]. I spoke to Roscoe from time to time. He was worried about Paul and felt the boy was out of control[15]. But there didn't seem to be very much he could do[16]."

"So is that what you want me for?[17]" Alex interrupted. "You want me to meet this boy and talk to him about his father's death?"

"No." Blunt shook his head and handed a file to[18] Mrs Jones.

She opened it. Alex caught a glimpse of[19] a photograph; a dark-skinned[20] man in military uniform. "Remember what we told you about Roscoe," she said. "Because now I want to tell

1. inquiet au sujet de son fils
2. où on voulait en venir
3. seul fils
4. relation
5. bien que le garçon ait décidé
6. ne s'entendaient pas vraiment
7. ces problèmes typiques de l'adolescence
8. tu grandis entouré de
9. avait de mauvais résultats
10. séchait les cours
11. de très mauvaises fréquentations
12. rien de grave
13. a réussi à l'étouffer
14. il était tout de même contrarié
15. incontrôlable
16. il ne semblait pas pouvoir y faire grand-chose
17. Alors c'est pour ça que vous avez besoin de moi ?
18. secoua la tête et tendit un dossier à
19. aperçut
20. à la peau mate

you about another man[1]." She slid the photograph round so that Alex could see it[2]. "This is General Viktor Ivanov. Ex-KGB. Until last December[3] he was head of the Foreign Intelligence Service[4] and probably the second or third most powerful man in[5] Russia after the president. But then something happened to him too. It was a boating[6] accident on the Black Sea. His cruiser exploded[7] ... nobody knows why."

"Was he a friend of Roscoe's?" Alex asked.

"They probably never met. But we have a department[8] here that constantly monitors world news[9], and their computers have thrown up[10] a very strange coincidence. Ivanov also had a fourteen-year-old son, Dimitry. And one thing is certain. The young Ivanov certainly knew[11] the young Roscoe because they went to the same school."

"Paul and Dimitry..." Alex was puzzled[12]. "What was a Russian boy doing at a school in New York?"

"He wasn't in New York." Blunt took over[13]. "As I told you, Roscoe was having trouble[14] with his boy. Trouble at school, trouble at home. So last year he decided to take action[15]. He sent Paul to Europe, to a place in France, a sort of finishing school[16]. Do you know what a finishing school is?"

"I thought it was the sort of place where rich people used to send their daughters[17]," Alex said. "To learn table manners.[18]"

1. te parler d'un autre homme
2. retourna la photo pour qu'Alex puisse la voir
3. Jusqu'en décembre dernier
4. dirigeait le Service des renseignements extérieurs
5. 2e ou 3e homme le plus puissant de
6. de bateau
7. yacht a explosé
8. service
9. qui surveille constamment les informations dans le monde
10. ont fait remonter
11. connaissait
12. perplexe
13. prit le relais
14. avait des problèmes
15. prendre des mesures
16. une sorte d'école privée
17. ce genre d'endroit où les gens riches envoient leurs filles
18. Pour apprendre les bonnes manières à table.

"That's the general idea.[1] But this school is for boys only, and not just ordinary boys[2]. The fees[3] are ten thousand pounds a term[4]. This is the brochure. You can have a look[5]." He passed a heavy, square booklet[6] to Alex. Written on the cover, gold letters on black[7], were the two words:

POINT BLANC

"It's right on the French-Swiss border[8]," Blunt explained. "South of Geneva. Just above Grenoble, in the French Alps. It's pronounced *Point Blanc*." He spoke[9] the words with a French accent. "Literally[10], *white point*. It's a remarkable place. Built as a private home by some lunatic[11] in the nineteenth century[12]. As a matter of fact, that's what it became[13] after he died ... a lunatic asylum[14]. It was taken over by the Germans in the Second World War[15]. They used it as a leisure centre[16] for their senior staff[17]. After that, it fell into disrepair[18] until it was bought by the current owner[19], a man called Grief. Dr Hugo Grief. He's the principal[20] of the school. What I suppose you'd call the head-teacher[21]."

Alex opened the brochure and found himself looking at a colour photograph of Point Blanc. Blunt was right. The school was like nothing he had ever seen[22]; something between a German castle and a French chateau, straight out of a Grimm's fairy tale[23]. But what drew Alex's breath[24], more

1. C'est un peu le principe.
2. pas n'importe lesquels
3. frais de scolarité
4. par trimestre
5. jeter un coup d'œil
6. lourde plaquette carrée
7. en lettres dorées sur fond noir
8. C'est juste à la frontière franco-suisse
9. prononça
10. Cela veut dire
11. Construit comme résidence privée par un fou
12. XIXe siècle
13. En fait, c'est ce que c'est devenu
14. asile d'aliénés
15. repris par les Allemands pendant la Seconde Guerre mondiale
16. lieu de villégiature
17. hauts dignitaires
18. a été laissé à l'abandon
19. propriétaire actuel
20. principal
21. chef d'établissement
22. ne ressemblait à rien de ce qu'il connaissait
23. sorti tout droit d'un conte de Grimm
24. ce qui lui coupa le souffle

1. décor
2. perchée sur le versant
3. uniquement entourée de montagnes
4. grand édifice de briques et de pierres
5. paysage enneigé
6. ne semblait pas à sa place, ici
7. arraché à une cité antique
8. jeté
9. héliport qui surplombait les remparts

than the building itself, was the setting[1]. The school was perched on the side[2] of a mountain, with nothing but mountains all around[3]; a great pile of brick and stone[4] surrounded by a snow-covered landscape[5]. It seemed to have no business being there[6], as if it had been snatched out of an ancient city[7] and accidentally dropped[8] there. No roads led to the school. The snow continued all the way to the front gate. But looking again, Alex saw a modern helicopter pad projecting over the battlements[9]. He guessed that was the only way to get there ... and to leave.

He turned the page.

10. Bienvenue

Welcome[10] to the Academy at

Point Blanc...

11. imprimée
12. caractères

the introduction began. It had been printed[11] in the sort of lettering[12] Alex would expect to find on the menu of an expensive restaurant.

13. qu'on leur apporte davantage que ce que permet le système éducatif traditionnel
14. De tous temps, on nous a qualifiés
15. ne pensons pas que ce terme soit approprié
16. Notre objectif est de séparer les deux.

...a unique school that is much more than a school, created for boys who need more than the ordinary education system can provide[13]. In our time, we have been called[14] a school for "problem boys", but we do not believe the term applies[15].

There are problems and there are boys. It is our aim to separate the two.[16]

"There's no need to read all that stuff[1]," Blunt said. "All you need to know is that the academy takes in[2] boys who have been expelled[3] from all their other schools. There are never very many of them there.[4] Just six or seven at a time[5]. And it's unique in other ways too[6]. For a start[7], it only takes the sons of the super-rich—"

"At ten thousand pounds a term, I'm not surprised," Alex said.

"You'd be surprised just how many parents have applied[8] to send their sons there," Blunt went on. "But I suppose you've only got to look at the newspapers to see how easy it is to go off the rails[9] when you're born with a silver spoon in your mouth[10]. It doesn't matter if they're[11] politicians or popstars; fame[12] and fortune for the parents often brings problems for the[13] children ... and the more successful the parents are, the more pressure there seems to be[14]. The academy went into business to sort the young people out[15], and by all accounts[16] it's been a great success."

"It was established twenty years ago," Mrs Jones said. "In that time it's had a client list you'd find hard to believe.[17] Of course, they've kept the names confidential[18]. But I can tell you that parents who have sent their children there include[19] an American vice-president, a Nobel Prize-winning scientist[20] and a member of our own royal family!"

1. Inutile de tout lire
2. intègre
3. renvoyés
4. Ils ne sont jamais très nombreux, là-bas.
5. à la fois
6. à d'autres égards, aussi
7. D'abord
8. du nombre de parents ayant fait une demande
9. de perdre les pédales
10. né avec une cuillère en argent dans la bouche
11. Peu importe qu'ils soient
12. la célébrité
13. des parents créent souvent des problèmes aux
14. plus la pression semble élevée
15. a été créée pour remettre les jeunes dans le droit chemin
16. de toute évidence
17. À cette époque, tu ne peux t'imaginer qui étaient leurs clients.
18. n'ont pas divulgué les noms
19. comptent entre autres
20. scientifique lauréat du prix Nobel

"As well as[1] Roscoe and this man, Ivanov," Alex said.

"Yes."

Alex shrugged[2]. "So it's a coincidence. Just like you said.[3] Two rich parents with two rich kids at the same school. They're both killed in accidents. Why are you so interested?"

"Because I don't like coincidence," Blunt replied. "In fact, I don't believe in[4] coincidence. Where some people see coincidence, I see conspiracy.[5] That's my job."

And you're welcome to it[6], Alex thought. He said, "Do you really think the school and this man Grief might have had something to do with the two deaths[7]? Why? Had they forgotten to pay the fees?"

Blunt didn't smile. "Roscoe telephones me because he's worried about his son. The next day he's dead. We've also learned from Russian intelligence sources[8] that a week before he died, Ivanov had a violent argument[9] with his son. Apparently Ivanov was worried about something. Now do you see the link?[10]"

Alex thought for a moment. "So you want me to go to this school," he said. "How are you going to manage that[11]? I don't have parents and they were never rich anyway."

"We've already arranged that[12]," Mrs Jones said. Alex realized that she must have made her

1. Ainsi que
2. haussa les épaules
3. C'est ce que vous avez dit.
4. ne crois pas aux
5. Là où les gens voient une coïncidence, moi je vois un complot.
6. je ne te l'envie pas
7. aient quelque chose à voir avec ces deux décès
8. été informés par les services secrets russes
9. s'est violemment disputé
10. Tu vois le lien, maintenant ?
11. organiser ça
12. C'est déjà organisé

plans before the business with the crane ever happened[1]. Even if he hadn't drawn attention to himself[2], they would have come for him[3]. "We're going to supply you with a wealthy father[4]. His name is Sir David Friend."

"Friend … as in Friend's supermarkets?" Alex had seen the name often enough in the newspapers.

"Supermarkets. Department stores.[5] Art galleries. Football teams." Mrs Jones paused. "Friend is certainly a member of the same club[6] as Roscoe. The billionaires'[7] club. He's also heavily involved in government circles, as personal adviser to the prime minister[8]. Very little happens[9] in this country without Sir David being involved in some way[10]."

"We've created a false[11] identity for you," Blunt said. "From this moment on[12], I want you to start thinking of yourself as[13] Alex Friend, the fourteen-year-old son of Sir David."

"It won't work[14]," Alex said. "People must know that Friend doesn't have a son."

"Not at all.[15]"? Blunt shook his head. "He's a very private person[16] and we've created the sort of son no father would want to talk about. Expelled from Eton[17]. A criminal record[18] … shoplifting[19], vandalism and possession of drugs. That's you, Alex. Sir David and his wife[20], Caroline, don't know what to do with you. So they've enrolled[21] you in the academy. And you've been accepted."

1. qu'elle devait avoir tout prévu avant même l'histoire de la grue
2. s'il n'avait pas attiré l'attention sur lui
3. seraient venus le chercher
4. te trouver un père riche
5. Grands magasins.
6. fait sûrement partie du même club
7. des milliardaires
8. également très proche du gouvernement, en qualité de conseiller particulier du Premier ministre
9. Très peu de choses se passent
10. sans que sir David ne soit concerné, d'une façon ou d'une autre
11. fausse
12. À partir de maintenant
13. te mettes dans la tête que tu es
14. Ça ne marchera pas
15. Pas du tout.
16. quelqu'un de très discret
17. [l'une des plus célèbres écoles privées pour garçons de la grande bourgeoisie et de l'aristocratie britanniques]
18. casier judiciaire
19. vol à l'étalage
20. femme
21. Alors ils t'ont inscrit

"And Sir David has agreed to all this[1]?" Alex asked.

Blunt sniffed[2]. "As a matter of fact, he wasn't very happy about it[3] – about using someone as young as you[4]. But I spoke to him at some length[5] and, yes, he agreed to help."

"So when am I going to the academy?"

"Five days from now[6]," Mrs Jones said. "But first you have to immerse yourself[7] in your new life. When you leave here, we've arranged for you to be taken to Sir David's home.[8] He has a house in Lancashire[9]. He lives there with his wife – and he has a daughter. She's one year older than you[10]. You'll spend[11] the rest of the week with the family, which should give you time to learn[12] everything you need to know. It's vital that you have a strong cover[13]. After that, you'll leave for Grenoble."

"And what do I do when I get there?"

"We'll give you a full briefing nearer the time[14]. Essentially, your job is to find out everything you can. It may be[15] that this school is perfectly ordinary and that there was in fact no connection between the deaths. If so, we'll pull you out.[16] But we want to be sure."

"How will I get in touch with you?[17]"

"We'll arrange all that." Mrs Jones ran an eye over Alex[18], then turned to Blunt. "We'll have to do something about his appearance[19]," she said. "He doesn't exactly look the part.[20]"

1. accepté tout ça
2. renifla
3. En fait, cela ne l'enchantait pas
4. le fait de se servir de quelqu'un d'aussi jeune que toi
5. longuement
6. Dans cinq jours
7. t'immerger
8. En partant d'ici, on te conduira chez sir David.
9. [comté du nord-ouest de l'Angleterre]
10. a un an de plus que toi
11. passeras
12. ce qui devrait te laisser le temps d'apprendre
13. couverture en béton
14. te ferons un briefing complet juste avant
15. Peut-être bien
16. Dans ce cas, on t'exfiltrera.
17. Comment je ferai pour vous contacter ?
18. parcourut Alex du regard
19. pour son allure
20. Il n'a pas vraiment le physique de l'emploi.

"See to it[1]," Blunt said.

Alex sighed. It was strange really. He was simply going from one school to another. From a London comprehensive to a finishing school[2] in France. It wasn't quite the adventure he'd been expecting[3].

He stood up[4] and followed Mrs Jones out of the room. As he left[5], Blunt was already sifting through documents[6] as if he'd forgotten that Alex had been there or even existed at all[7].

1. Occupez-vous de ça

2. D'un collège londonien à une école privée

3. qu'il avait imaginée

4. se leva

5. Tandis qu'il partait

6. parcourait déjà des documents

7. qu'il ait jamais existé

THE SHOOTING PARTY

The chauffeur-driven[1] Rolls-Royce Corniche cruised along a tree-lined avenue, penetrating ever deeper[2] into the Lancashire countryside[3], its 6.75 litre light pressure V8 engine barely a whisper[4] in the great green silence all around. Alex sat in the back, trying to be unimpressed[5] by a car that cost as much as a house. Forget the Wilton[6] wool carpets[7], the wooden panelling[8] and the leather seats[9], he told himself. It's only a car.

It was the day after his meeting[10] at MI6 and, as Mrs Jones had promised, his appearance had completely changed. He had to look like a rebel – the rich son[11] who wanted to live life by his own rules[12]. So Alex had been dressed in purposefully provocative[13] clothes. He was wearing a hooded[14] sweatshirt, Tommy Hilfiger jeans – frayed at the ankles[15] – and trainers that were falling apart[16] on his feet. Despite[17] his protests, his hair had been cut so short[18] that he almost looked like a skinhead

1. conduite par un chauffeur
2. roulait le long d'une avenue bordée d'arbres, s'enfonçant toujours plus
3. campagne
4. moteur V8 basse pression faisant à peine un murmure
5. de ne pas être impressionné
6. [type de tissage originaire de Wilton, Wiltshire]
7. tapis en laine
8. marqueterie
9. sièges en cuir
10. réunion
11. fils de riche
12. vivre sa vie selon ses propres règles
13. volontairement provocants
14. à capuche
15. effiloché en bas
16. des baskets avachies
17. Malgré
18. coupés si court

and his right ear had been pierced[1]. He could still feel it throbbing underneath[2] the temporary stud[3] that had been put in to stop the hole closing[4].

The car had reached a set of wrought-iron gates[5] which opened automatically to receive it[6]. And there was Haverstock Hall, a great mansion[7] with stone figures[8] on the terrace and seven figures in the price[9]. Sir David had bought it a few years ago, Mrs Jones had told him, because he wanted a place[10] in the country. Half the Lancashire countryside seemed to have come with it[11]. The grounds stretched for miles[12] in every direction, with sheep dotted across the hills[13] on one side and three horses watching from an enclosure[14] on the other. The house itself was Georgian[15]: white brick with slender windows and columns[16]. Everything looked very neat[17]. There was a walled garden[18] with evenly spaced beds[19], a square glass conservatory housing a swimming pool[20], and a series of ornamental hedges[21] with every leaf[22] perfectly in place.

The car stopped. The horses swung their necks round[23] to watch Alex get out, their tails[24] rhythmically beating at flies[25]. Nothing else moved.

The chauffeur walked round to the boot[26]. "Sir David will be inside," he said. He had disapproved of Alex from the moment he had set eyes on him. Of course, he hadn't said as much[27], he was too professional. But he showed it with his eyes[28].

1. oreille droite avait été percée
2. des élancements sous
3. clou [boucle d'oreille]
4. pour empêcher le trou de se refermer
5. portail en fer forgé
6. pour l'accueillir
7. grand manoir
8. des statues en pierre
9. valant une fortune [un prix à 7 chiffres]
10. résidence
11. en faire partie
12. terres s'étendaient sur des km
13. des moutons dispersés sur les collines
14. enclos
15. de style georgien [XVIIIe s.]
16. d'étroites fenêtres et des colonnes
17. soigné
18. jardin clos
19. plates-bandes bien espacées
20. véranda carrée abritant une piscine
21. haies décoratives
22. feuille
23. tournèrent leur encolure
24. leurs queues
25. chassant les mouches
26. coffre
27. n'en avait rien dit
28. cela se voyait dans son regard

Alex moved away[1] from the car, drawn towards[2] the conservatory on the other side of the drive[3]. It was a warm day, the sun beating down[4] on the glass, and the water on the other side looked suddenly inviting[5]. He passed through[6] a set of doors. It was hot inside the conservatory. The smell of chlorine rose up[7] from the water, stifling him[8].

He had thought the pool was empty[9], but as he watched, a figure swam up from the bottom[10], breaking through[11] the surface just in front of him. It was a girl, dressed in a white bikini. She had long black hair and dark eyes but her skin[12] was pale. Alex guessed[13] she must be about fifteen years old and remembered what Mrs Jones had told him about Sir David Friend. "He has a daughter ... one year older than you." So this must be her.[14] He watched her pull herself out[15] of the water. Her body was well-shaped, closer to[16] the woman she would become[17] than the girl she had been. She was going to be beautiful. That much was certain.[18] The trouble was, she already knew it[19]. When she looked at Alex, arrogance flashed[20] in her eyes.

"Who are you?" she asked. "What are you doing in here?"

"I'm Alex."

"Oh yes." She reached for a towel[21] and wrapped it around[22] her neck. "Daddy said you were coming – but I didn't expect you to just walk in like this[23]." Her voice was very adult and upper-class[24].

1. s'éloigna
2. attiré par
3. allée
4. dardant ses rayons
5. tentante
6. franchit
7. Une odeur de chlore émanait
8. suffocante
9. qu'il n'y avait personne dans la piscine
10. silhouette remonta du fond
11. fendant
12. peau
13. estima
14. Alors c'était sûrement elle.
15. se hisser hors
16. bien dessiné, s'approchant plus de
17. allait devenir
18. C'était une certitude.
19. le savait déjà
20. apparut
21. attrapa une serviette
22. l'enroula autour de
23. à ce que tu débarques comme ça
24. aristocratique

It sounded strange, coming out of that fifteen-year-old mouth[1]. "Do you swim?" she asked.

"Yes," Alex said.

"That's a shame.[2] I don't like having to share[3] the pool. Especially with a boy. And a smelly London boy at that[4]." She ran her eyes over Alex[5], taking in[6] the torn[7] jeans, the shaven[8] hair, the stud in his ear. She shuddered[9]. "I can't think *what* Daddy was doing, agreeing to let you stay[10]," she went on[11]. "And having to pretend you're my brother! What a ghastly[12] idea! If I did have[13] a brother, I can assure you he wouldn't look like you."

Alex was wondering whether to pick the girl up and throw her back[14] into the pool – or out through[15] a window – when there was a movement behind him and he turned to see a tall, rather[16] aristocratic man with curling grey[17] hair and glasses, wearing a sports jacket[18], an open-necked shirt[19] and cords[20]. He too seemed a little jolted[21] by Alex's appearance, but he recovered[22] quickly, extending a hand[23]. "Alex?" he enquired.

"Yes."

"I'm David Friend."

Alex shook his[24] hand. "How do you do[25]," he said politely.

"I hope you had a good journey[26]. I see you've met my daughter." He smiled at the girl who was now sitting beside[27] the pool drying herself[28], ignoring them both.

1. bouche
2. C'est dommage.
3. être obligée de partager
4. racaille de Londres, en plus
5. dévisagea Alex de la tête aux pieds
6. son regard englobant
7. déchiré
8. tondus
9. eut un frisson
10. en acceptant que tu viennes
11. poursuivit-elle
12. horrible
13. Si j'avais vraiment
14. s'il allait l'attraper et la jeter à nouveau
15. par
16. plutôt
17. gris bouclés
18. veste sport
19. chemise à col ouvert
20. pantalon en velours côtelé
21. un peu ébranlé
22. se ressaisit
23. lui tendant la main
24. lui serra la
25. [façon plutôt formelle de saluer une personne que l'on rencontre pour la première fois]
26. que tu as fait bon voyage
27. à côté de
28. en train de se sécher

"We haven't actually introduced ourselves[1]," Alex said.

"Her name is Fiona. I'm sure the two of you will get on fine[2]." Sir David didn't sound convinced[3]. He gestured back towards[4] the house. "Why don't we go and talk in my study[5]?"

Alex followed him back across the drive and into the house. The front door opened into[6] a hall that could have come straight out[7] of the pages of an expensive[8] magazine. Everything was perfect, the antique furniture, ornaments[9] and paintings placed exactly so[10]. There wasn't a speck of dust to be seen[11] and even the sunlight streaming in through[12] the windows seemed almost artificial, as if it was only there to bring out the best[13] in everything it touched. It was the house of a man who knows exactly what he wants and has the time and the money to get it[14].

"Nice place," Alex said.

"Thank you. Please come this way.[15]" Sir David opened a heavy, oak-panelled[16] door to reveal[17] a sophisticated, modern office beyond[18]. There was a desk with a chair on either side[19], a pair of computers, a white leather sofa and a series of metal bookshelves[20]. Sir David showed Alex to a chair[21] and sat down behind the desk.

He was unsure of himself[22]. Alex could see it immediately. Sir David Friend might run a business empire worth[23] millions – even billions[24] – of

1. En fait, nous n'avons pas fait les présentations
2. que vous vous entendrez bien, vous deux
3. convaincu
4. montra d'un geste
5. bureau
6. porte d'entrée donnait sur
7. aurait pu sortir tout droit
8. de luxe
9. meubles d'époque, les objets décoratifs
10. exactement disposés de cette façon
11. un seul grain de poussière
12. les flots de lumière pénétrant par
13. s'ils n'étaient là que pour faire ressortir le meilleur
14. pour se l'acheter
15. Par ici, s'il te plaît.
16. lambrissée de chêne
17. qui révéla
18. de l'autre côté
19. de chaque côté
20. d'étagères métalliques
21. invita Alex à s'asseoir
22. n'était pas sûr de lui
23. dirigeait peut-être un empire de sociétés valant
24. milliards

pounds[1], but this was a new experience for him. Having Alex there, knowing who and what he was. He wasn't quite sure how to react[2].

"I've been told very little[3] about you," he began. "Alan Blunt got in touch with me[4] and asked me to put you up[5] here for the rest of the week, to pretend that you're my son. I have to say, you don't look anything like me[6]."

"I don't look anything like myself either[7]," Alex said.

"You're on your way to some school[8] in the French Alps. They want you to investigate it[9]." He paused. "Nobody asked me my opinion," he said, "but I'll give it to you anyway[10]. I don't like the idea of a fourteen-year-old boy being used as a spy. It's dangerous—"

"I can look after myself[11]," Alex cut in[12].

"I mean[13], it's dangerous to[14] the government. If you manage to get yourself killed and anyone finds out[15], it could cause the prime minister a great deal of embarrassment[16]. I advised him against it[17], but for once he disagreed[18] with me. It seems that the decision had already been made[19]. This school – the academy – has already telephoned me to say that the assistant[20] director will be coming here to pick you up[21] next Saturday. It's a woman. A Mrs Stellenbosch. That's a South African name, I think..."

Sir David had a number of bulky files[22] on his desk. He pushed them forward[23]. "In the mean-

1. livres sterling
2. ne savait pas trop comment réagir
3. On m'a dit très peu de choses
4. m'a contacté
5. t'accueillir
6. tu ne me ressembles pas du tout
7. non plus
8. Tu vas partir dans une école
9. que tu y fasses une enquête
10. tout de même
11. Je peux me débrouiller
12. rétorqua
13. Ce que je veux dire
14. pour
15. que quelqu'un l'apprend
16. pourrait être très gênant pour le Premier ministre
17. Je le lui ai déconseillé
18. pour une fois, il n'était pas d'accord
19. déjà été prise
20. adjointe
21. viendra te chercher, ici
22. dossiers volumineux
23. les poussa devant lui

time[1], I understand you have to familiarize yourself with details about[2] my family. I've prepared a number of files. You'll also find information here about the school you're meant to have been expelled from[3], Eton. You can start reading them tonight. If you need to know anything more, just ask. Fiona will be with you the whole time." He glanced down at[4] his fingertips[5]. "I'm sure that in itself will be quite an experience[6] for you."

The door opened and a woman came in. She was slim and dark-haired[7], very much like her daughter. She was wearing a simple mauve dress with a string of pearls[8] around her neck. "David..." she began, then stopped, seeing Alex.

"This is my wife," Friend said. "Caroline, this is the boy I was telling you about[9], Alex."

"It's very nice to meet you[10], Alex." Lady Caroline tried to smile but her lips only managed a faint twitch[11]. "I understand you're going to stay with us for a while[12]."

"Yes Mother," Alex said.

Lady Caroline blushed[13].

"He has to pretend to be our son," Sir David reminded her[14]. He turned to Alex. "Fiona doesn't know anything about MI6 and the rest of it. I don't want to alarm her[15]. I've told her that it's connected with my work ... a social experiment[16], if you like. She's to pretend you're her brother. To give you a week in the country as

1. En attendant
2. si j'ai bien compris, tu dois apprendre tout ce qui concerne
3. d'où tu es censé t'être fait renvoyer
4. jeta un regard sur
5. le bout de ses doigts
6. que ce sera déjà une sacrée expérience
7. mince et brune
8. rang de perles
9. dont je t'ai parlé
10. Ravie de te rencontrer
11. se contractèrent à peine
12. pendant un certain temps
13. rougit
14. lui rappela
15. l'inquiéter
16. expérience

part[1] of the family. I'd prefer it if you didn't tell her the truth[2]."

"Dinner is in half an hour," Lady Caroline said. "Do you eat venison[3]?" She sniffed[4]. "Perhaps you'd like a wash[5] before you eat? I'll show you to[6] your room."

Sir David passed[7] the files to Alex. "You've got a lot of reading to do[8]. I'm afraid[9] I have to go back to London tomorrow – I have lunch with the president of France – so I won't be able to help you. But, as I say, if there's anything you don't know—"

"Fiona Friend," Alex said.

Alex had been given a small, comfortable room at the back of the house. He took a quick shower[10], then put his old clothes back on again[11]. He liked to feel clean[12], but he had to look grimy[13]. It suited the character[14] of the boy he was supposed to be.

He opened the first of the files. Sir David had been thorough[15]. He had given Alex the names and recent histories[16] of just about the entire family, as well as photographs of holidays, details of the house in Mayfair[17], the flats[18] in New York, Paris and Rome and the villa in Barbados[19]. There were newspaper clippings[20], magazine articles ... everything he could possibly need.

A gong sounded[21]. It was seven o'clock. Alex went downstairs and into the dining room[22]. This was a room with six windows and a polished[23]

1. Et t'accueillir à la campagne pendant une semaine, comme si tu faisais partie
2. que tu ne lui dises pas la vérité
3. du chevreuil
4. renifla
5. te rafraîchir
6. Je vais te conduire à
7. remit
8. beaucoup de choses à lire
9. Malheureusement
10. se doucha rapidement
11. remit ses anciens vêtements
12. se sentir propre
13. avoir l'air sale
14. correspondait à la personnalité
15. minutieux
16. les dernières anecdotes
17. [quartier chic de Londres]
18. appartements
19. de la Barbade
20. coupures de presse
21. résonna
22. salle à manger
23. cirée

table long enough to seat sixteen[1]. But there were only the three of them there: Sir David, Lady Caroline and Fiona. The food had already been served, presumably by a butler or maid[2]. Sir David gestured to[3] an empty chair. Alex sat down.

"Fiona was just talking about Don Giovanni," Lady Caroline said. There was a pause. "It's an opera. By Mozart."

"I'm sure Alex isn't interested in opera," Fiona said. She was in a bad mood[4]. "In fact, I doubt if we have *anything* in common. Why do I have to pretend he's my brother? The whole thing[5] is completely—"

"Fiona," Sir David muttered in a low voice[6].

"Well, it's all very well having him here[7], Daddy, but it *is* meant to be my Easter holiday[8]." Alex realized that Fiona must go to a private school. Her term would have ended earlier than[9] his. "I don't think it's fair[10]."

"Alex is here because of my work," Sir David continued. It was strange, Alex thought, the way they talked about him as if he wasn't actually there[11]. "I know you have a lot of questions, Fiona, but you're just going to have to do as I say[12]. He's only with us until the end of the week. I want you to look after him[13]."

"Is it something to do with the supermarkets?" Fiona asked.

1. accueillir 16 personnes
2. vraisemblablement par un majordome ou une domestique
3. indiqua
4. de mauvaise humeur
5. Tout ça
6. marmonna à voix basse
7. c'est bien beau qu'il soit là
8. là, ce sont mes vacances de Pâques
9. devait se terminer plus tôt que
10. juste
11. cette façon de parler de lui comme s'il n'était pas là
12. devras te contenter de faire ce que je te dis
13. que tu t'occupes de lui

"Fiona!" Sir David didn't want any more argument[1]. "It's what I told you. An experiment. And you will make him feel welcome[2]!"

Fiona picked up her glass and looked directly at[3] Alex for the first time since he had come into the room. "We'll see about that[4]," she said.

The week seemed endless[5]. After[6] only two days, Alex had decided that if he had really been a son in this frigid, self-important family[7], he probably *would* have ended up rebelling[8]. Sir David had left[9] at six o'clock the first morning and was still in London, sending messages to his wife and daughter by e-mail. Lady Caroline did her best to avoid[10] Alex. Once or twice[11] she drove into the town nearby[12], but otherwise[13] she seemed to spend a lot of time in bed. And Fiona...

When she wasn't quoting[14] opera, she was boasting about her lifestyle[15], her wealth[16], her holidays around the world. At the same time, she made it clear how much she disliked[17] Alex. She'd asked him several times[18] what he was really doing at Haverstock Hall. Alex had shrugged[19] and said nothing – which had made her dislike him all the more[20].

On the third day, she introduced him to some[21] of her friends.

"I'm going shooting[22]," she told him. "I don't suppose you want to[23] come."

1. voulait mettre un terme à la discussion
2. veilleras à ce qu'il se sente le bienvenu
3. dans les yeux
4. On verra bien
5. semblait interminable
6. Au bout de
7. le fils de cette famille prétentieuse et glaciale
8. aurait fini par se révolter
9. était parti
10. faisait tout pour éviter
11. Une ou deux fois
12. s'était rendue en voiture dans la ville voisine
13. à part ça
14. ne citait pas un
15. se vantait de son train de vie
16. fortune
17. montrait bien à quel point elle détestait
18. plusieurs fois
19. haussé les épaules
20. encore plus
21. lui présenta certains
22. Je vais chasser
23. J'imagine que tu ne veux pas

Alex shrugged. He had memorized most of the details[1] in the files and figured he could easily pass as[2] a member of the family. Now he was counting the hours until the woman from the academy arrived to take him away.

"Have you ever been shooting?[3]" Fiona asked.

"No," Alex said.

"I go hunting and shooting[4]," Fiona said. "But of course, you're a city boy. You wouldn't[5] understand."

"What's so great about[6] killing animals?" Alex asked.

"It's part of the country way of life.[7] It's traditional." Fiona looked at him as if he were[8] stupid. It was how she always looked at him.[9] "Anyway, the animals enjoy it[10]."

The shooting party turned out to be young[11] and – apart from Fiona – entirely male[12]. There were five of them[13] waiting on the edge of a wood[14] that was part of the Haverstock estate[15]. Rufus, the leader, was sixteen, well-built[16] with dark curly hair. He seemed to be Fiona's official boyfriend. The others – Henry, Max, Bartholomew and Fred – were about the same age[17]. Alex looked at them with a heavy heart[18]. They had uniform Barbour jackets, tweed trousers, flat caps[19] and Huntsman leather boots. They spoke with uniform public school accents[20]. Each of them carried a shotgun, with the barrel broken over his arm[21]. Two of them were smoking. They gazed at[22] Alex

1. informations
2. il considérait qu'il se ferait facilement passer pour
3. Es-tu déjà allé à la chasse ?
4. Moi, je tire et je chasse
5. ne peux pas
6. Qu'est-ce qu'il y a de si génial à
7. Cela fait partie de la vie à la campagne.
8. comme s'il était
9. Elle le regardait toujours comme ça.
10. aiment ça
11. Le groupe de chasseurs était jeune
12. totalement masculin
13. Ils étaient cinq
14. à la lisière d'une forêt
15. domaine
16. bien bâti
17. avaient à peu près le même âge
18. le cœur gros
19. casquettes plates
20. avaient tous ces mêmes intonations d'école privée
21. fusil, l'arme cassée sur le bras
22. dévisagèrent

with barely concealed contempt[1]. Fiona must have already told them about him. The London boy.

Quickly, she made the introductions. Rufus stepped forward[2].

"Nice to have you with us," he drawled[3]. He ran his eyes over Alex. "Up for a bit of shooting are we?[4]"

"I don't have a gun," Alex said.

"Well, I'm afraid I'm not going to lend you mine[5]." Rufus snapped the barrel back into place[6] and held it up[7] for Alex to see. It was eighty centimetres of gleaming steel stretching out of a dark walnut stock[8] decorated with ornately carved, solid silver sideplates[9]. "It's an over-under[10] shotgun with detachable trigger[11], hand-made by Abbiatico and Salvinelli," he said. "It cost me thirty grand[12] – or my mother, anyway. It was a birthday present."

"It can't have been easy to wrap[13]," Alex said. "Where did she put the ribbon[14]?"

Rufus's smile faded[15]. "You wouldn't know anything about guns[16]," he said. He nodded at[17] one of the other teenagers, who handed Alex a much more ordinary weapon. It was old and a little rusty[18]. "You can use[19] this one," he said. "And if you're very good and don't get in the way[20], maybe we'll let you have a cartridge[21]."

They all laughed at that.[22] Then the two smokers put out[23] their cigarettes and they set off into[24] the wood.

1. en dissimulant à peine leur mépris
2. s'avança
3. dit-il, la voix traînante
4. Alors, on est partant pour tirer ?
5. te prêter le mien
6. referma le canon d'un coup sec
7. le tint en l'air
8. d'acier étincelant se profilant d'une crosse en noyer foncé
9. des platines latérales en argent massif ornées de gravures
10. superposé
11. détente amovible
12. 30 000 livres
13. Elle a dû s'embêter pour l'emballer
14. ruban
15. disparut
16. Tu ne connais rien aux armes
17. fit signe de la tête à
18. rouillée
19. te servir de
20. gentil et que tu ne nous gênes pas
21. on te donnera une cartouche
22. Cela les fit éclater de rire.
23. écrasèrent
24. partirent dans

Thirty minutes later, Alex knew he had made a mistake in coming. The boys blasted away left and right, aiming at anything that moved[1]. A rabbit spun in a glistening red ball[2]. A wood pigeon tumbled out[3] of the branches and flapped around on the leaves below[4]. Whatever the quality of their weapons, the teenagers weren't good shots[5]. Many of the animals they shot were only wounded[6], and Alex felt a growing sickness[7] following this trail of blood[8].

They reached a clearing[9] and paused to reload[10]. Alex turned to Fiona. "I'm going back to the house," he said.

"Why? Can't stand the sight of a little blood?[11]"

Alex glanced at a rabbit about fifty metres away[12]. It was lying on its side[13] with its back legs kicking helplessly[14]. "I'm surprised they let you carry guns," he said. "I thought you had to be seventeen."

Rufus had overheard him[15]. He stepped forward, an ugly look in his eyes[16]. "We don't bother with rules[17] in the countryside," he muttered.

"Maybe Alex wants to call a policeman!" Fiona said.

"The nearest[18] police station is forty miles from here."

"Do you want to borrow[19] my mobile?"

They all laughed again. Alex had had enough[20]. Without saying another word[21], he turned round and walked off[22].

1. tiraient à tout bout de champ, visant tout ce qui bougeait
2. lapin tournoya en l'air, transformé en boule sanglante
3. dégringola
4. battant des ailes dans le feuillage au-dessous
5. tireurs
6. blessés
7. était de plus en plus dégoûté
8. trainée de sang
9. clairière
10. firent une halte pour recharger
11. Tu supportes pas la vue d'une goutte de sang ?
12. 50 m de là
13. gisait sur le flanc
14. pattes arrière battant en vain
15. l'avait entendu
16. le regard mauvais
17. On se fiche des lois
18. le plus proche
19. emprunter
20. en eut marre
21. Sans dire un mot
22. tourna les talons et s'en alla

It had taken them thirty minutes to reach[1] the clearing, but thirty minutes later he was still stuck[2] in the wood, completely surrounded by trees and wild shrubs[3]. Alex realized he was lost[4]. He was annoyed with himself[5]. He should have watched where he was going when he was following Fiona and the others. The wood was enormous. Walk in the wrong[6] direction and he might blunder onto the moors[7] ... and it could be days before he was found[8]. At the same time, the spring foliage was so thick[9] that he could barely see[10] ten metres in any direction. How could he possibly find his way[11]? And should he try to retrace his steps[12] or continue forward in the hope of stumbling[13] on the right path[14]?

Alex sensed danger before the first shot was fired[15]. Perhaps it was the snapping of a twig[16] or the click of a metal bolt being slipped into place[17]. He froze[18] – and that was what saved him. There was an explosion – loud, close[19] – and a tree one step ahead of him shattered, splinters of wood dancing in the air[20].

Alex turned round, searching for whoever[21] had fired the shot. "What are you doing?" he shouted. "You nearly hit[22] me!"

Almost immediately there was a second shot and, just behind it, a whoop of excited laughter[23]. And then Alex realized. They hadn't mistaken him for[24] an animal. They were aiming at him for fun[25]!

1. atteindre
2. coincé
3. buissons sauvages
4. comprit qu'il s'était perdu
5. s'en voulait
6. S'il partait dans la mauvaise
7. il pourrait atterrir sur la lande
8. avant qu'on ne le retrouve
9. feuillage printanier était si dense
10. voyait à peine à
11. pouvait-il retrouver son chemin
12. revenir sur ses pas
13. d'avancer en espérant tomber
14. bon chemin
15. coup de feu soit tiré
16. une branche sectionnée
17. bruit métallique
18. se figea
19. forte, proche
20. à un pas devant lui fut pulvérisé, envoyant des éclats de bois dans l'air
21. essayant de repérer celui qui
22. touché
23. éclat de rire nerveux
24. ne l'avaient pas pris pour
25. le visaient pour s'amuser

1. plongea en avant
2. lui foncer dessus
3. menaçant de lui barrer le chemin
4. sol au-dessous de
5. ramolli par la pluie qui était tombée
6. s'accrochait à
7. les coller sur place
8. baissa la tête
9. fendre l'air au-dessus de
10. déchirant le feuillage
11. on était au beau milieu
12. ces ados riches et désœuvrés avaient l'habitude de n'en faire qu'à leur tête
13. moquerie
14. d'emballage
15. se soucieraient des
16. Voulaient-ils vraiment
17. gravement blessé
18. s'en tireraient d'une façon ou d'une autre
19. terrible
20. ligne de tir
21. l'effrayer
22. fit irruption
23. plumes tournoyantes
24. poursuivit sa course
25. son souffle lui irritant la gorge
26. grosse ronce jaillit sur sa poitrine et lui déchira

He dived forward[1] and began to run. The trunks of the trees seemed to press in on him[2] from all sides, threatening to bar his way[3]. The ground beneath[4] him was soft from recent rain[5] and dragged at[6] his feet, trying to glue them into place[7]. There was a third explosion. He ducked[8], feeling the gunshot spray above[9] his head, shredding the foliage[10].

Anywhere else in the world, this would have been madness. But this was the middle[11] of the English countryside and these were rich, bored teenagers who were used to having things their own way[12]. Alex had insulted them. Perhaps it had been the jibe[13] about the wrapping[14] paper. Perhaps it was his refusal to tell Fiona who he really was. But they had decided to teach him a lesson and they would worry about the[15] consequences later. Did they mean to[16] kill him? "We don't bother with rules in the countryside," Rufus had said. If Alex was badly wounded[17] – or even killed – they would somehow get away with it[18]. A dreadful[19] accident. He wasn't looking where he was going and stepped into the line of fire[20].

No. That was impossible.

They were trying to scare him[21], that was all.

Two more shots. A pheasant erupted out[22] of the ground, a ball of spinning feathers[23], and screamed up into the sky. Alex ran on[24], his breath rasping in his throat[25]. A thick briar reached out across his chest and tore at[26] his clothes. He still had the gun he had been given and he used it to beat a way through[1]. A tangle of roots almost sent him sprawling.[2]

"Alex? Where *are* you?" The voice belonged to[3] Rufus. It was high-pitched[4] and mocking, coming from the other side of a barrier of leaves[5]. There was another shot, but this one went high over his head. They couldn't see him. Had he got away?[6]

Alex came to a stumbling, sweating halt[7]. He had broken out[8] of the wood but he was still hopelessly lost[9]. Worse – he was trapped[10]. He had come to the edge of a wide, filthy lake[11]. The water was a scummy brown[12] and looked almost solid[13]. No ducks or wild birds were anywhere near[14] the surface. The evening sun beat down on it[15] and the smell of decay drifted up[16].

"He went that way[17]!"

"No ... through here[18]!"

"Let's try the lake..."

Alex heard the voices and knew that he couldn't let them find him here. He had a sudden image of his body, weighed down with stones[19], at the bottom of the lake. But that gave him an idea. He had to hide.

He stepped into[20] the water. He would need something to breathe through[21]. He had seen people do this in films. They would lie[22] in the water and breathe through a hollow reed[23]. But there were no reeds here. Apart from grass and thick, slimy algae, nothing was growing at all[24].

1. pour se frayer un chemin
2. Il faillit s'étaler à cause d'un nœud de racines.
3. était celle de
4. aiguë
5. rideau de feuilles
6. S'était-il sauvé ?
7. s'arrêta, titubant et en nage
8. s'était échappé
9. totalement perdu
10. pris au piège
11. au bord d'un grand lac dégoûtant
12. marron, écumeuse
13. presque figée
14. ne se trouvait à proximité de
15. dardait ses rayons dessus
16. l'odeur de pourriture remontait
17. par là
18. par ici
19. lesté de pierres
20. entra dans
21. quelque chose pour respirer
22. s'allongeaient
23. par un brin de roseau creux
24. grosses algues gluantes, absolument rien ne poussait

One minute later, Rufus appeared at the edge of the lake, his gun hooked over[1] his arm. He stopped and looked around with eyes that knew the forest well. Nothing moved.

"He must have doubled back[2]," he said.

The other hunters had gathered[3] behind him. There was a tension between them now, a guilty[4] silence. They knew the game had gone too far[5].

"Let's forget him[6]," one of them said.

"Yeah."

"We've taught him[7] a lesson."

They were in a hurry[8] to get home. The group disappeared back the way they had come. Rufus was left on his own, still clutching[9] his gun, searching for Alex. He took one last look across[10] the water, then turned to follow them.

That was when Alex struck[11]. He had been lying under the water, watching the vague shapes[12] of the teenagers as if through a sheet of thick brown glass[13]. The barrel[14] of the shotgun was in his mouth[15]. The rest of the gun was just above the surface of the lake. He was using the hollow tubes to breathe through. Now he rose up[16] – a nightmare[17] creature oozing mud[18] and water, with fury in his eyes[19]. Rufus heard him, but he was too late. Alex swung[20] the shotgun, catching Rufus in the small of the back[21]. Rufus grunted and fell to his knees[22], his own gun falling out of his hands. Alex picked it up. There were two cartridges in the breach[23]. He snapped the gun shut[24].

1. replié sur
2. a dû rebrousser chemin
3. s'étaient rassemblés
4. coupable
5. était allé trop loin
6. Oublions-le
7. On lui a donné
8. pressés
9. resta seul, serrant toujours
10. jeta un dernier coup d'œil sur
11. attaqua
12. silhouettes
13. comme à travers une épaisse vitre marron
14. canon
15. bouche
16. se leva d'un coup
17. de cauchemar
18. dégoulinant de boue
19. le regard furieux
20. frappa avec
21. touchant Rufus au niveau des reins
22. grogna et tomba à genoux
23. dans l'ouverture
24. referma le fusil d'un coup sec

Rufus looked at him and suddenly all the arrogance had gone and he was just a stupid, frightened[1] teenager, struggling to get to his knees[2].

"Alex!" The single word came out as a whimper.[3] It was as if he was seeing Alex for the first time. "I'm sorry!" he snivelled[4]. "We weren't really going to hurt you[5]. It was a joke[6]. Fiona put us up to it.[7] We just wanted to scare you[8]. Please!"

Alex paused, breathing heavily[9]. "How do I get out of here?" he asked.

"Just follow the lake round[10]," Rufus said. "There's a path[11]..."

Rufus was still on his knees. There were tears in his eyes.[12] Alex realized that he was pointing the silver-plated[13] shotgun in his direction. He turned it away, disgusted with himself[14]. This boy wasn't the enemy. He was nothing.

"Don't follow me," Alex said, and began to walk.

"Please...!" Rufus called after him. "Can I have my gun back? My mother would kill me if I lost it."

Alex stopped. He weighed the weapon[15] in his hands, then threw it with all his strength[16]. The hand-crafted[17] Italian shotgun spun twice in the dying light[18] then disappeared with a splash[19] into the middle of the lake. "You're too young to play with guns," he said.

He walked away, letting the forest swallow him up[20].

1. effrayé

2. essayant de se relever

3. Le mot sortit sous la forme d'un gémissement.

4. pleurnicha-t-il

5. te faire du mal

6. blague

7. C'est Fiona qui nous a poussés à le faire.

8. te faire peur

9. bruyamment

10. le pourtour du lac

11. sentier

12. Il avait les larmes aux yeux.

13. plaqué argent

14. le détourna, écœuré de son propre geste

15. soupesa l'arme

16. puis la lança de toutes ses forces

17. fait main

18. tournoya deux fois dans le crépuscule

19. dans une éclaboussure

20. la forêt se refermant sur lui

THE TUNNEL

The man sitting in the gold[1], antique chair[2] turned his head slowly and gazed out of the window at[3] the snow-covered slopes[4] of Point Blanc. Dr Hugo Grief was almost sixty years old with short white hair and a face that was almost colourless[5] too. His skin[6] was white, his lips vague shadows[7]. Even his tongue was no more than grey[8]. And yet, against this blank background[9], he wore circular wire spectacles[10] with dark red lenses[11]. The effect was startling[12]. And, for him, the entire world would be the colour of blood[13]. He had long fingers, the nails beautifully manicured[14]. He was dressed in a dark suit buttoned up to his neck[15]. If there were such a thing as a vampire, it would look very much like[16] Hugo Grief.

"I have decided to move[17] the Gemini[18] Project into its last phase," he said. He spoke with a South African accent, biting into each word[19] before it left his mouth. "There can be no further delay.[20]"

1. doré
2. fauteuil
3. regarda par la fenêtre, fixant
4. pentes enneigées
5. diaphane
6. peau
7. lèvres à peine esquissées
8. langue était toute grise
9. pourtant, sur ce fond neutre
10. des lunettes rondes à monture métallique
11. verres rouges
12. saisissant
13. monde entier avait la couleur du sang
14. ongles magnifiquement soignés
15. boutonné jusqu'au cou
16. Si les vampires existaient, ils devaient beaucoup ressembler à
17. d'enclencher
18. Gémeaux
19. mordant dans chaque mot
20. On ne peut plus le reporter.

"I understand, Dr Grief."

There was a woman sitting opposite[1] Dr Grief, dressed in tight-fitting Lycra[2] with a sweat band[3] round her head. This was Eva Stellenbosch. She had just finished her morning work-out[4] – two hours of weightlifting[5] and aerobic exercise – and she was still breathing heavily[6], her huge muscles rising and falling[7]. Mrs Stellenbosch had a facial structure that wasn't quite human, with lips curving out far in front of[8] her nose and wisps of bright ginger hair hanging over a high-domed forehead[9]. She was holding a glass filled with some milky[10] green liquid. Her fingers were thick and stubby[11]. She had to be careful not to break the glass.

She sipped[12] her drink, then frowned[13]. "Are you sure we're ready?" she asked.

"We have no choice in the matter.[14] We have had two unsatisfactory results in the last few months[15]. First Ivanov. Then Roscoe in New York. Quite apart from the expense of arranging the terminations[16], it's possible that someone may have connected[17] the two deaths."

"Possible, but unlikely[18]," Mrs Stellenbosch said.

"The intelligence services are idle and inefficient[19], it is true. The CIA in America. MI6 in England. Even the KGB! They're all shadows of what they used to be.[20] But even so[21], there's always the chance that one of them might have accidentally

1. en face du
2. vêtue d'un juste-au-corps en Lycra moulant
3. bandeau en éponge
4. séance de sport matinale
5. haltérophilie
6. était encore essoufflée
7. énormes muscles se soulevant et s'abaissant
8. saillantes, loin devant
9. des touffes de cheveux d'un roux éclatant surplombant un front très haut et bombé
10. laiteux
11. boudinés
12. but une gorgée de
13. fronça les sourcils
14. Nous n'avons pas le choix.
15. au cours de ces derniers mois
16. Mis à part les frais d'organisation de ces assassinats
17. ait fait le lien entre
18. peu probable
19. paresseux et inefficaces
20. Ils ne sont plus que l'ombre de ce qu'ils étaient.
21. Mais quand même

stumbled onto[1] something. The sooner we end[2] this phase of the operation, the more chance we have of remaining ... unnoticed[3]." Dr Grief brought his hands together and rested his chin on his fingertips[4]. "When is the final boy arriving?" he asked.

"Alex?" Mrs Stellenbosch emptied[5] her glass and set it down. She opened her handbag[6] and took out a handkerchief which she used to wipe her[7] lips. "I am travelling to England tomorrow," she said.

"Excellent. You'll take the boy to Paris on the way here[8]?"

"Of course, Doctor. If that is what you wish[9]."

"It is very much[10] what I wish, Mrs Stellenbosch. We can do all the preliminary work there. It will save time.[11] What about the Sprintz boy?"

"I'm afraid we still need another few days[12]."

"That means[13] that he and Alex will be here at the same time."

"Yes."

Dr Grief considered[14]. He had to balance[15] the risk of the two boys meeting against the dangers of moving too fast[16]. It was fortunate[17] that he had a scientific mind[18]. His calculations were never wrong. "Very well," he said. "The Sprintz boy can stay with us for another few days."

Mrs Stellenbosch nodded.

"Alex Friend is an excellent catch[19] for us," Dr Grief said

1. ait pu tomber par hasard sur
2. Plus tôt nous aurons achevé
3. passer... inaperçus
4. joignit les mains et posa le menton sur l'extrémité de ses doigts
5. vida
6. sac à main
7. mouchoir dont elle se servit pour s'essuyer les
8. sur le chemin du retour
9. souhaitez
10. C'est précisément
11. Nous gagnerons du temps.
12. quelques jours de plus
13. veut dire
14. réfléchit
15. devait évaluer
16. que les deux garçons se rencontrent, par rapport aux dangers de précipiter les choses
17. Heureusement
18. esprit
19. prise

"Supermarkets?" The woman sounded unconvinced[1].

"His father has the prime minister's ear[2]. He is an impressive man. His son, I am sure, will meet all our expectations[3]." Dr Grief smiled. His eyes glowed red[4]. "Very soon, we'll have Alex here at the academy. And then, at last, the Gemini Project will be complete[5]."

"You're sitting all wrong[6]," Fiona said. "Your back isn't straight[7]. Your hands should be lower[8]. And your feet are pointing the wrong way[9]."

"What does it matter, so long as you're enjoying yourself?[10]" Alex asked, speaking through gritted teeth[11].

It was the fourth day of his stay[12] at Haverstock Hall and Fiona had taken him out riding[13]. Alex wasn't enjoying himself at all. Before the ride, he'd had to endure the inevitable lecture[14] – although he had barely listened[15]. The horses were Iberian or Hungarian[16]. They'd won a bucketful of gold medals[17]. Alex didn't care[18]. All he knew was that his horse was big and black and attracted flies[19]. And that he was riding it with all the style of a sack of potatoes on a trampoline.

The two of them had barely mentioned the business[20] in the forest. When Alex had limped back[21] to the house, soaked and freezing[22], Fiona had politely fetched him a towel[23] and offered him a cup of tea.

1. peu convaincue
2. a de l'influence auprès du Premier ministre
3. sera à la hauteur de nos attentes
4. se mirent à rougeoyer
5. bouclé
6. Tu ne te tiens pas bien du tout
7. dos n'est pas droit
8. devraient se trouver plus bas
9. ne sont pas orientés dans la bonne direction
10. Qu'est-ce que cela peut faire, du moment qu'on s'amuse ?
11. les dents serrées
12. séjour
13. l'avait emmené faire du cheval
14. cours
15. bien qu'il ait à peine écouté
16. ibériques ou hongrois
17. remporté plein de médailles d'or
18. s'en fichait
19. attirait les mouches
20. à peine évoqué l'affaire
21. était rentré en boitant
22. trempé et gelé
23. était allée poliment lui chercher une serviette

"You tried to kill me!" Alex said.

"Don't be silly[1]!" Fiona looked at Alex with something like pity[2] in her eyes. "We would never do that. Rufus is a very nice boy."

"What...?"

"It was just a game, Alex. Just a bit of fun.[3]"

And that was it.[4] Fiona had smiled as if everything had been explained and then gone to have a swim[5]. Alex had spent the rest of the evening with the files. He was trying to take in a fake history[6] that lasted[7] fourteen years. There were uncles and aunts, friends at Eton, a whole crowd of people[8] he had to know without ever having met any of them[9]. More than that[10], he was trying to get the feel of this luxurious lifestyle[11]. That was why he was here now, out riding with Fiona – she upright in her riding jacket and breeches[12], he bumping along[13] behind.

They had ridden for[14] about an hour and a half when they came to the tunnel. Fiona had tried to teach Alex a bit of technique – the difference, for example, between walking, trotting[15] and cantering[16]. But this was one sport[17] he had already decided he would never take up[18]. Every bone[19] in his body had been rattled out of place[20] and his bottom was so bruised[21] he wondered if he would ever be able to sit down again. Fiona was enjoying his torment[22]. He even wondered if she had chosen a particularly bumpy route[23] to add to

1. bête
2. de la pitié
3. Juste un peu de rigolade.
4. Et cela s'arrêtait là.
5. était partie nager
6. d'assimiler une histoire inventée
7. durait
8. tout un tas de gens
9. sans jamais les avoir rencontrés
10. En plus
11. s'habituer à ce style de vie luxueux
12. elle, bien droite en veste et pantalon d'équitation
13. et lui, brinquebalant
14. montaient depuis
15. le pas, le trot
16. le petit galop
17. bien un sport
18. ne pratiquerait jamais
19. os
20. disloqué
21. fesses étaient si meurtries
22. se réjouissait de ses souffrances
23. trajet accidenté

his bruises[1]. Or maybe it was just a particularly bumpy[2] horse.

There was a single railway line[3] ahead of them, with an automatic level-crossing equipped with a bell and flashing lights to warn motorists[4] of any approaching train. Fiona steered[5] her horse – a smaller grey[6] – towards it. Alex's horse automatically followed. He assumed[7] they were going to cross the line[8], but when she reached the barrier, Fiona stopped.

"There's a short-cut[9] we can take if you want to get home," she said.

"A short-cut would be great," Alex admitted.

"It's that way." Fiona pointed up the line, and there was the tunnel, a gaping black hole[10] in the side of a hill, surrounded by dark red Victorian brick[11]. Alex looked at her to see if she was joking[12]. She was obviously quite serious.[13] He turned back to the tunnel. It was like the barrel of a gun, pointing at him[14], warning him to keep away[15]. He could almost imagine the giant finger on the trigger[16], somewhere behind the hill. How long was it?[17] Looking more carefully, he could see a pin-prick of light at the other end[18]. Perhaps up to a kilometre away[19].

"You're not being serious[20]," he said.

"Actually[21], Alex, I don't usually tell jokes[22]. When I say something, I mean it[23]. I'm just[24] like my father."

1. bleus
2. agité
3. seule voie de chemin de fer
4. passage à niveau avec sonnerie et feu clignotant, pour avertir les automobilistes
5. guida
6. plus petit et gris
7. pensa
8. traverser la voie
9. raccourci
10. trou noir béant
11. versant de la colline, entouré de briques victoriennes rouge sombre
12. si elle plaisantait
13. Apparemment, elle était sérieuse.
14. canon de fusil pointé sur lui
15. de ne pas s'approcher
16. doigt géant sur la détente
17. Quelle distance faisait-il ?
18. imperceptible point lumineux à l'autre bout
19. à 1 km maximum
20. Tu plaisantes
21. Tu sais
22. n'ai pas l'habitude de faire des blagues
23. je suis sérieuse
24. exactement

"Your father isn't barking mad[1]," Alex muttered.

Fiona pretended not to hear him[2]. "The tunnel is exactly one kilometre long," she explained. "There's a bridge on the other side[3], then another level-crossing. If we go that way[4], we can be home in thirty minutes. Otherwise it's an hour and a half back the way we came.[5]"

"Then let's go the way we came."

"Oh Alex, don't be such a scaredy-cat[6]!" Fiona pouted at him[7]. "There's only one train an hour[8] on this line and the next one isn't due for[9]" – she looked at her watch – "twenty minutes. I've been through[10] the tunnel a hundred times and it never takes more than five minutes. Less if you canter.[11]"

"It's still crazy[12] to ride on a railway line."

"Well, you'll have to find your own way home if you turn back." She kicked with her heels[13] and her horse jerked forward, past the barrier and onto the line[14]. "I'll see you later.[15]"

But Alex followed her. He would never have been able to ride back to the house on his own[16]. He didn't know the way[17] and he could barely[18] control the horse. Even now it was following Fiona with no prompting from him[19]. Would the two animals really enter the darkness of the tunnel? It seemed incredible, but Fiona had said they'd done it before and sure enough[20] the horse walked into the side of the hill without even[21] hesitating.

1. fou à lier
2. fit la sourde oreille
3. de l'autre côté
4. par là
5. Sinon, il faut une heure et demie pour rentrer par où on est venu.
6. si froussard
7. lui dit Fiona, en faisant la moue
8. toutes les heures
9. le prochain ne passera pas avant
10. j'ai traversé
11. Encore moins au petit galop.
12. quand même dingue
13. éperonna
14. passa la barrière et s'engagea sur la voie
15. À tout à l'heure.
16. tout seul
17. ne connaissait pas le chemin
18. à peine
19. sans qu'il ne l'ait poussé à le faire
20. en effet
21. sans même

Alex shivered[1] as the light was suddenly cut off[2] behind him. It was cold and clammy[3] inside. The air smelled of soot[4] and diesel. The tunnel was a natural echo-chamber[5]. The horses' hooves[6] rattled all around them as they struck against the gravel between the sleepers[7]. What if[8] his horse stumbled[9]? Alex put the thought out of his mind[10]. The leather saddles creaked[11]. Slowly his eyes got used to the dark. A certain amount of sunshine was filtering in from behind. More comfortingly, the way out was visible straight ahead, the circle of light widening with every step as they drew nearer[12]. He tried to relax. Perhaps this wasn't going to be so bad after all.

And then Fiona spoke. She had slowed down, allowing his horse to catch up with hers[13]. "Are you still worried about the train, Alex?" she said. "Perhaps you'd like to go faster..."

He heard the riding crop whistle through the air[14] and felt his horse jerk[15] as Fiona whipped it hard on the rear[16]. The horse whinnied and leapt forward[17]. Alex was thrown backwards, almost off[18] the saddle. Digging in with his legs he just managed to cling on[19], but the top half[20] of his body was at a crazy angle, the reins tearing into the horse's mouth[21]. Fiona laughed. Alex was aware only of the wind rushing past him[22], the thick blackness spinning round his face and the horse's hooves striking heavily at[23] the gravel as the ani-

1. frissonna
2. disparut soudain
3. humide
4. sentait la suie
5. chambre de réverbération
6. sabots
7. résonnaient tout autour d'eux en percutant les graviers entre les traverses
8. Et si
9. trébuchait
10. chassa cette pensée
11. selles en cuir crissaient
12. s'élargissant à chaque pas, à mesure qu'ils approchaient
13. laissant son cheval rattraper le sien
14. cravache siffler dans l'air
15. sursauter
16. lui fouetta la croupe de toutes ses forces
17. hennit et bondit en avant
18. projeté en arrière, presque éjecté de
19. En serrant les jambes, il réussit tout juste à s'accrocher
20. partie supérieure
21. penchait dangereusement, les rênes s'enfonçant dans la bouche du cheval
22. ne sentait que le vent cinglant sur les côtés
23. frappant violemment

mal careered forward[1]. Dust blew into[2] his eyes, blinding him[3]. He thought he was going to fall.

But then, miraculously, they had burst out into[4] the light. Alex fought for his balance[5] and brought the horse back under control, pulling back with[6] the reins and squeezing[7] the horse's flanks with his knees. He took a deep breath, spat out an oath[8] and waited for Fiona to appear.

His horse had come to rest[9] on the bridge that she had mentioned. The bridge was fashioned out of thick iron girders and spanned[10] a river. There had been a lot of rain that month and, about fifteen metres below him, the water was racing past[11], dark green and deep. Carefully, he turned round to face the[12] tunnel. If he lost control here it would be easy to fall over the edge[13]. The sides of the bridge couldn't have been more than a metre high[14].

He could hear Fiona approaching. She had been cantering after him, probably laughing the entire way[15]. He gazed into the tunnel – and that was when the grey burst out, raced past him[16] and disappeared through the level-crossing on the other side of the bridge.

But Fiona wasn't on it.

The horse had come out alone[17].

It took Alex a few seconds to work it out[18]. His head was reeling[19]. She must have fallen off[20]. Perhaps her horse had stumbled. She could be lying[21] inside the tunnel. On the track.[22] How long

1. fonçait en avant
2. La poussière vola dans
3. l'aveuglant
4. débarquèrent en trombe dans
5. repris son équilibre à grand-peine
6. en tirant sur
7. en serrant
8. respira un grand coup, cria un gros mot
9. s'était arrêté
10. était formé de grosses poutres métalliques et enjambait
11. filait à toute allure
12. se retourna face au
13. de tomber du bord
14. faisaient à peine plus de 1 m de haut
15. tout le long
16. là, le cheval gris sortit en trombe et passa devant lui
17. seul
18. avant de comprendre
19. tournait
20. chuté
21. Peut-être était-elle à terre
22. Sur la voie.

was there until[1] the next train? Twenty minutes, she had said. But at least five of those minutes had gone[2], and she might have been exaggerating to begin with[3]. What should he do? He had only three choices.

Go back in on foot[4].

Go back in on the horse.

Go home and forget about her[5].

No. He had only two choices. He knew that. He swore[6] for a second time, then seized hold of the reins[7]. Somehow he would get this horse to obey him[8]. He had to get the girl out and he had to do it fast.

Perhaps his desperation managed to communicate itself to the horse's brain.[9] The animal wheeled round and tried to back away[10], but when Alex kicked with his heels it stumbled forward and reluctantly[11] entered the darkness of the tunnel for a second time. Alex kicked again. He didn't want to hurt it but he could think of no other way[12] to make it obey him.

The horse trotted on. Alex searched ahead[13]. "Fiona!" he called out. There was no reply. He had hoped[14] that she would be walking towards him, but he couldn't hear any footsteps[15]. If only there was more light!

The horse stopped and there she was, right in front of him[16], lying on the ground, her arms and chest actually on the line[17]. If a train came now,

1. Combien de temps restait-il avant
2. s'étaient écoulées
3. d'abord
4. à pied
5. la laisser tomber
6. lâcha un gros mot
7. puis s'empara des rênes
8. forcerait ce cheval à lui obéir
9. Peut-être que son désespoir réussit à atteindre le cerveau du cheval.
10. fit demi-tour en essayant de reculer
11. de mauvaise grâce
12. ne voyait aucun autre moyen
13. scruta devant lui
14. espéré
15. n'entendait aucun bruit de pas
16. elle était là, juste devant lui
17. les bras et le buste en plein sur la voie

1. la couperait en deux
2. entendit la douleur
3. que je me suis cassé la cheville
4. une toile d'araignée ou un truc comme ça
5. te suivre
6. Je l'ai prise en plein visage
7. j'ai perdu l'équilibre
8. À l'entendre, on aurait dit que c'était de sa faute à lui
9. fouetté
10. te lever
11. soupira
12. En tenant toujours fermement les rênes
13. se laissa glisser de
14. ne pouvait mieux avoir choisi son moment
15. Selon
16. ne devait pas passer avant au moins 10 mn
17. se baissa pour l'aider à se relever
18. Il avait posé le pied sur
19. Tremblant le long de
20. arrivait
21. chasser la peur
22. vrombissant sur la voie

it would cut her in half[1]. It was too dark to see her face, but when she spoke he heard the pain[2] in her voice.

"Alex," she said. "I think I've broken my ankle[3]."

"What happened?"

"There was a cobweb or something[4]. I was trying to keep up with you[5]. It went in my face[6] and I lost my balance[7]."

She'd been trying to keep up with him! She sounded as if she was blaming *him*[8] – as if she'd forgotten that she had whipped[9] his horse on in the first place.

"Can you get up[10]?" Alex asked.

"I don't think so."

Alex sighed[11]. Keeping a tight hold on the reins[12], he slid off[13] his horse. Fiona couldn't have timed it better[14]. She had fallen right in the middle of the tunnel. He forced himself not to panic. According to[15] her calculations, the next train must still be at least ten minutes away[16]. He reached down to help her up[17]. His foot came to rest on[18] one of the rails ... and he felt something. Under his foot. Shivering up[19] his leg. The track was vibrating.

The train was on its way[20].

"You've got to stand up," he said, trying to keep the fear out[21] of his voice. He could already see the train in his imagination, thundering along the line[22]. When it plunged into the tunnel, it would be a five hundred tonne torpedo[1] that would smash them to pieces[2]. He could hear the grinding of the wheels[3], the roar of the engine[4]. Blood and darkness. It would be a horrible way to die.

But he still had time. "Can you move your toes[5]?" he asked.

"I think so." Fiona was clutching onto him[6].

"Then your ankle's probably sprained[7], not broken. Come on."

He dragged her up[8], wondering if it would be possible to stay inside the tunnel, at the edge of the track[9]. If they hugged[10] the wall, the train might simply go past them. But Alex knew there wouldn't be enough space[11]. And even if the train missed them[12], it would still hit[13] the horse. Suppose it derailed?[14] Dozens of people could be killed.

"What train comes this way?" he asked. "Does it carry[15] passengers?"

"Yes." Fiona was sounding tearful[16]. "It's a Virgin train. Heading up to[17] Glasgow."

Alex sighed. It was just his luck to get a Virgin train that arrived on time.[18]

Fiona froze. "What's that?" she asked.

She had heard the clanging of a bell[19]. What was it? Of course – the level-crossing! It was signalling the approach of the train, the barrier lowering itself over[20] the road.

And then Alex heard a second sound that made his blood run cold[21]. For a moment he couldn't

1. torpille de 500 tonnes

2. les écraserait en mille morceaux

3. grincement des roues

4. rugissement du moteur

5. orteils

6. s'agrippait à lui

7. foulée

8. la releva

9. au bord de la voie

10. S'ils se plaquaient contre

11. qu'il n'y aurait pas assez d'espace

12. les ratait

13. heurterait quand même

14. Et s'il déraillait ?

15. transporte

16. avait des sanglots dans la voix

17. Il va à

18. Pas de bol que, pour une fois, un train Virgin soit à l'heure.

19. le bruit métallique de la sonnerie

20. s'abaissant au-dessus de

21. qui lui glaça le sang

breathe[1]. It was extraordinary. His breath had got stuck in his lungs[2] and refused to get up to his mouth. His whole body was paralysed as if some switch had been thrown in his brain[3]. He was simply terrified.

The screech of a train whistle.[4] It was still a mile[5] or more away but the tunnel was acting as a sound conductor[6] and he could feel it almost cutting into him[7]. And now there was another noise. The rolling thunder of the diesel engine[8]. It was moving fast towards them. Underneath his foot, the rail was vibrating more violently.

Alex gulped for air[9] and forced his legs to obey him. "Get on[10] the horse," he shouted. "I'll help you."

Not caring how much pain he caused her[11], he dragged[12] Fiona next to the horse and forced her up towards the saddle[13]. The noise was getting louder[14] with every second that passed. The rail was humming softly[15], like a giant tuning-fork[16]. The very air[17] inside the tunnel seemed to be in motion[18], spinning left and right as if trying to get out of the way[19].

Fiona squealed[20] and Alex felt her weight leave his arms as she fell onto[21] the saddle. The horse whinnied and took a half step sideways[22], and for a dreadful[23] moment Alex thought she was going to ride off[24] without him. There was just enough light to make out the shapes of both[25] the animal

1. eut le souffle coupé
2. respiration était coincée dans ses poumons
3. comme si l'on avait appuyé sur un interrupteur dans son cerveau
4. Le hurlement de l'avertisseur d'un train.
5. [1,6 km]
6. servait de conducteur sonore
7. c'était comme s'il le transperçait
8. roulements de tonnerre du moteur diesel
9. essaya de respirer un bon coup
10. Monte sur
11. Sans se demander s'il lui faisait mal
12. traîna
13. la hissa en haut de la selle
14. s'amplifiait
15. bourdonnait doucement
16. diapason
17. Même l'air
18. se déplacer
19. libérer le passage
20. poussa un cri perçant
21. ses bras se décharger de son poids lorsqu'elle se laissa tomber sur
22. fit un petit pas de côté
23. affreux
24. détaler
25. pour distinguer les deux silhouettes de

and its rider[1]. He saw Fiona grabbing[2] the reins. She brought the horse back under control. Alex reached up and caught hold of its mane[3], using the thick hair to pull himself onto the saddle[4] in front of Fiona. The noise of the approaching train was getting louder and louder[5]. Soot and loose cement were trickling out of the curving walls[6]. The wind currents were twisting faster[7], the rails singing. For a moment the two of them were tangled together[8], but then he had the reins and she was clinging onto[9] him, her arms around his chest.

"Go!" he shouted, and kicked the horse.

The horse needed no encouragement. It raced for[10] the light, galloping up the railway line, throwing[11] Alex and Fiona back and forth into each other[12].

Alex didn't dare[13] look behind him, but he felt the train as it reached the mouth[14] of the tunnel and plunged into it, travelling at one hundred and five miles per hour[15]. A shock wave hammered into them[16]. The train was punching the air out of its way[17], filling the space with solid steel[18]. The horse understood the danger and burst forward with new speed[19], its hooves flying over the sleepers in great strides[20]. Ahead of them the tunnel mouth opened up[21] but Alex knew, with a sickening[22] sense of despair, that they weren't going to make it[23]. Even when they got out of the tunnel, they would still be hemmed in by the sides[24] of the

1. cavalière
2. saisir
3. empoigna sa crinière
4. l'épaisse touffe de crins pour se hisser en selle
5. devenait de plus en plus fort
6. poussière de ciment s'échappaient de la voûte
7. courants d'air tourbillonnaient plus vite
8. ils se retrouvèrent enchevêtrés
9. s'accrochait à
10. fonça vers
11. rejetant
12. sans cesse l'un contre l'autre
13. n'osait pas
14. lorsqu'il atteignit l'entrée
15. dedans, se déplaçant à 168 km/h
16. onde de choc les percuta
17. repoussait l'air devant lui
18. d'acier massif
19. bondit en avant encore plus vite
20. à longues enjambées
21. sortie du tunnel apparut
22. atroce
23. n'allaient pas y arriver
24. pris entre les parapets

bridge. The second level-crossing was a hundred metres further down the line[1]. They might get out, but they would die in the open air[2].

The horse passed through[3] the end of the tunnel. Alex felt the circle of darkness slip over[4] his shoulders. Fiona was screaming, her arms wrapped around him so tightly[5] that he could barely breathe. He could hardly hear her[6]. The roar[7] of the train was right behind him. As[8] the horse began a desperate race[9] over the bridge, he sneaked a glance round[10]. He just had time to see the huge metallic beast roar out[11] of the tunnel, towering over them, its body painted the brilliant red of the Virgin colours[12], the driver staring in horror[13] from behind his window. There was a second blast from the train whistle[14], this one all-consuming, exploding all around them[15]. Alex knew what he had to do. He pulled on one rein, kicking with the opposite foot at the same time. He just hoped the horse would understand what he wanted.

And somehow it worked. The horse veered round[16]. Now it was facing the[17] side of the bridge. There was a final, deafening[18] blast from the train. Diesel fumes smothered them.[19]

The horse jumped.

The train roared past, barely missing them[20]. But now they were in the air, over the side[21] of the bridge. The carriages were still thundering past[22]; a red blur[23]. Fiona screamed again. Everything

1. encore 100 m plus bas
2. à l'air libre
3. franchit
4. glisser au-dessus de
5. serrés si fort autour de lui
6. l'entendait à peine
7. rugissement
8. Alors que
9. partait dans une course folle
10. jeta un regard derrière lui
11. énorme monstre métallique sortir en rugissant
12. les dominant, ses voitures peintes en rouge vif, aux couleurs Virgin
13. le regard fixe, horrifié
14. coup de sifflet
15. dévorant, cette fois, explosant tout autour d'eux
16. fit demi-tour
17. était face au
18. assourdissant
19. Ils furent enveloppés dans les vapeurs de diesel.
20. les évitant de peu
21. au-dessus du bord
22. wagons défilaient toujours dans un bruit de tonnerre
23. une traînée rouge

seemed to be happening in slow motion as[1] they fell. One moment[2] they were next to the bridge, a moment later underneath it[3] and still falling. The green river rose up to receive them.[4]

The horse with its two riders plummeted[5] through the air and crashed into the river. Alex just had time to snatch a breath[6]. He was afraid the water wouldn't be deep enough[7], that all three of them would end up with broken bones[8]. But then they had hit the surface and passed through, down[9] into a freezing[10], dark green whirlpool[11] that sucked at them greedily, threatening to keep them there for ever[12]. Fiona was torn away from[13] him. He felt the horse kick itself free[14]. Bubbles exploded out of his mouth and he realized he was yelling[15].

Finally, Alex rose to the surface again[16]. The water was rushing past[17] and, dragged back by[18] his clothes and shoes, he clumsily swam for the nearest bank[19].

The train driver hadn't stopped. Perhaps he had been too frightened by what had happened. Perhaps he wanted to pretend it hadn't happened at all. The train had gone.

Alex reached the bank and pulled himself, shivering, onto the grass[20]. There was a splutter and a cough[21] from behind him and Fiona appeared. She had lost her riding hat[22] and her long black hair was hanging over[23] her face. Alex looked

1. se dérouler au ralenti pendant
2. À un moment
3. et l'instant d'après, au-dessous
4. La rivière verdâtre se souleva, prête à les happer.
5. dégringolèrent
6. avaler de l'air
7. ne soit pas assez profonde
8. allaient se rompre les os
9. touché la surface, passant à travers avant de sombrer
10. glacial
11. tourbillon
12. les avala goulûment, menaçant de les garder à jamais
13. violemment séparée de
14. se dégager à coup de pattes
15. hurlait
16. remonta à la surface
17. Le courant filait autour de lui
18. freiné par
19. nagea péniblement vers la berge la plus proche
20. se hissa sur l'herbe en tremblant
21. un bruit de crachat et de toux
22. bombe
23. recouvraient

past her[1]. The horse had also managed to reach dry land[2]. It trotted forward[3] and shook itself, seemingly unharmed[4]. Alex was glad about that. At the end of the day, the horse had saved both their lives[5].

He stood up. Water dripped out of[6] his clothes. There was no feeling anywhere in his body.[7] He wondered if it was because of the cold water or the shock of what he had just been through[8]. He went over to[9] Fiona and helped her to her feet[10].

"Are you all right?" he asked.

"Yes." She was looking at him strangely. She wobbled[11] and he put out a hand to steady her[12]. "Thank you," she said.

"That's all right."

"No." She held onto his hand[13]. Her shirt had fallen open[14] and she threw back her head, shaking the hair out of her eyes[15]. "What you did back there[16] ... it was fantastic. Alex, I'm sorry I've been such a beast[17] to you all week. I thought – because you were only here for charity and all the rest of it – I thought you were just an oik[18]. But I was wrong about you[19]. You're really great[20]. And I know we're going to be friends now." She half closed her eyes and moved towards him, her lips slightly parted[21]. "You can kiss me if you like[22]," she said.

Alex let go of her and turned away[23]. "Thanks, Fiona," he said. "But frankly[24] I'd prefer to kiss the horse."

1. regarda ailleurs
2. réussi à regagner la terre ferme
3. s'avança en trottant
4. s'ébroua, apparemment indemne
5. leur avait sauvé la vie à tous les deux
6. ruisselait de
7. Son corps était totalement engourdi.
8. ce qu'il venait de subir
9. alla retrouver
10. l'aida à se lever
11. chancela
12. tendit la main pour la stabiliser
13. garda sa main dans la sienne
14. s'était ouverte
15. rejeta la tête en arrière pour chasser ses cheveux de ses yeux
16. là-bas
17. aussi mauvaise
18. plouc
19. me suis trompée à ton sujet
20. génial
21. entrouvertes
22. si tu veux
23. la lâcha et tourna les talons
24. honnêtement

SPECIAL EDITION

The helicopter circled twice[1] over Haverstock Hall before beginning its descent[2]. It was a Robinson R44 four-seater aircraft[3], American-built[4]. There was only one person – the pilot – inside. Sir David Friend had returned from London and he and his wife came outside to watch it land[5] in front of the house. The engine noise died down and the rotors began to slow[6]. The cabin door slid open[7] and the pilot got out, dressed in a one-piece leather flying suit[8], helmet and goggles[9].

The pilot walked up to them, extending a hand[10]. "Good morning," she said. "I'm Mrs Stellenbosch from the academy."

If Sir David and Lady Caroline had been thrown by their first sight of Alex[11], the appearance[12] of this assistant director, as she called herself, left them frozen to the spot[13]. Sir David was the first to recover[14]. "You flew[15] the helicopter yourself?"

1. décrivit deux cercles
2. d'amorcer sa descente
3. appareil 4 places
4. de fabrication américaine
5. atterrir
6. se coupa progressivement et les rotors ralentirent
7. coulissa
8. combinaison de vol en cuir
9. lunettes
10. la main tendue
11. décontenancés en voyant Alex pour la première fois
12. allure
13. les pétrifia sur place
14. premier à s'en remettre
15. avez piloté

1. j'ai mon brevet
2. pour couvrir
3. les conduisit dans
4. jusqu'à
5. les jambes écartées
6. à côté d'elle
7. en face d'elle
8. On apporta le thé sur un plateau.
9. Cela vous dérange
10. fouilla dans
11. en alluma un et rejeta la fumée
12. avec tellement de goût
13. est parti se promener
14. lui avait offerte
15. grande source de tracas
16. acquiesça de la tête
17. ne trahissaient rien
18. Au cours des minutes qui suivirent
19. s'était fait renvoyer
20. était devenu ingérable

"Yes, I'm qualified[1]." Mrs Stellenbosch had to shout over[2] the noise of the rotors, which were still turning.

"Would you like to come in?" Lady Caroline asked. "Perhaps you'd like some tea?"

She led them into[3] the house and through to[4] the living room, where Mrs Stellenbosch sat, her legs apart[5], her helmet on the sofa beside her[6]. Sir David and Lady Caroline sat opposite her[7]. Tea was brought in on a tray.[8]

"Do you mind[9] if I smoke?" Mrs Stellenbosch asked. She reached into[10] a pocket and took out a small packet of cigars without waiting for an answer. She lit one and blew smoke[11]. "What a very beautiful house you have, Sir David. Georgian, I would say, but decorated with such taste[12]! And where, may I ask, is Alex?"

"He went for a walk[13]," Sir David said.

"Perhaps he's a little nervous." She smiled again and took the teacup Lady Caroline had proffered[14]. "I understand that Alex has been a great source of concern[15] to you."

Sir David Friend nodded[16]. His eyes gave nothing away[17]. For the next few minutes[18], he told Mrs Stellenbosch about Alex, how he had been expelled[19] from Eton, how out of control he had become[20]. Lady Caroline listened to all this in silence, occasionally holding her husband's arm.

"I'm at my wit's end[1]," Sir David concluded. "We have an older[2] daughter and she's perfect. But Alex? He hangs around[3] the house. He doesn't read. He doesn't show any interest in anything[4]. His appearance ... well, you'll see for yourself[5]. Point Blanc Academy is our last resort[6], Mrs Stellenbosch. We're desperately hoping you can sort him out[7]."

The assistant director poked at the air with her cigar, leaving a grey trail[8]. "I'm sure you've been a marvellous father, Sir David," she purred[9]. "But these modern children! It's heart-breaking[10] the way some of them behave[11]. You've done the right thing in coming to us[12]. As I'm sure you know, the academy has had a remarkable success rate over the past eleven years[13]."

"What exactly do you do?" Lady Caroline asked.

"We have our methods." The woman's eyes twinkled[14]. She tapped ash into her saucer[15]. "But I can promise you, we'll sort out[16] all Alex's problems. Don't you worry![17] When he comes home, he'll be a completely different boy!"

Meanwhile[18], Alex was crossing a field[19] about a kilometre away from the house. He had seen the helicopter land[20] and knew that his time had come[21]. But he wasn't ready to leave yet. Mrs Jones had telephoned him the night before[22]. Once again, MI6 weren't going to send

1. Je n'en peux plus
2. plus âgée
3. traîne dans
4. ne s'intéresse à rien
5. constaterez par vous-même
6. notre dernier recours
7. vous pourrez le recadrer
8. agita son cigare, laissant un sillage gris dans l'air
9. ronronna-t-elle
10. Cela fait mal au cœur
11. se comportent
12. en vous adressant à nous
13. taux de réussite remarquable depuis onze ans
14. pétillèrent
15. tapota la cendre dans sa soucoupe
16. réglerons
17. Ne vous en faites pas !
18. Pendant ce temps
19. traversait un champ
20. atterrir
21. moment était venu
22. la veille au soir

1. en territoire éventuellement hostile, les mains vides
2. observa une moissonneuse-batteuse pétarader vers lui, coupant à travers
3. s'arrêta en faisant une embardée
4. si gros
5. s'extirper, une fesse après l'autre
6. à carreaux
7. salopette
8. une tenue d'agriculteur
9. chapeau de paille et une tige de blé
10. cultiver vraiment quoi que ce soit
11. lui sourit
12. mon pote
13. fourni les divers gadgets
14. fit un clin d'œil
15. On m'a dit de me fondre dans le paysage.
16. Sauf qu'on est en
17. Il n'y a rien à récolter.
18. dit-il en faisant un grand sourire
19. agent de terrain
20. [jeu de mots sur « field » qui signifie terrain et champ]
21. bien content

him into what might be enemy territory empty-handed[1].

He watched as a combine harvester rumbled slowly towards him, cutting a swathe through[2] the grass. It jerked to a halt[3] a short distance away and the door of the cabin opened. A man got out – with difficulty. He was so fat[4] that he had to squeeze himself out, first one buttock, then the next[5], finally his stomach, shoulders and head. The man was wearing a checked[6] shirt and blue overalls[7] – a farmer's outfit[8]. But even if he'd had a straw hat and a blade of corn[9] between his teeth, Alex could never have imagined him actually farming anything[10].

The man grinned at him[11]. "Hello, old chap[12]!" he said.

"Hello, Mr Smithers," Alex replied.

Smithers worked for MI6. He had supplied the various devices[13] Alex had used on his last mission.

"Very nice to see you again!" he exclaimed. He winked[14]. "What do you think of the cover? I was told to blend in with the countryside.[15]"

"The combine harvester's a great idea," Alex said. "Except this is[16] April. There isn't anything to harvest.[17]"

"I hadn't thought of that!" Smithers beamed[18]. "The trouble is, I'm not really a field agent[19]. *Field*[20] agent!" He looked around him and laughed. "Anyway, I'm jolly glad[21] to have the chance to work with you again, Alex. To think up a few bits and pieces[1] for you. It's not often I get a teenager. Much more fun than the adults!"

He reached into[2] the cabin and pulled out a suitcase[3]. "Actually, it's been a bit tricky[4] this time," he went on.

"Have you got another Nintendo DS?" Alex asked.

"No. That's just it.[5] The school doesn't allow[6] Game Boys – or any computers at all, for that matter[7]. They supply their own laptops. I could have hidden[8] a dozen gadgets inside a laptop, but there you are[9]! Now, let's see..." He opened the case. "I'm told there's still a lot of snow up at[10] Point Blanc, so you'll need this."

"A ski suit[11]," Alex said. That was what Smithers was holding.

"Yes. But it's highly insulated and also bulletproof[12]." He pulled out a pair of green-tinted[13] goggles. "These are ski goggles. But in case you have to go anywhere at night, they're actually infrared[14]. There's a battery concealed in the frame[15]. Just press the switch[16] and you'll be able to see for about[17] twenty metres, even if there's no moon[18]."

Smithers reached into the case a third time. "Now, what else would a boy of your age have with him? Fortunately, you're allowed to take[19] a rather basic[20] Sony Discman – provided[21] all the CDs are classical." He handed Alex the machine.

1. De mettre au point quelques petits trucs
2. passa le bras dans
3. valise
4. En fait, c'était un peu délicat
5. C'est ça le problème.
6. n'autorise pas
7. d'ailleurs
8. J'aurais pu cacher
9. voilà
10. là-haut, à
11. combinaison de ski
12. ultra thermique et pare-balles, aussi
13. teintées en vert
14. en fait, elles sont à infrarouge
15. pile cachée dans la monture
16. Appuie simplement sur l'interrupteur
17. à une distance d'environ
18. même sans clair de lune
19. tu as le droit d'emporter
20. assez simple
21. à condition que

"So while[1] people are shooting at me in the middle of the night, I get to listen to[2] music," Alex said.

"Absolutely. Only don't play[3] the Beethoven!" Smithers held up[4] the disc. "The Discman converts into an electric saw[5]. The CD is diamond-edged[6]. It'll cut through just about anything[7]. Useful if you need to get out in a hurry. There's also a panic button I've built in[8]. If the balloon goes up[9] and you need help, just press fast forward[10] three times. It'll send out a signal which our satellite will pick up[11]. And then we can fast forward you out[12]!"

"Thank you, Mr Smithers," Alex said. But he was disappointed and it showed[13].

Smithers understood. "I know what you want," he said, "but you know you can't have it. No guns![14] Mr Blunt is adamant[15]. He thinks you're too young."

"Not too young to get killed though[16]."

"Yes, well. I've given it a bit of thought[17] and rustled up[18] a couple of ... defensive measures, so to speak[19]. This is just between you and me, you understand. I'm not sure Mr Blunt would approve[20]."

He held out a hand. There was a gold ear-stud lying in two pieces in the middle of his palm[21]; a diamond shape for the front[22] and a catch to hold it at the back[23]. The stud looked tiny surrounded

1. pendant que
2. je peux écouter de la
3. Mais surtout n'écoute pas
4. brandit
5. se transforme en scie électrique
6. a une lame diamant
7. découpe absolument tout
8. bouton d'alarme que j'ai intégré
9. Si les choses se gâtent
10. la touche d'avance rapide
11. captera
12. te faire sortir rapidement [jeu de mots sur « fast forward »]
13. manifestement déçu
14. Pas d'armes !
15. catégorique
16. pour me faire tuer, pourtant
17. J'y ai un peu réfléchi
18. bricolé vite fait
19. moyens défensifs, pour ainsi dire
20. serait d'accord
21. boucle d'oreille en or en deux parties au creux de sa paume
22. à l'avant
23. fermoir pour la retenir à l'arrière

by so much flesh[1]. "They told me you'd had your ear pierced," he said. "So I made you this. Be very careful after you've put it in[2]. Bringing the two pieces together will activate it.[3]"

"Activate what?" Alex looked doubtful[4].

"The ear-stud is a small but very powerful explosive device[5]. Separating the two pieces again will set it off[6]. Count to ten and it'll blow a hole[7] in just about anything – or anyone, I should add[8]."

"Just so long as it doesn't blow my ear off[9]," Alex muttered.

"No, no. It's perfectly safe so long as the pieces remain attached[10]." Smithers smiled. "And finally – I'm *very* pleased with this. It's exactly what you'd expect any young boy leaving for school to be given, and I bought it specially for[11] you." He had produced a book.

Alex took it. It was a hardback edition[12] of *Harry Potter and the Chamber of Secrets*[13]. "Thanks," he said, "but I've already read it."

"This is a special edition. There's a gun built into the spine[14] and the chamber is loaded[15] with a stun dart[16]. Just point it and press the author's name on the spine. It'll knock out[17] an adult in less than five seconds."

Alex smiled. Smithers climbed back[18] into the combine harvester. For a moment he seemed to have wedged himself permanently in the doorway[19], but then, with a grunt[20], he managed to go

1. minuscule, entouré de cette masse de chair

2. après l'avoir mise

3. Elle s'active quand on assemble les deux morceaux.

4. peu convaincu

5. engin explosif

6. ça le déclenche

7. ça creuse un trou

8. n'importe qui, dois-je préciser

9. Du moment qu'il ne fait pas exploser mon oreille

10. restent reliées

11. exprès pour

12. une édition à couverture rigide

13. [Harry Potter et la chambre des secrets]

14. arme intégrée dans le dos

15. chambre est chargée

16. flèche incapacitante

17. Ça met K.-O.

18. remonta

19. s'être encastré irrémédiablement dans l'ouverture

20. grognement

the whole way[1]. "Good luck, old chap," he said. "Come back in one piece[2]! I really do quite enjoy having you around![3]"

It was time to go.

Alex's luggage[4] was being loaded[5] into the helicopter and he was standing next to[6] his "parents" clutching[7] the Harry Potter book. Eva Stellenbosch was waiting for him beneath the rotors. He had been shocked by her appearance and at first he'd tried to hide it[8]. But then he'd relaxed. He didn't have to be polite. Alex Rider might be well-mannered[9] but Alex Friend wouldn't give a damn what she thought[10]. He glanced at her scornfully[11] now and noticed that she was watching him carefully[12] as he said goodbye to the Friends.

Once again, Sir David Friend acted his part perfectly[13]. "Goodbye, Alex," he said. "You will write to us and let us know[14] you're OK?"

"If you want," Alex said.

Lady Caroline moved forward and kissed him. Alex backed away from her as if embarrassed[15]. He had to admit that she looked genuinely sad[16].

"Come, Alex." Mrs Stellenbosch was in a hurry to get away[17]. She told him that they would need to stop in Paris to refuel[18].

And then Fiona appeared, crossing the lawn[19] towards them. Alex hadn't spoken to her since the business at the tunnel. Nor had she spoken

1. à passer complètement
2. en un seul morceau
3. J'apprécie vraiment ta compagnie !
4. bagages
5. chargés
6. se tenait près de
7. serrant
8. le dissimuler
9. était peut-être bien élevé
10. se ficherait bien de ce qu'elle pensait
11. avec dédain
12. l'observait attentivement
13. joua son rôle à la perfection
14. pour nous informer que
15. recula pour s'éloigner d'elle, comme s'il était gêné
16. réellement triste
17. pressée de partir
18. faire le plein
19. traversant la pelouse

to him. He had rejected her[1] and he knew she would never forgive him[2]. She hadn't come down to breakfast this morning and he'd assumed she wouldn't show herself again until[3] he'd gone. So what was she doing here now?

Suddenly Alex knew. She'd come to cause trouble – one last jab below the belt[4]. He could see it in her eyes and in the way she flounced across[5] the lawn with her hands rolled into fists[6].

Fiona didn't know he was a spy. But she must know that he was here for a reason and she had probably guessed[7] it had something to do with the woman from Point Blanc. So she had decided to come out and spoil things for him[8]. Maybe she was going to ask questions. Maybe she was going to tell Mrs Stellenbosch that he wasn't really her brother. Either way[9], Alex knew that his mission would be over before it had even begun[10]. All his work memorizing[11] the files and all the time he had spent[12] with the family would have been for nothing[13].

"Fiona!" Sir David muttered. His eyes were grave. He had come to[14] the same conclusion as Alex.

She ignored him. "Are you here for Alex?" she asked, speaking directly to Mrs Stellenbosch.

"Yes, my dear."

"Well, I think there's something you should know."

1. l'avait repoussée
2. ne lui pardonnerait jamais
3. s'était dit qu'elle ne se montrerait plus jusqu'à
4. semer la zizanie, un ultime coup au-dessous de la ceinture
5. à sa façon théâtrale de traverser
6. les poings serrés
7. deviné
8. de tout gâcher
9. Dans les deux cas
10. serait terminée avant même d'avoir commencé
11. pour mémoriser
12. le temps passé
13. ne serviraient à rien
14. avait tiré

There was only one thing Alex could do.[1] He lifted[2] the book and pointed it at[3] Fiona, then pressed the spine once, hard[4]. There was no noise, but he felt the book shudder[5] in his hand. Fiona put her hand to the side of her leg. All the colour drained out of her face.[6] She crumpled[7] to the grass.

Lady Caroline ran over to[8] her. Mrs Stellenbosch looked puzzled. Alex turned to her, his face blank[9]. "That's my sister," he said. "She gets very emotional[10]."

Two minutes later the helicopter took off[11]. Alex watched through the window as Haverstock Hall got smaller and smaller[12] and then disappeared behind them. He looked at Mrs Stellenbosch hunched over the controls[13], her eyes hidden by her goggles. He eased himself[14] into his seat and let himself be carried away[15] into the darkening sky. Then the clouds rolled in[16]. The countryside was gone. So was his only weapon.[17] Alex was on his own[18].

1. Alex n'avait plus qu'une chose à faire.
2. souleva
3. le pointa sur
4. appuya avec force sur le dos, une seule fois
5. vibrer
6. Son visage devint livide.
7. s'écroula
8. courut vers
9. impassible
10. est très émotive
11. décolla
12. devenir de plus en plus petit
13. penchée sur ses commandes
14. s'installa confortablement
15. emporter
16. nuages affluèrent
17. Et avec elle, sa seule arme.
18. livré à lui-même

ROOM 13

It was raining in Paris. The city was looking tired and disappointed[1], the Eiffel Tower fighting against a mass of heavy cloud[2]. There was nobody sitting at the tables spread outside the[3] cafés and for once the little kiosks[4] selling paintings and postcards were being ignored by the tourists hurrying back to their hotels[5]. It was five o'clock in the afternoon and the evening was drawing in[6]. The shops and offices were emptying[7], but the city didn't care[8]. It just wanted to be left alone[9].

The helicopter had landed in a private area of Charles de Gaulle airport and a car had been waiting to drive them in[10]. Alex had said nothing during the flight[11] and now he sat on his own in the back[12], watching the buildings flash by[13]. They were following the Seine, moving surprisingly fast along a wide dual carriageway[14] that dipped above and below the water level[15]. Their route took them

1. avait l'air fatiguée et contrariée
2. luttant contre une masse de gros nuages
3. disposées à l'extérieur des
4. pour une fois, les bouquinistes
5. se dépêchant de rentrer à l'hôtel
6. soir tombait
7. se vidaient
8. s'en fichait
9. qu'on la laisse tranquille
10. les y attendait pour les conduire
11. vol
12. était assis seul, à l'arrière
13. passer à toute vitesse
14. le long d'une route à quatre voies, très large
15. s'inclinait au-dessus et au-dessous du niveau de l'eau

past[1] Notre Dame. Then they turned off, weaving their way through a series of back streets[2] with small restaurants and boutiques fighting for space on the pavements[3].

"The Marais," Mrs Stellenbosch said.

Alex pretended to show no interest[4]. In fact, he had stayed in the Marais district[5] once before and knew it as one of the smartest[6] and most expensive[7] quarters of Paris.

The car turned into a large square[8] and stopped. Alex glanced out of the window. He was surrounded on four sides by the tall, classical houses for which Paris is famous[9]. But the square had been disfigured[10] by a single modern hotel. It was a white rectangular block[11], the windows fitted with dark glass[12] that allowed no view to the inside[13]. It rose up four floors[14], with a flat roof[15] and the name Hotel du Monde in gold letters above the main door[16]. If a spaceship[17] had landed in the square, crushing[18] a couple of buildings to make room for itself[19], it couldn't have looked more out of place[20].

"This is where we're staying," Mrs Stellenbosch said. "The hotel is owned by[21] the academy."

The driver had taken their cases out[22] of the boot[23]. Alex followed the assistant director towards the entrance, the door sliding open[24] automatically to allow them in[25]. The reception was cold and faceless[26], white marble and mirrors, with a

1. trajet les fit passer devant
2. se faufilant dans un dédale de ruelles
3. se disputant l'espace sur les trottoirs
4. fit semblant de ne pas s'y intéresser
5. quartier
6. plus élégants
7. plus chers
8. grande place
9. célèbre
10. défiguré
11. immeuble
12. équipées de vitres sombres
13. empêchaient de voir l'intérieur
14. se dressait sur 4 étages
15. toit terrasse
16. au-dessus de la porte d'entrée
17. vaisseau spatial
18. en écrasant
19. pour se faire une place
20. plus déplacé
21. appartient à
22. sorti leurs valises
23. coffre
24. coulissant
25. pour les faire entrer
26. anonyme

single potted plant tucked into a corner as an afterthought[1]. There was a small reception desk with an unsmiling[2] male receptionist in a dark suit and glasses, a computer and a row of pigeon holes[3]. Alex counted them. There were fifteen. Presumably the hotel had fifteen rooms.

"*Bonsoir,* Madame Stellenbosch." The receptionist nodded his head slightly[4]. He ignored Alex. "I hope you had a good journey[5] from England," he continued, still speaking in French. Alex gazed blankly[6], as if he hadn't understood a word. Alex Friend wouldn't speak French[7]. He wouldn't have bothered to learn[8]. But Ian Rider had made certain[9] that his nephew spoke French almost as soon as he spoke English. Not to mention German and Spanish[10] as well.

The receptionist took down[11] two keys. He didn't ask either of them to sign in[12]. He didn't ask for a credit card. The school owned[13] the hotel, so there would be no bill when they left[14]. He gave Alex one of the keys.

"I hope you are not superstitious," he said, speaking in English now.

"No," Alex replied[15].

"It is room thirteen. On the first floor[16]. I am sure you will find it most[17] agreeable." The receptionist smiled.

Mrs Stellenbosch took her key. "The hotel has its own[18] restaurant," she said. "We might as well

1. plante verte posée dans un coin, comme si elle avait été ajoutée après coup
2. peu souriant
3. rangée de casiers
4. hocha légèrement la tête
5. fait bon voyage
6. le regarda bêtement
7. n'aurait pas parlé français
8. n'aurait pas pris la peine de l'apprendre
9. s'était assuré
10. Sans parler de l'allemand ni de l'espagnol
11. prit
12. à aucun d'eux de signer le registre
13. possédait
14. pas de note à payer en partant
15. répondit
16. premier étage
17. très
18. son propre

eat here tonight.[1] We don't want to go out in the rain. Anyway, the food here is excellent. Do you like French food, Alex?"

"Not much," Alex said.

"Well, I'm sure we'll find something that you like. Why don't you freshen up[2] after the journey?" She looked at her watch[3]. "We'll eat at seven. An hour and a half from now.[4] It will give us an opportunity to talk together. Might I suggest[5], perhaps, some smarter clothes[6] for dinner? The French are informal[7], but – if you'll forgive me saying so[8], my dear – you take informality a little far[9]. I'll call you at five to seven[10]. I hope the room is all right."

Room thirteen was at the end of a long, narrow[11] corridor. The door opened into[12] a surprisingly large space[13], with views over[14] the square. There was a double bed[15] with a black and white cover[16], a television and mini-bar, a desk and, on the wall, a couple of framed pictures[17] of Paris. A porter had carried up[18] Alex's cases and, as soon as he was gone, Alex kicked off[19] his shoes and sat down on the bed. He wondered why they had come here. He knew the helicopter had needed refuelling[20], but that shouldn't have necessitated an overnight stop[21]. Why not fly straight on to[22] the school?

He had more than an hour to kill[23]. First he went into the bathroom – more glass and white marble –

1. Autant dîner ici ce soir.
2. Et si tu faisais un brin de toilette
3. montre
4. Dans une heure et demie.
5. Puis-je te suggérer
6. des vêtements plus élégants
7. décontractés
8. pardonne-moi de le dire
9. tu pousses la décontraction un peu loin
10. sept heures moins cinq
11. étroit
12. révéla
13. pièce étonnamment spacieuse
14. une vue sur
15. grand lit
16. dessus-de-lit
17. photos encadrées
18. porteur avait monté
19. retira
20. besoin de faire le plein
21. de s'arrêter pour la nuit
22. ne pas repartir directement à
23. plus d'une heure devant lui

and took a long shower. Then, wrapped in a towel[1], he went back into the room and put the television on. Alex Friend would watch a lot of[2] television. There were about thirty channels to choose from[3]. Alex skipped past[4] the French ones and stopped on MTV. He wondered if he was being monitored[5]. There was a large mirror next to the desk and it would have been easy enough to conceal[6] a camera behind it. Well, why not give them something to think about[7]? He opened the mini-bar and poured himself[8] a glass of gin. Then he went into the bathroom, refilled[9] the bottle with water and put it back in the fridge. Drinking alcohol and stealing[10]! If she was watching, Mrs Stellenbosch would know that she had her hands full with him[11].

He spent the next[12] forty minutes watching television and pretending to[13] drink the gin. Then he took the glass into the bathroom and dumped it[14] in the sink[15], allowing the liquid to run out[16]. It was time to get dressed. Should he do what he was told[17] and put on smart clothes? In the end, he compromised[18]. He put on[19] a shirt, but kept the same jeans. A moment later, the telephone rang. His call to dinner.[20]

Mrs Stellenbosch was waiting for him in the restaurant, an airless[21] room in the basement. Soft lighting[22] and mirrors had been used to make it feel more spacious[23], but it was still the last place Alex would have chosen[24]. The restaurant could have

1. enveloppé dans une serviette
2. devait énormément regarder la
3. environ 30 chaînes au choix
4. zappa
5. s'il était filmé
6. assez facile de dissimuler
7. matière à réflexion
8. se versa
9. remplit à nouveau
10. voler
11. qu'elle aurait du boulot, avec lui
12. suivantes
13. en faisant semblant de
14. jeta le contenu
15. lavabo
16. laissant le liquide s'écouler
17. faire ce qu'on lui avait dit
18. trouva un compromis
19. mit
20. On l'appelait pour dîner.
21. qui manquait d'air
22. Des lumières tamisées
23. lui donner l'air plus spacieux
24. aurait choisi

been anywhere, in any part[1] of the world. There were two other diners – businessmen by the look of them[2] – but otherwise[3] they were alone. Mrs Stellenbosch had changed into a black evening dress[4] with feathers at the collar[5] and she wore an antique-looking necklace[6] of black and silver beads[7]. The smarter her clothes[8], Alex thought, the uglier she looked[9]. She was smoking another cigar.

"Ah, Alex!" She blew[10] smoke. "Did you have a rest?[11] Or did you watch TV?"

Alex didn't say anything. He sat down and opened the menu, then closed it again when he saw that it was all in French.

"You must let me order[12] for you. Some soup to start, perhaps? And then[13] a steak. I've never yet met a boy who doesn't like steak."

"My cousin Oliver is a vegetarian[14]," Alex said. It was something he had read in one of the files[15].

The assistant director nodded as if she already knew this[16]. "Then he doesn't know what he is missing[17]," she said. A pale-faced[18] waiter came over and she placed the order[19] in French. "What will you drink?" she asked.

"I'll have a Coke."

"A repulsive drink[20], I always think. I have never understood the taste.[21] But, of course, you shall have what you want."

The waiter brought Alex a Coke and a glass of champagne for Mrs Stellenbosch. Alex watched

1. n'importe où, dans n'importe quelle partie
2. d'après leur apparence
3. sinon
4. s'était changée, elle portait une robe de soirée noire
5. des plumes sur le col
6. collier de style ancien
7. perles
8. Plus ses vêtements étaient chics
9. plus elle paraissait laide
10. rejeta
11. Tu t'es reposé ?
12. Laisse-moi commander
13. ensuite
14. végétarien
15. dans l'un des dossiers
16. acquiesça comme si elle le savait déjà
17. ce qu'il rate
18. au visage pâle
19. passa la commande
20. boisson répugnante
21. Je n'ai jamais aimé ce goût.

the bubbles rising[1] in the two glasses, his black, hers a pale gold[2].

"*Santé*," she said.

"I'm sorry?[3]"

"It's French for 'good health[4]'."

"Oh. Cheers.[5]"

There was a moment's silence. The woman's eyes were fixed on him – as if she could see right through him[6]. "So, you were at Eton," she said casually[7].

"That's right." Alex was suddenly on his guard[8].

"What house[9] were you in?"

"The Hopgarden." It was the name of a real house at the school. Alex had read the file carefully[10].

"I visited Eton once. I remember a statue. I think it was a king. It was just through the main gate[11]..."

She was testing him. Alex was sure of it. Did she suspect him[12] – or was it simply a precaution, something she always did? "You're talking about[13] Henry VI," he said. "His statue's in College Yard. He founded Eton.[14]"

"But you didn't like it there[15]."

"No."

"Why not?"

"I didn't like the uniform and I didn't like the beaks[16]." Alex was careful not to use the word "teachers". At Eton, they're known as[17] beaks. He

1. bulles remonter
2. noires pour lui, et d'un or pâle pour elle
3. Pardon ?
4. bonne santé
5. Santé.
6. comme si elle pouvait lire en lui
7. l'air de rien
8. sur ses gardes
9. résidence
10. attentivement
11. juste après l'entrée principale
12. Est-ce qu'elle le soupçonnait
13. Vous voulez dire
14. C'est le fondateur d'Eton.
15. tu ne t'es pas plu, là-bas
16. profs
17. on les appelle les

half smiled to himself.[1] If she wanted a bit of Eton-speak, he'd give it to her[2]. "And I didn't like the rules[3]. Getting fined by the pop[4]. Or being put in the tardy book[5]. I was always getting rips[6] and infoes[7] or being put on the bill[8]. The divs were boring[9]—"

"I'm afraid I don't really understand a word[10] you're saying."

"Divs are lessons," Alex explained. "Rips are when your work is no good—"

"All right!" She drew a line with[11] her cigar. "Is that why you set fire to the library[12]?"

"No," Alex said. "That was just because I don't like books."

The first course[13] arrived. Alex's soup was yellow and had something floating in it[14]. He picked up his spoon and poked at it suspiciously[15]. "What's this?" he demanded.

"*Soupe de moules.*"

He looked at her blankly.

"Mussel soup. I hope you enjoy it[16]."

"I'd have preferred Heinz tomato[17]," Alex said.

The steaks, when they came, were typically French; barely cooked at all[18]. Alex took a couple of mouthfuls[19] of the bloody meat[20], then threw down[21] his knife and fork and used his fingers to eat the chips[22]. Mrs Stellenbosch talked to him about the French Alps, about skiing[23] and about her visits to various European cities. It was easy

1. Il sourit intérieurement.
2. du jargon d'Eton, elle allait être servie
3. le règlement
4. [membre de l'Eton Society, encadre l'assemblée matinale]
5. [registre des retards à signer avant le petit déjeuner plusieurs jours de suite]
6. [devoirs ratés à faire signer par son « tuteur » et le « préfet » de la résidence]
7. [version allégée de « rip »]
8. [en cas de faits graves, convocation chez le directeur]
9. cours m'ennuyaient
10. ne comprends vraiment pas un mot de
11. l'interrompit d'un geste de
12. as mis le feu à la bibliothèque
13. entrée
14. des trucs flottaient dedans
15. saisit sa cuillère et les tapota, l'air méfiant
16. que tu aimeras
17. [soupe à la tomate en conserve]
18. à peine cuits
19. bouchées
20. viande saignante
21. laissa tomber
22. frites
23. de ski

to look bored[1]. He *was* bored. And he was beginning to feel tired[2]. He took a sip[3] of Coke, hoping the cold drink would wake him up. The meal seemed to be dragging on[4] all night.

But at last the puddings[5] – ice cream with white chocolate sauce – had come and gone[6]. Alex declined[7] coffee.

"You look tired," Stellenbosch said. She had lit[8] another cigar. The smoke curled around[9] her head and made him feel dizzy[10]. "Would you like to go to bed?"

"Yes."

"We don't need to leave until midday[11] tomorrow. You'll have time for a visit to the Louvre, if you'd like that."

Alex shook his head[12]. "Actually[13], paintings bore me."

"Really? What a shame![14]"

Alex stood up. Somehow his hand knocked into[15] his glass, spilling[16] the rest of the Coke over the pristine white tablecloth[17]. What was the matter with him?[18] Suddenly he was exhausted[19].

"Would you like me to come up with you, Alex?" the woman asked. She was looking carefully at him, a tiny glimmer[20] of interest in her otherwise dead eyes[21].

"No. I'll be all right." Alex stepped away[22]. "Goodnight."

1. d'avoir l'air mort d'ennui
2. se sentir fatigué
3. gorgée
4. repas semblait s'éterniser
5. desserts
6. avaient été servis et débarrassés
7. refusa
8. allumé
9. encercla
10. l'étourdit
11. ne sommes pas obligés de partir avant midi
12. secoua la tête
13. En fait
14. Quel dommage !
15. Sans faire exprès, sa main heurta
16. renversant
17. nappe d'un blanc immaculé
18. Mais qu'est-ce qu'il avait ?
19. épuisé
20. petite lueur
21. son regard vide par ailleurs
22. s'éloigna

Getting upstairs was an ordeal[1]. He was tempted to take the lift but he didn't want to lock himself into[2] that small, windowless cubicle[3]. He would have felt suffocated[4]. He climbed[5] the stairs, his shoulder resting heavily against[6] the wall, stumbled down[7] the corridor and somehow got the key into the lock[8]. When he finally got inside, the room was spinning[9]. What was going on?[10] Had he drunk more of the gin than he had intended[11] or was he...?

Alex swallowed[12]. He had been drugged[13]. There had been something in the Coke. It was still on his tongue[14], a sort of bitterness[15]. There were only three steps between him and his bed, but it could have been a mile away[16]. His legs wouldn't obey him any more[17]. Just lifting[18] one foot took all his strength[19]. He fell forward, reaching out with his arms[20]. Somehow he managed to propel himself[21] far enough. His chest and shoulders hit[22] the bed, sinking into the mattress[23]. The room was spinning round him, faster and faster. He tried to stand up, tried to speak – but nothing came. His eyes closed. Gratefully[24], he allowed the darkness to take him[25].

Thirty minutes later, there was a soft[26] click and the room began to change[27].

If Alex had been able to open his eyes, he would have seen the desk, the mini-bar and the

1. fut une épreuve
2. se retrouver enfermé dans
3. cabine sans fenêtre
4. aurait eu l'impression d'étouffer
5. grimpa
6. s'appuyant de tout son poids contre
7. tituba le long de
8. réussit à insérer la clé dans la serrure
9. tournoyait
10. Que se passait-il ?
11. qu'il ne le pensait
12. avala sa salive
13. drogué
14. Il l'avait encore sur la langue
15. amertume
16. à des km
17. ne lui obéissaient plus
18. soulever
19. force
20. tomba les bras en avant
21. se hisser
22. touchèrent
23. s'enfonçant dans le matelas
24. Avec bonheur
25. se laissa sombrer dans l'obscurité
26. léger
27. se transformer

framed pictures of Paris begin to rise up the wall[1]. Or so it might have seemed to him.[2] But in fact the walls weren't moving. The floor was sinking on hidden hydraulics[3], taking the bed – with Alex on it – into the depths[4] of the hotel. The entire room was nothing more than a huge lift which was carrying him, one centimetre at a time[5], into the basement and beyond[6]. Now the walls were metal sheets[7]. He had left the wallpaper[8], the lights and the pictures high above him. He was dropping through[9] what might have been a ventilation shaft[10] with four steel rods guiding him to the bottom[11]. Brilliant light suddenly flooded over him[12]. There was another soft click. He had arrived.

The bed had come to rest[13] in the centre of a gleaming underground clinic[14]. Scientific equipment crowded in on him from all sides[15]. There were a number of cameras – digital, video, infrared and X-ray[16]. There were instruments of all shapes and sizes[17], many of them unrecognizable[18].

A tangle of wires spiralled out[19] from each machine to a bank of computers[20] that hummed[21] and blinked[22] on a long worktable[23] against one of the walls. A window had been cut into the wall on the other side. The room was air-conditioned. Had Alex been awake[24], he might have shivered in the cold[25]. His breath appeared as a faint white cloud hovering[26] around his mouth.

1. s'élever le long du mur
2. Ou bien il aurait eu cette impression.
3. sol descendait par un système hydraulique
4. dans les profondeurs
5. cm par cm
6. encore plus bas
7. parois métalliques
8. papier peint
9. descendait le long de
10. conduit
11. 4 montants en acier le guidant jusqu'au fond
12. l'inonda soudain
13. s'était posé
14. clinique souterraine rutilante
15. le cernait de tous côtés
16. rayons X
17. de toutes formes et dimensions
18. non identifiables
19. Des câbles en spirale sortaient pêle-mêle
20. station informatique
21. bourdonnait
22. clignotait
23. plan de travail
24. Si Alex avait été éveillé
25. aurait peut-être grelotté de froid
26. souffle formait un léger nuage blanc planant

1. grassouillet
2. blouse
3. lissés en arrière
4. déjà rattrapé par la cinquantaine
5. joues bouffies
6. épais et gras
7. livides
8. se mirent aussitôt au travail
9. Manipulant
10. légumes
11. cadavre
12. le déshabillèrent entièrement
13. et en remontant, prenant
14. s'allumant
15. se déroulant
16. Pas un centimètre de son corps n'échappa à l'examen.
17. mèche
18. sectionnée
19. glissée dans un sachet en plastique
20. fond de son œil
21. moulage
22. pâte
23. menton pour qu'il morde dedans
24. marque de naissance
25. cicatrice
26. empreintes digitales
27. se rongeait les ongles
28. Cette information
29. également enregistrée
30. le pesèrent sur une grande balance plate

A plump[1] man wearing a white coat[2] was waiting to receive him. The man was about forty, with yellow hair slicked back[3] and a face that was rapidly sinking into middle-age[4], with puffy cheeks[5] and a thick, fatty[6] neck. The man had glasses and a small moustache. He had two assistants with him. They were also wearing white coats. Their faces were blank[7].

The three of them set to work at once[8]. Handling[9] Alex as if he were a sack of vegetables[10] – or a corpse[11] – they picked him up and stripped off all his clothes[12]. Then they began to photograph him, using a conventional camera to begin with. Starting at his toes, they moved upwards, clicking off[13] at least a hundred pictures, the flash igniting[14] and the film automatically spooling forward[15]. Not one inch of his body escaped their examination.[16] A lock[17] of his hair was snipped off[18] and slid into a plastic envelope[19]. An opthalmoscope was used to produce a perfect image of the back of his eye[20]. They made a moulding[21] of his teeth, slipping a piece of putty[22] into his mouth and manipulating his chin to make him bite down[23]. They made a careful note of the birthmark[24] on his left shoulder, the scar[25] on his arm and even his fingerprints[26]. Alex bit his nails[27]. That[28] was recorded too[29].

Finally, they weighed him on a large, flat scale[30] and then measured him – his height, chest, waist, inside leg[1], hand size and so on[2] – making a note of every measurement on clipboards[3].

And all the time, Mrs Stellenbosch watched from the other side of the window. She never moved. The only sign of life anywhere in[4] her face was the cigar, clamped between her lips[5]. It glowed red[6] and the smoke trickled up[7].

The three men had finished. The one with the yellow hair spoke into a microphone. "We're all done[8]," he said.

"Give me your opinion, Mr Baxter." The woman's voice echoed out of a concealed speaker[9].

"It's a cinch.[10]" The man called Baxter was English. He spoke with an upper-class accent. And he was obviously pleased with himself[11]. "He's got a good bone structure[12]. Very fit.[13] Interesting face. You notice the pierced ear? He's had that done recently. Nothing else to say, really."

"When will you operate?"

"Whenever you say, old girl.[14] Just let me know."

Mrs Stellenbosch turned to the other two men. "*Rhabillez-le!*" She snapped[15] the two words.

The two assistants put Alex's clothes back on him again[16]. This took longer[17] than taking them off. As they worked, they made a careful note of all the brand names[18]. The Quiksilver shirt. The Gap socks[19]. By the time they had dressed him[20], they knew as much about him[21] as a doctor knows

1. taille, sa poitrine, son tour de taille, son entrejambe
2. etc.
3. notant chaque mesure sur des bloc-notes
4. présent sur
5. coincé entre ses lèvres
6. rougeoyait
7. de petits filets de fumée s'élevaient
8. On a fini
9. haut-parleur caché
10. C'est du gâteau.
11. content de lui
12. squelette
13. En pleine forme.
14. Dès que tu le diras, ma grande.
15. aboya
16. rhabillèrent Alex
17. prit plus de temps
18. marques
19. chaussettes
20. Après l'avoir habillé
21. en savaient autant sur lui

1. nouveau-né
2. Tout avait été noté.
3. transmis
4. Aussitôt
5. disparurent au-delà du plafond
6. dormait toujours
7. qu'on le remontait le long de
8. dans la pièce qui, pour lui, était la
9. Rien ne trahissait
10. Tout l'épisode s'était volatilisé
11. qu'un rêve

about a newborn baby[1]. It had all been noted down.[2] And the information would be passed on[3].

Mr Baxter walked over to the worktable and pressed a button. At once[4], the carpet, bed and hotel furniture began to rise up. They disappeared through the ceiling and kept going[5]. Alex slept on[6] as he was carried back up[7] the shaft, finally arriving in the space that he knew as[8] room thirteen.

There was nothing to show[9] what had happened. The whole experience had evaporated[10], as quickly as a dream[11].

"MY NAME IS GRIEF"

The academy at Point Blanc had been built[1] by a lunatic[2]. For a time[3] it had been used as an asylum[4]. Alex remembered what Alan Blunt had told him as[5] the helicopter began its final descent[6], the red and white helipad looming up to receive it[7]. The photograph in the brochure had been artfully taken[8]. Now that he could see the building for himself[9], he could only describe it as ... mad[10].

It was a jumble of towers and battlements[11], green sloping roofs[12] and windows of every shape and size. Nothing fitted together properly.[13] The overall design[14] should have been simple enough; a circular central area[15] with two wings[16]. But one wing was longer than the other. The two sides didn't match[17]. The academy was four floors high[18] but the windows were spaced in such a way[19] that it was hard to tell where one floor ended and the next began[20]. There was an internal courtyard[21]

1. construite
2. fou
3. Pendant un certain temps
4. servi d'asile d'aliénés
5. alors que
6. amorçait sa descente
7. héliport surgit pour l'accueillir
8. prise astucieusement
9. voyait de ses propres yeux l'édifice
10. dingue
11. fouillis de tours et de remparts
12. toits pentus
13. Rien n'était bien assorti.
14. L'architecture globale
15. zone circulaire au centre
16. ailes
17. n'allaient pas ensemble
18. faisait 4 étages
19. espacées de telle sorte
20. où finissait un étage et où débutait le suivant
21. cour intérieure

1. vraiment carrée
2. était totalement gelée
3. dépassant
4. mal fichu
5. écrasé les murs de briques pour s'y loger
6. coupa les commandes
7. faire la connaissance de
8. hélices
9. n'avait pas encore fondu
10. à perte de vue
11. sur le flanc d'une pente abrupte
12. en contrebas
13. immense langue de fer
14. au niveau du sol
15. se recourbait vers l'extérieur là où le versant tombait à pic
16. tremplin de saut à ski
17. jeux Olympiques d'hiver
18. courbe
19. à 50 m au-dessus du sol
20. tout en bas
21. distinguait une zone plane en forme de fer à cheval
22. sauteurs devaient atterrir
23. de se propulser dans l'espace
24. pour amortir sa chute
25. saisit
26. interdit
27. franchirent
28. descendirent un étroit escalier en colimaçon

that wasn't quite square[1], with a fountain that had frozen solid[2]. Even the helipad, jutting out[3] of the roof, was ugly and awkward[4], as if a spaceship had smashed into the brickwork and lodged in place[5].

Mrs Stellenbosch flicked off the controls[6]. "I will take you down to meet[7] the director," she shouted over the noise of the blades[8]. "Your luggage will be brought down later."

It was cold on the roof, the snow covering the mountain still hadn't melted[9] and everything was white for as far as the eye could see[10].

The academy was built into the side of a steep slope[11]. A little further down[12], Alex saw a great iron tongue[13] that started at ground level[14] but then curved outwards as the mountainside dropped away[15]. It was a ski-jump[16] – the sort of thing he had seen at the Winter Olympics[17]. The end of the curve[18] was at least fifty metres above the ground[19] and, far below[20], Alex could make out a flat area shaped like a horseshoe[21] where the jumpers were meant to land[22].

He was staring at it, imagining what it would be like to propel yourself into space[23] with only two skis to break your fall[24], when the woman grabbed[25] his arm. "We don't use it," she said. "It is forbidden[26]. Come now. Let's get out of the cold."

They went through[27] a door in the side of one of the towers and down a narrow spiral staircase[28] –

each step a different distance apart[1] – that took them all the way to the ground floor[2]. Now they were in a long, narrow corridor with plenty of doors but no windows.

"Classrooms," Mrs Stellenbosch explained. "You will see them later."

Alex followed her through the strangely silent building. The central heating[3] had been turned up high[4] inside the academy and the atmosphere was warm and heavy. They stopped at a pair of modern glass doors which opened into the courtyard that Alex had seen from above[5]. From the heat back into the cold again[6], Mrs Stellenbosch led him[7] through the doors and past the frozen fountain. A movement caught his eye[8] and Alex glanced up[9]. This was something he hadn't noticed earlier. A sentry stood[10] on one of the towers. He had a pair of binoculars[11] round his neck and a submachine-gun slung across one arm[12].

Armed guards? In a school? Alex had only been here a few minutes and already he was unnerved[13].

"Through here.[14]" Mrs Stellenbosch opened another door for him and he found himself in the main reception hall[15] of the academy. A log fire[16] was burning in a massive fireplace[17] with two stone dragons guarding the flames. A grand staircase led upwards[18]. The hall was lit by a chandelier[19] with at least a hundred bulbs[20]. The walls were wood panelled[21]. The carpet was thick, dark

1. marche inégalement espacée
2. rez-de-chaussée
3. chauffage central
4. mis à fond
5. d'en haut
6. Ils passèrent à nouveau du chaud au froid
7. le conduisit
8. capta son regard
9. leva les yeux
10. garde se tenait
11. jumelles
12. mitraillette en bandoulière
13. troublé
14. Par ici.
15. hall d'entrée principal
16. feu de bois
17. énorme cheminée
18. escalier monumental menait aux étages supérieurs
19. éclairé par un lustre
20. ampoules
21. recouverts de boiseries

red. A dozen pairs of eyes pursued[1] Alex as he followed Mrs Stellenbosch towards the next corridor. The hall was decorated with animal heads. A rhino, an antelope, a water buffalo[2] and, saddest of all[3], a lion. Alex wondered who had shot them.

They came to a single[4] door, which suggested they had come to the end of their journey[5]. So far[6] Alex hadn't encountered any boys[7] but, glancing out of the window, he saw two more guards marching slowly past, both of them cradling machine-guns[8].

Mrs Stellenbosch knocked on[9] the door.

"Come in!" Even with just two words, Alex caught[10] the South African accent.

The door opened and they went into a huge room that made no sense[11]. Like the rest of the building, its shape was irregular, none[12] of the walls running parallel[13]. The ceiling was about[14] seven metres high[15], with windows running the whole way[16] and giving an impressive view of the slopes. The room was modern, with soft lighting coming from units concealed[17] in the walls. The furniture was ugly[18], but not as ugly as the further[19] animal heads on the walls and the zebra skin[20] on the wooden floor[21]. There were three chairs next to a small fireplace. One of them was gold and antique. A man was sitting in it. His head turned as Alex came in.

"Good afternoon, Alex," he said. "Please come and sit down."

1. épiaient
2. buffle d'Inde
3. le plus triste de tout
4. arrivèrent devant une seule
5. à la fin du parcours
6. Jusqu'à présent
7. croisé aucun garçon
8. passer en marchant au pas, tous deux armés de mitraillettes
9. frappa à
10. repéra
11. était insensée
12. aucun
13. n'était parallèle
14. faisait environ
15. de haut
16. sur toute la hauteur
17. spots encastrés
18. meubles étaient laids
19. nouvelle série de
20. peau de zèbre
21. plancher

Alex sauntered into[1] the room and took one of the chairs. Mrs Stellenbosch sat in the other.

"My name is Grief," the man continued. "Dr Grief. I am very pleased to meet you and to have you here[2]."

Alex stared at[3] the man who was the director of Point Blanc, at the white paper[4] skin and the eyes burning behind the red spectacles. It was like meeting a skeleton[5] and for a moment he was lost for words[6]. Then he recovered[7]. "Nice place[8]," he said.

"Do you think so?" There was no emotion whatsoever[9] in Grief's voice. So far he had moved only his neck. "This building was designed in 1857 by a Frenchman[10] who was certainly the world's worst architect[11]. This was his only commission[12]. When the first owners moved in[13], they had him shot[14]."

"There are still quite a few people here with guns[15]." Alex glanced out of the window as another pair of[16] guards walked past[17].

"Point Blanc is unique," Dr Grief explained. "As you will soon discover[18], all the boys who have been sent here come from families of great wealth[19] and importance. We have had the sons of emperors and industrialists[20]. Boys like yourself. It follows that[21] we could very easily become a target for terrorists[22]. The guards are therefore[23] here for your protection."

1. entra d'un pas nonchalant
2. ravi de te rencontrer et que tu sois parmi nous
3. dévisagea
4. blanche comme du papier
5. squelette
6. il resta sans voix
7. se ressaisit
8. Bel endroit
9. Il n'y avait pas la moindre émotion
10. un Français
11. le pire architecte de la terre
12. son unique commande
13. propriétaires ont emménagé
14. l'ont fait fusiller
15. encore pas mal de monde armé, ici
16. alors que deux autres
17. passaient devant
18. le verras bientôt
19. très fortunées
20. d'industriels
21. Par conséquent
22. la cible de terroristes
23. donc

"That's very kind of you[1]." Alex felt he was being too polite. It was time to show this man what sort of person he was meant to be[2]. "But to be honest, I don't really want to be here myself. So if you'll just tell me how I get down into town[3], maybe I can get the next train home[4]."

"There is no way down[5] into town." Dr Grief lifted[6] a hand to stop Alex interrupting[7]. Alex looked at his long, skeletal fingers and at the eyes glinting red[8] behind the spectacles. The man moved as if every bone in his body had been broken and then put back together again[9]; he seemed both old and young at the same time[10] and somehow not completely human. "The skiing season[11] is over[12] ... it's too dangerous now. There is only the helicopter and that will take you from here only when I say so[13]." The hand lowered itself[14] again. "You are here, Alex, because you have disappointed your parents. You were expelled[15] from school. You have had difficulties with the police—"

"That wasn't my bloody fault![16]" Alex protested.

"Don't interrupt the doctor!" Mrs Stellenbosch said.

Alex glanced at her balefully[17].

"Your appearance is displeasing[18]," Dr Grief went on. "Your language also. It is our job to turn you into[19] a boy of whom[20] your parents can be proud[21]."

1. très gentil de votre part
2. était censé être
3. Alors dites-moi simplement comment descendre en ville
4. prendre le prochain train pour rentrer
5. Il n'y a aucun moyen de descendre
6. leva
7. de l'interrompre
8. à la lueur rouge
9. réassemblés
10. à la fois vieux et jeune
11. saison de ski
12. terminée
13. ne t'emmènera d'ici que lorsque je l'aurai ordonné
14. se rabaissa
15. as été renvoyé
16. Merde, c'était pas ma faute !
17. méchamment
18. allure est déplorable
19. de te transformer en
20. dont
21. fiers

"I'm happy as I am[1]," Alex said.

"That is of no relevance.[2]" Dr Grief fell silent[3].

Alex shivered[4]. There was something about this room; so big, so empty, so twisted out of shape[5]. "So what are you going to do with me?" Alex asked.

"There will be no lessons to begin with[6]," Mrs Stellenbosch said. "For the first couple of weeks we want you to assimilate[7]."

"What does that mean?"

"To assimilate. To conform ... to adapt ... to become like.[8]" It was as if she were reading out of a dictionary. "There are six boys at the academy at the moment. You will meet them and you will spend time[9] with them. There will be opportunities for sport[10] and for being social[11]. There is a good library here and you will read. Soon, you will learn our methods."

"I want to call my mum and dad," Alex said.

"The use of telephones is forbidden," Mrs Stellenbosch explained. She tried to smile sympathetically[12], but with *her* face it wasn't quite[13] possible. "We find it makes our students homesick[14]," she went on. "Of course, you may write letters if you wish."

"I prefer e-mails," Alex said.

"For the same reason, personal computers are not permitted."

Alex shrugged, and swore under his breath[15].

1. tel que je suis
2. Cela ne présente aucun intérêt.
3. se tut
4. eut un frisson
5. tellement difforme
6. Au départ, tu n'iras pas en cours
7. que tu t'intègres
8. Obéir... s'adapter... devenir comme.
9. passeras du temps
10. des occasions de faire du sport
11. d'échanger
12. avec compassion
13. n'était pas vraiment
14. cela donne le mal du pays à nos étudiants
15. jura dans sa barbe

Dr Grief had seen him. "You will be polite to[1] the assistant director!" he snapped[2]. He hadn't raised his voice[3] but the words came out acid[4]. "You should be aware[5], Alex, that Mrs Stellenbosch has worked with me[6] now for[7] twenty-six years and that when I met her she had been voted[8] Miss South Africa five years in a row[9]."

Alex looked at the ape-like[10] face. "A beauty contest?[11]" he asked.

"The weightlifting championships[12]." Dr Grief glanced at the fireplace. "Show him," he said.

Mrs Stellenbosch got up and went over to the fireplace. There was a poker lying in the grate[13]. She took it with both hands[14]. For a moment she seemed to concentrate. Alex gasped[15]. The solid metal poker, at least[16] two centimetres thick[17], was slowly bending[18]. Now it was u-shaped[19]. Mrs Stellenbosch wasn't even sweating[20]. She brought the two ends together[21] and dropped it back[22] into the grate. It clanged against[23] the stone.

"We enforce[24] strict discipline here at the academy," Dr Grief said. "Bedtime[25] is at ten o'clock – not a minute past[26]. We do not tolerate bad language[27]. You will have no contact with the outside world without our permission. You will not attempt to leave. And you will do as you are told instantly, without hesitation. And finally" – he leaned towards[28] Alex – "you are permitted only in certain parts of this building." He

1. Sois poli avec
2. dit-il sèchement
3. n'avait pas élevé la voix
4. paroles étaient mordantes
5. dois savoir
6. travaille avec moi
7. depuis
8. avait été élue
9. de suite
10. simiesque
11. Un concours de beauté ?
12. championnat d'haltérophilie
13. tisonnier dans le foyer
14. des deux mains
15. étouffa un cri
16. d'au moins
17. d'épaisseur
18. se tordait lentement
19. en forme de U
20. ne transpirait même pas
21. réunit les deux extrémités
22. le laissa retomber
23. fit un bruit métallique au contact de
24. appliquons
25. L'heure du coucher
26. de plus
27. les grossièretés
28. se pencha vers

gestured[1] with a hand and for the first time Alex noticed a second door at the far end of the room. "My private quarters[2] are through there. You will remain[3] on the ground floor and the first floor only. That is where the bedrooms and classrooms are located[4]. The second and third floors are out of bounds[5]. The basement also. This is again for your safety[6]."

"You're afraid I'll trip on[7] the stairs?" Alex asked.

Dr Grief ignored him. "You may leave[8]," he said.

"Wait outside the office, Alex," Mrs Stellenbosch said. "Someone will be along to collect you[9]."

Alex stood up.

"We will make you into what[10] your parents want," Dr Grief said.

"Maybe they don't want me at all[11]."

"We can arrange that too.[12]"

Alex went.

"An unpleasant boy ... a few days ... faster than usual[13] ... the Gemini Project ... closing down[14]..."

If the door hadn't been so thick, Alex would have been able to hear more[15]. The moment he had left the room he'd cupped his ear against the keyhole[16], hoping to pick up[17] something that might be useful to[18] MI6. Sure enough[19], Dr Grief and Mrs Stellenbosch were busily talking[20] on the other side, but Alex heard little and understood less[21].

1. fit un geste
2. appartements privés
3. resteras
4. situées
5. inaccessibles
6. sécurité
7. que je trébuche dans
8. Tu peux disposer
9. va venir te chercher
10. Nous allons faire de toi ce que
11. qu'ils ne veulent pas du tout de moi
12. On peut trouver une solution.
13. plus vite que d'habitude
14. fermeture définitive
15. en entendre davantage
16. collé son oreille au trou de la serrure
17. saisir
18. d'utile pour le
19. Effectivement
20. étaient en pleine conversation
21. avait du mal à entendre et comprenait encore moins

1. Une poigne s'abattit sur
2. fit volte-face, pas très content de lui
3. soi-disant
4. surpris en train d'écouter
5. déchiré
6. casquette
7. Il s'était bagarré récemment
8. apparemment, il n'avait pas eu le dessus
9. bleu
10. coupure
11. Ils te flingueront
12. le regard hostile
13. devina
14. n'accordait pas sa confiance à n'importe qui
15. te faire visiter
16. pour qu'on t'envoie dans ce trou
17. Je me suis fait jeter
18. qui me soit jamais arrivée
19. Il intervient sur les marchés financiers.
20. il en a plein
21. éteinte, neutre

A hand clamped down on[1] his shoulder and he twisted round, annoyed with himself[2]. A so-called[3] spy caught listening[4] at the keyhole! But it wasn't one of the guards. Alex found himself looking up at a round-faced boy with long dark hair, dark eyes and pale skin. He was wearing a very old *Star Wars* T-shirt, torn[5] jeans and a baseball cap[6]. Recently he had been in a fight[7], and it looked like he'd got the worst of it[8]. There was a bruise[9] around one of his eyes and a gash[10] on his lip.

"They'll shoot you[11] if they catch you listening at doors," the boy said. He looked at Alex with hostile eyes[12]. Alex guessed[13] he was the sort of boy who wouldn't trust anyone easily[14]. "I'm James Sprintz," he said. "They told me to show you round[15]."

"Alex Friend."

"So what did you do to get sent to this dump[16]?" James asked as they walked back down the corridor.

"I got expelled from Eton."

"I got thrown out[17] of a school in Düsseldorf." James sighed. "I thought it was the best thing that ever happened to me[18]. Until my dad sent me here."

"What does your dad do?" Alex asked.

"He's a banker. He plays the money markets.[19] He loves money and has lots of it[20]." James's voice was flat, unemotional[21].

"Dieter Sprintz?" Alex remembered the name. He'd made the front page[1] of every newspaper in England a few years before. The One Hundred Million Dollar Man.[2] That was how much he had made[3] in just twenty-four hours. At the same time the pound had crashed[4] and the British government had almost collapsed[5].

"Yeah. Don't ask me to show you a photograph because I don't have one. This way."

They had reached the main hall with the dragon fireplace. From here[6], James showed him to the dining-room[7], a long, high-ceilinged[8] room with six tables and a hatch[9] leading into the kitchen. After that, they visited two living-rooms, a games room[10] and a library. The academy reminded Alex of an expensive hotel in a ski resort[11] – and not just because of its setting[12]. There was a sort of heaviness about the place[13], a sense of being cut off[14] from the real world. The air was warm and silent and, despite[15] the size of the rooms, Alex couldn't help feeling claustrophobic[16]. If the place *had* been a hotel, it would have been an unpopular one[17]. Grief had said there were only six boys living there. The building could have housed[18] sixty. Empty space was everywhere.[19]

There was nobody in either of the living-rooms – just a collection of armchairs, desks and tables – but they found a couple of boys in the library. This was a long, narrow room with old-fashioned

1. la une
2. L'homme aux 100 millions de dollars.
3. C'était ce qu'il avait gagné
4. livre sterling s'était effondrée
5. avait failli tomber
6. En partant de là
7. salle à manger
8. avec une grande hauteur de plafond
9. passe-plat
10. salons, une salle de jeux
11. station de ski
12. pas seulement à cause de son cadre
13. d'atmosphère pesante dans cet endroit
14. sensation d'être coupé
15. malgré
16. ne pouvait s'empêcher de se sentir claustrophobe
17. très peu fréquenté
18. aurait pu en accueillir
19. Il y avait du vide partout.

oak shelves lined with[1] books in a variety of languages[2]. A suit of medieval Swiss armour[3] stood in an alcove at the far end[4].

"This is Tom. And Hugo," James said. "They're probably doing extra maths[5] or something, so we'd better not disturb them[6]."

The two boys looked up and nodded briefly[7]. One of them was reading a textbook[8]. The other was writing. They were both much more smartly[9] dressed than James and didn't look very friendly[10].

"Creeps[11]," James said as soon as they had left the room.

"In what way?[12]"

"When I was told about this place, they said *all* the kids had problems. I thought it was going to be wild[13]. Do you have a cigarette?"

"I don't smoke."

"Great.[14] I get here and it's like[15] a museum or a monastery or ... I don't know what. It looks like Dr Grief's been busy[16]. Everyone's quiet, hard-working, boring[17]. God knows how he did it.[18] Sucked their brains out with a straw[19] or something. A couple of days ago I got into a fight with a couple of them, just for the hell of it[20]." He pointed to[21] his face. "They beat the crap out of me[22] and then went back to their studies[23]. Really creepy![24]"

They went into the games room, which contained table tennis, darts[25], a wide-screen[26] TV and a snooker[27] table. "Don't try playing snooker,"

1. des étagères en chêne, démodées, remplies de
2. en différentes langues
3. Une armure suisse du Moyen Âge
4. une niche, à l'autre bout
5. des maths renforcées
6. il vaut mieux ne pas les déranger
7. levèrent les yeux et hochèrent à peine la tête
8. manuel scolaire
9. avec beaucoup plus d'élégance
10. sympathiques
11. Bande de fayots
12. Comment ça ?
13. que ça allait déchirer
14. Magnifique.
15. Je débarque ici et ça ressemble à
16. a bien travaillé
17. se tient tranquille, travaille dur, est ennuyeux
18. Dieu sait comment il a fait.
19. Il a aspiré leurs cerveaux à la paille
20. juste comme ça
21. montra
22. m'ont tabassé comme des fous
23. se sont remis à étudier
24. Vraiment flippant !
25. ping-pong, des jeux de fléchettes
26. grand écran
27. de billard

James said. "The room's on a slant[1] and all the balls roll to the side[2]."

Then they went upstairs. This was where the boys had their study bedrooms[3]. Each one contained a bed, an armchair, a television ("It only shows the programmes[4] Dr Grief wants you to see," James said), a wardrobe[5] and a desk, with a second door leading into a small bathroom with a toilet and shower. None of the rooms were locked[6].

"We're not allowed to[7] lock them," James explained. "We're all stuck here with nowhere to go[8], so nobody bothers to steal[9] anything. Hugo Vries – the boy in the library – used to nick anything he could get his hands on[10]. He was arrested for shoplifting[11] in Amsterdam."

"But not any more[12]?"

"He's another success story.[13] He's flying home next week. His father owns diamond mines. Why bother shoplifting when you can afford to buy the whole shop[14]?"

Alex's study was at the end of the corridor, with views over[15] the ski-jump. His suitcases had already been carried up and were waiting for him on the bed. Everything felt very bare[16] but, according to[17] James, the study bedrooms were the only part of the school which the boys were allowed to decorate themselves. They could choose their own duvets[18] and cover the walls with their own posters.

1. penche
2. roulent d'un côté
3. [chambres d'étudiants]
4. émissions
5. armoire
6. n'était fermée à clé
7. Nous n'avons pas le droit de
8. coincés ici sans pouvoir aller nulle part
9. ne s'embête à voler
10. piquait tout ce qu'il trouvait
11. vol à l'étalage
12. il ne le fait plus
13. Son cas est aussi une réussite.
14. t'as les moyens d'acheter tout le magasin
15. et donnait sur
16. faisait très dépouillé
17. d'après
18. couettes

1. de pouvoir s'exprimer

2. [surnom qui signifie poche de colostomie]

3. Je l'appelle comme ça.

4. Cet endroit est super bizarre

5. renvoyé

6. celle-là, c'est l'horreur

7. je n'ai presque jamais eu cours

8. font des soirées musique

9. me faire lire

10. à part ça, on me laisse dans mon coin

11. C'est ce qu'ils disent.

12. comme si on était

13. Mais réfléchis !

14. étudia

15. Ce serait cool d'imaginer qu'il y a enfin quelqu'un avec qui je peux communiquer

"They say it's important that you express yourself[1]," James said. "If you haven't brought anything with you, Miss Stomach-bag[2] will take you into Grenoble."

"Miss Stomach-bag?"

"Mrs Stellenbosch. That's my name for her.[3]"

"What do the other boys call her?"

"They call her Mrs Stellenbosch." James paused by the door. "This is a deeply weird place[4], Alex. I've been to a lot of schools because I've been thrown out[5] of a lot of schools. But this one is the pits[6]. I've been here for six weeks now and I've hardly had any lessons[7]. They have music evenings[8] and discussion evenings and they try to get me to read[9]. But otherwise I've been left on my own[10]."

"They want you to assimilate," Alex said, remembering what Dr Grief had said.

"That's *their* word for it.[11] But this place ... they may call it a school, but it's more like being[12] in prison. You've seen the guards."

"I thought they were here to protect us."

"If you think that, you're a bigger idiot than I thought. Think about it![13] There are about thirty of them. Thirty armed guards for seven kids. That's not protection. That's intimidation." James examined[14] Alex for a second time. "It would be nice to think that someone has finally arrived who I can relate to[15]," he said.

"Maybe you can," Alex said.

"Yeah. But for how long?"

James left, closing the door behind him.

Alex began to unpack[1]. The bullet-proof ski suit and infrared goggles were at the top[2] of the first case. It didn't look as if he would be needing them.[3] It wasn't as if he even had any skis.[4] Then came[5] the Discman. He remembered the instructions Smithers had given him. "If the balloon goes up[6], just press fast forward[7] three times." He was almost tempted[8] to do it now. There was something unsettling about[9] the academy. He could feel it even now, in his room. He was like a goldfish in a bowl[10]. Looking up[11], he almost expected to see a pair of huge eyes looming over him[12] and he knew that they would be wearing red-tinted glasses[13]. He weighed[14] the Discman in his hand. He couldn't hit[15] the panic button – yet[16]. He had nothing to report back[17] to MI6. There was nothing to connect the school with the deaths of the two men in New York and the Black Sea.

But if there was anything, he knew where he would find it. Why were two whole floors[18] of the building out of bounds[19]? Presumably the guards slept up there but even though[20] Dr Grief seemed to employ a small army, that would still leave a lot of empty rooms[21]. The second and third floors. If something was going on[22] at the academy, it had to be going on there.

1. défaire ses valises

2. sur le dessus

3. Il semblait bien qu'il n'en aurait pas besoin.

4. Il n'avait même pas de skis.

5. Ensuite, il y avait

6. Si ça se gâte

7. la touche avance rapide

8. presque tenté

9. de perturbant dans

10. poisson rouge dans un bocal

11. En levant les yeux

12. il s'attendait presque à voir deux yeux géants surgir au-dessus de lui

13. porteraient des lunettes aux verres rouges

14. soupesa

15. appuyer sur

16. encore

17. à apprendre

18. étages complets

19. inaccessibles

20. même si

21. cela faisait quand même beaucoup de chambres inoccupées

22. S'il se passait quelque chose

A bell sounded[1] downstairs. Alex swung his case shut[2], left his room and walked down the corridor. He saw another couple of boys walking ahead of him, talking quietly[3] together. Like the boys he had seen in the library, they were both clean and well-dressed[4], with hair cut short and smartly groomed[5]. Majorly creepy[6], James had said. Even on first sight[7], Alex had to agree[8].

He reached the main staircase. The two boys had gone down. Alex glanced in their direction, then went up. The staircase turned a corner and stopped. Ahead of him was a sheet of metal that rose up[9] from the floor to the ceiling and all the way across[10], blocking off the view. The wall had been added recently, like the helipad. Someone had carefully and deliberately cut the building in two[11].

There was a door set[12] in the metal wall and beside it a key pad with nine buttons demanding[13] a code. Alex reached for the door handle[14], his hand closing around it[15]. He didn't expect the door to open – but nor did he expect what happened next[16]. The moment[17] his fingers came into contact with the handle, an alarm went off[18], a shrieking[19] siren that echoed throughout[20] the building. A few seconds later he became aware of footsteps[21] on the stairs and turned to find[22] two guards facing him, their guns raised[23].

Neither of them[24] spoke to him. One of them pushed past him[25] and punched a code[26] into the

1. cloche sonna
2. referma sa valise d'un coup
3. tranquillement
4. propres et bien habillés
5. l'allure soignée
6. Totalement flippant
7. à première vue
8. était bien de cet avis
9. une paroi de métal qui se dressait
10. sur toute la largeur
11. avait pris soin, délibérément, de séparer le bâtiment en deux
12. ménagée
13. Digicode à neuf touches exigeant
14. posa la main sur la poignée
15. se refermant dessus
16. il ne s'attendait pas non plus à ce qui arriva ensuite
17. Dès que
18. se déclencha
19. hurlante
20. résonna dans tout
21. entendit des bruits de pas
22. se trouva face à face avec
23. armes relevées
24. Aucun des deux
25. passa devant lui en le bousculant
26. tapa un code

key pad. The alarm stopped. And then Mrs Stellenbosch was there, hurrying forward on her short, stubby legs[1].

"Alex!" she exclaimed. Her eyes were filled with suspicion[2]. "What are you doing here? The director told you that the upper[3] floors are forbidden."

"Yeah ... well I forgot." Alex looked straight at her[4]. "I heard the bell go[5] and I was on my way to[6] the dining-room."

"The dining-room is downstairs."

"Right."

Alex walked past[7] the two guards, who stepped aside[8] to let him pass. He felt Mrs Stellenbosch watching him as he went[9]. Metal doors, alarms and guards with machine-guns. What were they hiding? And then he remembered something else. The Gemini Project. Those were the words[10] he had heard when he was listening at Dr Grief's door.

Gemini. The twins[11]. One of the twelve star signs.[12]

But what did it mean?

Turning the question over in his mind[13], Alex went down to meet the rest of the school.

1. avançant à toute allure sur ses petites jambes boudinées

2. pleins de méfiance

3. supérieurs

4. droit dans les yeux

5. sonner

6. j'allais à

7. passa devant

8. firent un pas de côté

9. le regard de Mme Stellenbosch dans son dos

10. C'était bien les mots qu'

11. jumeaux

12. L'un des douze signes astrologiques.

13. En tournant et retournant la question dans sa tête

THINGS THAT GO CLICK IN THE NIGHT[1]

1. Un clic dans la nuit

At the end of his first week at Point Blanc, Alex drew up[2] a list of the six boys with whom he shared[3] the school. It was mid-afternoon[4] and he was alone in his room. There was a note-pad[5] open in front of him. It had taken him about half an hour to put together the names and the few details[6] that he had. He only wished he had more[7].

2. dressa
3. qui étaient avec lui à
4. le milieu de l'après-midi
5. bloc-notes
6. une demi-heure pour réunir les noms et les quelques informations
7. aurait bien aimé en avoir plus

HUGO VRIES (14) Dutch[8], lives in Amsterdam. Brown hair, green eyes. Father's name: Rudi, owns diamond mines. Speaks little English[9]. Reads and plays guitar. Very solitary. Sent to PB for shoplifting and arson[10].

8. néerlandais
9. ne parle pas bien l'anglais
10. incendie criminel

TONY McMORIN (14) Canadian, from Vancouver. Parents divorced. Mother runs media empire[1] (newspapers, TV). Reddish[2] hair, blue eyes. Well-built, chess player[3]. Car thefts[4] and drunken driving[5].

1. magnat de la presse et des médias
2. roux
3. joueur d'échecs
4. vols de voitures
5. conduite en état d'ivresse

NICOLAS MARC (14) French, from Bordeaux? Expelled from private School in Paris, cause unknown[6] – drinking? Brown hair, brown eyes, very fit all-rounder[7]. Good at sport but hates losing. Tattoo of devil[8] on left shoulder. Father: Anthony Marc – airlines[9], pop music, hotels. Never mentions his mother.

6. inconnue
7. très bon sportif dans tous les domaines
8. Diable tatoué
9. compagnies aériennes

1. dirige un studio de cinéma
2. parle très fort
3. dit beaucoup de gros mots
4. délits liés à la drogue
5. trafic

CASSIAN JAMES (14) American. Fair hair, brown eyes. Mother: Jill, studio chief[1] in Hollywood. Parents divorced. Loud voice.[2] Swears a lot.[3] Plays jazz piano. Expelled from three schools. Various drug offences[4] – sent to PB after smuggling[5] arrest but won't talk about it now. One of the kids who beat up James. Stronger than he looks.

6. poste important
7. absentéisme

JOE CANTERBURY (14) American. Spends a lot of his time with Cassian. (helped him with James). Brown hair, blue eyes. Mother (name unknown) New York senator. Father something big[6] at the Pentagon. Vandalism, truancy,[7] shoplifting. Sent to PB after stealing and smashing up car. Vegetarian. Permanently chewing gum. Has he given up smoking?

JAMES SPRINTZ (14) German, lives in Düsseldorf. Brown hair, brown eyes, pale. Father: Dieter Sprintz, banker, well-known financier (the One Hundred Million Dollar Man). Mother living in England. Expelled for wounding[1] a teacher with an air-pistol[2]. My only friend at PB! And the only one who really hates it here.

Lying[3] on his bed, Alex studied the list. What did it tell him?[4] Not a great deal.[5]

First, all the boys were the same age – fourteen. The same age as him. At least three of them, and possibly[6] four, had parents who were either divorced or separated. They all came from hugely wealthy backgrounds[7]. Blunt had already told him that was the case, but Alex was surprised by just how diverse the parents were[8]. Airlines, diamonds, politics and movies[9]. France, Germany, Holland, Canada and America. All of the parents were at the top of his or her field[10] and those fields covered just about every human activity. He himself was supposed to be the son of a supermar-

1. pour avoir blessé
2. pistolet à air comprimé
3. Allongé
4. Que pouvait-il en retirer ?
5. Pas grand-chose.
6. peut-être
7. milieux immensément riches
8. de l'extrême diversité de leurs parents
9. cinéma
10. au sommet de leur secteur d'activité

ket king. Food. That was another world industry he could tick off[1].

At least two of the boys had been arrested for shoplifting. Two of them had been involved with drugs[2]. But Alex knew that the list somehow hid more than it revealed[3]. With the exception of[4] James, it was hard to pin down[5] what made the boys at Point Blanc different. In a strange way, they all looked the same[6].

Their eyes and hair were different colours. They wore different clothes. All the faces were different: Tom handsome and confident[7], Joe quiet and watchful[8]. And of course they spoke not only with different voices but in several languages[9]. James had talked about brains being sucked out with straws[10] and he had a point[11]. It was as if the same consciousness had somehow invaded them all[12]. They had become puppets[13] dancing on the same string[14].

The bell rang downstairs. Alex looked at his watch. It was exactly one o'clock – lunch-time[15]. That was another thing about the school. Everything was done to the exact minute[16]. Lessons from nine until twelve. Lunch from one to two. And so on. James made a point of being late[17] for everything and Alex had taken to joining him[18]. It was a tiny[19] rebellion, but a satisfying one[20]. It showed they still had a little control over[21] their lives[22]. The other boys, of course, turned up

1. cocher
2. impliqués dans des affaires de drogue
3. cachait plus de choses qu'elle n'en révélait
4. À part
5. difficile de cerner
6. se ressemblaient tous
7. plein d'assurance
8. attentif
9. en plusieurs langues
10. de cerveaux aspirés à la paille
11. avait raison
12. la même conscience les avait tous envahis
13. marionnettes
14. au bout de la même ficelle
15. l'heure du déjeuner
16. réglé comme du papier à musique
17. s'appliquait à être en retard
18. s'était mis à faire pareil
19. toute petite
20. cela faisait du bien
21. contrôlaient encore un peu
22. vies

like clockwork[1]. They would be in the dining-room now, waiting quietly for the food to be served[2].

Alex rolled over[3] on the bed and reached for a pen[4]. He wrote a single word on the pad, underneath[5] the names.

Brainwashing[6]?

Maybe that was the answer. According to James, the other boys had arrived at the academy two months before him. He had been there for[7] six weeks. That added up to just[8] fourteen weeks in total and Alex knew that you didn't take a bunch[9] of delinquents and turn them into[10] perfect students just by giving them good books. Dr Grief had to be doing something else[11]. Drugs? Hypnosis?[12] Something.

He waited five more[13] minutes, then hid the note-pad under his mattress and left the room. He wished he could[14] lock the door. There was no privacy[15] at Point Blanc. Even the bathrooms had no locks. And Alex still couldn't shake off the feeling[16] that everything he did, even everything he thought, was somehow being monitored, noted down. Evidence to be used[17] against him.

It was ten past one when he reached[18] the dining-room and, sure enough[19], the other boys

1. arrivaient pile à l'heure
2. sagement que le repas soit servi
3. se retourna
4. attrapa un stylo
5. au-dessous de
6. lavage de cerveau
7. était là depuis
8. Cela faisait exactement
9. on ne prenait pas une bande
10. pour la transformer en
11. faisait sûrement autre chose
12. L'hypnose ?
13. de plus
14. Si seulement il pouvait
15. Il n'y avait aucune intimité
16. ne pouvait se débarrasser de cette sensation
17. Des preuves qu'on utiliserait
18. arriva à
19. en effet

were already there, eating their lunch and talking quietly amongst themselves[1]. Nicolas and Cassian were at one table. Hugo, Tom and Joe were at another. Nobody was flicking peas[2]. Nobody even had their elbows[3] on the table. Tom was talking about a visit he had made to some museum in Grenoble. Alex had only been in the room for a few seconds but already his appetite had gone[4].

James had arrived just ahead of him[5] and was standing at the hatch, helping himself to food[6]. Most of the food[7] arrived pre-cooked[8] and one of the guards heated it up[9]. Today it was stew[10]. Alex got his lunch and sat next to James. The two of them had their own[11] table. They had become friends quite effortlessly[12]. Everyone else ignored them.

"You want to go out after lunch?" James asked.

"Sure. Why not?"

"There's something I want to talk to you about.[13]"

Alex looked past James at[14] the other boys. There was Tom, at the head of the table, reaching out for a jug[15] of water. He was dressed in a polo jersey[16] and jeans. Next to him was Joe Canterbury, the American. He was talking to Hugo now, waving a finger to emphasize a point[17]. Where had Alex seen that movement[18] before? Cassian was just behind them, round-faced, with fine, light brown hair, laughing at a joke[19].

1. entre eux
2. ne faisait des batailles de petits pois
3. ne posait même ses coudes
4. avait déjà perdu l'appétit
5. avant lui
6. debout devant le passe-plat, en train de se servir
7. La plupart des plats
8. déjà cuisinés
9. les réchauffait
10. du ragoût
11. leur propre
12. assez naturellement
13. Je veux te parler de quelque chose.
14. Le regard d'Alex se détourna de James et se posa sur
15. en train de saisir un pichet
16. polo
17. levant le doigt pour insister sur quelque chose
18. geste
19. riant d'une blague

Different but the same.[1] Watching them closely[2], Alex tried to work out what that meant[3].

It was all in the details, the things you wouldn't notice unless you saw them[4] all together like they were now. The way they were all sitting with their backs straight and their elbows close to their sides[5]. The way they held their knives[6] and forks[7]. Hugo laughed and Alex realized that for a moment he had become a mirror image[8] of Cassian. It was the same laugh[9]. He watched Joe eat a mouthful[10] of food. Then he watched Nicolas. They were two different boys. There was no doubting that.[11] But they ate in the same way[12], as if they were mimicking each other[13].

There was a movement at the door and suddenly Mrs Stellenbosch appeared. "Good afternoon, boys," she said.

"Good afternoon, Mrs Stellenbosch." Five people answered, but Alex heard only one voice[14]. He and James remained silent[15].

"Lessons this afternoon will begin at three o'clock. The subjects will be Latin and French."

The lessons would be taught[16] by Dr Grief or Mrs Stellenbosch. There were no other teachers at the school. Alex hadn't yet been taught anything[17]. James dipped in and out of class, depending on his mood[18].

"There will be a discussion this evening in the library," Mrs Stellenbosch went on. "The subject

1. Ils sont différents mais tous pareils.
2. attentivement
3. comprendre ce que cela signifiait
4. qu'on ne remarquerait pas à moins de les voir
5. les coudes près du corps
6. tenaient leurs couteaux
7. fourchettes
8. était devenu la réplique exacte
9. même rire
10. bouchée
11. Cela ne faisait aucun doute.
12. mangeaient de la même façon
13. s'ils s'imitaient
14. une seule et même voix
15. restèrent silencieux
16. cours étaient dispensés
17. n'avait pas eu cours, encore
18. allait et venait en cours, selon son humeur

is 'violence in television and film'. Mr McMorin will be opening the debate[1]. Afterwards there will be hot chocolate and Dr Grief will be giving a lecture[2] on the works[3] of Mozart. Everyone is welcome to attend.[4]"

James jabbed[5] a finger into his open mouth and stuck out his tongue[6]. Alex smiled. The other boys were listening quietly.

"Dr Grief would also like to congratulate[7] Cassian James on winning the poetry competition[8]. His poem is pinned to the notice-board[9] in the main hall. That is all."

She turned and left the room. James rolled his eyes[10]. "Let's go out and get some fresh air," he said. "I'm feeling sick.[11]"

The two of them went upstairs and put on their coats[12]. James had the room next door to[13] Alex and had done his best to make it more homely[14]. There were posters of old sci-fi movies[15] on the walls and a mobile of the solar system dangling above[16] the bed. A lava lamp[17] bubbled and swirled[18] on the bedside[19] table, casting an orange glow[20]. There were clothes everywhere. James obviously didn't believe in hanging them up[21]. Somehow he managed to find a scarf and a single glove[22]. He shoved[23] one hand into a pocket. "Let's go!" he said.

They went back down and along the corridor, passing the games room. Nicolas and Cassian were

1. ouvrira la discussion
2. donnera un cours
3. œuvres
4. Tout le monde est le bienvenu.
5. fourra
6. tira la langue
7. féliciter
8. qui a gagné le concours de poésie
9. affiché sur le tableau d'information
10. roula les yeux
11. J'ai envie de vomir.
12. manteaux
13. à côté de celle d'
14. de son mieux pour s'y sentir chez lui
15. films de science-fiction
16. était suspendu au-dessus de
17. lampe à lave [lampe transparente contenant un liquide dans lequel des bulles colorées montent et descendent]
18. faisait des bulles et des remous
19. de chevet
20. en projetant une lueur orange
21. ne jugeait pas utile de les suspendre
22. écharpe et un seul gant
23. enfonça

playing table tennis and Alex stopped at the door to watch them. The ball was bouncing back and forth[1] and Alex found himself mesmerized[2]. He stood there for about sixty seconds, watching. Kerplink, kerplunk[3], kerplink, kerplunk – neither[4] of the boys were scoring[5]. There it was again.[6] Different but the same. Obviously there were[7] two boys there. But the way they played, the style of their game, was identical. If it had been one boy, knocking a ball up against[8] a mirror, the result would have looked much the same. Alex shivered. James was standing at his shoulder[9]. The two of them moved away.

Hugo was sitting in the library. The boy who had been sent to Point Blanc for shoplifting was reading a Dutch[10] edition of *National Geographic* magazine. They reached the hall and there was Cassian's poem, prominently[11] pinned to the notice-board. He had been sent to Point Blanc for smuggling drugs[12]. Now he was writing about daffodils[13].

Alex pushed open the main door and felt the cold wind hit[14] his face. He was grateful for it.[15] He needed to be reminded[16] that there was a real world outside.

It had begun to snow again. The two boys walked slowly round the[17] building. A couple of guards walked towards them, speaking softly[18] in German. Alex had counted thirty guards at Point

1. rebondissait d'un côté et de l'autre
2. se laissa hypnotiser
3. [bruit de la balle heurtant la table]
4. aucun
5. ne marquait de point
6. Et rebelote.
7. Il y avait bien
8. frappant une balle contre
9. près de lui
10. hollandaise
11. de façon bien visible
12. pour trafic de drogue
13. jonquilles
14. le vent froid fouetter
15. Il en fut heureux.
16. qu'on lui rappelle
17. autour du
18. à voix basse en allemand

Blanc, all of them young German men, dressed in uniform black roll-neck sweaters[1] and black padded waistcoats[2]. The guards never spoke to the boys. They had pale, unhealthy[3] faces and close-cropped[4] hair. Dr Grief had said they were there for his protection, but Alex still wondered[5]. Were they there to keep intruders out – or the boys in[6]?

"This way," James said.

James walked ahead[7], his feet sinking into[8] the thick snow. Alex followed, looking back at the windows on the second and third floors. It was maddening.[9] Half of the castle – perhaps more – was closed off to him[10] and he still couldn't think of a way of getting up there. He couldn't climb[11]. The brickwork was too smooth[12] and there was no convenient ivy to provide handholds[13]. The drain-pipes[14] looked too fragile to take his weight[15].

Something moved. Alex stopped in his tracks[16].

"What is it?" James asked.

"There!" Alex pointed at the third floor. He thought he'd seen a figure[17] watching them from a window two floors above his room. It was only there for a moment. The face seemed to be covered – a white mask with narrow slits[18] for the eyes. But even as he pointed[19], the figure stepped back, out of sight[20].

"I don't see anything," James said.

"It's gone."

1. portaient les mêmes pulls noirs à col roulé
2. des gilets matelassés
3. fatigués
4. coupés en brosse
5. se posait toujours la question
6. pour repousser les intrus ou forcer les garçons à rester
7. devant
8. s'enfonçant dans
9. Ça le rendait fou.
10. lui était inaccessible
11. escalader
12. murs de briques étaient trop lisses
13. pas de lierre, bien commode pour avoir une prise
14. gouttières
15. pour supporter son poids
16. s'arrêta net
17. silhouette
18. masque blanc percé d'étroites fentes
19. au moment même où il la montrait du doigt
20. recula, hors de vue

They walked on, heading for[1] the abandoned ski-jump. According to James, the jump had been built just before Grief had bought the academy. There had been plans to turn[2] the building into a winter sports training centre[3]. The jump had never been used. They reached the wooden barriers that lay across the entrance[4] and stopped.

"Let me ask you something," James said. His breath was misting[5] in the cold air. "What do you think of this place?"

"Why do we have to talk out here?" Alex asked. Despite[6] his coat, he was beginning to shiver[7].

"Because when I'm inside the building, I get the feeling that someone is listening to every word I say[8]."

Alex nodded[9]. "I know what you mean." He considered the question James had put to him[10]. "I think you were right the first day we met," he said. "This place is creepy."

"So how would you feel about[11] getting out of here?"

"You know how to fly[12] the helicopter?"

"No. But I'm going[13]." James paused and looked around. The two guards had gone into the school. There was nobody else in sight. "I can trust you[14], Alex, because you've only just got here[15]. He hasn't got to you yet[16]." *He* was Dr Grief. James didn't need to say the name. "But believe me," he went on, "it won't be long[17]. If you stay here,

1. continuèrent à marcher, se dirigeant vers

2. des projets pour convertir

3. centre de formation aux sports d'hiver

4. barrières en bois barrant l'entrée

5. souffle se transformait en buée

6. Malgré

7. trembler

8. écoute tout ce que je dis

9. acquiesça

10. réfléchit à la question que James lui avait posée

11. que penserais-tu de

12. comment piloter

13. je m'en vais

14. peux te faire confiance

15. viens juste d'arriver

16. ne s'est pas encore occupé de toi

17. ça ne va pas tarder

you're going to end up[1] like the others. Model students – that's exactly the term for them. It's like they're all made out of Plasticene[2]! Well, I've had enough[3]. I'm not going to let him do that to me!"

"Are you going to run away[4]?" Alex asked.

"Who needs to run?" James looked down the slope[5]. "I'm going to ski."

Alex looked at the slope. It plunged steeply down, stretching on for ever[6]. "Is that possible?" he asked. "I thought—"

"I know Grief says it's too dangerous. But he would, wouldn't he.[7] It's true it's black runs all the way down[8] and there'll be tons of moguls[9]—"

"Won't the snow have melted?[10]"

"Only further down[11]." James pointed. "I've been right down to the bottom[12]," he said. "I did it the first week I was here. All the slopes run into[13] a single valley. It's called La Vallée de Fer. You can't actually make it as far as the[14] town because there's a train track[15] that cuts across[16]. But if I can get to[17] the track, I reckon[18] I can walk the rest of the way."

"And then?"

"A train back to[19] Düsseldorf. If my dad tries to send me back here, I'll go to my mum in England. If she doesn't want me, I'll disappear. I've got friends in Paris and Berlin. I don't care. All I know is, I've got to split[20] and if you know what's good for you[21], you'll come too."

1. finir
2. pâte à modeler
3. j'en ai marre
4. t'enfuir
5. regarda en bas de la pente
6. plongeait en pente raide, s'étendant à perte de vue
7. il a raison, non ?
8. c'est une piste noire jusqu'en bas
9. il doit y avoir des tonnes de bosses
10. La neige n'aura pas fondu ?
11. un peu plus bas
12. tout en bas
13. aboutissent dans
14. vraiment aller jusqu'en
15. voie ferrée
16. la traverse
17. atteindre
18. j'estime que
19. pour rentrer à
20. c'est qu'il faut que je me casse
21. dans ton propre intérêt

Alex considered. He was tempted to join the other boy, if only to help him on his way[1]. But he had a job to do. "I don't have any skis," he said.

"Nor do I.[2]" James spat[3] into the snow. "Grief took all the skis when the season ended. He's got them locked up somewhere.[4]"

"On the third floor?"

"Maybe. But I'll find them. And then I'm out of here[5]." He reached out to[6] Alex with his ungloved hand[7]. "Come with me."

Alex shook his head. "I'm sorry, James. You go, and good luck to you. But I'll stick it out a bit longer[8]. I don't want to break my neck[9]."

"OK. That's your lookout.[10] I'll send you a postcard."

The two of them walked back towards the school. Alex gestured at[11] the window where he had seen the masked face. "Have you ever wondered[12] what goes on up there?" he asked.

"No." James shrugged. "I suppose that's where the guards live."

"Two whole[13] floors?"

"There's a basement as well. And Dr Grief's rooms. Do you think he sleeps with[14] Miss Stomach-bag?" James made a face[15]. "That's a pretty gross thought[16], the two of them together. Darth Vader[17] and King Kong. Well, I'm going to find my skis and get out of here, Alex. And if you've got any sense[18], you'll come too."

1. au moins pour l'aider à partir
2. Moi non plus.
3. cracha
4. Il les a enfermés quelque part.
5. alors je partirai
6. tendit vers
7. sa main dépourvue de gant
8. Je vais rester encore un peu
9. me rompre le cou
10. C'est tes oignons.
11. désigna
12. Tu t'es jamais demandé
13. complets
14. couche avec
15. fit une grimace
16. C'est assez dégueulasse à imaginer
17. [Dark Vador, La Guerre des étoiles]
18. si tu n'es pas fou

Alex and James were skiing together down the slope, the blades cutting smoothly[1] *through the surface snow*[2]*. It was a perfect night. Everything frozen and still*[3]*. They had left the academy behind them. But then Alex saw a figure ahead of them. Dr Grief was there! He was standing motionless*[4]*, wearing his dark suit*[5]*, his eyes quite hidden*[6] *by his red-lensed spectacles. Alex veered away from him*[7]*. He lost control. He was moving*[8] *faster and faster down the slope*[9]*, his poles flailing at the air*[10]*, his skis refusing to turn. He could see the ski-jump*[11] *ahead of him. Someone had removed*[12] *the barriers. He felt his skis leave the snow and shoot forward onto solid ice*[13]*. And then it was a screaming drop down, tearing ever further*[14] *into the night, knowing there was no way back*[15]*. Dr Grief laughed and at the same moment there was a click and Alex shot into space*[16]*, spinning a mile above the ground and then falling, falling, falling…*

He woke up.

He was lying in bed, the moonlight spilling onto the covers[17]. He looked at his watch. Two-fifteen. He played back the dream[18] he had just had. Trying to escape with James. Dr Grief waiting for them. He had to admit, the academy was beginning to get to him[19]. He didn't usually have bad dreams. But the school and the people in it were slipping under his skin, working their way into his mind[20].

1. skis glissant en douceur
2. poudreuse
3. gelé et silencieux
4. immobile
5. costume
6. bien cachés
7. le contourna
8. se déplaçait
9. le long de la pente
10. bâtons cinglant l'air
11. voyait le tremplin
12. enlevé
13. foncer sur une épaisse couche de glace
14. ce fut la chute vertigineuse, en s'enfonçant toujours plus
15. qu'il ne pouvait pas faire marche arrière
16. s'envola
17. clair de lune inondant ses couvertures
18. se repassa le rêve
19. lui taper sur le système
20. lui filaient la chair de poule et commençaient à lui faire perdre les pédales

He thought about what he had heard. Dr Grief laughing – and something else ... a clicking sound[1]. That was strange. What had gone "click"?[2] Had it actually been part of the dream? Suddenly Alex was completely awake[3]. He got out of bed, went to the door and turned the handle[4]. He was right. He hadn't imagined the sound. While[5] he was asleep, the door had been locked from outside[6].

Something had to be happening[7] – and Alex was determined to see what it was. He got dressed as quickly as possible, then knelt down[8] and examined the lock. He could make out two bolts[9], at least a centimetre in diameter, one at the top and one at the bottom. They must have been activated automatically. One thing was sure. He wasn't going to get out through the door.

That left[10] the window. All the bedroom windows were fastened with a steel rod that allowed them to open[11] ten centimetres but no more. Alex picked up[12] his Discman, put in[13] the Beethoven CD and turned it on[14]. The CD spun round[15] – moving at a fantastic speed[16] – then slowly edged forward[17], still spinning, until it protruded from the casing[18]. Alex pressed the edge[19] of the CD against[20] the steel rod. It took just a few seconds. The CD cut through[21] the steel like scissors[22] through paper. The rod fell away, allowing the window to swing fully open[23].

1. un cliquetis
2. C'était quoi, ce « clic » ?
3. réveillé
4. tourna la poignée
5. Pendant qu'
6. verrouillée de l'extérieur
7. Il devait se passer quelque chose
8. s'agenouilla
9. distingua deux verrous
10. Il ne restait que
11. fixées avec une tige métallique permettant une ouverture de
12. récupéra
13. inséra
14. le mit en marche
15. tournoya
16. vitesse
17. se rapprocha du bord
18. jusqu'à ce qu'il dépasse du boîtier
19. appliqua le bord
20. contre
21. découpa
22. des ciseaux
23. de s'ouvrir complètement

It was snowing. Alex turned the CD player off and threw it back[1] on his bed. Then he put on his coat and climbed out of[2] the window. He was one floor up[3]. Normally a fall from that height[4] would have broken an ankle[5] or a leg. But it had been snowing for the best part of[6] ten hours and a white bank had built up[7] against the wall right beneath[8] him. Alex lowered himself[9] as far as he could, then let go[10]. He fell through the air and hit[11] the snow, disappearing as far as his waist[12]. He was freezing and damp before he had even started[13]. But he was unhurt[14].

He climbed out[15] of the snow and began to move round the side of the building, making for[16] the front. He would just have to hope[17] that the main entrance wasn't locked too. But somehow he was sure it wouldn't be. His door had been locked automatically. Presumably a switch had been thrown[18] and all the others had been locked too. Most of the boys would be asleep. Even the ones who were awake wouldn't be going anywhere[19], leaving Dr Grief free to do whatever[20] he wanted, coming and going as he pleased[21].

Alex had just made it to[22] the side of the building when he heard[23] the guards approach, boots crunching[24]. There was nowhere to hide so he threw himself face-down[25] into the snow, hugging the shadows[26]. There were two of them. He could hear them talking softly in German but he didn't

1. le jeta
2. enjamba
3. au premier étage
4. chute de cette hauteur
5. cheville
6. depuis au moins
7. congère s'était formée
8. juste au-dessous de
9. se laissa descendre
10. lâcha prise
11. atterrit dans
12. s'enfonçant jusqu'à la taille
13. gelé et mouillé avant même de commencer
14. n'était pas blessé
15. s'extirpa
16. en se dirigeant vers
17. n'avait plus qu'à espérer
18. quelqu'un avait appuyé sur un interrupteur
19. n'iraient nulle part
20. libre de faire tout ce qu'
21. d'aller et venir à son gré
22. venait d'arriver sur
23. entendit
24. dans un crissement de bottes
25. se jeta à plat ventre
26. en se plaquant au maximum

dare look up[1]. If he made any[2] movement, they would see him. If they came too close[3], they would probably see him anyway. He held his breath[4], his heart pounding[5].

The guards walked past and round the corner[6]. Their path would take them[7] under his room. Would they see the open window? Alex had left the light off[8]. Hopefully[9] there would be no reason for them to look up. But he was still aware[10] that he might not have much time. He had to move – now.

He lifted himself up[11] and ran forward. His clothes were covered in snow and more flakes[12] were falling, drifting into[13] his eyes. It was the coldest[14] part of the night and Alex was shivering by the time he reached[15] the main door. What would he do if it was locked after all? He certainly wouldn't be able to stay out in the open[16] until morning.

But the door was unlocked. Alex pushed it open and slipped into the warmth[17] and darkness of the main hall. The dragon fireplace was in front of him. There had been a fire earlier in the evening and the burnt-out logs were still smouldering[18] in the hearth[19]. Alex held his hands against the glow[20], trying to draw a little warmth into himself[21]. Everything was silent. The empty corridors stretched into the distance[22], illuminated by a few low-watt bulbs[23] that had been left on at intervals[24]. Only now did it occur to Alex[25] that he could have been mistaken from

1. n'osa pas lever les yeux
2. le moindre
3. venaient trop près
4. retint sa respiration
5. cœur battant la chamade
6. passèrent et tournèrent à l'angle
7. chemin les mènerait
8. la lumière éteinte
9. Avec un peu de chance
10. avait tout de même conscience
11. se releva
12. flocons
13. entrant dans
14. la plus froide
15. le temps qu'il arrive à
16. à découvert
17. chaleur
18. bûches brûlées se consumaient encore
19. l'âtre
20. plaça ses mains face à cette lueur
21. se réchauffer un peu
22. s'étiraient au loin
23. quelques ampoules de faible intensité
24. étaient restées allumées à intervalles
25. Pour la première fois, Alex se dit

the start[1]. Perhaps the doors were locked every night as part of the security. Perhaps he had jumped too quickly to the wrong conclusion[2] and there was nothing going on after all.

"No...!"

It was a boy's voice. A long, quavering shout[3] that echoed[4] through the school. A moment later, Alex heard feet stamping along[5] a wooden corridor somewhere above[6]. He looked for somewhere to hide and found it inside the fireplace, right next to the logs. The actual fire was contained in a metal basket[7]. There was a wide space[8] on each side between the basket and the brickwork that swept up to become[9] the chimney. Alex crouched low[10], feeling the heat on the side of his face and legs. He looked out[11], past the two dragons, waiting to see what would happen.

Three people were coming down[12] the stairs. Mrs Stellenbosch was the first. She was followed by two of the guards, dragging[13] something between them. It was a boy! He was face-down[14], dressed only in[15] his pyjamas, his bare feet sliding down the stone steps[16]. Mrs Stellenbosch opened the library door and went in. The two guards followed. The door crashed shut[17]. The silence returned.

It had all happened very quickly. Alex had been unable to see[18] the boy's face. But he was sure he knew who it was. He had known just from the sound of his voice.

James Sprintz.

1. s'était peut-être trompé depuis le début
2. avait-il tiré trop vite la mauvaise conclusion
3. cri chevrotant
4. résonna
5. taper le long de
6. quelque part au-dessus
7. panier métallique
8. grand espace
9. s'élevait majestueusement pour former
10. s'accroupit le plus possible
11. jeta un regard à l'extérieur
12. descendaient
13. traînant
14. avait la tête penchée en avant
15. n'était vêtu que de
16. pieds nus traînant sur les marches de pierre
17. se ferma en claquant
18. n'avait pas pu voir

Alex eased himself out[1] of the fireplace and crossed the hall, making for the library door. There was no sound coming from the other side. He knelt down[2] and looked through[3] the keyhole. No lights were on[4] inside the room. He could see nothing. What should he do? If he went back upstairs, he could make it back to[5] his room without being seen[6]. He could wait until[7] the doors were unlocked[8] and then slip[9] into bed. Nobody would know he had been out[10].

But the only person in the school who had shown him any kindness[11] was on the other side of the library door. He had been dragged down here.[12] Perhaps he was being brainwashed[13] ... beaten[14], even. Alex couldn't just turn round and leave him[15].

Alex had made his decision. He threw open the door and walked in.

The library was empty.

He stood in the doorway, blinking[16]. The library only had one door. All the windows were closed. There was no sign that anyone had been there. The suit of armour stood in its alcove[17] at the end, watching him as he moved forward[18]. Could he have been mistaken? Could Mrs Stellenbosch and the guards have gone into a different room?

Alex went over to[19] the alcove and looked behind the armour, wondering if it might conceal a second exit[20]. There was nothing. He tapped a knuckle against[21] the wall. Curiously, it seemed to be made

1. se dégagea
2. s'agenouilla
3. par
4. Aucune lumière n'était allumée
5. regagner
6. sans être vu
7. jusqu'à ce que
8. déverrouillées
9. se glisser
10. qu'il était sorti
11. qui avait été sympa avec lui
12. On l'y avait traîné de force.
13. qu'on était en train de lui laver le cerveau
14. de le tabasser
15. ne pouvait pas tourner les talons et le laisser tomber
16. resta à l'entrée, clignant des yeux
17. L'armure était dans sa niche
18. lorsqu'il avança
19. alla jusqu'à
20. elle dissimulait une deuxième sortie
21. Du poing, il tapota

of metal, but unlike the wall across[1] the stairs there was no handle[2], nothing to suggest a way through[3].

There was nothing more he could do here. Alex decided to go back to his room before he was discovered.

But he had only just made it to the[4] first floor when he heard voices once again ... more guards, walking slowly down the corridor. Alex saw a door and slipped inside, once again ducking out of sight[5]. He was in the laundry room[6]. There was a washing-machine, a tumble-drier[7] and two ironing-boards[8]. At least it was warm in here. He felt himself surrounded by soap fumes[9].

The guards had gone. There was a metallic click that seemed to stretch the length of the[10] corridor and Alex realized that all the doors had been unlocked at the same time. He could go back to bed.

He crept out[11] and hurried forward[12]. His footsteps took him past[13] James Sprintz's room, next to his own. He noticed that James's door was open. And then a voice called out from inside.

"Alex?" It was James.

No. That wasn't possible. But there was someone in his room.

Alex looked inside. The light went on[14].

It *was* James. He was sitting up in[15] bed, bleary-eyed[16], as if he had just woken up. Alex stared at him[17]. He was wearing the same pyjamas as the boy he had just seen dragged[18] into the library

1. à la différence du mur en travers de
2. poignée
3. n'indiquant un passage
4. venait juste d'arriver au
5. se glissa à l'intérieur du local, se recroquevillant à nouveau pour se cacher
6. buanderie
7. machine à laver, un sèche-linge
8. planches à repasser
9. des odeurs de lessive
10. se propager tout le long du
11. sortit à pas de loup
12. s'élança à toute allure
13. En chemin, il passa devant
14. s'alluma
15. assis dans son
16. le regard ensommeillé
17. le dévisagea
18. que l'on avait traîné sous ses yeux

… but that *couldn't* have been him. It must have been someone else.

"What are you doing?" James asked.

"I thought I heard[1] something," Alex said.

"But you're dressed. And you're soaking wet[2]!" James looked at his watch. "It's almost three…"

Alex was surprised that so much time had passed[3]. It had only been two-fifteen when he'd woken up. "Are you all right?" he asked.

"Yeah."

"You haven't…?"

"What?"

"Nothing. I'll see you later.[4]"

Alex crept back[5] to his own room. He closed the door, then stripped off[6] his wet clothes, dried himself[7] with a towel and got back into bed. If it wasn't James he had seen being taken into the library, who was it? And yet it *had* been[8] James. He had heard the cry, seen the limp form[9] on the stairs. So why was James lying[10] now?

Alex closed his eyes and tried to get back to sleep[11]. The movements of the night had created more puzzles[12] and had solved nothing[13]. But at least he'd got something out of it all[14].

He now knew how to get up to the second floor.

1. J'ai cru entendre
2. trempé
3. se soit écoulé
4. À plus tard.
5. retourna sans bruit
6. retira
7. se sécha
8. pourtant, c'était bien
9. silhouette inerte
10. Pourquoi James mentait-il
11. se rendormir
12. Les événements de la nuit avaient généré de nouveaux mystères
13. n'avaient rien résolu
14. tout cela lui avait appris une chose

SEEING DOUBLE[1]

James was already eating his breakfast when Alex came down; eggs, bacon, toast and tea. He had the same breakfast[2] every day. He raised a hand in greeting as[3] Alex came in. But the moment[4] he saw him, Alex got the feeling[5] that something was wrong. James was smiling but he seemed somehow distant, as if his thoughts were on other things[6].

"So what was all that about[7] last night?" James asked.

"I don't know..." Alex was tempted[8] to tell James everything – even the fact that he was here under a false name and had been sent to spy on the school. But he couldn't do it. Not here, so close[9] to the other boys. "I think I had some sort of bad dream."

"Did you go sleepwalking[10] in the snow?"

"No. I thought I saw[11] something, but I couldn't have[12]. I just had a weird[13] night." He changed the

1. Double vision
2. prenait le même petit déjeuner
3. salua d'un geste de la main lorsque
4. dès que
5. eut l'impression
6. s'il avait la tête ailleurs
7. c'était quoi le problème
8. eut envie
9. si près
10. Tu as fait le somnambule
11. J'ai cru avoir vu
12. ce n'est pas possible
13. bizarre

subject, lowering his voice[1]. "Have you thought any more about[2] your plan?" he asked.

"What plan?"

"Skiing."

"We're not allowed to ski."

"I mean ... escaping."

James smiled as if he'd only just[3] remembered what Alex was talking about. "Oh – I've changed my mind[4]," he said.

"What d'you mean?[5]"

"If I ran away, my dad would only send me back again. There's no point.[6] I might as well grin and bear it.[7] Anyway, I'd never get all the way down the mountain. The snow's too thin[8]."

Alex stared at[9] James. Everything he was saying was the exact opposite[10] of what he had said the day before[11]. He almost wondered if this was the same boy. But of course it was. He was as untidy as ever[12]. The bruises – fading now[13] – were still there on his face. Dark hair, dark brown eyes, pale skin – it was James. And yet[14] at the same time, something had happened. He was sure of it.

Then James twisted round[15] and Alex saw that Mrs Stellenbosch had come into the room, wearing a particularly nasty lime-green dress[16] that just came down to her knees[17]. "Good morning, boys!" she announced. "We're starting today's lessons in ten minutes. The first lesson is history in the tower room[18]." She walked over to[19]

1. changea de sujet, baissant la voix
2. réfléchi un peu plus à
3. s'il venait juste de
4. changé d'avis
5. Comment ça ?
6. Ça ne sert à rien.
7. Autant prendre mon mal en patience.
8. [couche de] neige est trop mince
9. dévisagea
10. tout le contraire
11. la veille
12. aussi débraillé que d'habitude
13. qui s'estompaient à présent
14. pourtant
15. se retourna
16. une robe particulièrement laide, vert jaune
17. lui arrivait au niveau des genoux
18. salle de la tour
19. s'approcha de

Alex's table. "James, I hope you're going to join us today?"

James shrugged[1]. "All right, Mrs Stellenbosch."

"Excellent. We're looking at the life of Adolf Hitler. Such an interesting man. I'm sure you'll find it most valuable[2]." She walked away.

Alex turned to James. "You're going to lessons[3]?"

"Why not?" James had finished eating. "I'm stuck here[4] and there isn't much else[5] to do. Maybe I should have gone to lessons before. You shouldn't be so negative, Alex." He waved a finger to underline[6] what he was saying. "You're wasting[7] your time."

Alex froze[8]. He had seen that movement before – the way he had waved[9] his finger. Joe Canterbury, the American boy, had done exactly the same thing yesterday.

Puppets dancing on the same string.[10]

What had happened the night before?

Alex watched James leave with the others. He felt he had lost[11] his only[12] friend at Point Blanc and suddenly he wanted to be away[13] from this place, off[14] the mountain and back in the safe world[15] of Brookland School. There might have been a time when[16] he had wanted this adventure. Now he just wanted out of it[17]. Press fast forward three times on his Discman and MI6 would come for him[18]. But he couldn't do that until he had something to report.

1. haussa les épaules
2. vous trouverez cela très instructif
3. en cours
4. coincé ici
5. il n'y a pas grand-chose d'autre
6. agita son doigt pour souligner
7. perds
8. se figea
9. cette façon d'agiter
10. Des marionnettes qui dansent au bout de la même ficelle.
11. sentit qu'il avait perdu
12. seul
13. eut envie d'être loin
14. hors de
15. de retrouver l'univers protégé
16. Même si à un moment
17. voulait juste en sortir
18. viendrait le récupérer

Alex knew what he had to do. He got up and left the room.

He had seen the way[1] the night before when he was hiding in the fireplace. The chimney bent and twisted its way to the open air[2] – he had been able to see a chink of light[3] from the bottom. Moonlight. The bricks outside the academy might be too smooth to climb[4], but inside the chimney they were broken and uneven[5], with plenty of hand and foot-holds[6]. Maybe there would be a fireplace[7] on the second or third floor. But even if there wasn't[8], the chimney would still lead him[9] to the roof and – assuming[10] there weren't any guards waiting for him there – he might then be able to find a way down[11].

Alex reached the fireplace with the two stone dragons. He looked at his watch. Nine o'clock. Lessons would continue until lunch and nobody would wonder where he was. The fire had finally gone out, although the ashes were still warm[12]. Would one of the guards come to clean it? He would just have to hope they would leave it until[13] the afternoon. He looked up the chimney. He could see a narrow slit of bright blue[14]. The sky seemed a very long way away and the chimney was narrower[15] than he had thought. What if he got stuck?[16] He forced the thought out of his head[17], reached for a crack[18] in the brickwork and pulled himself up[19].

1. repéré un chemin
2. conduit de cheminée remontait, tortueux, jusqu'à l'air libre
3. rayon de lumière
4. trop lisses pour être escaladées
5. cassées et inégales
6. plein de prises pour les mains et les pieds
7. foyer
8. même s'il n'y en avait pas
9. le mènerait tout de même
10. en supposant
11. un moyen de descendre
12. s'était enfin éteint, bien que les cendres soient encore chaudes
13. ne le feraient pas avant
14. aperçut le ciel bleu vif, comme par une étroite meurtrière
15. plus étroite
16. Et s'il restait bloqué ?
17. chassa cette idée de son esprit
18. plaça sa main dans une fissure
19. se hissa

1. exhalait l'odeur de mille feux
2. La suie flottait dans l'air
3. sans en aspirer
4. réussit à trouver une prise
5. se hissant de 1 mètre environ
6. encastré, bloqué en position assise
7. les fesses suspendues dans le vide
8. étirer
9. pour se propulser
10. pour se maintenir
11. glisser
12. faisait tomber un peu plus de suie
13. n'osait pas
14. aveuglé
15. dérapaient
16. retomberait jusqu'en bas
17. loin au-dessus de
18. Quelle distance avait-il parcourue ?
19. ce qui voulait dire
20. hauteur
21. devenait plus sombre et se resserrait
22. se rapprocher
23. gorge
24. enduite de
25. se cognèrent contre
26. propageant un élancement de douleur jusqu'à

The inside of the chimney smelled of a thousand fires[1]. Soot hung in the air[2] and Alex couldn't breathe without taking it in[3]. He managed to find some purchase[4] for his feet and pushed, sliding himself about one metre up[5]. Now he was wedged inside, forced into a sitting position[6] with his feet against one wall, his back against the other and his legs and bottom hanging in the air[7]. He wouldn't need to use his hands at all. He only had to straighten[8] his legs to push himself up[9], using the pressure of his feet against the wall to keep himself[10] in place. Push and slide[11]. He had to be careful. Every movement brought more soot trickling down[12]. He could feel it in his hair. He didn't dare[13] look up. If it went into his eyes he would be blinded[14]. Push and slide again, then again. Not too fast. If his feet slipped[15] he would fall all the way back down[16]. He was already a long way above[17] the fireplace. How far had he come?[18] At least one floor ... meaning[19] that he had to be on his way to the second. If he fell from this height[20] he would break both his legs.

The chimney was getting darker and tighter[21]. The light at the top didn't seem to be getting any nearer[22]. Alex found it difficult to manoeuvre himself. He could barely breathe. His entire throat[23] seemed to be coated in[24] soot. He pushed again and this time his knees banged into[25] brickwork, sending a spasm of pain down to[26] his feet. Pinning himself in place[1], Alex reached up and tried to feel[2] where he was going. There was an L-shaped[3] wall jutting out[4] above his head. His knees had hit[5] the bottom part of it. But his head was behind the upright section[6]. Whatever the obstruction was[7], it effectively cut the passageway in half[8], leaving only the narrowest of gaps[9] for Alex's shoulders and body to pass through[10].

Once again, the nightmare prospect[11] of getting stuck flashed into[12] his mind. Nobody would ever find him. He would suffocate in the dark.

He gasped for breath[13] and swallowed[14] soot. One last try![15] He pushed again, his arms stretching out over[16] his head. He felt his back slide up the wall, the rough[17] brickwork tearing at[18] his shirt. Then his hands hooked over what he realized must be the top of the L[19]. He pulled himself up and found himself looking into[20] a second fireplace, sharing the main chimney[21]. That was the obstruction he had just climbed round[22]. Alex levered himself over the top[23] and dived clumsily forward[24]. More logs and ashes broke his fall[25]. He had made it to the second floor!

He crawled out[26] of the fireplace. Only a few weeks before, at Brookland, he'd been reading about Victorian chimney-sweeps[27]; how boys as young as six[28] had been forced into virtual slave labour[29]. He'd never thought he would

1. En se bloquant en position
2. tâtonna vers le haut pour évaluer
3. en forme de L
4. qui dépassait
5. heurté
6. partie toute droite
7. Quel que soit l'obstacle
8. réduisait de moitié le passage
9. qu'une ouverture très étroite
10. se faufilent
11. perspective cauchemardesque
12. traversa
13. chercha de l'air
14. avala
15. Dernière tentative !
16. étirés au-dessus de
17. rugueux
18. déchirer
19. agrippèrent ce qui, d'après lui, devait être le dessus du L
20. se retrouva face à
21. desservi par le conduit principal
22. venait de contourner
23. se hissa par-dessus
24. plongea maladroitement en avant
25. amortirent sa chute
26. sortit en rampant
27. ramoneurs de l'époque victorienne
28. de six ans
29. réduits à un véritable esclavage

learn how they had felt[1]. He coughed and spat into[2] the palm[3] of his hand. His saliva was black. He wondered what he must look like[4]. He would need to take a shower before he was seen[5].

He stood up. The second floor was as silent as the ground and the first[6]. Soot trickled out[7] of his hair and for a moment he was blinded. He propped himself against[8] a statue while he wiped[9] his eyes. Then he looked again. He was leaning[10] on a stone dragon, identical to the one on the[11] ground floor. He looked at the fireplace. That too[12] was identical. In fact—

Alex wondered if he hadn't somehow made a terrible mistake. He was standing[13] in a hall that was the same in every detail as the[14] hall on the ground floor. There were the same corridors, the same staircase, the same fireplace – even the same animal heads staring miserably[15] from the walls. It was as if he had climbed in a circle, arriving back where he had begun[16]. He turned round. No. Here was[17] one difference. There was no main door. He could look down on the front courtyard[18] from the window; there was a guard leaning against a wall, smoking a cigarette. This *was*[19] the second floor. But it had been constructed as a perfect replica of the ground[20].

Alex tiptoed forward[21], worried that somebody might have heard him climb out[22] of the fireplace. But there was no one around. He followed the corridor as far as[23] the first door. On the ground floor,

1. saurait ce qu'ils avaient pu ressentir
2. toussa et cracha dans
3. paume
4. à quoi il devait ressembler
5. qu'on le voie
6. que le rez-de-chaussée et le premier
7. s'échappa
8. s'appuya contre
9. s'essuyait
10. s'appuyait
11. à celui du
12. Celle-là aussi
13. se trouvait
14. identique en tous points au
15. au regard triste et fixe
16. tourné en rond et qu'il était revenu au point de départ
17. Là, il y avait
18. cour d'honneur
19. C'était bien
20. à l'identique du rez-de-chaussée
21. avança sur la pointe des pieds
22. ait pu l'entendre s'extraire
23. jusqu'à

this would be the library. Gently, a centimetre at a time[1], he opened the door. It led into[2] a second library – again the spitting image[3] of the first. It had the same tables and chairs, the same suit of armour guarding the same alcove[4]. He ran an eye along[5] one of the shelves[6]. It even had the same books.

But there was one difference – at least[7], one difference that Alex could see. He felt as if he had strayed into one of those puzzles they sometimes print in comics[8] or magazines. Two identical pictures. But ten deliberate mistakes[9]. Can you spot them?[10] The mistake here was that there was a large television set on a bracket built into the wall[11]. The television was on[12]. Alex found himself looking at an image of yet another[13] library. He was beginning to feel dizzy.[14] What was the[15] library on the television screen? It couldn't be this one because Alex himself was not being shown[16]. So it had to be the library on the ground floor.

Two identical libraries. You could sit in one[17] and watch the other[18]. But why? What was the point?[19]

It took Alex about ten minutes to discover that the entire second floor was a carbon copy[20] of the ground floor, with the same dining-room, living-room and games room. Alex went over to the snooker table and placed a ball in the middle[21]. It rolled into the corner pocket[22]. The room was on

1. En douceur, centimètre par centimètre
2. donnait dans
3. copie parfaite
4. montant la garde dans la même niche
5. Il parcourut du regard
6. étagères
7. du moins
8. C'était comme s'il s'était égaré dans un de ces jeux que l'on trouve parfois dans les bandes dessinées
9. dix erreurs glissées délibérément
10. Pouvez-vous les retrouver ?
11. accroché au mur
12. allumée
13. encore une autre
14. Sa tête commençait à tourner.
15. C'était quoi, cette
16. n'y était pas visible
17. être assis dans l'une
18. surveiller l'autre
19. Pour quoi faire ?
20. duplicata
21. au centre
22. roula dans le trou, à l'angle

the same slant[1]. A television screen showed the games room downstairs. It was the same as the library; one room spying on another[2].

He retraced his steps[3] and climbed the stairs to the third floor. He wanted to find his own room, but first he went into James's[4]. It was another perfect copy; the same sci-fi posters, the same mobile hanging over[5] the bed, the same lava lamp on the same table. Even the same clothes strewn over the floor[6]. So these rooms weren't just built to be the same. They were carefully maintained[7]. Whatever happened downstairs[8], happened upstairs. But did that mean there had been somebody living here, watching every[9] movement that James Sprintz made, doing everything he did[10]? And if so[11], had somebody else been doing the same for him[12]?

Alex went next door. It was like stepping into his own[13] room. Again there was the same bed, the same furnishings[14] – and the same television. He turned it on[15]. The picture showed his room on the first floor. There was the Discman, lying on[16] the bed. There were his wet clothes[17] from the night before[18]. Had somebody been watching[19] when he cut through[20] the window and climbed out into the night? Alex felt a jolt of alarm[21], then forced himself to relax. This room – the copy of his room – was different. Nobody had moved in here yet[22]. He could tell, just by looking around[23] him. The bed hadn't been slept in.[24] And the smaller details hadn't been copied.

1. avait la même inclinaison
2. espionnant l'autre
3. revint sur ses pas
4. celle de James
5. suspendu au-dessus de
6. jonchant le sol
7. entretenues avec soin
8. Tout ce qui se passait en bas
9. que quelqu'un avait vécu ici, épiant chaque
10. faisant tout ce qu'il faisait
11. si c'était bien le cas
12. la même chose avec lui
13. comme s'il entrait dans sa propre
14. mobilier
15. l'alluma
16. posé sur
17. vêtements mouillés
18. nuit dernière
19. Est-ce que quelqu'un l'observait
20. avait scié
21. sursauta d'inquiétude
22. n'y avait encore emménagé
23. Cela se voyait rien qu'en regardant autour de
24. Personne n'avait dormi dans le lit.

There was no Discman in the duplicate room. No wet clothes. He had left the wardrobe door open[1] downstairs. In here[2] it was closed.

The whole thing was like[3] some sort of mind-bending puzzle[4]. Alex forced himself to think it through[5]. Every single[6] boy who arrived at the academy was watched[7]. All his actions were duplicated. If he hung[8] a poster on the wall of his room, an identical poster was hung in an identical room. There would be someone living[9] in this room doing everything that Alex did. He remembered the figure he had glimpsed[10] the day before ... someone wearing what looked like a white mask. Perhaps that person had been about to move in[11]. But all the evidence suggested[12] that for some reason[13] he wasn't here yet.

And that still left the biggest question of all[14]. What was the point? To spy on the boys was one thing[15]. But to copy everything they did?

A door swung shut[16] and he heard voices, two men walking down the corridor outside. Alex crept over to the door and looked out. He just had time to see Dr Grief walk through[17] a door with another man, a short, plump figure[18] in a white coat. They had gone into the laundry room. Alex slipped out[19] of the duplicate bedroom and followed them.

"...you have completed[20] the work. I am grateful to you[21], Mr Baxter."

"Thank you, Dr Grief."

1. laissé la porte du placard ouverte
2. Ici
3. Tout ça ressemblait à
4. casse-tête hallucinant
5. à l'analyser
6. Chaque
7. épié
8. accrochait
9. Quelqu'un allait vivre
10. qu'il avait aperçue
11. s'apprêtait à emménager
12. tout semblait prouver
13. pour une raison ou une autre
14. la question la plus importante demeurait
15. c'était une chose
16. se ferma d'un coup
17. franchir
18. une petite silhouette grassouillette
19. se glissa hors
20. terminé
21. vous suis reconnaissant

They had left the door open. Alex crouched down[1] and looked through[2]. Here at last[3] was a section of the third floor that didn't mirror[4] the first. There were no washing-machines or ironing-boards here. Instead[5], Alex found himself looking into a room with a row of sinks[6] and through a second set of doors leading into a fully equipped operating theatre[7] at least twice as big[8] as the laundry room on the first floor. At the centre of the room was an operating[9] table. The walls were lined with shelves[10] containing surgical[11] equipment, chemicals[12] and – scattered across the surface[13] – what looked like black and white[14] photographs.

An operating theatre! What was its role[15] in this bizarre, devilish jigsaw puzzle[16]? The two men had walked into it and were talking together, Grief standing with one hand in his pocket[17]. Alex chose his moment[18], then slipped into the outer room[19], crouching down beside[20] one of the sinks. From here he could watch and listen as the two of them talked[21].

"So, I hope you're pleased with[22] the last operation." It was Mr Baxter who was speaking. He had half turned towards[23] the doors and Alex could see a round, flabby[24] face with yellow hair and a thin[25] moustache. Baxter was wearing a bow tie[26] and a checked suit[27] underneath his white coat[28]. Alex had never seen the man before. He was certain of

1. s'accroupit
2. par l'ouverture
3. enfin
4. qui ne reflétait pas
5. À la place
6. rangée d'éviers
7. bloc opératoire totalement équipé
8. deux fois plus grand
9. d'opération
10. garnis d'étagères
11. chirurgicaux
12. des produits chimiques
13. éparpillées sur toute la surface
14. en noir et blanc
15. À quoi servait-il
16. puzzle démoniaque
17. était debout, une main dans la poche
18. attendit le moment propice
19. pièce attenante
20. à côté de
21. les deux hommes qui parlaient
22. content de
23. s'était à moitié tourné vers
24. flasque
25. fine
26. nœud papillon
27. costume à carreaux
28. blouse blanche

it. And yet at the same time, he thought he knew him[1]. Another puzzle!

"Entirely[2]," Dr Grief replied. "I saw him as soon as the bandages came off[3]. You have done extremely well[4]."

"I always *was* the best. But that's what you paid for." Baxter chuckled[5]. His voice was oily[6]. "And while we're on that subject[7], maybe we should talk about my final[8] payment?"

"You have already been paid the sum of one million American dollars."

"Yes, Dr Grief." Baxter smiled. "But I was wondering if you might not like to think about[9] a little ... bonus?"

"I thought we had an agreement[10]." Dr Grief turned his head very slowly. The red spectacles homed in on[11] the other man like searchlights[12].

"We had an agreement for my work, yes. But my silence is another matter[13]. I was thinking of another quarter of a million[14]. Given[15] the size and the scope[16] of your Gemini Project, it's not so much to ask[17]. Then I'll retire to[18] my little house in Spain and you'll never hear from me again."

"I will never hear from you again[19]?"

"I promise."

Dr Grief nodded. "Yes. I think that is a good idea."

His hand came out of his pocket. Alex saw that it was holding[20] an automatic pistol with a thick

1. avait l'impression de le connaître
2. Absolument
3. dès que l'on a retiré les bandages
4. fait un excellent travail
5. gloussa
6. mielleuse
7. pendant que nous y sommes
8. dernier
9. si vous n'envisageriez pas
10. accord
11. se braquèrent sur
12. projecteurs
13. c'est une autre histoire
14. 250 000 de plus
15. Étant donné
16. portée
17. ce n'est pas trop demander
18. je me retirerai dans
19. n'entendrai plus jamais parler de vous
20. tenait

silencer protruding[1] from the barrel[2]. Baxter was still smiling as Grief shot him once[3], through the middle of the forehead[4]. He was thrown off his feet and onto[5] the operating table. He lay still[6].

Dr Grief lowered the gun. He went over to a telephone, picked it up and dialled[7] a number. There was a pause while his call was answered[8].

"This is Grief. I have some garbage[9] in the operating theatre that needs to be removed[10]. Could you please inform the disposal team[11]?"

He put down[12] the phone and, glancing one last time at[13] the still[14] figure on the operating table, walked to the other side of the room. Alex saw him press a button. A section[15] of the wall slid open to reveal[16] a lift on the other side. Dr Grief got in. The lift doors closed.

Alex straightened up[17], too shocked to think straight[18]. He staggered forward[19] and went into the operating theatre. He knew he had to move fast[20]. The disposal team that Dr Grief had called for would be on their way[21]. But he wanted to know what sort of operations took place[22] here. Mr Baxter had presumably been the surgeon[23]. But for what sort of work had he been paid a million dollars?

Trying not to look at the body, Alex looked around[24]. On one shelf was a collection of surgical knives, as horrible as anything he had ever seen[25], the blades so sharp[26] that he could almost

1. gros silencieux dépassant
2. canon
3. souriait encore lorsque Grief le tua d'un seul coup de feu
4. front
5. fut soulevé du sol et projeté sur
6. ne bougeait plus
7. le décrocha et composa
8. pendant que l'on répondait à son appel
9. Il y a des déchets
10. dont on doit se débarrasser
11. équipe de ramassage
12. raccrocha
13. jetant un dernier regard sur
14. inerte
15. pan
16. s'ouvrit en coulissant et révéla
17. se redressa
18. pour avoir les idées claires
19. avança en titubant
20. agir vite
21. en route
22. se déroulaient
23. chirurgien
24. autour de lui
25. scalpels, les plus horribles qu'il ait jamais vus
26. lames si tranchantes

feel their touch[1] just looking at them. There were rolls of gauze, syringes, bottles[2] containing various liquids. But nothing to say why Baxter had been employed. Alex realized it was hopeless[3]. He knew nothing about medicine. This room could have been used for anything from ingrown toenails to full-blown heart surgery[4].

And then he saw the photographs. He recognized himself, lying[5] on a bed that he thought he knew too. It was Paris! Room thirteen at the Hotel du Monde. He remembered the black and white bedspread, as well as[6] the clothes he had been wearing[7] that night. The clothes had been removed[8] in most of the photographs. Every inch of him[9] had been photographed, sometimes close-up[10], sometimes wider[11]. In every picture, his eyes were closed. Looking at himself[12], Alex knew[13] that he had been drugged and remembered how the dinner with Mrs Stellenbosch had ended[14].

The photographs disgusted him. He had been manipulated by people who thought he was worth nothing at all[15]. From the moment he had met them[16], he had disliked[17] Dr Grief and his assistant director. Now he felt pure loathing[18]. He still didn't know what they were doing. But they were evil[19]. They had to be stopped.

He was shaken out of his thoughts[20] by the sound of footsteps[21] coming up the stairs. The disposal team! He looked around him and cursed[22].

1. sentir leur effet
2. des rouleaux de gaze, des seringues, des flacons
3. se rendit compte qu'il n'avait aucune chance
4. n'importe quoi, des ongles incarnés à la chirurgie à cœur ouvert
5. se reconnut, allongé
6. dessus-de-lit, ainsi que
7. qu'il portait
8. Il n'avait pas de vêtements
9. Chaque centimètre de son corps
10. en gros plan
11. de façon plus panoramique
12. En s'observant
13. comprit
14. s'était terminé
15. qu'il ne valait rien du tout
16. Dès qu'il les avait rencontrés
17. détesté
18. une véritable haine
19. démoniaques
20. Ses réflexions furent interrompues
21. bruit de pas
22. lâcha un gros mot

He didn't have time to get out and there was nowhere[1] in the room to hide[2]. Then he remembered the lift. He went over to it and urgently stabbed at[3] the button. The footsteps were getting nearer. He heard voices. Then the panels slid open. Alex stepped into a small silver[4] box. There were five buttons: S, R, 1, 2, 3. He pressed R. He had remembered enough French to know that the R must stand for[5] *rez-de-chaussée*, or ground floor. Hopefully, the lift would take him back where he had begun[6].

The doors slid shut[7] a few seconds before the guards entered the theatre[8]. Alex felt his stomach lurch as he was carried down[9]. The lift slowed[10]. He realized that the doors could open anywhere[11]. He might find himself surrounded by[12] guards – or by the other boys in the school. Well, it was too late now. He had made his choice. He would just have to cope with whatever he found[13].

But he was lucky[14]. The doors slid open to reveal the library. Alex assumed this was the real library and not another copy. The room was empty. He stepped out[15] of the lift, then turned round. He was facing[16] the alcove. The lift doors formed the alcove wall. They were brilliantly[17] camouflaged, with the suit of armour now sliced exactly in two, one half on each side[18]. As the doors closed automatically, the armour slid back together again, completing the disguise[19]. Despite himself[20], Alex

1. nulle part
2. où se cacher
3. appuya impatiemment sur
4. argentée
5. devait signifier
6. le ramènerait à son point de départ
7. se refermèrent
8. bloc
9. estomac se retourner pendant qu'il descendait
10. ralentit
11. s'ouvrir n'importe où
12. entouré de
13. n'aurait qu'à se débrouiller quoi qu'il arrive
14. eut de la chance
15. sortit
16. était face à
17. remarquablement
18. bien séparée en deux, une moitié de chaque côté
19. se reforma en coulissant, finalisant le camouflage
20. Malgré lui

had to admire[1] the simplicity of it. The entire building was a fantastic box of tricks[2].

Alex looked at his hands. They were still filthy[3]. He had forgotten that he was completely covered in soot[4]. He crept out of the library, trying not to leave black footprints[5] on the carpet. Then he hurried back to his room. When he got there, he had to remind himself that it was indeed[6] his room and not the copy two floors above. But the Discman was there – and that was what he most needed[7].

He knew enough.[8] It was time to call for the cavalry.[9] He pressed the fast forward button three times, then went to have a shower[10].

1. ne put s'empêcher d'admirer

2. fabuleusement truqué

3. dégoûtantes

4. recouvert de suie

5. de traces de pas noires

6. bien

7. ce dont il avait le plus besoin

8. Il en savait suffisamment.

9. Il était temps d'appeler la cavalerie.

10. alla prendre une douche

DELAYING TACTICS[1]

It was raining in London, the sort of rain that seems never to stop. The early evening traffic was huddled together, going nowhere[2]. Alan Blunt was standing at the window looking out over[3] the street when there was a knock at the door. He turned away reluctantly[4], as if the city at its most damp and dismal held some attraction for him[5]. Mrs Jones came in. She was carrying a sheet of paper. As Blunt sat down behind his desk he noticed the words *Most*[6] *Urgent* printed in red across the top[7].

"We've heard[8] from Alex," Mrs Jones said.

"Oh yes?"

"Smithers gave him a Euro-satellite transmitter built[9] into a portable CD player. Alex sent a signal to us this morning ... at ten twenty-seven hours, his time[10]."

"Meaning?[11]"

1. Report stratégique
2. circulation de la fin d'après-midi formait des bouchons et n'avançait pas
3. donnant sur
4. se détourna à contrecœur
5. sous la pluie et lugubre comme jamais, l'attirait
6. Très
7. inscrits en rouge en haut [du document]
8. Nous avons eu des nouvelles
9. émetteur Euro-satellite intégré
10. à 10 h 27, heure locale
11. Ce qui veut dire ?

"Either he's in trouble or he's found out enough for us to go in.[1] Either way[2], we have to pull him out[3]."

"I wonder..." Blunt leaned back[4] in his chair, deep in thought[5]. As a young man, he had gained a first class honours degree[6] in mathematics at Cambridge University[7]. Thirty years later, he still saw life as[8] a series of complicated calculations. "Alex has been at Point Blanc for how long[9]?" he asked.

"A week."

"As I recall, he didn't want to go. According to Sir David Friend, his behaviour at Haverstock Hall was, to say the least[10], anti-social. Did you know that he knocked out[11] Friend's daughter with a stun dart[12]? Apparently he also nearly got her killed[13] in an incident in a railway tunnel."

"He was playing a part[14]," she said. "Exactly what you told him to do."

"Playing it too well, perhaps," Blunt murmured. "Alex may no longer be one hundred per cent reliable[15]."

"He sent the message." Mrs Jones couldn't keep the exasperation out of her voice[16]. "For all we know, he could be in serious trouble.[17] We gave him the device[18] as an alarm signal. To let us know[19] if he needed help. He's used it. We can't just sit back and do nothing[20]."

"I wasn't suggesting that." Alan Blunt looked curiously at her. "You're not forming some sort of attachment[21] to Alex Rider, are you[22]?" he asked.

1. Soit qu'il a des problèmes, soit qu'il en a découvert suffisamment pour que nous intervenions.
2. Dans les deux cas
3. l'exfiltrer
4. se pencha en arrière
5. absorbé dans ses pensées
6. obtenu un diplôme avec mention « très bien »,
7. [prestigieuse université britannique]
8. voyait toujours la vie comme
9. depuis combien de temps
10. pour le moins
11. a mis K.-O.
12. flèche incapacitante
13. a failli la faire mourir
14. jouait un rôle
15. n'est peut-être plus fiable à 100 %
16. s'empêcher d'avoir un ton exaspéré
17. Tout ce que l'on sait, c'est qu'il a peut-être de sérieux ennuis.
18. cet instrument
19. Pour nous informer
20. rester sans rien faire
21. pas en train de vous attacher
22. n'est-ce pas

Mrs Jones looked away. "Don't be ridiculous."

"You seem worried about him."

"He's fourteen years old, Alan! He's a child, for heaven's sake[1]!"

"You used to have[2] children."

"Yes." Mrs Jones turned to face him again. "Perhaps that does make[3] a difference. But even you must admit that he's special. We don't have another agent like him. A fourteen year old boy! The perfect secret weapon[4]. My feelings about him[5] have nothing to do with it. We can't afford to[6] lose him."

"I just don't want to go blundering into[7] Point Blanc without any firm[8] information," Blunt said. "First of all, this is France we're talking about[9] – and you know what the French are like[10]. If we're seen to be invading their territory they'll kick up one hell of a fuss[11]. Secondly, Grief has got hold of[12] boys from some of the wealthiest[13] families in the world. If we go storming in[14] with the SAS or whatever[15], the whole thing could blow up into a major international incident[16]."

"You wanted proof[17] that the school was connected to the deaths of Roscoe and Ivanov," Mrs Jones said. "Alex may have it."

"He may have it and he may not. A twenty-four hour delay[18] shouldn't make a great deal of[19] difference."

"Twenty-four hours?"

1. pour l'amour du ciel
2. avez eu
3. que cela fait effectivement
4. arme
5. sentiments le concernant
6. ne pouvons pas nous permettre de
7. débarquer n'importe comment à
8. solide
9. il s'agit de la France
10. comment sont les Français
11. ils crieront au scandale
12. a mis la main sur
13. les plus fortunées
14. on leur tombe dessus
15. quoi que ce soit
16. tout ça pourrait dégénérer en énorme incident international
17. des preuves
18. Un report de 24 heures
19. grande

"We'll put a unit on standby[1]. They can keep an eye on things. If Alex is in trouble, we'll find out soon enough[2]. It could play to our favour[3] if he's managed to stir things up[4]. It's exactly what we want. Force Grief to show us his hand[5]."

"And if Alex contacts us again?"

"Then we'll go in."

"We may be too late.[6]"

"For Alex?" Blunt showed no[7] emotion. "I'm sure you don't need to worry about him, Mrs Jones. He can look after himself[8]."

The telephone rang and Blunt answered it. The interview was over. Mrs Jones got up and left to make the arrangements for an SAS unit to fly into Geneva[9]. Blunt was right[10], of course. Delaying tactics[11] might work in their favour. Clear it with the French.[12] Find out what was going on. And it was only twenty-four hours.

She would just have to hope[13] Alex could survive that long[14].

Alex found himself eating his breakfast on his own[15]. For the first time, James Sprintz had decided to join the other boys. There they were – the six of them[16], suddenly the best of friends[17]. Alex looked carefully at the boy who had once been[18] his friend, trying to see what it was that had changed about him[19]. He knew the answer. It was everything and nothing. James was exactly

1. allons placer une unité prête à intervenir
2. on le saura bien assez tôt
3. jouer en notre faveur
4. a réussi à lever un lièvre
5. à dévoiler son jeu
6. Peut-être qu'on arrivera trop tard.
7. ne trahit aucune
8. sait se débrouiller
9. partit faire le nécessaire afin qu'une unité SAS prenne l'avion pour Genève
10. avait raison
11. Un report stratégique
12. Avoir l'accord des Français.
13. n'avait plus qu'à espérer qu'
14. puisse survivre jusque-là
15. tout seul
16. Ils était là, tous les six
17. meilleurs amis du monde
18. avait été
19. en quoi il avait changé

the same[1] and completely different at the same time[2].

Alex finished his food and got up. James called out to him[3]. "Why don't you come to class this morning, Alex? It's Latin."

Alex shook his head. "Latin's a waste of time[4]."

"Is that what you think?" James couldn't keep the sneer out of his voice[5] and for a moment Alex was startled[6]. For just one second it hadn't been James talking at all[7]. It had been James who had moved his mouth[8]. But it had been Dr Grief speaking the words.

"You enjoy it[9]," Alex said. He hurried out[10] of the room.

Almost twenty-four hours had passed since[11] he had pressed the fast forward[12] on the Discman. Alex wasn't sure what he had been expecting[13]. A fleet[14] of helicopters flying[15] the Union Jack[16] would have been reassuring. But so far[17] nothing had happened. He even wondered if the alarm signal had worked[18]. At the same time, he was annoyed with himself[19]. He had seen Grief shoot the man called Baxter in the operating theatre and he had panicked. He knew that Grief was a killer. He knew that the academy was far more[20] than the finishing school it pretended to be. But he still didn't have[21] all the answers. What exactly was Dr Grief doing? Was he responsible for the deaths of Michael J. Roscoe and Viktor Ivanov? And if so[22], why?

1. exactement le même
2. à la fois
3. l'interpella
4. perte de temps
5. ne put dissimuler son ton méprisant
6. étonné
7. ce n'était pas du tout James qui avait parlé
8. remué la bouche
9. Amuse-toi bien
10. sortit précipitamment
11. s'étaient écoulées depuis
12. la touche « avance rapide »
13. de ce à quoi il s'était attendu
14. flotte
15. aux couleurs de
16. [drapeau officiel du Royaume-Uni]
17. jusqu'à présent
18. fonctionné
19. s'en voulait
20. bien plus
21. n'avait toujours pas
22. si oui

The fact was[1], he didn't know enough. And by the time MI6 arrived, Baxter's body would be buried somewhere[2] in the mountains and there would be nothing to prove[3] there was anything wrong. Alex would look like a fool[4]. He could almost imagine Dr Grief telling his side[5] of the story...

"Yes. There is an operating theatre here. It was built years ago[6]. We never use the second and third floors. There is a lift, yes. It was built before we came. We explained to Alex about[7] the armed guards. They're here for his protection. But as you can see, gentlemen, there is nothing unpleasant happening here. The other boys are fine[8]. Baxter? No, I don't know anyone by that name[9]. Obviously[10] Alex has been having bad dreams. I'm amazed[11] that he was sent here to spy on us[12]. I would ask you to take him with you when you leave..."

He had to find out more – and that meant going back up to[13] the second floor. Or perhaps down. Alex remembered the letters in the secret lift. R for *rez-de-chaussée*. S had to stand for *sous-sol*. The French for[14] basement.

He went over to the Latin classroom and looked in through the half-open door[15]. Dr Grief was out of sight[16], but Alex could hear his voice.

"*Felix qui potuit rerum cognoscere causas*[17]..."

There was the sound of scratching[18]; chalk on a blackboard.[19] And there were the six boys, sitting at their desks, listening intently[20]. James was

1. En fait
2. enterré quelque part
3. plus rien pour prouver que
4. passerait pour un imbécile
5. en train de raconter sa version
6. il y a des années
7. Nous avons fourni des explications à Alex concernant
8. vont bien
9. ne connais personne de ce nom
10. De toute évidence
11. stupéfait
12. pour nous espionner
13. remonter au
14. L'équivalent en français de
15. regarda par la porte entrouverte
16. n'étais pas visible
17. Heureux celui qui a pu pénétrer les causes secrètes des choses
18. un crissement
19. la craie sur le tableau noir
20. écoutant attentivement

sitting between Hugo and Tom, taking notes[1]. Alex looked at his watch. They would be there for another hour[2]. He was on his own.

He walked back down the corridor and slipped into the library. He had woken up still smelling faintly of[3] soot and had no intention of making his way back up[4] the chimney. Instead he crossed over to[5] the suit of armour. He knew now that the alcove disguised[6] a pair of elevator doors. They could be opened from inside[7]. Presumably there was some sort of control[8] on the outside too.

It took him just a few minutes to find it. There were three buttons built into the breast-plate[9] of the armour. Even close to[10], the buttons looked like part[11] of the suit – something the medieval knight[12] would have used to strap the thing on[13]. But when Alex pressed the middle[14] button, the armour moved. A moment later, it split in half again and he found himself looking into the waiting lift[15].

This time he pressed the bottom button. The lift seemed to travel a long way[16], as if the basement of the building had been built far underground[17]. Finally the doors slid open again. Alex looked out into a curving passageway[18] with tiled[19] walls that reminded him a little of[20] a London tube station[21]. The air was cold down here[22]. The passage was lit by naked bulbs, screwed[23] into the ceiling at intervals.

He looked out[24], then ducked back[25]. There was a guard at the end of the corridor, sitting at a

1. en train de prendre des notes
2. pendant une heure encore
3. en sentant encore vaguement la
4. remonter par
5. Il se dirigea plutôt vers
6. dissimulait
7. de l'intérieur
8. Il devait bien y avoir un bouton
9. intégrés dans le plastron
10. Même de près
11. semblaient faire partie
12. chevaliers du Moyen Âge
13. pour fixer l'armure sur eux
14. central
15. l'ascenseur qui était déjà là
16. parcourir une longue distance
17. dans de lointaines profondeurs
18. couloir faisant un coude
19. carrelés
20. lui rappelèrent un peu
21. station de métro
22. en bas
23. ampoules nues, vissées
24. regarda au-dehors
25. rentra vivement la tête

table reading a newspaper. Would he have heard[1] the lift doors open? Alex leaned forward again[2]. The guard was absorbed in the sports pages[3]. He hadn't moved. Alex slipped out[4] of the lift and crept down the passage, moving away[5] from him. He reached the corner[6] and turned into a second passageway lined with steel doors[7]. There was nobody else in sight[8].

Where was he? There had to be[9] something down here or there wouldn't be any need for a guard. Alex went over to the nearest of the doors[10]. There was a spy-hole set in the front[11] and he looked through into a bare white cell[12] with two bunk beds, a toilet and a sink. There were two boys in the cell. One he had never seen before, but he recognized the other. It was the red-haired[13] boy called Tom McMorin. But he had seen Tom in Latin just a few minutes ago! What was he doing here?

Alex moved on to[14] the next[15] cell. This one also held[16] two boys. One was a fair-haired, fit-looking[17] boy with blue eyes and freckles[18]. Once again, he recognized the other. It was James Sprintz. Alex examined the door. There were two bolts[19], but as far as he could see, no key. He drew back the bolts[20] and jerked the door handle down[21]. The door opened. He went in.

James stood up, astonished[22] to see him. "Alex! What are you doing here?"

1. Avait-il entendu
2. se pencha à nouveau en avant
3. rubrique sportive
4. se glissa hors
5. s'éloignant
6. au coin
7. avec des portes métalliques tout du long
8. personne d'autre en vue
9. Il devait bien y avoir
10. la porte la plus proche
11. judas inséré devant
12. à travers, il vit une cellule aux murs blancs, dépouillée
13. roux
14. alla vers
15. suivante
16. était occupée par
17. blond, l'air en forme
18. taches de rousseur
19. deux verrous
20. tira les verrous en arrière
21. abaissa la poignée d'un coup
22. stupéfait

Alex closed the door. "We haven't got much time," he said. He was speaking in a whisper even though[1] there was little chance of being overheard[2]. "What happened to you?"

"They came for me the night before last[3]," James said. "They dragged me out[4] of bed and into the library. There was some sort of lift—"

"Behind the armour."

"Yes. I didn't know what they were doing. I thought they were going to kill me. But then they threw me in here[5]."

"You've been here for[6] two days?"

"Yes."

Alex shook his head. "I saw you having breakfast upstairs[7] fifteen minutes ago."

"They've made duplicates of us.[8]" The other boy had spoken for the first time. He had an American accent. "All of us! I don't know how they've done it or why. But that's what they've done." He glanced at the door with anger[9] in his eyes. "I've been here for months[10]. My name's Paul Roscoe."

"Roscoe? Your dad's—"

"Michael Roscoe."

Alex fell silent[11]. He couldn't tell this boy what had happened to his father and he looked away[12], afraid that Paul would read it in his eyes[13].

"How did you get down here?" James asked.

"Listen," Alex said. He was speaking rapidly now. "I was sent here by MI6. My name isn't Alex

1. en chuchotant, même si
2. qu'on l'entende
3. en pleine nuit, avant-hier
4. m'ont traîné hors
5. m'ont jeté là-dedans
6. Tu es là depuis
7. prendre le petit déjeuner là-haut
8. Ils ont créé nos sosies.
9. de la colère
10. depuis des mois
11. se tut
12. détourna le regard
13. ne le voie dans ses yeux

Friend. It's Alex Rider. Everything's going to be OK. They'll send people in and get you all freed[1]."

"You're ... a *spy?*" James was obviously startled[2].

Alex nodded. "I'm a sort of spy, I suppose," he said.

"You've opened the door. We can get out of here!" Paul Roscoe stood up, ready to move[3].

"No!" Alex held up his hands[4]. "You've got to wait. There's no way down the mountain. Stay here for now[5] and I'll come back with help[6]. I promise you. It's the only way.[7]"

"I can't—"

"You have to. Trust me[8], Paul. I'm going to have to lock you back in so that[9] nobody will know I've been here. But it won't be for long[10]. I'll come back!"

Alex couldn't wait for any more argument[11]. He went back to the door and opened it.

Mrs Stellenbosch was standing outside.

He only just had time to register the shock of seeing her[12]. He tried to bring up[13] a hand to protect himself, to twist his body into position[14] for a karate kick[15]. But it was already too late. Her arm shot out, the heel of her hand driving into[16] his face. It was like being hit[17] by a brick wall. Alex felt every bone in[18] his body rattle[19]. White light exploded behind his eyes. Then he was out[20].

1. vont envoyer du monde et vous libérer tous

2. afficha son étonnement

3. prêt à partir

4. leva les mains

5. pour l'instant

6. avec du renfort

7. C'est la seule solution.

8. Fais-moi confiance

9. vous enfermer à nouveau là-dedans afin que

10. ça ne sera pas long

11. n'avait plus le temps de discuter

12. de ressentir un choc en la voyant

13. lever

14. de se mettre en position

15. coup de karaté

16. bras s'abattit, la base de sa paume percutant

17. comme s'il avait été frappé

18. os de

19. vibrer

20. perdit connaissance

1. Comment régner sur le monde

HOW TO RULE THE WORLD[1]

2. souhaite
3. de très loin [de l'autre côté d'un océan]
4. grogna
5. assis, les bras maintenus dans le dos
6. Tout un côté
7. avait l'air meurtri et enflé
8. un goût de sang
9. attendit que la pièce se matérialise
10. le poing relâché dans son autre main
11. du coup
12. lui avait fait perdre connaissance
13. Toute sa tête lui faisait mal
14. passa sa langue
15. s'il n'en manquait pas
16. Il avait de la chance d'avoir roulé sous l'impact.
17. Sinon
18. aurait pu lui rompre le cou

"Open your eyes, Alex. Dr Grief wishes[2] to speak to you."

The words came from across an ocean[3]. Alex groaned[4] and tried to lift his head. He was sitting down, his arms pinned behind his back[5]. The whole side[6] of his face felt bruised and swollen[7] and there was the taste of blood[8] in his mouth. He opened his eyes and waited for the room to come into focus[9]. Mrs Stellenbosch was standing in front of him, her fist curled loosely in her other hand[10]. Alex remembered the force of the blow[11] that had knocked him out[12]. His whole head was throbbing[13] and he ran his tongue[14] over his teeth to see if there were any missing[15]. It was fortunate he had rolled with the punch.[16] Otherwise[17] she might have broken his neck[18].

Dr Grief was sitting in his golden chair, watching Alex with what might have been curiosity or distaste or perhaps a little of both[1]. There was nobody else[2] in the room. It was still snowing outside and there was a small fire burning in the hearth[3], but the flames weren't as red as Dr Grief's eyes.

"You have put us to a great deal of inconvenience[4]," he said.

Alex straightened his[5] head. He tried to move his hands, but they had been chained together behind the chair[6].

"Your name is not Alex Friend. You are not the son of Sir David Friend. Your name is Alex Rider and you are employed by the British Secret Service." Dr Grief was simply stating facts[7]. There was no emotion in his voice.

"We have microphones concealed in the cells[8]," Mrs Stellenbosch explained. "Sometimes it is useful for us to hear the conversations between our young guests[9]. Everything you said was overheard[10] by the guard who summoned me[11]."

"You have wasted our time[12] and our money," Dr Grief continued. "For that you will now be punished. It is not a punishment you will survive[13]."

The words were cold and absolute[14] and Alex felt the fear that they triggered[15]. It coursed through his bloodstream, closing in on his heart.[16] He took a deep breath, forcing himself back under control.[17] He had signalled[18] MI6. They would be on

1. du dégoût, ou un peu des deux
2. personne d'autre
3. l'âtre
4. nous a créé bien des désagréments
5. redressa la
6. enchaînées au dos de la chaise
7. énonçait simplement les faits
8. Nous avons caché des micros dans les cellules
9. jeunes invités
10. a été entendu
11. qui m'a appelée
12. nous a fait perdre notre temps
13. punition à laquelle tu survivras
14. sans appel
15. ressentit la frayeur qu'ils avaient déclenchée
16. Elle lui glaça le sang et lui serra le cœur.
17. Il respira un grand coup, se forçant à se ressaisir.
18. alerté le

their way to Point Blanc. They might appear any minute now. He just had to play for time[1].

"You can't do anything to me," he said.

Mrs Stellenbosch lashed out[2] and he was thrown backwards as the back of her hand sliced into the side of his head[3]. Only the chair kept him upright[4]. "When you speak to the director, you refer to him as[5] 'Dr Grief'," she said.

Alex looked round again, his eyes watering[6]. "You can't do anything to me, Dr Grief," he said. "I know everything. I know about the Gemini Project. And I've already told London what I know. If you do anything to me, they'll kill you. They're on their way here[7] now."

Dr Grief smiled and in that single moment[8] Alex knew that nothing he said would make any difference to[9] what was about to happen to him. The man was too confident[10]. He was like a poker player[11] who had not only managed to[12] see all the cards but had stolen the four aces for himself[13].

"It may well be[14] that your friends are on their way," he said. "But I do not think you have told them anything. We have been through[15] your luggage and found the transmitting device concealed in the Discman. I noted also that it is an ingenious electric saw[16]. But as for the transmitter, it can send out a signal but not a message. Quite how you have learned about[17] the Gemini Project is of no interest to me. I assume[18] you overheard the

1. gagner du temps
2. attaqua
3. projeté en arrière suite au coup qu'elle lui porta à la tempe
4. le maintint d'aplomb
5. tu l'appelles
6. les larmes aux yeux
7. sont en route
8. à ce moment précis
9. quoi qu'il dise, cela ne changerait rien à
10. trop sûr de lui
11. joueur de poker
12. non seulement avait réussi à
13. avait mis la main sur les 4 as
14. Il se pourrait bien
15. avons fouillé
16. scie électrique
17. Comment tu as fait exactement pour découvrir
18. J'imagine que

name whilst eavesdropping at a door[1]. We should have been more careful – but for British intelligence to send in a child[2] ... that was something we could not expect[3].

"Let us assume[4] then that your friends do come calling[5]. They will find nothing wrong[6]. You yourself will have[7] disappeared. I shall tell them that you ran away[8]. I will say that my men are looking for you even now[9], but I very much fear[10] you will have died a cold and lingering death[11] on the mountainside. Nobody will guess[12] what I have done here. The Gemini Project will succeed[13]. It has *already* succeeded. And even if your friends do take it upon themselves to kill me[14], that will make no difference. I cannot be killed, Alex. The world is already mine[15]."

"You mean it belongs to the kids you've hired to act as doubles[16]," Alex said.

"Hired?" Dr Grief muttered[17] a few words to Mrs Stellenbosch in a harsh, guttural[18] language. Alex assumed it must be Afrikaans[19]. Her thick lips parted[20] and she laughed, showing heavy, discoloured teeth[21]. "Is that what you think?" Dr Grief asked. "Is that what you believe?"

"I've seen them."

"You don't know what you've seen. You have no understanding of my genius[22]! Your little mind[23] couldn't begin to encompass what I have achieved[24]." Dr Grief was breathing heavily[25]. He

1. en écoutant aux portes
2. que les services secrets britanniques envoient un enfant
3. nous ne pouvions nous attendre à une chose pareille
4. Imaginons
5. nous rendent bien visite
6. ne trouveront rien qui cloche
7. Toi, tu auras
8. que tu t'es enfui
9. sont toujours à ta recherche
10. je crains fort
11. seras mort de froid lentement
12. ne devinera
13. réussira
14. décident vraiment de me tuer
15. m'appartient déjà
16. avez engagés pour jouer les sosies
17. marmonna
18. dure et gutturale
19. [une des langues officielles de l'Afrique du Sud]
20. s'écartèrent
21. exhibant de grosses dents décolorées
22. ne comprends rien à mon génie
23. petite cervelle
24. jamais comprendre ce que j'ai accompli
25. respirait bruyamment

seemed to come to a decision. "It is rare enough for me to come face to face[1] with the enemy," he said. "It has always been my frustration[2] that I will never be able to communicate to the world the brilliance[3] of what I have done. Well, since I have you here – a captive audience, so to speak[4] – I shall allow myself the luxury[5] of describing the Gemini Project. And when you go, screaming, to your death[6], you will understand that there was never any hope for you[7]. That you could not hope to come up against[8] a man like me and win[9]. Perhaps that will make it easier for you."

"I will smoke, if you don't mind[10], Doctor," Mrs Stellenbosch said. She took out her cigars and lit one. Smoke danced in front of her eyes.

"I am, as I am sure you are aware[11], South African," Dr Grief began. "The animals in the hall and in this room are all souvenirs of my time there[12]; shot on[13] safari. I still miss my country.[14] It is the most beautiful place on this planet.

"What you may not know, however, is that for many years I was one of South Africa's foremost biochemists[15]. I was head of[16] the biology department at the University of Johannesburg. I later ran[17] the Cyclops Institute for Genetic Research[18] in Pretoria. But the height of my career[19] came in the 1960s[20] when, although I was still in my twenties[21], John Vorster, the prime minister of South Africa, appointed me[22] Minister for Science—"

1. de me retrouver face à face
2. J'ai toujours été frustré à l'idée
3. le génie
4. audience captive, pour ainsi dire
5. vais m'offrir le luxe
6. quand tu iras à la mort, en hurlant
7. tu n'avais aucune chance
8. affronter
9. gagner
10. si cela ne vous dérange pas
11. tu le sais
12. de l'époque où je vivais là-bas
13. tués au cours de
14. Mon pays me manque toujours.
15. l'un des biochimistes les plus éminents d'Afrique du Sud
16. Je dirigeais
17. J'ai dirigé ensuite
18. recherche génétique
19. l'apogée de ma carrière
20. les années 1960
21. bien que n'ayant qu'une vingtaine d'années
22. m'a nommé

"You've already said you're going to kill me," Alex said, "but I didn't think that meant you were going to bore me to death[1]."

Mrs Stellenbosch coughed on[2] her cigar and advanced on Alex, her fist clenched[3]. But Dr Grief stopped her. "Let the boy have his little joke[4]," he said. "There will be pain enough for him later.[5]"

The assistant director glowered at[6] Alex.

Dr Grief went on[7]. "I am telling you this, Alex, only because it will help you understand. You perhaps know nothing about South Africa. English schoolchildren are, I have found[8], the laziest[9] and most ignorant in the world. All that will soon change! But let me tell you a little bit about[10] my country, as it was when I was young.

"The white people[11] of South Africa ruled everything[12]. Under the laws that came to be known to the world as apartheid[13], black people were not allowed[14] to live near[15] white people. They could not marry white people. They could not share white toilets[16], restaurants, sports halls[17] or bars. They had to carry passes[18]. They were treated like animals."

"It was disgusting," Alex said.

"It was wonderful!" Mrs Stellenbosch murmured.

"It was indeed[19] perfect," Dr Grief agreed[20]. "But as the years passed[21], I became aware[22] that it would also be short-lived[23]. The uprising[24] at Soweto[25], the growing[26] resistance and the way

1. me faire mourir d'ennui
2. s'étouffa avec
3. le poing serré
4. faire sa petite blague
5. Il souffrira bien assez plus tard.
6. jeta un regard noir à
7. poursuivit
8. je l'ai constaté
9. plus paresseux
10. permets-moi de te parler un peu de
11. Les Blancs
12. régnaient sur tout
13. Selon les lois que le monde entier a qualifiées d'apartheid
14. n'avaient pas le droit
15. près des
16. aller dans les toilettes des Blancs
17. salles de sport
18. être munis de laissez-passer
19. effectivement
20. approuva
21. au fil des ans
22. me suis rendu compte
23. cela n'allait pas durer
24. insurrections
25. [banlieue noire en périphérie de Johannesburg]
26. grandissante

the entire world[1] – including your own, stinking country[2] – ganged up on us[3], I knew that white South Africa was doomed[4] and I even foresaw[5] the day when power would be handed over[6] to a man like Nelson Mandela."

"A criminal!" Mrs Stellenbosch added. Smoke was dribbling out of her nostrils[7].

Alex said nothing. It was clear enough that both Dr Grief and his assistant were mad. Just how mad they were[8] was becoming clearer with every word they spoke[9].

"I looked at the world," Dr Grief said, "and I began to see just how weak and pathetic it was becoming[10]. How could it happen that a country like mine could be given away[11] to people who would have no idea how to run it[12]? And why was the rest of the world so determined for it to be so? I looked around me and I saw that the people of America and Europe had become stupid and weak. The fall of the Berlin Wall only made things worse.[13] I had always admired the Russians, but they quickly became infected with the same disease[14]. And I thought to myself[15], if I ruled the world[16], how much stronger it would be. How much better—"

"For you, perhaps, Dr Grief," Alex said. "But not for anyone else[17]."

Grief ignored him. His eyes, behind the red glasses, were brilliant. "It has been the dream

1. la façon dont le monde entier
2. ton propre misérable pays
3. s'est ligué contre nous
4. condamnée
5. j'ai même prévu
6. où le pouvoir serait remis
7. ressortait par ses narines
8. L'étendue de leur folie
9. de plus en plus évidente à chaque mot
10. à quel point il devenait faible et pitoyable
11. abandonné
12. ne sauraient pas comment le diriger
13. La chute du mur de Berlin n'a fait qu'empirer les choses.
14. ont vite été contaminés par la même maladie
15. me suis dit
16. je régnais sur le monde
17. pour personne d'autre

of very few men[1] to rule the entire world," he said. "Hitler was one[2]. Napoleon another. Stalin, perhaps, a third[3]. Great men![4] Remarkable men! But to rule the world in the twenty-first century requires something more than military strength[5]. The world is a more complicated place now. Where does real power lie?[6] In politics.[7] Prime ministers and presidents. But you will also find power in industry, in science, in the media, in oil[8], in the Internet... Modern life is a great tapestry[9] and if you wish to take control of it all, you must seize hold of every strand[10].

"This is what I decided to do, Alex. And it was because of my unique position[11] in the unique place that was South Africa that I was able to attempt it[12]." Grief took a deep breath[13]. "What do you know about nuclear transplantation?" he asked.

"I don't know anything," Alex said. "But as you said, I'm an English schoolboy. Lazy and ignorant."

"There is another word for it. Have you heard of cloning[14]?"

Alex almost burst out laughing[15]. "You mean ... like Dolly the sheep[16]?"

"To you it may be a joke[17], Alex. Something out[18] of science fiction. But scientists have been searching for a way[19] to create exact replicas of themselves for more than[20] a hundred years.

1. Très peu d'hommes ont rêvé
2. fut l'un d'entre eux
3. troisième
4. De grands hommes !
5. exige plus qu'une force militaire
6. Où se situe le véritable pouvoir ?
7. Dans la politique.
8. le pétrole
9. immense tapisserie
10. t'emparer de chaque fil
11. grâce à ma position exceptionnelle
12. que j'ai pu le tenter
13. profonde respiration
14. clonage
15. faillit éclater de rire
16. la brebis Dolly [premier mammifère cloné]
17. Pour toi, c'est peut-être une plaisanterie
18. tiré
19. les scientifiques cherchent un moyen
20. depuis plus de

The word itself is Greek for 'twig'[1]. Think how a twig starts as one branch[2] but then splits into two[3]. This is exactly what has been achieved[4] with lizards, with sea urchins[5], with tadpoles and frogs, with mice[6] and, yes, on 5 July 1996, with a sheep. The theory is simple enough[7]. Nuclear transplantation. To take the nucleus out of an egg and replace it with a cell taken from[8] an adult. I won't tire you[9] with the details, Alex. But it is not a joke. Dolly was the perfect copy of a sheep that had died[10] six years before Dolly was born[11]. She was the end result[12] of no less than[13] one hundred years of experimentation. And in all that time, the scientists shared a single dream[14]. To clone an adult human.[15] I have achieved that dream!"

He paused.

"If you want a round of applause[16], you'll have to take off the handcuffs[17]," Alex said.

"I don't want applause," Grief snarled[18]. "Not from you. What I want from you is your life ... and that I will take."

"So who did you clone?" Alex asked. "Not Mrs Stellenbosch, I hope. I'd have thought one of her was more than enough.[19]"

"Who do you *think*[20]? I cloned myself![21]" Dr Grief grabbed hold of the arms[22] of his chair, a king on the throne of his own imagination. "Twenty years ago I began my work," he explained. "I told you – I was Minister for Science. I had all the equip-

1. grec lui-même, signifie « brindille »
2. est d'abord une branche
3. elle se divise en deux
4. ce qui a été accompli
5. les oursins
6. les têtards et les grenouilles, avec les souris
7. assez
8. On extrait le noyau d'un ovule et on le remplace par une cellule prélevée chez
9. ne vais pas t'ennuyer
10. était morte
11. soit née
12. résultat final
13. pas moins de
14. avaient le même rêve
15. Cloner un humain adulte.
16. séance d'applaudissements
17. m'enlever les menottes
18. grogna
19. Je pense qu'un seul exemplaire suffit.
20. à ton avis
21. Je me suis cloné moi-même !
22. saisit les accoudoirs

ment and money that I needed. Also – this was South Africa! The rules that hampered[1] other scientists around the world did not apply to me[2]. I was able to use human beings[3] – political prisoners – for my experiments[4]. Everything was done in secret. I worked without stopping for twenty years. And then, when I was ready, I stole a very large amount[5] of money from the South African government and moved here[6].

"This was in 1981. And six years later, almost a whole decade[7] before an English scientist astonished[8] the world by cloning a sheep, I did something far, far more[9] extraordinary – here, at Point Blanc. I cloned myself. Not just once![10] Sixteen times. Sixteen exact copies of me. With my looks[11]. My brains.[12] My ambition. And my determination."

"Were they all as mad as you too?" Alex asked, and flinched[13] as Mrs Stellenbosch hit him again, this time in the stomach. But he wanted to make them angry[14]. If they were angry, they might make mistakes[15].

"To begin with[16] they were babies," Dr Grief said. "Sixteen babies from[17] sixteen mothers – who were themselves biologically irrelevant[18]. They would grow up to become[19] replicas of myself. I have had to wait fourteen years for the babies to become boys and the boys to become teenagers[20]. Eva here has looked after all of them[21]. You have met them – some of them."

1. Les lois qui freinaient
2. ne s'appliquaient pas à moi
3. pouvais utiliser des êtres humains
4. expériences
5. j'ai volé une énorme somme
6. je me suis installé ici
7. presque dix ans révolus
8. n'étonne
9. de bien, bien plus
10. Et pas qu'une seule fois !
11. mon physique
12. Mon intelligence.
13. eut un mouvement de recul
14. qu'ils se mettent en colère
15. peut-être feraient-ils des erreurs
16. Au départ
17. venant de
18. qui, biologiquement, ne représentaient aucun intérêt
19. En grandissant, ils allaient devenir
20. adolescents
21. s'est occupée de tous

"Tom, Cassian, Nicolas, Hugo, Joe. And James..." Now Alex understood why they had somehow all looked the same[1].

"Do you see, Alex? Do you have any idea what I have done? I will never die because even[2] when this body is finished with, I will live on in them[3]. I am them and they are me. We are one and the same.[4]"

He smiled again. "I was helped in all this by Eva Stellenbosch, who had also worked with me in the South African government. She had worked in the SASS[5] – our own secret service. She was one of their principal interrogators[6]."

"Happy days!" Mrs Stellenbosch smiled.

"Together we set up[7] the academy. Because, you see, that was the second part of my plan. I was creating sixteen copies of myself. But that wasn't enough. You remember what I said about the strands[8] of the tapestry? I had to bring them[9] here, to draw them together[10]—"

"To replace them with copies of yourself!" Suddenly Alex saw it all[11]. It was totally insane[12]. But it was the only way to make sense of[13] everything he had seen.

Dr Grief nodded. "It was my observation[14] that families with wealth and power frequently had children who were ... troubled[15]. Parents with no time for[16] their sons. Sons with no love for[17] their parents. These children became my targets, Alex.

1. d'une manière ou d'une autre, ils se ressemblaient tous
2. même
3. n'existera plus, je continuerai à vivre à travers eux
4. Nous ne faisons qu'un.
5. [South African Secret Service]
6. spécialistes de l'interrogatoire
7. avons fondé
8. fils
9. J'ai dû les faire venir
10. les réunir
11. pour Alex, tout devint clair
12. démentiel
13. la seule façon d'expliquer
14. J'avais constaté
15. à... problèmes
16. qui ne s'occupent pas de
17. qui n'aiment pas

Because, you see, I wanted what these children had.

"Take[1] a boy like Hugo Vries. One day his father will leave him with a fifty per cent stake[2] in the world's diamond market[3]. Or Tom McMorin; his mother has newspapers all over[4] the world. Or Joe Canterbury; his father at the Pentagon, his mother a senator[5]. What better start for a life in politics?[6] What better start for a future president of the United States, even? Fifteen of the most promising[7] children who have been sent here to Point Blanc, I have replaced with[8] copies of myself. Surgically altered[9], of course, to look exactly like the originals."

"Baxter, the man you shot—"

"You have been busy[10], Alex." For the first time, Dr Grief looked surprised. "The late Mr Baxter[11] was a plastic surgeon[12]. I found him working in Harley Street[13], London. He had gambling debts[14]. It was easy to bring him under my control[15] and it was his job to operate on[16] my family, to change their faces, their skin colour[17] – and where necessary[18] their bodies – so that they would exactly resemble the teenagers they replaced. From the moment the real teenagers arrived here at Point Blanc, they were kept[19] under observation—"

"With identical rooms on the second and third floors."

1. Prenons par exemple
2. participation de 50 %
3. marché mondial du diamant
4. des journaux partout dans
5. sénatrice
6. Rien de tel pour débuter une carrière politique, non ?
7. les plus prometteurs
8. que j'ai remplacés par
9. Transformés par opération chirurgicale
10. Tu n'as pas chômé
11. Le regretté M. Baxter
12. chirurgien esthétique
13. [la rue des médecins, quartier de Westminster, Londres]
14. des dettes de jeu
15. le contrôler
16. son travail, c'était d'opérer
17. la couleur de leur peau
18. si nécessaire
19. placés

1. épier leurs cibles sur des écrans
2. chacun de leurs
3. Pour apprendre leurs manies.
4. devenir eux
5. se tortilla
6. une prise
7. serré
8. auraient découvert
9. étaient des faux
10. N'importe quelle mère
11. ricana
12. Tu te trompes complètement
13. D'abord
14. très occupés, qui travaillent dur
15. quasiment jamais de temps
16. dès le départ
17. la raison même pour laquelle
18. amélioreront leurs enfants, les rendront plus intelligents, plus sûrs d'eux
19. revenaient sans avoir changé
20. Au moment où il rentre chez lui

"Yes. My doubles were able to watch their targets on television monitors[1]. To copy their every[2] movement. To learn their mannerisms.[3] To eat like them. To speak like them. In short, to become them[4]."

"It would never have worked!" Alex twisted[5] in his chair, trying to find some leverage[6] in the handcuffs. But the metal was too tight[7]. He couldn't move. "Parents would know[8] that the children you sent back were fakes[9]!" he insisted. "Any mother[10] would know it wasn't her son, even if he looked the same."

Mrs Stellenbosch giggled[11]. She had finished her cigar. Now she lit another.

"You are quite wrong[12], Alex," Dr Grief said. "In the first place[13], you are talking about busy, hard-working[14] parents who had little or no time[15] for their children in the first place[16]. And you forget that the very reason why[17] these people sent their sons here was because they *wanted* them to change. It is the reason why all parents send their sons to private schools. Oh yes – they think the schools will make their children better, more clever, more confident[18]. They would actually be disappointed if those children came back the same[19].

"And nature, too, is on our side. A boy of fourteen leaves home for six or seven weeks. By the time he gets back[20], nature will have made its mark[1]. The boy will be taller[2]. He will be fatter[3] or thinner[4]. Even his voice will have changed[5]. It's all part of puberty[6] and the parents when they see him will say, 'Oh Tom, you've got so big – and you're so grown up[7]!' And they will suspect nothing[8]. In fact, they would be worried if the boy had *not* changed."

"But Roscoe guessed[9], didn't he?" Alex knew he had arrived at the truth[10], the reason why he had been sent here in the first place. He knew why Roscoe and Ivanov had died.

"There have been two occasions when the parents did not believe what they saw," Dr Grief admitted. "Michael J. Roscoe in New York. And General Viktor Ivanov in Moscow. Neither man completely guessed[11] what had happened. But they were unhappy[12]. They argued[13] with their sons. They asked too many questions."

"And the sons told you what had happened."

"You might say that I told myself.[14] The sons, after all, are me. But yes. Michael Roscoe knew something was wrong[15] and called MI6 in London. I presume that is how you were unlucky enough to become involved[16]. I had to pay to have Roscoe killed just as[17] I paid for the death of Ivanov. But it was to be expected that there would be[18] problems. Two out of sixteen[19] is not so catastrophic, and of course it makes no difference to[20] my plans. In many ways[21], it even helps me. Michael

1. a pris ses marques
2. est plus grand
3. plus gros
4. plus mince
5. a changé
6. Tout cela fait partie de la puberté
7. que tu as grandi
8. ne se douteront de rien
9. a deviné
10. qu'il connaissait enfin la vérité
11. Ni l'un ni l'autre de ces hommes n'a totalement deviné
12. mécontents
13. se disputaient
14. C'est plutôt moi qui me le suis dit.
15. clochait
16. pour ça que tu as eu la malchance de te faire embarquer là-dedans
17. pour faire tuer Roscoe, tout comme
18. il fallait bien s'attendre à ce qu'il y ait
19. Deux sur seize
20. cela ne change rien à
21. À de nombreux égards

J. Roscoe left his entire[1] fortune to his son. And I understand that[2] the Russian president is taking a personal interest in Dimitry Ivanov following the loss[3] of his father.

"In short[4], the Gemini Project has been an outstanding success[5]. In a few days' time[6], the last of the children will leave Point Blanc to take their places in the heart[7] of their families. Once I am satisfied[8] that they have all been accepted, I will, I fear, have to dispose of the originals[9]. They will die painlessly[10].

"The same cannot be said[11] for you, Alex Rider. You have caused me a great deal of annoyance[12]. I propose, therefore[13], to make an example of you." Dr Grief reached into[14] his pocket and took out a device[15] that looked like a pager[16]. It had a single[17] button, which he pressed[18]. "What is the first lesson tomorrow morning, Eva?" he asked.

"Double biology," Mrs Stellenbosch replied.

"As I thought.[19] You have perhaps been to biology lessons where a frog or a rat has been dissected[20], Alex," he said. "For some time now, my children have been asking to see[21] a human dissection. This is no surprise to me. At the age of fourteen, I first attended a[22] human dissection myself. Tomorrow morning, at nine-thirty, their wish will be granted[23]. You will be brought into the laboratory and we will open you up[24] and have a look at you. We will not be using anaesthetic[25]

1. a laissé toute sa
2. d'après ce que j'ai compris
3. suite à la disparition
4. En bref
5. réussite éclatante
6. Dans quelques jours
7. au cœur
8. Une fois que je serai sûr
9. je me débarrasserai, je le crains, des originaux
10. mourront sans souffrances
11. On ne peut pas en dire autant
12. beaucoup d'ennuis
13. Par conséquent, je vais
14. fouilla dans
15. instrument
16. bip
17. un seul
18. sur lequel il appuya
19. C'est ce que je pensais.
20. étaient disséqués
21. me réclament d'assister à
22. j'ai assisté à ma première
23. vœu sera exaucé
24. on t'ouvrira
25. Il n'y aura pas d'anesthésie

and it will be interesting to see how long[1] you survive before your heart gives out[2]. And then, of course, we shall dissect your heart."

"You're sick![3]" Alex yelled[4]. Now he was thrashing about[5] in the chair, trying to break the wood, trying to get the handcuffs to come apart[6]. But it was hopeless. The metal cut into him[7]. The chair rocked[8] but stayed in one piece[9]. "You're a madman[10]!"

"I am a scientist!" Dr Grief spat the words[11]. "And that is why I am giving you a scientific death[12]. At least in your last minutes you will have been some use to me[13]." He looked past Alex. "Take him away and search him thoroughly[14]. Then lock him up[15] for the night. I'll see him again first thing[16] tomorrow morning."

Alex had seen Dr Grief summon[17] the guards but he hadn't heard them come in. He was seized[18] from behind, the handcuffs were unlocked and he was jerked backwards out[19] of the room. His last sight of Dr Grief was of the man stretching out[20] his hands to warm them[21] at the fire, the twisting flames reflected[22] in his glasses. Mrs Stellenbosch smiled and blew out smoke.

Then the door slammed shut[23] and Alex was dragged down[24] the corridor knowing that Blunt and the secret service had to be on their way – but wondering if they would arrive before it was too late.

1. combien de temps
2. que ton cœur ne lâche
3. Vous êtes un grand malade !
4. hurla
5. se démenait
6. casser en deux les menottes
7. le coupait
8. se balançait
9. en un seul morceau
10. fou
11. cracha ses paroles
12. t'offre une mort scientifique
13. dans tes derniers instants, tu me seras utile
14. fouillez-le complètement
15. enfermez-le
16. à la première heure
17. appeler
18. On l'empoigna
19. on le traîna à reculons, sans ménagement, hors
20. tendant
21. pour les réchauffer
22. l'ondulation des flammes se reflétant
23. se referma en claquant
24. traîné le long de

BLACK RUN[1]

The cell measured[2] two metres by[3] four metres and contained a bunk bed with no mattress[4] and a chair. The door was solid steel[5]. Alex had heard a key turn in the lock after it was closed. He had not been given anything[6] to eat or drink. The cell was cold but there were no blankets[7] on the bed.

At least the guards had left the handcuffs off[8]. They had searched[9] Alex expertly, removing[10] everything they had found in his pockets. They had also removed his belt and the laces[11] of his shoes. Perhaps Dr Grief had thought he would hang himself[12]. He needed Alex fresh and alive[13] for the biology lesson.

It was about two o'clock in the morning but Alex hadn't slept. He had tried to put out of his mind[14] everything Grief had told him. That wasn't important now. He knew that he had to escape[15] before

1. La piste noire
2. cellule mesurait
3. sur
4. couchette sans matelas
5. en acier massif
6. On ne lui avait rien donné
7. il n'y avait pas de couvertures
8. lui avaient enlevé les menottes
9. fouillé
10. méthodiquement, retirant
11. ceinture et les lacets
12. qu'il allait se pendre
13. frais et dispos
14. essayé de chasser de son esprit
15. devait s'échapper

nine-thirty because – like it or not[1] – it seemed he was on his own[2]. More than thirty-six hours had passed since[3] he had pressed the panic button that Smithers had given him – and nothing had happened[4]. Either the machine hadn't worked or[5] for some reason MI6 had decided not to come. Of course it was possible that something might happen before breakfast the next day[6]. But Alex wasn't prepared to risk it[7]. He had to get out. Tonight.

For the twentieth time[8] he went over to the door and knelt down[9], listening carefully. The guards had dragged him back down to the basement[10]. He was in a corridor separate from the other[11] prisoners. Although[12] everything had happened very quickly, Alex had tried to remember where he was being taken[13]. Out of the lift and turn left. Round the corner and then down a second passageway[14] to a door at the end. He was on his own. And listening through[15] the door, he was fairly sure[16] that they hadn't posted a guard outside.

It had to be now[17] – the middle of the night. When they had searched him, the guards hadn't quite taken everything[18]. Neither of them had even noticed[19] the gold stud in his ear. What had Smithers said? "It's a small but very powerful explosive[20]. Separating[21] the two pieces activates it[22]. Count to ten and it'll blow a hole[23] in just about anything..."

1. qu'il le veuille ou non
2. être livré à lui-même
3. s'étaient écoulées depuis que
4. rien ne s'était passé
5. Soit la machine n'avait pas fonctionné, soit
6. le jour suivant
7. refusait de courir ce risque
8. vingtième fois
9. s'agenouilla
10. ramené de force en bas, dans le sous-sol
11. à l'écart des
12. Bien que
13. où on l'emmenait
14. [Ils avaient] tourné à l'angle et parcouru ensuite un second couloir
15. à
16. quasiment certain
17. C'était le bon moment
18. ne lui avaient pas vraiment tout pris
19. Aucun d'entre eux n'avait même remarqué
20. explosif très puissant
21. En séparant
22. on l'active
23. cela percera un trou

Now was the time to put it to the test.[1]

Alex reached up and unscrewed the ear-stud[2]. He pulled it out[3] of his ear, slipped the two pieces into[4] the keyhole of the door, stepped back[5] and counted to ten.

Nothing happened. Was the stud broken, like the Discman transmitter? Alex was about to give up[6] when there was a sudden flash, an intense sheet of orange flame[7]. Fortunately there was no noise[8]. The flare continued for[9] about five seconds, then went out[10]. Alex went back to the door. The stud had burned a hole in it, the size of a two pound coin[11]. The melted[12] metal was still glowing[13]. Alex reached out[14] and pushed. The door swung open[15].

Alex felt a momentary surge of excitement[16], but he forced himself to remain[17] calm. He might be out[18] of the cell but he was still in the basement of the academy. There were guards everywhere. He was on top of a mountain with no skis and no obvious way down[19]. He wasn't safe yet[20]. Not by a long way.[21]

He slipped out of the room and followed the corridor back round to the lift[22]. He was tempted to[23] find the other boys and release them[24] but he knew that they couldn't help. Taking them out of their cells would only[25] put them in danger. Somehow, he found his way back to[26] the lift. He noticed that the guard-post[27] he had seen that

1. Le moment était venu de le tester.
2. saisit la boucle et la dévissa
3. la retira
4. glissa les deux parties dans
5. recula
6. sur le point de renoncer
7. éclair fulgurant, une flamme orange intense
8. cela ne fit aucun bruit
9. Le flamboiement dura encore
10. cessa
11. en brûlant, avait fait un trou dedans, de la taille d'une pièce de 2 livres sterling
12. fondu
13. rougeoyait encore
14. tendit le bras
15. s'ouvrit d'un coup
16. bref élan d'exaltation
17. à rester
18. était peut-être sorti
19. sans savoir comment descendre
20. n'était toujours pas en sécurité
21. Loin de là.
22. suivit le couloir pour regagner l'ascenseur
23. eut envie de
24. pour les libérer
25. ne ferait que
26. retrouva le chemin de
27. poste de garde

morning was empty. Either the man had gone to make himself a coffee or Grief had relaxed security[1] in the academy. With Alex and all the other boys locked up, there was nobody left to guard[2]. Or so they thought.[3] Alex hurried forward[4]. It seemed that luck was on his side.

He took the lift back to[5] the first floor. He knew that his only way off[6] the mountain lay[7] in his bedroom. Grief would certainly have[8] examined everything he had brought with him. But what would he have done with it[9]? Alex crept down[10] the dimly lit[11] corridor and into[12] his room. And there it all was, lying in a heap[13] on his bed. The ski suit. The goggles. Even the Discman with the Beethoven CD. Alex heaved a sigh of relief[14]. He was going to need all of it.

He had already worked out[15] what he was going to do. He couldn't ski off the mountain[16]. He still had no idea where the skis were kept[17]. But there was more than one way to take to the snow[18]. Alex froze as a guard walked along[19] the corridor outside the room. So not everyone at the academy was asleep![20] He would have to move fast[21]. As soon as the broken cell door[22] was discovered, the alarm would be raised[23].

He waited until the guard had gone, then stole into[24] the laundry room a few doors down[25]. When he came out, he was carrying a long flat object[26] made of lightweight[27] aluminium. He carried it

1. relâché la sécurité
2. sous les verrous, il n'y avait plus personne à garder
3. Ça, c'était ce qu'ils croyaient.
4. se dépêcha
5. pour remonter au
6. le seul moyen de quitter
7. se trouvait
8. avait sûrement
9. qu'avait-il pu en faire
10. parcourut sur la pointe des pieds
11. faiblement éclairé
12. [entra] dans
13. tout était là, entassé
14. soupira de soulagement
15. défini
16. quitter la montagne à ski
17. étaient entreposés
18. il y avait d'autres moyens d'aborder la neige
19. passa dans
20. Donc, tout le monde ne dormait pas, dans l'école !
21. agir vite
22. porte endommagée de la cellule
23. déclenchée
24. se faufila dans
25. à quelques portes de là
26. transportait un objet long et plat
27. léger

1. planche à repasser
2. n'avait fait du snowboard que
3. passé l'essentiel de la journée
4. sur les fesses
5. bien plus difficile
6. dès que vous avez pris le coup
7. progresser rapidement
8. Au bout du 3e jour
9. à surfer, en se faufilant et se frayant un chemin sur des pistes pour débutants
10. devrait faire l'affaire
11. tournoya puis s'avança
12. lame diamant dépassant
13. trop large à son goût
14. plus la planche serait longue
15. Sans aucune courbe à l'avant
16. [extrémité avant]
17. bosse
18. racine retournée
19. appuya [sur l'appareil]
20. le disque tournoyer et entamer
21. Avec précaution
22. le dévia pour former une courbe
23. se détacha

into his bedroom, closed the door and turned on one small lamp. He was afraid that the guard would see the light if he returned. But he couldn't work in the dark. It was a risk he had to take.

He had stolen an ironing-board[1].

Alex had only been snowboarding[2] three times in his life. The first time, he had spent most of the day[3] falling or sitting on his bottom[4]. Snowboarding is a lot harder[5] to learn than skiing – but as soon as you get the hang of it[6], you can advance fast[7]. By the third day[8], Alex had learned how to ride, edging and cutting his way down the beginner slopes[9]. He needed a snowboard now. The ironing-board would have to do[10].

He picked up the Discman and turned it on. The Beethoven CD spun, then slid forward[11], its diamond edge jutting out[12]. Alex made a mental calculation, and began to cut. The ironing-board was wider than he would have liked[13]. He knew that the longer the board[14], the faster he could go, but if he left it too long he would have no control. The ironing-board was flat. Without any curve at the front[15] – or the nose[16], as it was called – he would be at the mercy of every bump[17] or upturned root[18]. But there was nothing he could do about that. He pressed down[19] and watched as the spinning disc sliced through[20] the metal. Carefully[21] Alex drew it round, forming a curve[22]. About half the ironing-board fell away[23]. He picked up the other half. It almost reached his chest[1], with a point at one end[2] and a curve at the back. Perfect.

Now he sliced off the supports[3], leaving about six centimetres sticking up[4]. He knew that the rider and the board can only[5] work together if the bindings are right[6] and he had nothing; no boots, no straps[7], no highback[8] to support his heel[9]. He was just going to have to improvize. He tore two strips of sheet[10] from the bed, then slipped into[11] his ski suit. He would have to tie one of his trainers[12] to what was left[13] of the ironing-board supports. It was horribly dangerous. If he fell, he would dislocate his foot.

But he was almost ready. Quickly Alex zipped up[14] the ski suit. Smithers had said it was bullet-proof[15] and it occurred to him[16] that he was probably going to need it. He put the goggles[17] around his neck. The window still hadn't been repaired. He dropped[18] the ironing-board out[19], then climbed out after it[20].

There was no moon now. Alex found the switch concealed[21] in the goggles and turned it. He heard a soft hum as the hidden battery activated[22], and suddenly the side[23] of the mountain glowed an eerie green[24] and Alex was able to see the trees and the deserted ski-run falling away.

He carried the ironing-board over to the edge of the snow[25] and used the sheet to tie it to his foot. Carefully he took up his position[26], his right

1. atteignait presque sa poitrine
2. pointe à une extrémité
3. trancha les pieds
4. qui dépassaient
5. snowboarder et la planche ne peuvent
6. que si les fixations sont correctes
7. pas de sangle
8. [partie montante, à l'arrière de la fixation]
9. pour maintenir ses talons
10. déchira deux pans de drap
11. enfila
12. attacher l'une de ses baskets
13. ce qui restait
14. remonta la fermeture Éclair de
15. pare-balles
16. il se dit
17. masque
18. laissa tomber
19. à l'extérieur
20. prit le même chemin
21. l'interrupteur caché
22. léger bourdonnement, lorsque la pile invisible s'activa
23. versant
24. s'illumina, teinté d'un vert inquiétant
25. jusqu'au bord de la piste enneigée
26. se mit en position

foot at forty degrees[1], his left foot at twenty. He was goofy-footed[2]. That was what the instructor had told him. His feet should have been the other way round[3]. But this was no time to[4] worry about technique. Alex stood where he was, contemplating[5] what he was about to do. He had only ever done green and blue runs[6] – the colours given to the beginner and intermediate[7] slopes. He knew from[8] James that this mountain was an expert black[9] all the way down. His breath rose up in green clouds[10] in front of his eyes. Could he do it? Could he trust himself?[11]

An alarm bell[12] exploded behind him. Lights came on throughout[13] the academy. Alex pushed forward and set off, picking up speed with[14] every second. The decision had been made for him[15]. Now, whatever happened, there could be no going back[16].

Dr Grief, wearing a long silver dressing-gown[17], stood beside the open window in Alex's room. Mrs Stellenbosch was also in a robe[18] – hers was pink silk[19] and looked strangely hideous[20], hanging off her lumpy body[21]. Three guards stood watching them, waiting for instructions.

"Who searched the boy?" Dr Grief asked. He had already been shown[22] the cell door with the circular hole burnt[23] into the lock.

None of the[24] guards answered, but their faces had gone pale[25].

1. à 40°
2. [le pied droit en avant sur le surf]
3. dans l'autre sens
4. ce n'était pas le moment de
5. méditant sur
6. n'avait pratiqué que des pistes vertes et bleues
7. pour débutant et [skieur] intermédiaire
8. grâce à
9. piste noire pour skieurs avertis
10. formait une buée verte remontant
11. En était-il capable ?
12. sirène d'alarme
13. s'allumèrent partout dans
14. se propulsa et partit, accélérant à
15. prise à sa place
16. quoi qu'il arrive, il ne pouvait plus faire marche arrière
17. longue robe de chambre argentée
18. en peignoir
19. soie
20. hideux
21. pendouillant sur son corps noueux
22. On lui avait déjà montré
23. le trou rond calciné
24. Aucun des
25. avaient pâli

"This is a question to be answered in the morning," Dr Grief continued. "For now, all that matters[1] is that we find him and kill him."

"He must be walking down the mountainside!" Mrs Stellenbosch said. "He has no skis. He won't make it.[2] We can wait until morning and pick him up[3] in the helicopter."

"I think the boy may be more inventive than we believe[4]." Dr Grief picked up the remains[5] of the ironing-board. "You see? He has improvized some sort of sleigh or toboggan[6]. All right..." He had come to[7] a decision. Mrs Stellenbosch was glad[8] to see the certainty return to his eyes. "I want two men on snowmobiles[9], following him down. Now!" One of the guards hurried out[10] of the room.

"What about the unit at the foot[11] of the mountain?" Mrs Stellenbosch said.

"Indeed.[12]" Dr Grief smiled. He had always kept a guard and a driver[13] at the end of the last valley in case anybody ever tried to leave the academy on skis. It was a precaution that was about to pay off[14]. "Alex Rider will have to arrive in la Vallée de Fer. Whatever he's using to get down[15], he'll be unable to cross the railway line[16]. We can have a machine-gun set up[17] waiting for him. Assuming he does manage to get that far[18], he'll be a sitting duck[19]."

"Excellent," Mrs Stellenbosch purred[20].

1. tout ce qui compte
2. Il n'y arrivera pas.
3. le récupérer
4. plus inventif que nous ne le pensons
5. les restes
6. traîneau ou de luge
7. avait pris
8. contente
9. motoneiges
10. se précipita hors
11. Et cette unité au pied
12. Effectivement.
13. maintenait un garde et un chauffeur en permanence
14. allait s'avérer payante
15. Quoi qu'il utilise pour descendre
16. ne pourra pas traverser la voie ferrée
17. pouvons installer une mitraillette
18. En considérant qu'il parvienne jusque-là
19. cible facile
20. ronronna

"I would have liked to watch him die. But, yes. The Rider boy has no hope at all. And we can return to bed."

Alex was on the edge of space, seemingly falling to certain death[1]. In snowboarding language, he was catching air[2] – meaning that he had shot away from the ground[3]. Every ten metres he went forward[4], the mountainside disappeared another five metres downward[5]. He felt the world spin around him. The wind whipped into[6] his face. Then somehow he brought himself in line with[7] the next section of the slope and shot down, steering[8] the ironing-board ever further[9] from Point Blanc. He was moving at a terrifying speed, trees and rock formations passing in a luminous green blur across[10] his night-vision goggles. In some ways the steeper slopes made it easier[11]. At one point[12] he had tried to make a landing[13] on a flat part of the mountain – a tabletop[14] – to slow himself down[15]. He had hit the ground with such a bone-shattering crash[16] that he had nearly blacked out[17] and had taken the next twenty metres[18] almost totally blind.

The ironing-board was shuddering and shaking crazily[19] and it took all his strength to make the turns[20]. He was trying to follow the natural fall-line[21] of the mountain but there were too many obstacles in the way[22]. What he most dreaded[23]

1. volait dans les airs, fonçant apparemment tout droit vers la mort
2. [sensation de voler dans les airs et d'atterrir fermement]
3. décollé du sol
4. Tous les 10 mètres
5. le dénivelé augmentait de 5 mètres
6. fouettait
7. parvenait à s'aligner à
8. fonçait en guidant
9. toujours plus loin
10. dans un flou lumineux verdâtre, à travers
11. pentes les plus abruptes lui facilitaient la tâche
12. À un moment
13. atterrissage
14. plateau
15. pour se ralentir
16. avec une telle violence, à se rompre les os
17. s'était presque évanoui
18. parcouru les 20 m suivants
19. vibrait et tremblait follement
20. prendre les virages
21. ligne de pente
22. sur son passage
23. Ce qu'il redoutait le plus

was melted[1] snow. If the board landed on a patch of mud[2] at this speed, he would be thrown[3] and killed. And he knew that the further down he went, the greater the danger would become[4].

But he had been travelling for five minutes and so far[5] he had only fallen twice – both times into thick banks of snow[6] that had protected him. How far down could it be?[7] He tried to remember what James Sprintz had told him, but thinking was impossible at this speed. He was having to use every ounce of his conscious thought[8] simply to stay upright[9].

He reached a small lip[10] where the surface was level[11] and drove the edge[12] of the board into the snow, bringing himself to a skidding halt[13]. Ahead of him the ground fell away alarmingly[14]. He hardly dared look down[15]. There were thick clumps[16] of trees to the left and to the right. In the distance there was just a green blur.[17] The goggles could only see so far[18].

And then he heard the noise coming up[19] behind him. The scream of at least two – maybe more – engines[20]. Alex looked back over his shoulder[21]. For a moment there was nothing. But then he saw them – black flies swimming into his field of vision[22]. There were two of them, heading his way[23].

Grief's men were riding[24] specially adapted Yamaha Mountain Max snowmobiles equipped with

1. fondue
2. flaque de boue
3. serait éjecté
4. plus il descendait, plus ce serait dangereux
5. jusqu'à présent
6. deux fois, et les deux fois dans d'épaisses congères
7. Quelle distance avait-il pu couvrir ?
8. devait se servir de toute sa concentration
9. rester droit
10. arriva à un petit monticule de neige
11. aplanie
12. enfonça la carre
13. s'arrêtant en dérapant
14. tombait dangereusement à pic
15. n'osait pas regarder en bas
16. bouquets
17. Au loin, tout était flou et vert.
18. ne permettait pas de voir plus loin
19. ce bruit monter
20. moteurs
21. regarda par-dessus son épaule
22. des mouches noires déferlant dans son champ de vision.
23. venant vers lui
24. pilotaient

700cc[1] triple-cylinder[2] engines. The bikes[3] were flying over the snow on their 141-inch tracks[4], effortlessly moving five times faster[5] than Alex. The 300-watt headlights had already picked him out[6]. Now the men sped towards him[7], cutting the distance between them with every second that passed.

Alex leapt forward[8], diving into the next slope. At the same moment, there was a sudden chatter, a series of distant cracks[9], and the snow leapt up[10] all around him. Grief's men had machine-guns built into[11] their snowmobiles! Alex yelled as he swooped down[12] the mountainside, barely able to control the sheet of metal under his feet. The makeshift binding was tearing at his ankle[13]. The whole thing was vibrating crazily. He couldn't see. He could only keep going, trying to keep his balance[14], hoping that the way ahead was clear[15].

The headlights of the nearest[16] Yamaha shot out[17] and Alex saw his own shadow stretching ahead of him[18] on the snow. There was another chatter from the machine-gun and Alex ducked down[19], almost feeling the fan of bullets spray over[20] his head. The second bike screamed up[21], coming parallel with him. He *had* to get off[22] the mountainside. Otherwise[23] he would be shot or run over[24]. Or both[25].

He forced the board onto its edge[26], making a turn. He had seen a gap[27] in the trees and he

1. 700 cm^3
2. trois cylindres
3. motos
4. patins de 3,58 m
5. se déplaçant naturellement cinq fois plus vite
6. phares de 300 W l'avaient déjà balayé
7. fonçaient vers lui
8. bondit en avant
9. claquement soudain, une série de crépitements lointains
10. jaillit
11. embarquées sur
12. en descendant en piqué
13. fixation de fortune cisaillait sa cheville
14. préserver son équilibre
15. qu'il n'y avait rien devant
16. la plus proche
17. surgirent
18. s'étirer devant lui
19. se recroquevilla
20. le souffle des balles au-dessus de
21. s'approcha, moteur hurlant
22. Il fallait absolument qu'il quitte
23. Sinon
24. se ferait tirer dessus ou écraser
25. les deux
26. força la planche à se mettre sur la carre
27. trouée

made for it[1]. Now he was racing through[2] the forest, with branches and trunks whipping past[3] like crazy animations in a computer game. Could the snowmobiles follow him through here? The question was answered by another burst[4] from the machine-guns, ripping through the leaves[5] and branches. Alex searched for a narrower path[6]. The board shuddered and he was almost thrown forward head first[7]. The snow was getting thinner[8]! He edged[9] and turned, heading for two of the thickest[10] trees. He passed between them with millimetres to spare[11]. Now – follow that!

The Yamaha snowmobile had no choice. The rider had run out of paths[12]. He was travelling too fast to stop. He tried to follow Alex between the trees, but the snowmobile was too wide[13]. Alex heard the collision. There was a terrible crunch[14], then a scream, then an explosion. A ball of orange flame leapt over the[15] trees, sending black shadows in a crazy dance[16]. Ahead of him Alex saw another hillock[17] and, beyond it, a gap in the trees. It was time to leave the forest.

He swooped up the[18] hillock and out, once again catching air. As he left the trees behind him, two metres above the ground, he saw the second snowmobile. It had caught up with him[19]. For a moment the two of them were side by side[20]. Alex doubled forward and grabbed the nose[21] of his board. Still in mid-air, he twisted the tip[22]

1. prit cette direction
2. filait à toute allure à travers
3. des troncs défilant sur les côtés
4. salve
5. déchirant les feuilles
6. chercha un chemin plus étroit
7. projeté en avant, la tête la première
8. se réduisait en épaisseur
9. se faufila
10. les plus touffus
11. au mm près
12. n'avait pas d'autre chemin
13. large
14. craquement
15. boule de feu orange surgit au-dessus des
16. projetant des ombres dans un ballet infernal
17. monticule
18. piqua vers le haut du
19. l'avait rattrapé
20. se trouvèrent côte à côte
21. se pencha en avant et attrapa l'extrémité
22. Toujours en l'air, il dévia le bout

of the board, bringing the tail swinging round[1]. He had timed it perfectly. The tail slammed into[2] the second rider's head, almost throwing him out of his seat. The rider yelled and lost control. His snowmobile jerked sideways[3] as if trying to make an impossibly tight turn[4]. Then it left the ground, cartwheeling over and over again[5]. The rider was thrown off[6], then screamed as the snowmobile completed its final turn[7] and landed on top of him. Man and machine were bounced across[8] the surface of the snow and then lay still[9]. Alex slammed into[10] the snow and skidded to halt, his breath clouding green[11] in front of his eyes.

A second later he pushed off again[12]. Ahead of him he could see that all the pistes were leading into a single valley[13]. This must be the bottleneck[14] called la Vallée de Fer. So he'd actually done it[15]! He'd reached the bottom of the mountain. But now he was trapped[16]. There was no other way round.[17] He could see lights in the distance. A city. Safety.[18] But he could also see the railway line stretching right across[19] the valley, from left to right, protected on both sides by an embankment and a barbed wire fence[20]. The glow from[21] the city illuminated everything. On one side the track[22] came out of the mouth of a tunnel. It ran for about a hundred metres in a straight line[23] before a sharp bend carried it round the other side[24] of the valley and it disappeared from sight.

1. en ramenant l'arrière vers l'avant
2. percuta
3. fit une embardée de côté
4. un virage trop serré
5. faisant tonneau sur tonneau
6. éjecté
7. acheva son dernier tonneau
8. rebondirent sur
9. s'immobilisèrent
10. s'enfonça violemment dans
11. formant un brouillard vert
12. se propulsa à nouveau
13. débouchaient dans une seule vallée
14. goulet d'étranglement
15. vraiment réussi
16. pris au piège
17. Il n'y avait pas d'autre chemin.
18. La sécurité.
19. qui s'étendait sur toute la largeur de
20. de chaque côté par un talus et une clôture en barbelés
21. rayonnement de
22. voie
23. s'étendait en ligne droite sur une centaine de mètres
24. qu'une courbe raide ne la déporte de l'autre côté

The two men in the grey van[1] saw Alex snowboarding towards them. They were parked[2] on a road on the other side of the railway line and had been waiting for only a few[3] minutes. They hadn't seen the explosion and wondered what had happened to the two guards on their snowmobiles. But that wasn't their concern[4]. Their orders were to kill the boy. And there he was, right out in the open, expertly managing[5] the last black run through the valley. Every second brought him closer to[6] them. There was nowhere for him to hide. The machine-gun was a Belgian FN MAG and would cut him in half[7].

Alex saw the van. He saw the machine-gun aiming at him[8]. He couldn't stop. It was too late to change direction. He had come this far[9], but now he was finished[10]. He felt the strength draining out of him[11]. Where were MI6? Why did he have to die, out here, on his own?

And then there was a sudden blast[12] as a train thundered out[13] of the tunnel. It was a goods[14] train, travelling[15] at about twenty miles an hour[16]. It had at least thirty carriages, pulled by a diesel engine[17], and it formed a moving wall[18] between Alex and the gun, protecting him. But it would only be there for a few seconds. He had to move fast.

Barely knowing what he was doing[19], Alex found a last mound[20] of snow and, using it as a launch

1. camionnette
2. garés
3. n'avaient attendu que quelques
4. ce n'était pas leur problème
5. totalement à découvert, négociant habilement
6. le rapprochait de
7. le couperait en deux
8. le viser
9. fait tout ce chemin
10. fichu
11. ses forces l'abandonner
12. détonation
13. sortit en trombe
14. de marchandises
15. se déplaçant
16. 30 km/h
17. wagons, tirés par une locomotive diesel
18. mur mobile
19. Sans trop savoir ce qu'il faisait
20. monticule

pad, swept up[1] into the air. Now he was level with[2] the train ... now above it[3]. He shifted his weight[4] and came down onto the roof[5] of one of the carriages. The surface was covered in ice and for a moment he thought he would fall off the other side[6], but he managed to swing round so that he was snowboarding[7] along the carriage tops, jumping[8] from one to another, at the same time being swept along the track[9] – away from the gun – in a blast of freezing air[10].

He had done it! He had got away![11] He was still sliding forward[12], the train adding its speed to his own. No snowboarder had ever moved so fast. But then the train reached the bend[13] in the track. The board had no purchase[14] on the icy[15] surface. As the train sped round to the left[16], the centrifugal[17] force threw[18] Alex to the right. Once again he soared into[19] the air. But he had finally run out of snow[20].

Alex hit the ground like a rag doll[21]. The snowboard was torn off his feet[22]. He bounced twice[23], then hit a wire fence[24] and came to rest with blood spreading around a deep gash[25] in his head. His eyes were closed.

The train ploughed on[26] through the night.

Alex lay still.

1. s'en servant de rampe de lancement, s'élança
2. au même niveau que
3. au-dessus
4. s'appuya sur l'autre jambe
5. atterrit sur le toit
6. retomber de l'autre côté
7. à faire demi-tour, afin de surfer
8. sautant
9. tout en se faisant transporter le long de la voie
10. bourrasque d'air glacial
11. Il s'en était sorti !
12. avançait toujours
13. arriva à la courbe
14. aucune prise
15. verglacée
16. tournait à gauche à toute allure
17. centrifuge
18. projeta
19. s'envola dans
20. il n'y avait plus de neige
21. poupée de chiffon
22. fut arraché de ses pieds
23. rebondit deux fois
24. grillage
25. s'immobilisa, du sang s'écoulant d'une profonde coupure
26. poursuivit sa route laborieusement

AFTER THE FUNERAL

The ambulance raced down[1] the Avenue Maquis du Gresivaudan in the north of Grenoble, heading towards[2] the river. It was five o'clock in the morning and there was no traffic yet, no need for the siren[3]. Just before the river it turned off into a compound[4] of ugly modern buildings. This was the second biggest hospital in the city. The ambulance pulled up[5] outside the *Service des Urgences*. Paramedics[6] ran towards it as the back doors flew open[7].

Mrs Jones got out of her hired car[8] and watched as the limp, unmoving body was lowered on a stretcher, transferred to a trolley[9] and rushed in[10] through the double doors. There was already a saline drip attached to[11] his arm. An oxygen mask covered his face. It had been snowing up in the mountains but down here there was only a dull drizzle, sweeping across the pavements[12]. A doctor in a white coat was bending over[13] the

1. fonça dans

2. en direction de

3. pas encore de circulation, la sirène était inutile

4. tourna brusquement dans un complexe

5. s'arrêta

6. Une équipe de soignants

7. portières arrière s'ouvraient en grand

8. voiture de location

9. tandis que le corps inerte sortait sur un brancard, avant d'être transféré sur un chariot

10. emmené d'urgence à l'intérieur

11. perfusion fixée à

12. bruine maussade balayant les trottoirs

13. était penché au-dessus de

stretcher. He sighed and shook[1] his head. Mrs Jones saw this. She crossed the road and followed the stretcher in[2].

A thin man with close-cropped hair[3], wearing a black jersey[4] and padded waistcoat[5], had also been watching the hospital. He saw Mrs Jones without knowing who she was. He had also seen Alex. He took out a mobile telephone and made a call[6]. Dr Grief would want to know…

Three hours later the sun had risen over the city. Grenoble is largely modern[7] and even with its perfect mountain setting it struggles to be attractive[8]. On this damp, cloudy[9] day it was clearly failing[10].

Outside the hospital, a car drew up[11] and Eva Stellenbosch got out. She was wearing a silver and white chessboard[12] suit, with a hat perched on her ginger[13] hair. She carried a leather handbag[14] and for once she had put on make-up[15]. She wanted to look elegant. She looked like a man in drag[16].

She walked into the hospital and found the main reception desk[17]. There was a young nurse[18] sitting behind a bank of telephones and computer screens[19]. Mrs Stellenbosch addressed her in fluent French[20].

"Excuse me," she said. "I understand that[21] a young boy was brought[22] here this morning. His name is Alex Friend."

1. secoua
2. suivit le brancard à l'intérieur
3. cheveux coupés court
4. pull
5. un gilet matelassé
6. passa un appel
7. en grande partie moderne
8. décor montagneux, elle a du mal à paraître attrayante
9. pluvieuse et nuageuse
10. elle n'y parvenait pas du tout
11. s'arrêta
12. à damier
13. roux
14. sac à main en cuir
15. pour une fois, elle s'était maquillée
16. travesti
17. réception principale
18. infirmière
19. îlot d'écrans d'ordinateurs et de téléphones
20. s'adressa à elle dans un français courant
21. D'après ce que je sais
22. a été conduit

"One moment, please." The nurse entered[1] the name into her computer. She read the information on the screen and her face became serious[2]. "May I ask who you are?"

"I am the assistant director of the academy at Point Blanc. He is one of our students."

"Are you aware of the extent of his injuries[3], madame?"

"I was told that he was involved in[4] a snowboarding accident." Mrs Stellenbosch took out a small handkerchief[5] and dabbed at her[6] eyes.

"He tried to snowboard down the mountains at night. He was involved in a collision[7] with a train. His injuries are very serious, madame. The doctors are operating on him now."

Mrs Stellenbosch nodded, swallowing her tears[8]. "My name is Eva Stellenbosch," she said. "May I wait for any news[9]?"

"Of course, madame."

Mrs Stellenbosch took a seat in the reception area. For the next hour she watched as[10] people came and went, some walking, some in wheel-chairs[11]. There were other people waiting for news of other patients. One of them, she noticed, was a serious-looking[12] woman with black hair, badly cut[13], and very black eyes. She was from England – glancing occasionally[14] at a copy[15] of the London *Times*.

Then a door opened and a doctor came out. Doctors have a certain face[16] when they come to

1. entra
2. grave
3. Êtes-vous au courant de l'étendue de ses blessures
4. On m'a dit qu'il avait eu
5. mouchoir
6. se tamponna les
7. est entré en collision
8. hocha la tête, ravalant ses larmes
9. que l'on me donne des nouvelles
10. Elle passa l'heure suivante à regarder
11. fauteuils roulants
12. avec l'air grave
13. mal coupés
14. jetait un coup d'œil, de temps à autre
15. exemplaire
16. une expression particulière

give bad news. This doctor had it now. "Madame Stellenbosch?" he asked.

"Yes?"

"You are the director of the school...?"

"The assistant director, yes."

The doctor sat next to her. "I am very sorry, madame. Alex Friend died a few minutes ago[1]." He waited while she absorbed the news[2]. "He had multiple fractures. His arms, his collar-bone[3], his leg. He had also fractured his skull[4]. We operated, but unfortunately there had been massive internal bleeding[5]. He went into shock[6] and we were unable to bring him round[7]."

Mrs Stellenbosch nodded, struggling for words[8]. "I must notify[9] his family," she whispered[10].

"Is he from this country?"

"No. He is English. His father ... Sir David Friend ... I'll have to tell him." Mrs Stellenbosch got to her feet[11]. "Thank you, doctor. I'm sure you did everything you could."

Out of the corner of her eye[12], Mrs Stellenbosch noticed that the woman with the black hair had also stood up, letting her newspaper fall to the floor. She had overheard[13] the conversation. She was looking shocked[14].

Both[15] women left the hospital at the same time. Neither of them spoke.[16]

* * *

1. est mort il y a quelques minutes
2. tandis qu'elle intégrait la nouvelle
3. clavicule
4. également une fracture du crâne
5. hémorragie interne massive
6. est entré en état de choc
7. le ranimer
8. cherchant ses mots
9. informer
10. chuchota-t-elle
11. se leva
12. Du coin de l'œil
13. entendu
14. avait l'air sous le choc
15. Les deux
16. Aucune des deux ne parla.

The aircraft[1] waiting on the runway[2] was a Lockheed Martin C-130 Hercules. It had landed just after midday[3]. Now it waited beneath[4] the clouds while three vehicles drove towards it[5]. One was a police car, one a Jeep and one an ambulance.

The Saint-Geoirs airport at Grenoble does not see many international flights[6], but the plane had flown out from[7] England that morning. From the other side of the perimeter fence[8], Mrs Stellenbosch watched through a pair of high-powered binoculars[9]. A small military escort had been formed. Four men in French uniforms. They had lifted up a coffin[10] which seemed pathetically small when balanced on their broad shoulders[11]. The coffin was simple. Pinewood with silver handles.[12] A Union Jack was folded in a square[13] in the middle.

Marching in time[14], they carried the coffin towards the waiting plane. Mrs Stellenbosch focused the binoculars[15] and saw the woman from the hospital. She had been travelling[16] in the police car. She stood watching as the coffin was loaded into the plane[17], then got back into the car and was driven away. By now[18], Mrs Stellenbosch knew who she was. Dr Grief kept extensive files[19] and had quickly identified her as Mrs Jones[20]; deputy to[21] Alan Blunt, head[22] of Special Operations for MI6.

Mrs Stellenbosch stayed until the end. The doors of the plane were closed. The Jeep and the

1. avion
2. la piste
3. midi
4. sous
5. roulaient dans sa direction
6. vols
7. était venu de
8. clôture du périmètre extérieur
9. des jumelles très puissantes
10. soulevé le cercueil
11. une fois posé sur leurs larges épaules
12. En pin avec des poignées argentées.
13. était plié en carré
14. En marchant au pas cadencé
15. zooma avec ses jumelles
16. fait le trajet
17. assista à l'embarquement du cercueil
18. À présent
19. possédait d'innombrables dossiers
20. avait rapidement identifié Mme Jones
21. l'adjointe d'
22. directeur

ambulance left. The plane's propellers[1] began to turn and it lumbered forward[2] onto the runway. A few minutes later it took off[3]. As it thundered into the air[4], the clouds opened as if[5] to receive it and for a moment its silver wings were bathed in brilliant sunlight[6]. Then the clouds rolled back[7] and the plane disappeared.

Mrs Stellenbosch took out her mobile. She dialled[8] a number and waited until she was connected. "The little swine[9] has gone," she said.

She got back into her car and drove away.

After Mrs Jones had left the airport, she returned to the hospital and took the stairs to the[10] second floor. She came to a pair of doors guarded by a policeman[11] who nodded and let her pass through[12]. On the other side was a corridor leading to a private wing[13]. She walked down to a door, this one also guarded. She didn't knock. She went straight in[14].

Alex Rider was standing by[15] the window, looking out at the view of[16] Grenoble on the other side of the River Isère. Outside, high above him, five steel and glass bubbles moved[17] slowly along a cable, ferrying[18] tourists up to the[19] Fort de la Bastille. He turned round as[20] Mrs Jones came in. There was a bandage around his head but otherwise he seemed unhurt[21].

"You're lucky to be alive[22]," she said.

1. hélices
2. avança lourdement
3. décolla
4. Lorsqu'il s'envola dans un bruit de tonnerre
5. s'écartèrent comme pour
6. la lumière éclatante du soleil inonda ses ailes argentées
7. s'amoncelèrent à nouveau
8. composa
9. petite ordure
10. prit l'escalier menant au
11. où un policier montait la garde
12. la laissa entrer
13. aile privée
14. entra directement
15. se tenait près de
16. vue sur
17. cinq bulles d'acier et de verre se déplaçaient
18. transportant
19. en haut, au
20. se retourna lorsque
21. à part ça, il avait l'air indemne
22. d'être en vie

"I thought I was dead," Alex replied.

"Let's hope Dr Grief believes as much[1]." Despite herself[2], Mrs Jones couldn't keep the worry out of her eyes[3]. "It really was a miracle," she said. "You should have at least broken something[4]."

"The ski suit protected me," Alex said. He tried to think back[5] to the whirling, desperate moment[6] when he had been thrown off the train. "There was undergrowth[7]. And the fence sort of caught me[8]." He rubbed his[9] leg and winced[10]. "Even if it was barbed wire."

He walked back to the bed and sat down. After they had finished examining him, the French doctors had brought him fresh clothes[11]. Military clothes, he noticed. Combat jacket and trousers.[12] He hoped they weren't trying to tell him something.

"I've got three questions," he said. "But let's start with the big one[13]. I called for help[14] two days ago. Where were you?"

"I'm very sorry, Alex," Mrs Jones said. "There were ... logistical problems."

"Yes? Well, while you were having your logistical problems, Dr Grief was getting ready to cut me up[15]!"

"We couldn't just storm[16] the academy. That could have got you killed.[17] It could have got you all killed. We had to move in slowly[18]. Try and work out[19] what was going on. How do you think we found you so quickly?"

1. le croit aussi
2. Malgré elle
3. ne put cacher son inquiétude
4. aurais dû te casser quelque chose, au minimum
5. repenser
6. cet instant déboussolant et désespéré
7. des broussailles
8. grillage m'a retenu, on dirait
9. se frotta la
10. fit une grimace
11. des vêtements de rechange
12. Une veste et un pantalon de treillis.
13. la plus importante
14. J'ai appelé à l'aide
15. s'apprêtait à me découper
16. attaquer
17. Tu aurais pu te faire tuer.
18. devions nous engager peu à peu
19. Essayer de comprendre

"That was my second question."

Mrs Jones shrugged[1]. "We've had people[2] in the mountains ever since[3] we got your signal. They've been closing in on[4] the academy. They heard the machine-gun fire when the snowmobiles were chasing you[5] and followed you down on skis. They saw what happened with the train and radioed for help[6]."

"All right. So why all the business[7] with the funeral? Why do you want Dr Grief to think I'm dead?"

"That's simple, Alex. From what[8] you've told us, he's keeping fifteen boys prisoner[9] in the academy. These are the boys that he plans to replace[10]." She shook her head. "I have to say, it's the most incredible thing I've ever heard[11]. And I wouldn't have believed it if I'd heard it from anyone else except you[12]."

"You're too kind[13]," Alex muttered[14].

"If Dr Grief thought you'd survived last night, the first thing he would do is kill every one of those boys. Or perhaps he'd use them as hostages[15]. We only had one hope if we were going to take him by surprise[16]. He had to believe you were dead."

"You're going to take him by surprise?"

"We're going in[17] tonight. I told you, we've assembled an attack squad[18] here in Grenoble. They were up in the mountains last night. They

1. haussa les épaules
2. avons placé du monde
3. dès l'instant où
4. cernent
5. te pourchassaient
6. ont demandé de l'aide par radio
7. toute cette histoire
8. D'après ce que
9. retient 15 garçons prisonniers
10. qu'il a l'intention de remplacer
11. que j'aie jamais entendue
12. si quelqu'un d'autre que toi me l'avait racontée
13. C'est trop gentil
14. marmonna
15. s'en servirait comme otages
16. n'avions qu'une seule chance de le prendre par surprise
17. Nous allons y pénétrer
18. unité de combat

plan to set off[1] as soon as it's dark. They're armed and they're experienced." Mrs Jones hesitated. "There's just one thing they don't have."

"And what's that?" Alex asked, feeling a sudden sense of unease[2].

"They need someone who knows the building," Mrs Jones said. "The library, the secret lift, the placement[3] of the guards, the passage with the cells—"

"No way![4]" Alex exclaimed. Now he understood the military clothes. "Forget it![5] I'm not going back up there! I almost got killed trying to get away! Do you think I'm mad?"

"Alex, you'll be looked after[6]. You'll be completely safe[7]—"

"No!"

Mrs Jones nodded. "All right. I can understand your feelings[8]. But there's someone I want you to meet."

As if on cue, there was a knock on the door[9] and it opened to reveal a young man, also in combat dress[10]. The man was well-built[11] with black hair, square shoulders[12] and a dark, watchful[13] face. He was in his late twenties[14]. He saw Alex and shook his head. "Well, well, well. There's a turn up for the books[15]," he said. "How's it going, Cub?[16]"

Alex recognized him at once[17]. It was the soldier he had known as[18] Wolf. When MI6 had sent

1. ont l'intention de se mettre en route

2. se sentant soudain mal à l'aise

3. disposition

4. Pas question !

5. Laissez tomber !

6. on s'occupera de toi

7. totalement en sécurité

8. ce que tu ressens

9. Comme par hasard, on frappa à la porte

10. en tenue de combat

11. robuste

12. des épaules carrées

13. attentif

14. approchait de la trentaine

15. En voilà une surprise

16. Comment ça va, Louveteau ?

17. tout de suite

18. qu'il avait connu sous le nom de

him for eleven days' SAS training[1] in Wales[2], Wolf had been in charge of his unit. If training had been hell, Wolf had only made it worse, picking on[3] Alex from the start and almost getting him thrown out[4]. In the end though[5], it had been Wolf who had nearly lost his place with[6] the SAS and Alex who had saved him. But Alex still wasn't sure where that left him[7], and the other man was giving nothing away[8].

"Wolf!" Alex said.

"I heard you got busted up.[9]" Wolf shrugged. "I'm sorry. I forgot the flowers and the bunch of grapes[10]."

"What are you doing here?" Alex asked.

"They called me in to clear up the mess you left behind you[11]."

"So where were you when I was being chased down[12] the mountain?"

"It seems you were doing fine on your own[13]."

Mrs Jones took over[14]. "Alex has done a very good job up to now[15]," she said. "But the fact is that there are fifteen young prisoners up at Point Blanc and our first priority[16] must be to save them. From what Alex has told us, we know there are about thirty guards in and around[17] the school. The only chance those boys have is for an SAS unit to break in[18]. It's happening tonight.[19]" She turned to Alex. "The unit will be commanded by Wolf."

1. en stage
2. pays de Galles
3. Le stage était déjà infernal, et Wolf n'avait fait qu'empirer les choses en s'en prenant à
4. en le faisant presque expulser
5. toutefois
6. qui avait failli perdre sa place au sein de
7. ne savait toujours pas à quoi s'en tenir
8. ne laissait rien paraître
9. Il paraît que tu t'es fait tabasser.
10. grappe de raisin
11. pour réparer la pagaille que tu as laissée derrière toi
12. lorsqu'on me poursuivait jusqu'en bas de
13. que tu t'en es bien sorti tout seul
14. prit le relais
15. jusqu'à présent
16. notre priorité absolue
17. à l'intérieur et autour de
18. c'est qu'un commando SAS donne l'assaut
19. C'est pour ce soir.

The SAS never use rank[1] when they are on active service. Mrs Jones was careful only to use[2] Wolf's code-name.

"Where does the boy come into this?[3]" Wolf demanded.

"He knows the school. He knows the position of the guards and the location[4] of the prison cells. He can lead you to the lift—"

"He can tell us everything we need to know here and now[5]," Wolf interrupted. He turned to Mrs Jones. "We don't need a kid[6]," he said. "He's just going to be baggage[7]. We're going in on skis. Maybe there'll be blood.[8] I can't waste one of my men holding his hand[9]—"

"I don't need to have my hand held[10]," Alex retorted angrily[11]. "She's right. I know more about Point Blanc than any of you. I've been there – and got out of there, no thanks to you[12]. Also, I've met some of those boys. One of them is a friend of mine. I promised I'd help him and I will[13]."

"Not if you get killed."

"I can look after myself.[14]"

"Then it's agreed[15]," Mrs Jones said. "Alex will lead you in there but then will take no further part in the operation[16]. And as for[17] his safety, Wolf, I hold you personally responsible[18]."

"Personally responsible. Right," Wolf growled.

Alex couldn't resist a smile[19]. He'd held his ground[20] and he'd be going back in with the SAS.

1. n'employait jamais de grades
2. prit soin de n'utiliser que
3. Qu'est-ce que le gosse vient faire dans tout ça ?
4. l'emplacement
5. là, tout de suite
6. d'un môme
7. ne sera qu'un boulet
8. Du sang sera peut-être versé.
9. sacrifier un homme pour lui tenir la main
10. qu'on me tienne la main
11. riposta avec colère
12. et c'est pas grâce à toi
13. c'est ce que je ferai
14. Je peux me débrouiller seul.
15. Alors c'est d'accord
16. sa participation s'arrêtera là
17. en ce qui concerne
18. vous en serez personnellement responsable
19. ne put s'empêcher de sourire
20. Il avait tenu bon

Then he realized[1]. A few moments ago, he'd been arguing violently against doing just that.[2] He glanced at Mrs Jones. She'd manipulated him, of course, bringing[3] Wolf into the room. And she knew it.

Wolf nodded. "All right, Cub," he said. "Looks like you're in.[4] Let's go play."

"Sure, Wolf," Alex sighed. "Let's go play."

1. il se rendit compte
2. Quelques instants auparavant, il s'insurgeait exactement contre ça.
3. en faisant venir
4. On dirait que tu es des nôtres.

NIGHT RAID

They came skiing down[1] from the mountain. There were seven of them. Wolf was the leader. Alex was at his side. The other five men followed. They had changed into white trousers, jackets and hoods[2] – camouflage that would help them blend into[3] the snow. A helicopter had dropped them[4] two kilometres north[5] of and two hundred metres above[6] Point Blanc and, equipped with[7] night vision goggles, they had quickly made their way down[8]. The weather had settled again[9]. The moon was out[10]. Despite himself[11], Alex enjoyed the journey[12], the whisper[13] of the skis cutting through the ice[14], the empty mountainside bathed in[15] white light. And he was part of a crack[16] SAS unit. He felt safe[17].

But then the academy loomed up below[18] him, and once again he shivered[19]. Before they had left, he had asked for a gun – but Wolf had shaken his head[20].

1. descendirent à ski
2. cagoules
3. à se fondre dans
4. les avait déposés
5. au nord
6. au-dessus de
7. munis de
8. étaient descendus rapidement
9. temps s'était calmé à nouveau
10. sortie
11. Malgré lui
12. apprécia le trajet
13. murmure
14. fendant la glace
15. baignée de
16. d'élite
17. se sentait en sécurité
18. se dressa au-dessous de
19. eut un frisson
20. secoué la tête

"I'm sorry, Cub. It's orders. You get us in[1], then you get out of sight[2]."

There were no lights showing[3] in the building. The helicopter crouched on[4] the helipad like a glittering[5] insect. The ski-jump stood to one side[6], dark and forgotten. There was nobody in sight. Wolf held up[7] a hand and they slid to a halt[8].

"Guards?" he whispered.

"Two patrolling. One on the roof."

"Let's take him out first.[9]"

Mrs Jones had made her instructions clear. There was to be no bloodshed unless absolutely necessary.[10] The mission was to get the boys out. The SAS could take care[11] of Dr Grief, Mrs Stellenbosch and the guards at a later date[12].

Now Wolf held out a hand[13] and one of the other men passed him something. It was a crossbow[14] – not the medieval sort[15] but a sophisticated, high-tech weapon with a microflite aluminium barrel[16] and laser scope[17]. He loaded it with an anaesthetic dart[18], lifted it up and took aim. Alex saw him smile to himself. Then his finger curled[19] and the dart flashed across the night, travelling at[20] one hundred metres a second. There was a faint[21] sound from the roof of the academy. It was as if someone had coughed[22]. Wolf lowered[23] the crossbow.

"One down[24]," he said.

1. nous fais entrer
2. disparais
3. On ne voyait aucune lumière
4. était posé sur
5. étincelant
6. se trouvait d'un côté
7. leva
8. s'arrêtèrent
9. Neutralisons-le en premier.
10. Sauf absolue nécessité, il ne devait pas y avoir d'effusion de sang.
11. s'occuperait
12. ultérieurement
13. tendit la main
14. arbalète
15. du genre médiéval
16. corps en aluminium
17. lunette de visée laser
18. Il chargea une flèche anesthésiante
19. se courba
20. fila dans la nuit, à une vitesse de
21. à peine audible
22. toussé
23. abaissa
24. Un de moins

"Sure," Alex muttered. "And about twenty-nine to go.[1]"

Wolf signalled and they continued down, more slowly now. They were about twenty metres from the school when they saw the main door open. Two men walked out, machine-guns hanging from their shoulders. As one[2], the SAS men veered to the right[3], disappearing round the side[4] of the school. They stopped within reach[5] of the wall, dropping down to lie flat on their stomachs[6]. Two of the men had moved slightly ahead[7]. Alex noticed that they had kicked off[8] their skis at the very same moment[9] they had come to a halt.

The two guards approached. One of them was talking quietly in German. Alex's face was half buried[10] in the snow. He knew that the combat clothes would make them invisible. He half-lifted[11] his head just in time to see two figures rise out[12] of the ground like ghosts from the grave[13]. Two coshes swung[14] in the moonlight. The guards crumpled[15]. In seconds they were tied up[16] and gagged[17]. They wouldn't be going anywhere that night.

Wolf signalled again. The men got up and ran forward, making for[18] the main door. Alex hastily pulled his own skis off[19] and followed. They reached the door in a line, their backs[20] against the wall. Wolf looked inside to check that it was safe[21]. He nodded. They went in.

1. Et il en reste encore 29.

2. Comme un seul homme

3. virèrent à droite

4. sur le côté

5. tout près

6. se jetant à plat ventre

7. s'étaient déplacés légèrement à l'avant

8. déchaussé

9. au moment même où

10. à moitié enfoui

11. souleva légèrement

12. silhouettes se dresser

13. des fantômes surgissant d'une tombe

14. matraques s'abattirent

15. s'écroulèrent

16. En quelques secondes, ils furent ligotés

17. bâillonnés

18. se précipitèrent vers

19. se dépêcha de retirer ses propres skis

20. en file indienne, dos [plaqué]

21. pour vérifier qu'il n'y avait pas de danger

1. aux côtés de
2. lui indiqua rapidement la direction, en désignant
3. Par ici.
4. fit un pas en avant
5. s'accroupit
6. fourrageant dans
7. pochettes
8. gilet [d'intervention]
9. ne prenait plus de risques
10. soit passé
11. lui emboîta le pas
12. choc sourd
13. fracas d'une arme qui tombait
14. Jusqu'ici, ça va
15. comment appeler
16. siffla doucement lorsque
17. en douceur
18. C'est un sacré endroit
19. Il y avait juste assez de place
20. averti
21. à portée de vue
22. en tirant

They were in the hall with the stone dragons and the animal heads. Alex found himself next to[1] Wolf and quickly gave him his bearings, pointing out[2] the different rooms.

"The library?" Wolf whispered. He was totally serious now. Alex could see the tension in his eyes.

"Through here.[3]"

Wolf took a step forward[4], then crouched down[5], his hand whipping into[6] one of the pouches[7] of his jacket[8]. Another guard had appeared, patrolling the lower corridor. Dr Grief was taking no more chances[9]. Wolf waited until the man had gone past[10], then nodded. One of the other SAS men went after him[11]. Alex heard a thud[12] and the clatter of a gun dropping[13].

"So far, so good[14]," Wolf whispered.

They went into the library. Alex showed Wolf how to summon[15] the lift and Wolf whistled softly as[16] the suit of armour smoothly[17] divided into two parts. "This is quite a place[18]," he muttered.

"Are you going up or down?"

"Down. Let's make sure the kids are all right."

There was just room[19] for all seven of them in the lift. Alex had warned[20] Wolf about the guard at the table, within sight[21] of the lift, and Wolf took no chances – he came out firing[22]. In fact, there were two guards there. One of them was holding a mug of coffee, the other lighting a cigarette.

Wolf fired twice[1]. Two more anaesthetic darts travelled[2] the short distance along the corridor and found their targets[3]. Again, it had all happened in almost total silence. The two guards collapsed[4] and lay still. The SAS men stepped out into[5] the corridor.

Suddenly Alex remembered. He was angry with himself for not mentioning it before[6]. "You can't go into the cells," he whispered. "They're wired up for sound[7]."

Wolf nodded. "Show me!"

Alex showed Wolf the passage with the steel doors. Wolf pointed to[8] one of the men. "I want you to stay here. If we're found[9], this is the first place Grief will come."

The man nodded. He understood. The rest of them went back to the lift, up to the library and out into the hall.

Wolf turned to Alex. "We're going to have to deactivate the alarm," he explained. "Do you have any idea—?"

"This way. Grief's private rooms are on the other side..."

But before he could finish, three more guards appeared, walking down the passageway. Wolf shot one of them – another anaesthetic dart – and one of his men took out[10] the other two. But this time they were a fraction of a second too slow[11]. Alex saw one of the guards bring his

1. à deux reprises
2. franchirent
3. atteignirent leurs cibles
4. s'écroulèrent
5. pénétrèrent dans
6. s'en voulut de ne pas l'avoir dit plus tôt
7. sont sur écoute
8. désigna
9. Si on nous découvre
10. neutralisa
11. avaient réagi une fraction de seconde trop tard

gun round[1]. He was probably unconscious before he managed to fire. But at the last moment, his finger tightened on the trigger[2]. Bullets sprayed upwards, smashing into the ceiling, bringing plaster and wood splinters showering down[3]. Nobody had been hit[4], but the damage had been done[5]. The lights flashed on[6]. An alarm began to ring.

Twenty metres away, a door opened and more guards poured through[7].

"Down![8]" Wolf shouted.

He had produced[9] a grenade. He tugged the pin out[10] and threw it. Alex hit the ground and a second later there was a soft[11] explosion as a great cloud of tear gas filled the far end[12] of the passage. The guards staggered, blind and helpless[13]. The SAS men quickly took them out.

Wolf grabbed hold of[14] Alex and dragged him close[15]. "Find somewhere to hide[16]!" he shouted. "You've got us in. We'll do the rest now."

"Give me a gun!" Alex shouted back. Some of the gas had reached him[17] and he could feel his eyes burning.

"No. I've got orders. At the first sign of trouble, you're to get out of the way.[18] Find somewhere safe[19]. We'll come for you[20] later."

"Wolf...!"

But Wolf was already up and running[21]. Alex heard machine-gun fire coming from somewhere below[22]. So Wolf had been right. One of the guards

1. retourna son arme
2. se resserra sur la détente
3. jaillirent en l'air, rentrèrent dans le plafond et une pluie de débris de plâtre et de bois déferla
4. touché
5. le mal était fait
6. s'allumèrent d'un coup
7. d'autres gardes se précipitèrent
8. À terre !
9. sorti
10. la dégoupilla
11. légère
12. grand nuage de gaz lacrymogène envahissait l'autre bout
13. titubèrent, aveuglés et sans défense
14. empoigna
15. l'approcha de lui
16. où te cacher
17. Du gaz l'avait atteint
18. Au moindre problème, tu dois dégager.
19. un endroit sûr
20. On viendra te récupérer
21. était déjà parti en courant
22. quelque part en bas

had been sent to take care[1] of the prisoners – but there had been an SAS man waiting for him. And now the rules[2] had changed. The SAS couldn't afford to risk the lives[3] of the prisoners. There was going to be bloodshed. Alex could only imagine the battle that must be taking place. But he was to be no part of it. His job was to hide.

More explosions. More gunfire. There was a bitter taste[4] in Alex's mouth as he made his way back[5] to the stairs. It was typical of[6] MI6. Half the time[7] they would happily get him killed. The other half they treated him like a child.

Suddenly a guard appeared, running towards the sound of the fighting[8]. Alex's eyes were still smarting from the[9] gas and now he made use of it[10]. He brought his hand up to[11] his face, pretending to[12] cry. The guard saw a fourteen-year-old boy in tears[13]. He stopped. At that moment Alex twisted round[14] on his left foot, driving the upper part[15] of his right foot sideways[16] into the man's stomach – the roundhouse kick[17] or *mawashi geri* he had learned in karate. The guard didn't even have time to cry out[18]. His eyes rolled and he went limp[19]. Alex felt a little better after that.

But there was still nothing more for him to do. There was another round of gunfire[20], then the quiet blast[21] of a second gas grenade. Alex went into the dining-room. From here he could look out through the windows at the side of the build-

1. pour s'occuper
2. règles
3. ne pouvait se permettre de risquer la vie
4. goût amer
5. en retournant vers
6. C'était classique avec le
7. La moitié du temps
8. courant vers les bruits de combat
9. piquaient encore sous l'effet du
10. s'en servit
11. porta la main à
12. en faisant semblant de
13. en larmes
14. pivota
15. expédiant le haut
16. de côté
17. coup de pied circulaire
18. crier
19. s'affaissa
20. série de coups de feu
21. explosion

1. pales
2. se rapprocha de
3. avoir l'air aussi inhumain
4. déformé par
5. protubérantes
6. le regard enflammé
7. Elle gémissait presque
8. ce n'était vraiment pas juste
9. as tout gâché
10. Qu'est-ce qui m'a poussée à
11. ricana intérieurement
12. le peu de raison qu'il lui restait était en train de s'envoler
13. voilà une partie du boulot
14. se crispa, pieds écartés, abaissant son centre de gravité
15. inutile
16. lui rentra dedans
17. effrayante
18. comme se faire renverser
19. l'empoignèrent
20. le jetèrent la tête la première dans la pièce
21. s'écrasa contre
22. la renversant
23. s'écarta en roulant
24. complétait

ing and the helipad above. He noticed that the blades[1] of the helicopter were turning. Somebody was inside it. He moved closer to[2] the window. It was Dr Grief! He had to let Wolf know.

He turned round.

Mrs Stellenbosch was standing in front of him.

He had never seen her look less human[3]. Her entire face was contorted with[4] anger, her lips rolled outwards[5], her eyes ablaze[6].

"You didn't die!" she exclaimed. "You're still alive!" Her voice was almost a whine[7], as if somehow none of it had been fair[8]. "You brought them here. You ruined everything[9]!"

"That's my job," Alex said.

"What was it that made me[10] look in here?" Mrs Stellenbosch giggled to herself[11]. Alex could see what little sanity she had left was slipping away[12]. "Well, at least this is one bit of business[13] I'm finally going to be able to finish."

Alex tensed himself, feet apart, centre of gravity low[14]. Just like he had been taught. But it was useless[15]. Mrs Stellenbosch lurched into him[16], moving with frightening[17] speed. It was like being run over[18] by a bus. Alex felt the full impact of her body weight, then cried out as two massive hands seized hold of him[19] and threw him head first across the room[20]. He crashed into[21] a table, knocking it over[22], then rolled out of the way[23] as Mrs Stellenbosch followed up[24] her first attack, lashing out with a kick[1] that would have taken his head off his shoulders if it hadn't missed by less than a centimetre[2].

He scrambled to his feet[3] and stood there, panting for breath[4]. For a moment his vision was blurred[5]. Blood trickled out[6] of the corner of his mouth. Mrs Stellenbosch charged again. Alex threw himself forward, using another of the tables for leverage[7]. His feet swung round, scything through the air, both his heels catching her on the back of the head[8]. Anyone else[9] would have been knocked out by the blow[10]. But although Alex felt the jolt of it running all the way up his body[11], Mrs Stellenbosch hardly faltered[12]. As Alex left the table, her hands swung down, smashing through[13] the thick wood. The table fell apart and she walked through it, grabbing him[14] again, this time by the neck. Alex felt his feet leave the floor. With a grunt[15] she hurled him[16] against the wall. Alex yelled, wondering if his back had been broken. He slid to the floor. He couldn't move.

Mrs Stellenbosch stopped, breathing heavily. She glanced out of the window. The helicopter's blades were at full speed[17] now. The helicopter rocked forward[18] then rose into the air. It was time to go.

She reached down[19] and picked up[20] her handbag. She took out a gun and aimed at Alex. Alex stared at her. There was nothing he could do.

1. en décochant un coup de pied

2. lui aurait arraché la tête s'il ne l'avait manqué d'à peine 1 centimètre

3. se releva péniblement

4. haletant

5. floue

6. gouttait

7. pour avoir plus d'appui

8. fendant l'air, ses deux talons la heurtant à la nuque

9. N'importe qui d'autre

10. par ce coup

11. l'ait senti vibrer dans tout son corps

12. chancela à peine

13. s'abattirent, brisant

14. l'empoignant

15. grognement

16. le précipita

17. tournaient à leur vitesse maximale

18. bascula en avant

19. se baissa

20. ramassa

Mrs Stellenbosch smiled. "And this is *my* job," she said.

The dining-room door swung open.

"Alex!" It was Wolf. He was holding a machine-gun.

Mrs Stellenbosch lifted the gun up and fired three shots. Each one of them found its target.[1] Wolf was hit in the shoulder, the arm and the chest. But even as he fell back[2], he opened fire himself[3]. The heavy bullets slammed into[4] Mrs Stellenbosch. She was hurled backwards into[5] the window, which smashed behind her. With a scream she disappeared out into the night and the snow, head first, her heavy stockinged legs trailing behind her[6].

The shock of what had happened gave Alex new strength. He got to his feet and ran over to Wolf. The SAS man wasn't dead but he was badly hurt, his breath rattling[7].

"I'm OK," he managed to say. "Came looking for you. Glad I found you."

"Wolf..."

"OK." He tapped at[8] his chest and Alex saw that he was wearing body armour[9] under his jacket. There was blood coming from his arm but the other two bullets hadn't reached him. "Grief..." he said.

Wolf gestured[10] and Alex looked round[11]. The helicopter had left its launch pad[12]. It was flying

1. Toutes les trois touchèrent leur cible.
2. même en tombant en arrière
3. tira lui aussi
4. percutèrent
5. projetée en arrière, contre
6. ses grosses jambes gainées de bas la suivant dans sa chute
7. gravement blessé, la respiration haletante
8. tapota
9. portait un gilet pare-balles
10. fit un geste
11. jeta un coup d'œil
12. plateforme de décollage

low[1] outside the academy. Alex saw Dr Grief in the pilot's seat. He had a gun. He fired. There was a yell and a body fell from somewhere above. One of the SAS men.

Suddenly Alex was angry. Grief was a freak[2], a monster. He was responsible for all this – and he was going to get away[3]. Not knowing what he was doing, he snatched up[4] Wolf's gun and ran through[5] the broken window, past[6] the dead body of Mrs Stellenbosch and into[7] the night. He tried to aim. The blades of the helicopter were whipping up the surface snow[8], blinding him, but he pointed the gun up and fired. Nothing happened. He pulled the trigger again. Still nothing.[9] Either Wolf had used all his ammunition[10] or the gun had jammed[11].

Dr Grief pulled at the controls[12] and the helicopter banked away[13], following the slope of the mountain. It was too late. Nothing could stop him.

Unless...[14]

Alex threw down[15] the gun and ran forward. There was a snowmobile lying idle[16] a few metres away, its engine still running[17]. The man who had been riding it was lying face down[18] in the snow. Alex leapt onto the seat[19] and turned the throttle full on[20]. The snowmobile roared away, skimming over[21] the ice, following the path[22] of the helicopter.

1. volait bas
2. taré
3. allait s'échapper
4. s'empara de
5. franchit en courant
6. [passa] devant
7. [s'enfonça] dans
8. soulevaient la neige poudreuse
9. Toujours rien.
10. toutes ses munitions
11. s'était enrayé
12. actionna les commandes
13. s'éloigna en virant
14. À moins que...
15. jeta par terre
16. garé
17. toujours en marche
18. gisait sur le ventre
19. bondit sur le siège
20. tourna l'accélérateur à fond
21. partit en vrombissant, effleurant
22. dans le sillage

1. pour lui faire au revoir

2. aperçut

3. fins

4. levés, un ultime geste de défi

5. agrippant

6. guidon

7. se mit debout sur les repose-pieds, se raidissant à l'avance, sachant ce qu'il devait faire

8. prenant de

9. se dressa

10. se déplaçait

11. filant sur ses côtés

12. en forme de croix

13. passa en la défonçant

14. s'éjecta

15. débris

16. réussit à se mettre à genoux

17. arriva au bout

18. décoller comme une fusée, propulsée

19. l'immense tremplin métallique

20. foncer à toute vitesse

21. phares éclatants

22. rouge vif, s'écarquillèrent sous le choc

Dr Grief saw him. The helicopter slowed and turned. Grief raised a hand – waving goodbye[1].

Alex caught sight of[2] the red spectacles, the slender[3] fingers raised in one last gesture of defiance[4]. With his hands gripping[5] the handlebars[6] Alex stood up on the foot-grips, tensing himself for what he knew he had to do[7]. The helicopter moved away again, gaining[8] altitude. In front of Alex, the ski-jump loomed up[9]. He was travelling[10] at seventy, eighty kilometres an hour, snow and wind rushing past him[11]. Ahead of him there was a wooden barrier shaped like a cross[12].

Alex smashed through it[13], then threw himself off[14].

The snowmobile plunged down, its engine screaming.

Alex rolled over and over in the snow, ice and wood splinters[15] in his eyes and mouth. He managed to get to his knees[16].

The snowmobile reached the end[17] of the ski-jump.

Alex watched it rocket into the air, propelled[18] by the huge metal slide[19].

In the helicopter Dr Grief just had time to see 225 kilograms of solid steel come hurtling[20] towards him out of the night, its headlights blazing[21], its engine still screaming. His eyes, bright red, opened wide in shock[22].

The explosion lit up[1] the entire mountain. The snowmobile had become a torpedo[2] and it hit its target with perfect accuracy[3]. The helicopter disappeared in a huge fireball[4], then plunged down. It was still burning when it hit the ground.

Behind him, Alex became aware[5] that the shooting[6] had stopped. The battle was over[7]. He walked slowly back to the academy, shivering[8] suddenly in the cold night air. As he approached, a man appeared at the broken window and waved[9]. It was Wolf, propping himself[10] against the wall but still very much alive[11]. Alex went over to him.

"What happened to Grief?" he asked.

"It looks like I sleighed[12] him," Alex replied.

On the slopes, the wreckage[13] of the helicopter flickered and burned[14] as the morning sun began to rise.

1. illumina
2. s'était transformée en torpille
3. une parfaite précision
4. énorme boule de feu
5. se rendit compte
6. les tirs
7. terminée
8. frissonnant
9. agita la main
10. s'appuyant
11. toujours bien vivant
12. [jeu de mots avec « sleigh », le traîneau (motoneige) et « slay », qui veut dire tuer : mais attention, le jeu de mots fonctionne même si le passé de slay est slew]
13. épave
14. luisait et brûlait

DEAD RINGER[1]

1. Le sosie

A few days later, Alex found himself sitting opposite[2] Alan Blunt in the faceless[3] office in Liverpool Street, with Mrs Jones twisting another sweet between her fingers[4]. It was 1 May, a bank holiday[5] in England – but somehow he knew that holidays never came to the building that called itself[6] the Royal & General bank. Even the spring[7] seemed to have stopped at the window. Outside, the sun was shining[8]. Inside, there were only shadows[9].

"It seems that once again we owe you a debt of thanks[10]," Blunt was saying.

"You don't owe me anything," Alex said.

Blunt looked genuinely puzzled[11]. "You have quite possibly[12] changed the future of this planet," he said. "Of course, Grief's plan was monstrous, crazy. But the fact remains[13] that his..." He searched for a word[14] to describe the test-tube creations[15] that had been sent out of[16] Point

2. était assis en face de
3. impersonnel
4. manipulant encore un bonbon entre ses doigts
5. jour férié
6. n'existaient pas, dans ce bâtiment soi-disant dénommé
7. printemps
8. brillait
9. il n'y avait que des ombres
10. nous te devons toute notre reconnaissance
11. avait l'air vraiment perplexe
12. très probablement
13. il n'en demeure pas moins
14. chercha un mot
15. créations in vitro
16. expédiées de

Blanc. "...his *offspring*[1] could have caused a great many[2] problems. At the very least[3] they would have had money. God knows what they would have got up to had they remained undiscovered.[4]"

"What's happened to them?" Alex asked.

"We've traced all fifteen of them[5] and we have them under lock and key[6]," Mrs Jones answered. "They were quietly arrested[7] by the intelligence services of each country where they lived. We'll take care of them.[8]"

Alex shivered. He had a feeling he knew[9] what Mrs Jones meant[10] by those last words. And he was certain that nobody would ever see the fifteen Grief replicas again.

"Once again, we've had to hush this up[11]," Blunt continued. "This whole business[12] of ... cloning[13]. It causes a great deal of public disquiet.[14] Sheep are one thing[15] – but human beings!" He coughed[16]. "The families involved in[17] this business have no desire for publicity[18], so they won't be talking. They're just glad to have their real sons returned to them[19]. The same, of course, goes for you[20], Alex. You've already signed the Official Secrets Act. I'm sure we can trust you to be discreet[21]."

There was a moment's pause. Mrs Jones looked carefully at Alex. She had to admit that she was worried about him. She knew everything that had happened at Point Blanc – how close he had come to a horrible death, only to be sent back[22] into

1. rejetons
2. d'innombrables
3. Au minimum
4. Dieu sait ce qu'ils auraient pu faire si on ne les avait jamais démasqués.
5. On les a retrouvés, tous les quinze
6. ils sont sous les verrous
7. ont été arrêtés discrètement
8. On va s'occuper d'eux.
9. crut comprendre
10. voulait dire
11. avons dû étouffer cette affaire
12. Toute cette histoire
13. clonage
14. Cela trouble énormément la population.
15. c'est une chose
16. toussota
17. concernées par
18. ne souhaitent pas que cela s'ébruite
19. qu'on leur ait rendu leurs véritables fils
20. vaut pour toi
21. pouvons compter sur ta discrétion
22. à quel point il avait frôlé une mort effroyable avant d'être envoyé à nouveau

the academy for a second time. The boy who had come back from the French Alps was different to the boy who had left. There was a coldness about him, as tangible as[1] the mountain snow.

"You did very well[2], Alex," she said.

"How is Wolf?" Alex asked.

"He's fine. He's still in hospital but the doctors say he'll make a complete recovery[3]. We hope to have him back on operations[4] in a few weeks."

"That's good."

"We only had one fatality in the[5] raid on Point Blanc. That was the man you saw falling from the roof[6]. Wolf and another man were injured[7]. Otherwise[8], it was a complete success." She paused. "Is there anything else you want to know?"

"No." Alex shook his head. He stood up. "You left me in there[9]," he said. "I called for help[10] and you didn't come. Grief was going to kill me, but you didn't care[11]."

"That's not true, Alex!" Mrs Jones looked at Blunt for support but he didn't meet her eyes[12]. "There were difficulties..."

"It doesn't matter. I just want you to know that I've had enough[13]. I don't want to be a spy any more and if you ask me again, I'll refuse. I know you think you can blackmail me[14]. But I know too much about you[15] now, so that won't work any more." He walked over to the door. "I used to think[16] that being a spy would be excit-

1. froideur en lui, aussi palpable que
2. as fait du bon travail
3. se rétablira totalement
4. qu'il sera à nouveau opérationnel
5. Il n'y a eu qu'un mort, au cours du
6. as vu tomber du toit
7. ont été blessés
8. À part ça
9. m'avez abandonné là-bas
10. J'ai appelé à l'aide
11. vous vous en fichiez
12. pour qu'il la soutienne mais il évita son regard
13. j'ai assez donné
14. pouvoir me faire chanter
15. sur vous
16. Je pensais

ing and special … like in the films. But you just used me[1]. In a way, the two of you are as bad as[2] Grief. You'll do anything[3] to get what you want. Well, I want to go back to school. Next time, you can do it without me[4]."

There was a long silence after Alex had left. At last, Blunt spoke. "He'll be back[5]," he said.

Mrs Jones raised an eyebrow[6]. "You really think so?"

"He's too good at what he does[7] … too good at the[8] job. And it's in his blood[9]." He stood up. "It's rather odd[10]," he said. "Most schoolboys dream of being spies[11]. With Alex, we have a spy who dreams of being a schoolboy."

"Will you really use him again?" Mrs Jones asked.

"Of course. There was a file that came in only this morning.[12] An interesting situation[13] in the Zagros Mountains of Iraq. Alex may be the only answer[14]." He smiled at his number two. "We'll give him a while to settle down[15] and then we'll call him."

"He won't answer."

"We'll see," Blunt said.

Alex walked home[16] from the bus-stop and let himself into[17] the elegant Chelsea[18] house that he shared with[19] his housekeeper and closest friend[20], Jack Starbright. Alex had already told

1. vous vous êtes juste servis de moi
2. Dans un sens, vous deux, vous êtes aussi mauvais que
3. Vous êtes prêts à tout
4. ce sera sans moi
5. reviendra
6. haussa un sourcil
7. doué pour ce qu'il fait
8. pour ce
9. il a ça dans le sang
10. plutôt étrange
11. rêvent d'être espions
12. Un dossier nous est parvenu, pas plus tard que ce matin.
13. cas
14. notre seule solution
15. On va lui laisser le temps de se poser
16. rentra à pied
17. pénétra dans
18. [quartier chic de Londres, situé à l'ouest]
19. qu'il partageait avec
20. gouvernante et meilleure amie

Jack where he had been and what he had been doing, but the two of them had made an agreement never to[1] discuss his involvement with[2] MI6. She didn't like it and she worried about him. But at the end of the day[3] they both knew[4] there was nothing more to be said.

She seemed surprised to see him. "I thought you'd just gone out[5]," she said.

"No."

"Did you get the message by the phone[6]?"

"What message?"

"Mr Bray wants to see you this afternoon. Three o'clock at the school."

Henry Bray was the head-teacher at[7] Brookland. Alex wasn't surprised by the summons[8]. Bray was the sort of head[9] who managed to run a busy comprehensive[10] and still find time to take a personal interest in every pupil[11] who went there. He had been worried by Alex's long absences. So he had called a meeting[12].

"Do you want lunch?" Jack asked.

"No thanks." Alex knew that he would have to pretend he had been ill again. Doubtless[13] MI6 would produce[14] another doctor's note in due course[15]. But the thought of lying[16] to his head-teacher spoiled his appetite[17].

He set off[18] an hour later, taking his bicycle, which had been returned to the house by the Putney police. He cycled slowly[19]. It was good

1. tous deux étaient convenus de ne jamais
2. de ce qu'il faisait au
3. en fin de compte
4. savaient tous les deux
5. que tu venais à peine de sortir
6. par téléphone
7. principal de
8. de cette convocation
9. principal
10. parvenait à gérer un grand collège
11. trouvait encore le temps de s'intéresser personnellement à chaque élève
12. l'avait convoqué
13. Sans aucun doute
14. fournirait
15. en temps et en heure
16. l'idée de mentir
17. lui coupait l'appétit
18. se mit en route
19. pédala lentement

to be back in London, to be surrounded by normal life. He turned off the King's Road[1] and pedalled down the side road[2] where – it felt like a month ago[3] – he had followed the man in the white Skoda. The school loomed up ahead of him. It was empty now and would remain so[4] until the summer term[5].

But as Alex arrived, he saw a figure walking across the yard to[6] the school gates and recognized Mr Lee, the elderly school caretaker[7].

"You again![8]"

"Hello, Bernie," Alex said. That was what everyone called him.[9]

"On your way to see[10] Mr Bray?"

"Yeah."

The caretaker shook his head. "He never told me he was going to be here today. But he never tells me anything! I'm just going down to the shops[11]. I'll be back at five to lock up[12] – so make sure you're out by then[13]."

"Right[14], Bernie."

There was nobody in the playground. It felt strange[15], walking across the tarmac[16] on his own. The school seemed bigger with nobody there[17], the yard stretching out too far[18] between the red-brick buildings, with the sun beating down, reflecting off[19] the windows. Alex was dazzled[20]. He had never seen the place[21] so empty and so quiet[22]. The grass[23] on the playing-fields[24] looked

1. Dans King's Road, il tourna
2. petite rue
3. il avait l'impression qu'il s'était écoulé un mois
4. le resterait
5. [la rentrée du] dernier trimestre
6. traverser la cour vers
7. vieux concierge de l'école
8. Encore toi !
9. Tout le monde l'appelait comme ça.
10. Tu vas voir
11. vais faire une course
12. pour tout fermer
13. alors fais en sorte de partir avant
14. D'accord
15. Cela faisait bizarre
16. macadam
17. sans tout le monde
18. s'étendant démesurément
19. qui tapait, ses rayons reflétés par
20. ébloui
21. cet endroit
22. aussi silencieux
23. herbe
24. terrains de sport

almost too green. Any school without[1] schoolchildren has its own peculiar atmosphere[2] and Brookland was no exception.

Mr Bray had an office in D block[3], which was next to the science building. Alex reached the swing-doors[4] and opened them. The walls here would normally be covered in posters but they had all been taken down[5] at the end of term. Everything was blank, off-white[6]. There was another door open to one side[7]. Bernie had been cleaning the main[8] laboratory. He had rested his mop and bucket[9] to one side when he'd gone to the shops – to pick up twenty cigarettes, Alex presumed. The man had been a chain smoker all his life[10] and Alex knew he'd die[11] with a cigarette between his lips[12].

Alex climbed up the stairs, his heels rapping against the stone surface[13]. He reached a corridor – left for biology, right for physics[14] – and continued straight ahead[15]. A second corridor, with full-length windows on both sides[16], led into D block. Bray's study[17] was directly ahead of[18] him. He stopped at the door, vaguely wondering[19] if he should have smartened up[20] for the meeting. Bray was always snapping at[21] boys with their shirts hanging out[22] or ties crooked[23]. Alex was wearing a denim[24] jacket, T-shirt, jeans and Nike trainers – the same clothes he had worn[25] that morning at MI6. His hair was still too short for his liking[26],

1. Une école sans
2. dégage une étrange atmosphère
3. bâtiment
4. portes battantes
5. décrochés
6. vide, blanc cassé
7. d'un côté
8. principal
9. laissé son balai à franges et son seau
10. toujours fumé comme un pompier
11. mourrait
12. au bec
13. talons tapant sur la surface en pierre
14. à droite, les sciences physiques
15. tout droit
16. des fenêtres sur toute la longueur, des deux côtés
17. bureau
18. juste devant
19. se demandant plus ou moins
20. aurait dû faire un effort vestimentaire
21. grondait toujours les
22. dont la chemise dépassait
23. la cravate était de travers
24. en jean
25. qu'il avait portés
26. à son goût

although it had begun to grow back[1]. All in all[2], he still looked like a juvenile delinquent – but it was too late now. And anyway, Bray didn't want to see him to discuss his appearance[3]. His non-appearance at school was more to the point.[4]

He knocked on the door.

"Come in!" a voice called.

Alex opened the door and walked into the head-teacher's study, a cluttered[5] room with views over the playground[6]. There was a desk, piled high with papers[7], and a black leather chair with its back towards the door[8]. A cabinet full[9] of trophies stood against one wall. The others were mainly lined with[10] books.

"You wanted to see me," Alex said.

The chair turned slowly round.

Alex froze[11].

It wasn't Henry Bray sitting behind the desk.

It was himself.[12]

He was looking at[13] a fourteen-year-old boy with fair hair cut very short, brown eyes and a slim[14], pale face. The boy was even dressed identically to him[15]. It took[16] Alex what felt like[17] an eternity to accept[18] what he was seeing. He was standing in a room looking at himself sitting in a chair. The boy *was* him.

With just one difference. The boy was holding a gun.

"Sit down," he said.

1. repousser
2. Globalement
3. tenue
4. Il s'agissait plutôt de son absence de l'école.
5. encombrée
6. donnant sur la cour de récréation
7. recouvert de piles de papiers
8. tournant le dos à la porte
9. meuble rempli
10. contenaient surtout des rangées de
11. se figea
12. C'était lui-même.
13. Il était face à
14. fin
15. habillé exactement comme lui
16. Il fallut à
17. ce qui lui sembla
18. pour admettre

Alex didn't move. He knew what he was facing[1] and he was angry with himself for not having expected it[2]. When he had been handcuffed[3] at the academy, Dr Grief had boasted to him that he had cloned himself[4] sixteen times. But that morning Mrs Jones had traced[5] "all fifteen of them". That left one spare[6] – one boy waiting to take his place in the family of Sir David Friend. Alex had glimpsed him[7] while he was at the academy. Now he remembered the figure with the white mask, watching him from[8] a window as he walked over to the ski-jump. The white mask had been[9] bandages. The new Alex had been spying on him as he recovered from the plastic surgery[10] that had made the two of them identical.

And even today there had been clues[11]. Perhaps it had been the heat[12] of the sun – or the fall-out from[13] his visit to MI6. But he had been too wrapped up in his own thoughts[14] to see them: Jack, when he got home – "I thought you'd just gone out"; Bernie, at the gate – "You again!"

They had both thought they'd just seen him.[15] And in a sense, they had[16]. They had seen the boy sitting opposite him now. The boy who was aiming[17] a gun at his heart.

"I've been looking forward to this[18]," the other boy said. Despite the hatred in[19] his voice, Alex couldn't help marvelling[20]. The voice wasn't the same as his[21]. The boy hadn't had enough time

1. à quoi il était confronté
2. de ne pas s'y être attendu
3. menotté
4. s'était vanté, devant lui, de s'être cloné
5. retrouvé
6. Il en restait donc un
7. l'avait aperçu
8. silhouette au masque blanc l'observant depuis
9. c'était des
10. pendant sa convalescence suivant la chirurgie esthétique
11. il y avait eu des indices
12. chaleur
13. contrecoup de
14. absorbé par ses propres pensées
15. Tous deux pensaient qu'ils venaient juste de le voir.
16. dans un sens, c'était vrai
17. pointait
18. J'attendais ce moment avec impatience
19. haine [contenue] dans
20. ne put s'empêcher d'être émerveillé
21. la même que la sienne

to get it right[1]. But otherwise he was a dead ringer[2].

"What are you doing here?" Alex said. "It's all over.[3] The Gemini Project is finished[4]. You might as well turn yourself in.[5] You need help."

"I need just one thing," the second Alex sneered[6]. "I need to see you dead. I'm going to shoot you. I'm going to do it now. You killed my father!"

"Your father was a test-tube[7]," Alex said. "You never had a mother or a father. You're a freak[8]. Hand-made[9] in the Alps ... like a cuckoo clock[10]. What are you going to do when you've killed me? Take my place? You wouldn't last a week[11]. You may look like me, but too many people know what Grief was trying to do. And I'm sorry, but you've got *fake* written all over you[12]."

"We would have had everything! We would have had the whole world!" The replica Alex[13] almost screamed the words and for a moment Alex thought he heard[14] Dr Grief somewhere in there, blaming him from beyond the grave[15]. But then[16] the creature in front of him *was*[17] Dr Grief ... or part of him. "I don't care what happens to me[18]," he went on, "just so long as[19] you're dead."

The hand with the gun stretched out[20]. The barrel was pointing at him[21]. Alex looked the boy straight in the eye[22].

And he saw the hesitation.

1. pour la mettre au point
2. sosie
3. Tout est fini.
4. mort
5. Tu ferais mieux de te rendre.
6. dit le second Alex, d'un ton méprisant
7. éprouvette
8. monstre
9. Fabriqué à la main
10. pendule à coucou
11. ne tiendrais pas une semaine
12. tu fais faux de la tête aux pieds
13. Le double d'Alex
14. crut entendre
15. là, quelque part, l'accusant d'outre-tombe
16. en même temps
17. était bien
18. Je me fiche de ce qu'il m'arrivera
19. du moment que
20. se tendit
21. canon pointé vers lui
22. droit dans les yeux

The fake Alex couldn't quite bring himself to do it[1]. They were too similar. The same height[2], the same build[3] – the same *face*. For the other boy, it would be like shooting himself[4]. Alex still hadn't closed the door. He threw himself backwards, out into[5] the corridor. At the same time, the gun went off[6], the bullet exploding millimetres above[7] his head and crashing into the far wall[8]. Alex hit the ground on his back[9] and rolled out of the doorway[10] as a second bullet slammed into[11] the floor. And then he was running, putting as much space between himself and his double as he could[12].

There was a third shot as he sprinted down[13] the corridor and the window next to him shattered, glass showering down[14]. Alex reached the stairs and took them three at a time, afraid that he would trip[15] and break an ankle[16]. But then he was at the bottom, heading for the main door, swerving only when he realized[17] that he would make too easy a target as he crossed[18] the playground. Instead he dived into[19] the laboratory, almost falling head first over Bernie's bucket and mop.

The laboratory was long and rectangular, divided into work stations[20] with Bunsen burners, flasks and dozens of bottles of chemicals spread out on shelves that stretched the full length[21] of the room. There was another door at the far end.

1. vraiment se résoudre à le faire
2. taille
3. corpulence
4. comme s'il se tirait dessus
5. D'un bond en arrière, il se jeta dans
6. coup partit
7. quelques millimètres à peine au-dessus de
8. mur du fond
9. se jeta à terre sur le dos
10. roula hors de la porte
11. percutait
12. autant de distance que possible entre lui et son double
13. tandis qu'il courait le long de
14. se brisa dans une pluie de verre
15. le descendit quatre à quatre, au risque de trébucher
16. cheville
17. ne déviant qu'après s'être rendu compte
18. cible trop facile s'il traversait
19. Il préféra plonger dans
20. réparti en postes de travail
21. dispersés sur des étagères qui faisaient toute la longueur

Alex dived behind the furthest[1] desk. Would his double have seen him[2] come in? Might he be looking for him, even now[3], out in the yard?

Cautiously[4] Alex poked his head over[5] the surface, then ducked down[6] as four bullets ricocheted around him, splintering[7] the wood and smashing one of the gas pipes[8]. Alex heard the hiss of escaping gas[9], then there was another gunshot and an explosion that hurled him backwards, sprawling onto the floor[10]. The last bullet had ignited[11] the gas. Flames leapt up, licking at the ceiling[12]. Then the sprinkler system went off, spraying[13] the entire room. Alex tracked back on his hands and feet, searching for shelter[14] behind fire and water, hoping that the other Alex would be blinded. His shoulders hit[15] the far[16] door. He scrambled to his feet[17]. There was another shot. But then he was through[18] – with another corridor and a second flight of stairs[19] straight ahead.

The stairs led nowhere[20]. He was halfway up before[21] he remembered. There was a single classroom at the top, used for biology. It had a spiral[22] staircase leading to the roof[23]. The school had so little land[24] that they'd planned to build a roof garden[25]. Then they'd run out of money[26]. There were a couple of greenhouses[27]. Nothing more.

There was no way down! Alex looked over his shoulder and saw the other Alex reloading[28] his gun, already on his way up[29]. He had no choice.

1. le plus éloigné
2. Son double l'avait-il vu
3. Était-il à sa recherche, en ce moment même
4. Prudemment
5. passa la tête au-dessus de
6. se baissa vivement
7. entaillant
8. tuyaux de gaz
9. le sifflement de la fuite de gaz
10. le projeta en arrière et il s'étala par terre
11. enflammé
12. jaillirent, léchant le plafond
13. se déclencha, arrosant
14. revint sur ses pas, à quatre pattes, en essayant de s'abriter
15. touchèrent
16. du fond
17. se releva péniblement
18. il était passé
19. escalier
20. ne menait nulle part
21. à mi-hauteur lorsqu'
22. en colimaçon
23. menant au toit
24. si peu de terrain
25. prévu de créer un jardin sur le toit
26. manqué d'argent
27. deux ou trois serres
28. qui rechargeait
29. déjà en train de monter

He had to continue even though[1] he knew that he was soon going to be trapped[2].

He reached the biology classroom and slammed the door shut behind him. There was no lock and the tables were all bolted into the floor, otherwise[3] he might have been able to make a barricade. The spiral staircase was ahead of him. He ran up it[4] without stopping, through[5] another door and out onto[6] the roof. Alex stopped to catch his breath[7] and see what he could do next[8].

He was standing on a wide, flat area with a fence running all the way round[9]. There were half a dozen terracotta[10] pots filled with earth[11]. A few plants sprouted out[12], looking more dead than alive. Alex sniffed[13] the air. Smoke was curling up[14] from the windows two floors below and he realized that the sprinkler system had failed to put out[15] the fire. He thought of the gas pouring into[16] the room and the chemicals stacked up[17] on the shelves[18]. He could be standing on a time-bomb[19]! He had to find a way down[20].

But then he heard feet on metal[21] and realized that his double had reached the top[22] of the spiral staircase. Alex ducked[23] behind one of the greenhouses. The door crashed open[24].

Smoke followed the fake Alex out onto the roof. He took a step forward. Now Alex was behind him.

"Where are you?" shouted the double. His hair was soaked[25] and his face contorted with anger[26].

1. même si
2. serait bientôt pris au piège
3. fixées au sol, autrement
4. le grimpa en courant
5. franchit
6. sortit sur
7. pour reprendre son souffle
8. ce qu'il pourrait faire ensuite
9. clôture faisant tout le tour
10. en terre cuite
11. de la terre
12. en surgissaient
13. renifla
14. Des tourbillons de fumée s'élevaient
15. n'avait pas réussi à éteindre
16. envahissant
17. produits chimiques entassés
18. étagères
19. se trouvait peut-être au-dessus d'une bombe à retardement
20. un moyen de descendre
21. des pas sur une surface métallique
22. était arrivé en haut
23. se cacha
24. s'ouvrit avec fracas
25. étaient trempés
26. crispé de colère

Alex knew his moment had come. He would never have a better chance. He ran forward[1]. The other Alex twisted round[2] and fired. The bullet creased his shoulder, a molten sword drawn across his flesh[3]. But then he had reached[4] his replica, grabbing him around the neck with one hand[5] and seizing hold of his wrist with the other, forcing the gun away[6]. There was a huge[7] explosion in the laboratory below and the entire building shook[8], but neither of the boys seemed to notice it. They were locked in an embrace[9], two reflections[10] that had become tangled up[11] in the mirror, the gun over their heads, fighting for control[12].

The flames were tearing through[13] the building. Fed by a variety of[14] chemicals, they burst through[15] the roof, melting[16] the asphalt. In the far distance the scream of fire engines penetrated[17] the sun-filled air[18]. Alex pulled with all his strength[19], trying to bring the gun down[20]. The other Alex clawed at him, swearing[21] – not in English but in Afrikaans.

The end came very suddenly.

The gun twisted[22] and fell to the ground.

One Alex lashed out, knocking the other down[23], then dived for[24] the gun.

There was another explosion and a sheet of chemical flame[25] leapt up. A crater had suddenly appeared in the roof, swallowing up[26] the gun. The

1. s'élança en courant
2. pivota
3. érafla son épaule, parcourant la chair comme un sabre incandescent
4. il était déjà sur
5. lui empoignant le cou d'une main
6. attrapant son poignet de l'autre, l'obligeant à lâcher l'arme
7. énorme
8. trembla
9. agrippés l'un à l'autre
10. reflets identiques
11. s'étaient enchevêtrés
12. luttant pour avoir le dessus
13. se propageaient à toute vitesse dans
14. Alimentées par toutes sortes de
15. transpercèrent
16. faisant fondre
17. Au loin, le hurlement de la sirène des pompiers déchira
18. l'atmosphère ensoleillée
19. de toutes ses forces
20. d'abaisser l'arme
21. le griffa en jurant
22. tourna
23. L'un des Alex attaqua, expédiant l'autre par terre
24. plongea pour récupérer
25. une langue de feu nourrie de produits chimiques
26. avalant

boy saw it too late and fell through[1]. With a yell[2], he disappeared into the smoke and fire.

One Alex Rider walked over to the hole[3] and looked down.

The other Alex Rider lay on his back[4], two floors below[5]. He wasn't moving. The flames were closing in[6].

The first fire engines[7] had arrived at the school. A ladder slanted up towards[8] the roof.

A boy with short fair hair and brown eyes, wearing a denim jacket, T-shirt and jeans, walked to the edge[9] of the roof and began to climb down[10].

1. tomba dedans
2. Dans un hurlement
3. s'approcha du trou
4. était étendu sur le dos
5. étages au-dessous
6. l'encerclaient
7. camions de pompiers
8. échelle s'éleva vers
9. gagna le bord
10. descendre

AN AFTERWORD[1] BY ANTHONY HOROWITZ

1. postface

THE BAD GUYS[2]

2. les méchants

Point Blanc was actually meant to be[3] the first Alex Rider book ... and it was inspired by a sheep[4]!

I'd decided I was going to write about a teenage spy and I was looking around for a story. It had to be something that was current[5]. And – equally[6] important – it had to involve an area of science[7] that had never appeared in any of the James Bond novels[8] ... a great source of inspiration for me, as you'll know[9] if you've read the afterword to[10] *Stormbreaker*. Well, by chance[11], I opened a magazine at[12] an article about Dolly the Sheep[13] which was the first animal to be cloned – which is to say[14], reproduced from a single cell[15]. Dolly was born[16] in 1996 with a huge fanfare of publicity[17] (although people had forgotten that another animal had already been cloned – a

3. devait être, en fait
4. brebis
5. d'actuel
6. tout aussi
7. il fallait que cela parle d'un domaine scientifique
8. romans
9. comme vous le savez
10. de
11. par hasard
12. à [la page d']
13. concernant la brebis Dolly
14. c'est-à-dire
15. à partir d'une seule cellule
16. est née
17. dans un déchaînement médiatique

1. têtard
2. Malheureusement
3. n'ont pas ce côté nounours des
4. ce qui explique peut-être pourquoi
5. Bref
6. du
7. J'ai mis un certain temps à résoudre cette énigme
8. j'ai eu l'idée de l'intrigue que vous venez de lire
9. ce projet un peu dément de dominer le monde
10. au cœur
11. immensément riches
12. Mais il y a quelque chose d'étrange.
13. préféré
14. qui est cité le plus souvent
15. péniche
16. grand point d'interrogation
17. m'a supplié
18. afin que les lecteurs sachent
19. pour une fois, j'ai tenu bon
20. j'ai toujours trouvé l'intrigue
21. trop proche de la science-fiction
22. précise et crédible
23. d'y croire vraiment moi-même
24. réserver ça pour
25. toujours en partant du principe

tadpole[1] in 1952. Sadly[2], tadpoles are less cuddly than[3] sheep which may be why[4] it's been forgotten).

Anyway[5], the newspaper article gave me the idea for[6] Dr Grief and his plan to clone human beings. Why was he doing it? It took me a while to work out that one[7], and in the end I came up with the plot you have just read[8] ... a slightly insane scheme to take over the world[9] by placing copies of himself at the heart[10] of massively wealthy[11] and powerful families.

Now here's the strange thing.[12] When I ask young people which is their favourite[13] Alex Rider novel, *Point Blanc* is the title that gets mentioned most often[14]. But it's not my favourite. There are things in it that I love: the canal boat[15], the ironing board that becomes a snowboard, the last line of chapter six, the fight in the last chapter with the big question mark[16] at the end (my American publisher begged me[17] to change it so that readers would know[18] who lived and who died – but for once I dug my heels in[19]). But the plot always struck me as[20] a little bit too close to sci-fi[21]. I worked hard to make the science in *Point Blanc* accurate and believable[22]. But I was never sure I entirely believed it myself[23].

That's why I decided to leave it for[24] number two (always assuming[25] that there was going to be a new book ... I'd have to wait and see if we managed to sell any copies[1] of the first). I then thought up[2] a second plot about a crazed businessman taking his revenge on the UK[3] by putting[4] a virus into thousands of computers. The result was *Stormbreaker*.

All of which brings me to the main subject[5] of this afterword and one of the hardest jobs that I have writing[6] the Alex Rider books. And that is – creating the bad guys.

Here's the problem. Herod Sayle, Dr Grief, Colonel Sarov ... all of my villains have to be larger than life[7]. They need to have big ideas. Alex Rider and MI6 aren't going to waste their time[8] fighting against someone who wants to break into a sweet shop[9] or get away without paying their television licence[10]. We're talking about[11] the sort of bad guys you see in a James Bond film. But at the end of the day, what is it, exactly, that they might want to do?

Take over the world. That's the obvious one.[12] But isn't that a bit comic book[13]? Isn't it what Doctor Doom wants to do in the *Fantastic Four*[14]? I wonder if it's even believable in the twenty-first century[15]. I mean[16], if you look at the mess that the world is in[17] at the moment, with everything from global warming to third world poverty[18], AIDS[19] and famine, would you want to take it over? Money, of course, is a good motivator[20]. But it's also a bit ordinary[21]. After all, these days[22], if you want to be

1. si nous arrivions à vendre des exemplaires
2. Alors, j'ai imaginé
3. homme d'affaires dingue qui se venge sur le Royaume-Uni
4. introduisant
5. Tout cela m'amène au thème principal
6. l'une des choses les plus difficiles à faire lorsque j'écris
7. méchants doivent être plus vrais que nature
8. perdre leur temps
9. braquer une confiserie
10. ne pas régler sa redevance audiovisuelle
11. Il s'agit de
12. Bien évidemment.
13. cela ne fait-il pas un peu BD
14. Quatre Fantastiques
15. XXIe siècle
16. Ce que je veux dire, c'est que
17. la pagaille qui règne dans le monde
18. du réchauffement climatique à la pauvreté du tiers-monde
19. le sida
20. constitue une bonne motivation
21. un peu banal
22. de nos jours

insanely wealthy[1], you don't have to destroy half the planet. You can just become a footballer or a judge on *The X Factor*. What else is there?[2]

Er...

And that's the big question. That's where I start every time I come to a new Alex Rider book. Before I can think up any of the action sequences or work out how Alex is going to get involved[3] in the adventure, I have to go to the very centre of the dart board, to the bullseye, so to speak[4]. The bad guy holds everything together.[5] He (or she) has to be original. He (or she) has to be trying to do something which may be mad and which may be almost impossible, but which is nonetheless[6] still believable and which adds up to a real threat[7] to both Alex and the world.

There are eight Alex Rider books so far[8]. And here's what the eight villains have been aiming at[9]. (DANGER: if you haven't read all the books, this section contains spoilers[10].)

HEROD SAYLE (*Stormbreaker*)

Wants revenge against the British Prime Minister who bullied him[11] at school. Aiming to kill[12] all the children in the UK.

DR GRIEF (*Point Blanc*)

Mad scientist creating clones of himself to insert[13] into wealthy families. A new angle on[14] taking over the world.

1. follement riche
2. Que reste-t-il d'autre ?
3. va rentrer
4. frapper au cœur même de la cible, dans le mille, pour ainsi dire
5. Tout repose sur le méchant.
6. néanmoins
7. représente une menace réelle
8. jusqu'à présent
9. voici l'objectif des 8 méchants
10. [indications résumant l'intrigue d'une histoire]
11. qui le harcelait
12. Il veut tuer
13. les infiltrer
14. Une nouvelle façon de

COLONEL SAROV (*Skeleton Key*)

Plans to bring back[1] Communism to save his country (and the world). He will do this by engineering[2] a nuclear accident.

1. A l'intention de rétablir
2. en provoquant

DAMIAN CRAY (*Eagle Strike*)

Multi-millionaire pop singer and anti-drugs campaigner[3]. Also, sadly, insane. Planning to bomb all the drugs fields[4] in the world.

3. militant anti-drogue
4. bombarder toutes les plantations de drogue

JULIA ROTHMAN (*Scorpia*)

Head[5] of a secret organization. She has been paid to destroy the special friendship[6] between the UK and the USA by killing thousands of children.

5. À la tête
6. amitié

NIKOLEI DREVIN (*Ark Angel*)

All the evidence that proves[7] he is a major[8] criminal is being kept[9] in the Pentagon in Washington. So he's going to destroy the Pentagon. And all of[10] Washington too.

7. Tous les éléments qui prouvent que
8. grand
9. sont conservés
10. toute la ville de

MAJOR WINSTON YU (*Snakehead*)

Another agent of Scorpia, he has been paid to disrupt a peace conference[11] on an island. He's going to do it by creating a tsunami.

11. perturber une conférence sur la paix

DESMOND McCAIN (*Crocodile Tears*[12])

A former MP[13], arrested for fraud. All he wants is money. But he's going to kill off a whole[14] continent to get it.

12. larmes
13. ancien député
14. anéantir tout un

1. personnages
2. vous faire
3. du premier au dernier
4. gallois
5. Comme
6. les services secrets, il semble normal
7. soient étrangers
8. cela m'a valu d'être accusé de racisme
9. dois faire attention à ma façon de les décrire
10. origines raciales de quelqu'un
11. l'endroit où ils sont nés
12. qui font d'eux des méchants
13. L'autre question, c'est de savoir si
14. En réalité, j'ai beaucoup de mal à créer une femme diabolique.
15. menacent
16. de
17. véritablement
18. dénuées de tout sens de l'humour
19. Cela dit, j'aime beaucoup
20. qui doit son nom à
21. [station balnéaire de la côte amalfitaine, au sud de l'Italie]
22. le séduire
23. plaisante

When you look at all eight of these characters[1] together, you begin to get[2] an idea of the way the villains are created.

Often I start with their nationality. Going from top to bottom[3], they are, in order: Lebanese, South African, Russian, Welsh[4], Russian, Chinese and English. Since[5] many of these characters are fighting against British intelligence, it seems only reasonable[6] that the majority of them should be foreign[7]. Unfortunately, this has left me open to accusations of racism[8] and when I'm writing about someone who is Arabic or Chinese, I have to be careful how I describe them[9]. I never make any judgement about anyone's racial origins[10]. It isn't where they're born[11] or the colour of their skin that makes them bad[12]!

The next question is whether[13] they're going to be male or female. I actually find it quite hard to create evil women.[14] When they threaten[15] Alex with[16] torture or death they seem genuinely[17] unpleasant and lacking in humour[18]. And when they get killed, also, they somehow die without making me smile. I don't know why this is. That said, I'm very fond of[19] Julia Rothman (named after[20] the cigarette) and like the scene where she takes Alex out to dinner in Positano[21]. It's almost as if she's trying to seduce him[22]! And her death is particularly satisfying[23]. I probably shouldn't say this but I was thinking of the actress Catherine Zeta-Jones when I created her.

Another thing about the bad guys is that they almost all have some sort of deformity[1]. In *Point Blanc*, as I'm sure you will have noticed, Dr Grief is an albino. It seemed to me quite funny that someone who was a racist, who disliked black people, should be totally white. His side-kick[2], Mrs Stellenbosch (named after the wine-growing district[3] near Cape Town[4], which I visited when I was writing the book) is a muscle-bound freak of nature[5]. Major Winston Yu has a brittle bone disease[6] which leads to a climax that is shattering in every sense[7]. And one of my favourite villains, the Reverend Desmond McCain, has a face that has been bizarrely disfigured as a result of a boxing match.

I know I'm treading on dangerous ground[8] here. It's quite wrong to poke fun[9] at people because they have an illness or a disability[10] and I will never forget a letter I received from a girl with vitiligo, the skin disease that afflicts[11] Nile, Julia Rothman's assistant in *Scorpia* (Michael Jackson supposedly suffered from it too[12]). She took me to task and quite rightly[13]. But at the same time, I want the bad guys to be different, to stand out[14]. I'm partly inspired by Ian Fleming, the author of James Bond. His Mr Big (*Live and Let Die*) had a weak heart[15] that had turned him from

1. souffrent presque tous de quelque malformation
2. sous-fifre
3. région de vignobles
4. Le Cap [l'une des capitales (siège du Parlement) de l'Afrique du Sud]
5. monstre de la nature, hyper-musclé
6. la maladie des os de verre
7. atteint un paroxysme à vous briser les os dans tous les sens du terme
8. que je marche sur un terrain miné
9. très mal de se moquer
10. infirmité
11. atteinte de vitiligo, cette maladie de la peau dont souffre
12. en aurait également souffert
13. m'a réprimandé, et à juste titre
14. qu'ils ressortent du lot
15. une maladie cardiaque

black to grey. He gave Dr No amputated hands. And who will forget the mute Korean midget[1] with his butler's suit[2] and bowler hat[3] ... Oddjob in *Goldfinger*?

The strange thing is that I find my inspiration for all the bad guys in the newspapers. Since[4] we're talking about *Point Blanc*, Dr Grief is largely[5] based on a man called PW Botha, the leader of the South African National Party and a supporter of apartheid[6]. I noticed him in the newspapers when he suffered a stroke[7] (he's now dead). A story about Sir Elton John and the enormous sums of money that he allegedly spent[8] on flowers gave me the idea for a mad pop singer ... the result was Damian Cray. And I actually met[9] Desmond McCain last year, although the person in question was nothing like[10] the villain of my book. He was in fact a very delightful[11] man working with disadvantaged[12] children in East London.

I've mentioned one or two of the sidekicks[13] and I have to say that I have enormous fun creating them[14] because they're usually even more unpleasant than the people they work for[15]. They don't have plans or ambitions. They're just hired hands[16] and seem to revel[17] in being violent and cruel. Take[18] Conrad in *Skeleton Key*. A terrorist who manages to blow himself up[19] and is then sewn back together again[20], he tries to crush[21] Alex between the rollers[22] of a sugar cane factory

1. nain coréen muet
2. tenue de majordome
3. chapeau melon
4. Puisque
5. en grande partie
6. partisan de l'apartheid
7. a eu un AVC
8. qu'il aurait, paraît-il, dépensées
9. j'ai réellement rencontré
10. n'avait rien à voir avec
11. adorable
12. défavorisés
13. acolytes
14. je m'amuse énormément en les créant
15. pour qui ils travaillent
16. Ce sont juste des hommes de main
17. semblent s'épanouir
18. Par exemple
19. arrive à se faire exploser
20. totalement recousu
21. d'écraser
22. cylindres

... just for the hell of it[1]. In the end, Alex has to be saved by General Sarov, who is, in every respect[2], a much more sympathetic character. At least he has something he believes in. I'm also fond of Kaspar in *Ark Angel*. He works for Drevin and has a map[3] of the world tattooed[4] on his head. At the end of the book he is blasted into space[5]. I cannot imagine why he has agreed to all this[6]. I suppose he must have been very well-paid[7].

Finally, a brief word on[8] the way in which the bad guys die. Because they're all larger than life, it follows that they must have[9] a truly[10] memorable death and often when I'm creating them I'm already thinking about how I'm going to get rid of them[11]. There are certain rules[12] concerning violence and death in Alex Rider books which I will discuss elsewhere[13] – but I will mention here that the death of Dr Grief is one of my favourites. It's different. It's unexpected[14]. And best of all[15] it's very visual ... as I wrote it[16], it was easy to imagine it happening.

The truth is, everyone loves a bad guy. Alex Rider may be the hero of all these books but they wouldn't work[17] if he didn't have memorable opponents[18]. And when I start writing a new story, I always look forward to the scene when[19] Sayle or Grief or whoever it is, ties Alex down[20] and explains, at great length[21], their evil scheme[22] to destroy the world. Why do they bother?[23] One day

1. juste pour le plaisir
2. à tous égards
3. carte
4. tatouée
5. une explosion l'expédie dans l'espace
6. accepté tout ça
7. très bien payé
8. petit mot à propos de
9. il faut forcément qu'ils aient
10. vraiment
11. à la façon dont je vais m'en débarrasser
12. règles
13. dont je parlerai ailleurs
14. inattendue
15. la meilleure, c'est que
16. en l'écrivant
17. ne fonctionneraient pas
18. adversaires
19. j'attends toujours avec impatience la scène où
20. ligote Alex
21. en long et en large
22. plan démoniaque
23. Pourquoi se donnent-ils cette peine ?

1. qu'ils ne s'en tireront pas impunément

2. cela fait peut-être partie de la méchanceté

3. Il ne leur vient jamais à l'esprit

4. perdre

they'll realize that they're not going to get away with it[1]. But maybe that's part of being bad[2]. It never occurs to them[3] that they're going to lose[4].

Anthony Horowitz
January 2010

Imprimé en Italie par La Tipografica Varese Srl
Dépôt légal : août 2015
315432-01/11029093-août 2015